A GLASS VILLAGE

Chris Cohen

A GLASS
VILLAGE

Matador
9 De Montfort Mews
Leicester LE1 7FW, UK
Tel: (+44) 116 255 9311 / 9312
Email: books@troubador.co.uk
Web: www.troubador.co.uk/matador

This book is based on fact from the author's experiences on a smallholding
in Bedfordshire, at the Chawston Estate of the Land Settlement
Association. However, the characters, settings and events are fictitious and
any similarities to any persons either living or dead are purely
coincidental.

ISBN 1 905237 27 8

Cover illustration: Chris Cohen

Typeset in 11pt Stempel Garamond by Troubador Publishing Ltd, Leicester, UK
Printed by Cromwell Press Trowbridge, Wiltshire

Matador is an imprint of Troubador Publishing Ltd

The author, who is married with grown up children and now lives in Newcastle upon Tyne, would like to thank her family and friends for their support for this work, with special acknowledgement to Catherine, Gillian and Linda, for their proof reading skills.

To all who believed in this book, they know who they are.

One

Some people can pinpoint a day when their life changed forever. It might have been circumstances beyond their control like 9/11, a lottery win or a car crash, or perhaps a positive intervention which altered what seemed to be in store. To *really* try to change things involves a certain amount of risk. To attempt something knowing there's a full bank account and your old bedroom waiting is not the same thing at all.

One grey December morning in 1980, a family were about to set out on their particular version of a lifetime's adventure. They were leaving friends and family behind in the same way emigrants in the 1960's left for Australia, not so far in distance but probably just as different. After settling their mortgage the small profit would be used to buy glasshouses and equipment for the five acres of land which they were to rent from the government. As urban as the rows of chimney stacks around them, they were about to jump into the great green unknown. Just about everybody thought they were mad.

'When the Land Settlement Association said they'd move us, I thought it'd be a proper removals van!' Karen hissed at Steve, as he broke from assisting the driver to grab a cigarette.

For her there'd been nothing to compare with the mix of emotions as the lorry pulled up forcing its nearside wheels upon the pavement outside her terraced home. The farewell parties were behind them and the leaving was as they'd wished, a low key affair. A dream which had once seemed impossible was about to be realised, and she'd made it happen.

It had involved lying and cheating, but she'd got there. Steve had been on hand to support her, but he'd never have made the move himself. Now they were on the brink of a new life and the cocktail of apprehension and excitement was almost too much. This became tempered with embarrassment when the driver rolled back the side-curtain and she realised their shabby belongings were about to be laid bare for all to see. Now she watched people squeezing past on the restricted pavement, some with pushchairs taking their children to school through the recently thawed slush and peering in at her privacy. She watched them gossiping, discussing the grime on the side of her fridge she'd been unable to reach and the punctured under-fabric of the settee, ripped further in transit and now flapping in the breeze. Oh, and there was the purple stain on the armchair where Steve had spilt a bottle of red one drunken night, fuzzy around the edges where she'd tried to scrub it out, and the grubby patch where Sandy sat and sweated after his run. All were usually hidden by a patterned throw but that was nowhere to be seen right now.

Karen flushed with shame. Any spare money had been saved to buy into their new life as their faded possessions now bore witness.

'I bet it's the lorry they use for taking the produce to market. There's all bits of lettuce and cabbage leaves in the back! And have you *smelt* it?'

Steve laughed. 'Makes it more of an adventure, lass,' he said. 'Where's your pioneering spirit? How d'you think the wagons looked when they set off for the wild west? Hey, I've just had a thought.'

'What?'

'Well, the kids'll grow up talking funny. Good job they've got Yorkshire on their birth certificates.'

2

'Oh, there's folk from all over, there,' said Karen.

'Aye, but words like *kallin'*, and *lakin'*, they'll be lost. Even *ginnel.*'

'I can absolutely guarantee there'll be no ginnels where we're going,' she said. 'But we can send the girls to your mam for revision. Or mine, but yours is richer.'

Steve looked at her. 'Eh?'

'In dialect, I mean!'

They were standing at the front room window looking out for the first time without the safety of a net curtain. Instead of terraced houses opposite, windows studded with Christmas lights, there was a panorama of their chattels, lit like a stage by the glow of an out-of-sync street lamp. The lorry completely blocked their view in the same way double-deckers blocked the window of the house next door. They heard the hiss as a bus pulled up behind the lorry, spilling yet more people onto the pavement. Everybody, it seemed, was unable to resist a stare, first into their empty room, and then to the hurriedly loaded lorry.

Karen glanced around her, seeing what they'd see. This had been the best room, their parlour, a haven slightly less battered by the kids. Now it was bare and echoey and a single light bulb hung inadequately from the magnificent ceiling rose. She'd loved this house, been happy here.

A neighbour they'd had little to do with stepped over the low wall with unaccustomed boldness, her heel sinking into Karen's flower border. She leaned against the windowsill.

'You're off then, are you, to your new life?' she called unnecessarily loudly, it wasn't as if they had double glazing. 'Rather you than me, but I *do* admire you! All that mud and muck, when will them little lassies get the chance to wear their pretty dresses?'

Karen gave her a forced smile. 'Who needs pretty dresses when they're healthy and sun-tanned from the fresh air?'

she said. She really couldn't remember when she'd last said two words to this woman, who now gestured towards the wagon.

'Where was it you said you wa' goin' again, cock?'

'Hong Kong,' mumbled Karen and the woman couldn't have heard her for she continued:

'Aye well, it's better than doin' a moonlight.'

There was quite an audience now. Moonlight flits were not quite common and not quite folklore.

'There's advantages to moonlights,' said Karen, pointedly.

'Still, you know what they say?' persisted the woman.

No, thought Karen, but I have the feeling you're about to tell me. 'What do they say?'

'Where there's muck there's brass. You'll not want to know the likes of us then!' Laughing heartily, she gestured at the filthy wagon as she spoke. The words "*Land Settlement Association*" were just visible through the grime on the cab door. Karen didn't bother to tell her the dirt was likely motorway filth, why waste her breath? Soon her mother would arrive with the girls and the dog, and they'd be away.

Two

April 1981

He remembered taking her Britvic orange to this very doorway, to the tune of '*Yes My Darling Daughter.*' Now as he picked up a pint of Guinness for himself and a pint of lager for her, his wife's words rang in his ears: Lay it on the line, Eric. Tell it to her straight.

She was sitting at the table, his darling daughter, dainty white hands clenched emphasising her oversized silver rings. She smiled at him, the same warm smile but anxiety, nerves, something showed through her green eyes. On the shiny tabletop next to her delicate hands was a bunch of keys to whatever sports car she was currently driving. No common ground there, for Eric viewed cars like he viewed tables – a necessity of life and the sturdier the better.

'Hello, Dad!'

They kissed continental style, a custom he'd learnt from his wife. He approved of it, a clarity lacking in the confusion that was English etiquette.

'Gail! You're looking great!'

And she was, sharply cut fair hair gleaming, sculptured tweed jacket and silver choker, same style as her rings.

'I am? How's Mum? Apart from hating me, I mean.'

Eric sighed, adjusting his back on the hard wooden settle. The lunchtime sun crept through the window, and he shaded his eyes to see his daughter, tense as a cat, ready to run.

'She doesn't hate you. She's just concerned, bothered that –'

' –he'll die next year? The neighbours will hear? In the supermarket they'll think he's my grandad? He'll be eighty when the children are teenagers? Needn't worry about the last one, because we don't want children.'

This was a bit of a blow to Eric, she was their only child. But as an employee of the Agriculture Department Advisory Service (ADAS) he measured everything in horticultural terms and saw this as an affliction which would probably right itself. Most importantly, he didn't want to lose his daughter. They had once been close, a father daughter bond, which was why he'd been sent. Since she'd become a journalist there'd been little in common, and more than breaking it had looked as if the bond would just peter out. Then Colin, a forty-eight year old reporter on the Mirror had pounced, with his cockney accent and three ex-wives. Eric's lovely young daughter had moved in with him. Two months later, the shock was only starting to subside.

'Your Mum and I,' said Eric slowly, licking the froth from his beard expertly and politely, 'just want you to know that -'

'I can come home if I need to? Come on Dad, I live in London, remember? I'm twenty-five. Can we talk about something else, or shall I just leave now?' She put her hand over her keys defensively.

He struggled with his emotions. After a long gulp of Guinness he said: 'So how's the paper?'

She held up the flat of her hand, silver bangles falling back over her slender wrist. 'No Dad. We can't talk about that. It's a temporary taboo subject. Tell me about you, you're looking knackered. Reassure me it's not me keeping you up in the small hours.'

It wasn't just her. It was work too, but Eric was afraid he'd bore her away. Then he remembered as a child she'd always liked to visit the Land Settlement with him on a

Saturday morning. Horticulture and growing didn't interest her in the slightest but she'd liked the Estate, the way the houses were spread out along the Drift in zigzags, the way the huge glasshouses crept up to the roadside. And she'd liked the people, they chatted to her in a way the arable farmers didn't. If they'd kept animals they'd show her, lift her up as she fed them.

'D'you remember the Land Settlement Association? The LSA?'

'Up the Drift? Of course. Is old Maisie still there? She used to give me hot cakes, and what's her husband called?'

'George. Yes, they're still there. Don't know how long for, though. That's what's keeping me awake, not you. It's tough for growers now, since we joined the EC. Going to get worse, too. I'm especially worried about the latest tenants, the girl's about your age, come down from Yorkshire. They've got a couple of kids..'

Gail narrowed those green eyes.

'No, I'm just saying,' her Dad continued nervously, but the crisis passed. 'They know nothing about horticulture, must've lied to get in, I would think. But they let anybody in anyway, nowadays, whereas you used to have to have a lot of knowledge. They've got Jonathan the fieldsman to show them what to do. I think he might have gone to school with you. Jonathan Foster, skinny, blond hair.'

Gail laughed, and her hands relaxed. 'Five hands Foster! For real? Always brainy, mind you. We called him that because he was always touching our knees, and pinging our bra straps. But I remember the LSA as such a happy place, not like some of the dismal old places you took me to.'

'It still is,' said Eric. Would Jonathan have been worse than Colin? Maybe. 'Karen, that's the one I was telling you about, loves it. Can't get over the space, they've all got about five acres, you know. They're both hardworking and want to learn. And Hazel and Eddie, a similar age and relatively

7

new, they're about to lose thousands of celery because it's bolting.' An image of Hazel's back in her strappy top crept into his mind, smooth skin speckled with tiny moles like the translucent skin of a new potato, Horrified, he forced it out. Was there a bit of Colin in every man?

'What about him who never grew much, the wheeler-dealer square-deal finger-in-every-pie guy? Is he still there?' Gail was relaxing, her smile natural now, her keys pushed away to the edge of the table.

'Scofflaw Sammy? Yes, he's there, Still don't grow much, his holding's like a fortress now. I haven't been on it for ages.'

'D'you remember that family, I used to play with the lad, John I think it was. You'd drop me off and pick me up later. Yes, John. We had a great time, building dens, and that. They had lots of animals, and I remember we put the buck rabbit in with a dozen does, to give it a treat. Was stiff in the run next day. I felt terrible!'

'Yes, Vic's lad. He and Ruby, they're still there, he's still brewing his home brew no one's quite man enough for. But times are hard now for small units, with the foreign competition. They all blame the Land Settlement Association staff. It's not quite all out war but hostilities have certainly begun. I seem to have gotten myself into a position where I'm the only one some will trust, being an independent advisor.'

Gail leaned forward, the journalist in her taking over. 'What's the set-up, I mean, I can't remember. The holdings are owned by the Government aren't they?'

Two plates of Ploughman's arrived, and automatically, without speech, they exchanged pickled onions for salad with each other, a ritual which had survived the passage of time and the recent alienation.

'Yes, that's right,' said her father. 'But the agent, the Land Settlement, runs the Estate. They do the marketing, the propagation and repair to the houses. The Government owns the land, the houses and three outbuildings. The growers accumulate glass themselves, and that's theirs.'

'We're talking co-operative farming, aren't we, like in Russia?'

Her father nodded, as a pickled onion burst in his mouth. 'Essentially we are.'

'I used to think it was like a spread out council estate, those red brick houses not grand enough for their large grounds.' Gail dissected her cheese, there was far too much. She considered passing half over to her dad, but his belly had grown recently and she didn't want to contribute to a thrombosis.

'It's the community, it's something special. A bit like college, all those people thrown together from different parts of the country and with something in common. In a time warp too, I suppose, a bubble. And a bit like a mining village, hence the attitude of those like Red Vera. But I can't keep up this level of calls, I'm the ADAS advisor to an area much wider than the Estate. And I'm going to have to break the news that the service will shortly no longer be free. It's things like that which keep me awake, Gail.'

'Dad, you should've been a vicar. Always interested in people.'

'Says the journalist!'

'Okay, point taken. I take after you. Remember that boyfriend I had, the one who got caught nicking lead from the church roof?'

Eric could see the little runt, big mouth and skinny body, now he had him scampering along the ridge tiles. Colin was beginning to look quite human in comparison. Perhaps a move from the Mirror to the Guardian might help. 'I certainly do, and I still think he was behind the loss of the fourteenth century nave window!'

Gail laughed, her eyes sparkling now. 'He worked for

the man with the huge holding, acres of glass. Is he still there?'

'Ah, Dennis, yes, he's there, still employing casuals, and Sylvia works in a bank, I believe. It's not a problem for the big growers, they can compete. It's the new ones, and the ones who haven't built up glass for whatever reason. Like Karen and Steve, I was telling you about. If I don't help them, it just leaves Jonathan, and he has split loyalties.'

'He always did,' laughed Gail. 'Whether to take you behind the bike sheds or the assembly hall.'

'You didn't go out with *him*, did you?' A pickled onion shot from the plate as he tried to spear it.

'No I didn't! The church roof cat burglar was as bad as it got. Dad, d'you think Mum will ever come round?'

'Of course,' said her father, with an ease he didn't wish to analyse. A belly full of Ploughman's and a successful lunch with his estranged daughter. Why should he want to look ahead?

૪૦ ૦૪

Sylvia removed her black leather court shoe from her accelerator foot and laid it carefully on the passenger seat. She didn't want her heel scuffed, but she didn't like to drive totally barefoot. Wife of one of the most successful growers, she was on her way to work and about to reverse onto the Drift. She shielded her eyes from the sun, still low but bright on this spring morning. The glare reflected harshly from the huge glasshouses, big as warehouses, which bordered the straight road at varying proximity. Inching out from her driveway she had to wait as two tractors, each trailing extravagant metal implements rattled past, vibrating the concrete.

This short length of roadway from her house to the junction was all she really saw of the horticultural industry which shaped everyone else's lives. Neatly clipped thirty foot conifers, golden ones of course, not the common blue-green, entirely enclosed her sweeping lawns and with her gazebo and scenic pond she could have been living in luxury somewhere in Surrey. At least, she reminded herself, if you didn't look at the house.

The design of her house was identical to the others on the Estate. She thought it a brick hutch more suited to some industrious animal which climbed into the eaves to sleep. She detested its pokiness, especially the bedrooms built into the roof with their sloping ceilings resistant to fitted furniture, and the downstairs toilet and bathroom designed to keep the upstairs clear from mud but problematic at night if you had a weak bladder. How many times had she mentally created a Dallas style ranch, or dreamed that her doll's house had become a four-bedroomed villa with latticed windows? Sylvia, however, was confident her dream would soon be realised. The government were selling off council houses like the Women's Institute sold jam, and she knew that she and husband Dennis, unlike most of their neighbours, would be well able to afford the discounted price should the scheme be extended to smallholdings.

As she straightened the car and began to move up through the gears she passed two young women on cycles. She watched through her mirror as they swung into the separate driveway to her husband's nursery. She glimpsed their stretch jeans and cut away tee-shirts, and the carefree way they shouted to each other as they swerved into the gap. Sylvia was grateful she didn't have to slave on the nursery, bent double in the steamy lettuce houses clad in dirty clothes with sweat running down her cleavage. She worked upstairs in a bank and her day would be spent taking bearable amounts of responsibility while swinging her long skirt from desk to desk in a pleasantly ordered atmosphere.

She knew through the nature of her job the horrific debt

some of the growers were in, not just to the bank but to the Land Settlement Association, the marketing agent for the Government. She sympathised with these neighbours but didn't really associate with them, and she probably wouldn't recognise them in the High Street although everyone raised a hand to each other on the Drift, familiarity of vehicle being enough. Sylvia also knew second-hand through her cleaning lady of their scruffy kitchens, neglected through pressure of work and had observed first hand the tatty gardens, all their energy going into the crops and none left for titivation. She felt a sort of detached sadness, all mixed in with her own aspirations for the future. As she turned out of the Estate the few independent buildings gave way to open road and she noted with pleasure that the hedgerows were softening with green. She began to plan her weekend in the garden.

                        80   CR

As Sylvia was contemplating her good fortune, activity was increasing in two bays of her husband's acres of glass. A perfectly even blanket of lush lettuce, patterned by the individual swirls of the hearts, was being eaten away systematically by a human band of cutters. The two cyclists, now wearing plastic aprons, were securing plastic bags around their waists. Four other women and two teenage boys were bent double in front of a trail of bagged lettuce, the plastic of these bags already misty with condensation. The four women moved with the sweep and flow of experts; Kitchen Devils flashing in the right hand, perfectly co-ordinated with the left which scooped the severed lettuce and stuffed it into a bag with just enough pressure to remove that bag from the bunch and toss the packed lettuce aside, all in one sweep!

The boys, new to the job and looking for cash before the

start of the summer term, looked gangly and awkward as might be expected on their second day. One of them slashed at a lettuce but his knife was fractionally too high, so he was left holding a bunch of leaves and no heart. He considered stuffing it in anyway but thought better of it. He straightened up with effort, clutching his back, his swear word just audible over the beat of the 'ghetto-blaster'. The women turned, still bent like hairpins.

'Listen to him! Did I hear that right?'

'Shall we make 'im wash his mouth out?'

They loved to tease. The boy rubbed his aching back. Then one asked:

'Did you wake up stiff this morning, Michael?'

'Yes I flippin' did –' Too late he realised what he'd said. The women hooted with laughter, pressing him for details. Poor Michael flushed and his mate quickly joined in with the women in case they turned on him.

The boys had been surprised at these women, all in their late twenties and early thirties and most of them mothers. Swear words and innuendoes bounced off the glass all day long and there seemed no limit to the personal questions they would ask the boys who were having to think quickly to keep up with the repartee. They had to admit the humour helped the day pass by.

The music stopped with a squawk as their boss pulled the plug. Dennis had fetched in a tray with mugs of coffee. The workers slung their bags and picked their way through the cut lettuce to the doorway. Already the glasshouse was heating up in the April sunshine and the cool fresh air was welcome. This wasn't a proper tea-break; there wouldn't be one of those until the the lorry, referred to as the "pick-up", arrived at about eleven. Sometimes, though, it didn't come until one o'clock, and then activity continued unhindered. Nobody stopped for long until the first load of boxed lettuce had been safely despatched. There was a vague notion amongst the workers that this wasn't legal, but nobody voiced this to the boss. It wasn't necessary really, because like most bosses, Dennis would do anything rather than actually cut lettuce himself, so there was plenty of opportunity to catch the break back later.

The banter continued as the workers sipped coffee and sucked hurriedly on cigarettes. Dennis, standing apart from them and leaning against the doorway, studied his early crop of outdoor lettuce, recovering now from the battering by cold weather which had yellowed them so severely. The rows, nicely straight, merged together in the distance but in reality there were still gaps between them. Speckles of a different green were starting to appear and Dennis wondered whether his crop would beat these weeds.

He became aware of a movement in the distance, across his vital early crop, a silver streak looping like a Russian gymnast's ribbon. That bloody dog! He identified it as it melted from view. Newcomers to the Estate, recently arrived from Birmingham or Yorkshire or somewhere, had moved in a couple of holdings away, and as well as two young children they had an Afghan. Of all the breeds to bring to a place like this, with valuable crops everywhere. Dennis knew it was called Sandy, because they were always having to call it. He suspected the family's connection with horticulture was tenuous; maybe they visited the park daily and this qualified them as far as the Estate Manager and the Board were concerned! Amongst recent tenants had been a cowman and even a fertiliser salesman as properly qualified horticulturists failed to apply any more. Wryly he remembered how his own application had been dissected at interview ten years ago, and he with an HND from Writtle and fifteen years experience. Was it any wonder so many new growers were failing? Together with a dearth of knowledge and faulty advice from that fieldsman Jonathan, they just didn't stand a chance. Suddenly he heard the purr of a petrol engine, and walked along his driveway to investigate, cup in hand. It was Eric Dobson, the ADAS advisor. Now here was somebody, mused Dennis, who knew his stuff.

Eric pulled alongside, squinting at the sun as he wound down the window. 'Got any celery this year, Dennis?'

This was one holding where the grower rarely exercised his right to free consultation, so Dennis was conscious something was amiss.

'Yes, I've a couple of spans.' Dennis lit another cigarette. 'Do you want a cuppa, mate?'

Eric shook his head. He stroked his hairy chin. 'Any sign of bolting? I've just had a look at a crop down the road.' He indicated a skinny yellow stick of immature celery laying on a double spread of the *Guardian* across the back seat. It was sliced in two, showing the cross-section which displayed the tell tale signs. They both knew that once celery started to go to seed then the whole crop had to be cut at once, and in this case it hadn't gained enough weight. It was also necessary for other growers to check their crops, especially if they had bought in seedlings from the same source, as the problem was sometimes initiated there.

'Which plant producer?' Dennis blew smoke casually to disguise his apprehension. This question was much more vital than the identity of the unfortunate grower.

'Westersea Plants.'

This was a relief. A new company, probably cowboy, offering them at a knockdown price. When would these growers ever learn, wondered Dennis. All growers were supposed to buy their young plants from the Land Settlement propagation department, but these plants although quality were costly. Several growers bought them more cheaply elsewhere, pretending they'd grown them from seed themselves.

'I'll check them anyway, and thanks for warning me,

mate,' Dennis answered. There was a small possibility that freak weather conditions at the planting out stage were responsible. As he walked off to examine his crop, Dennis remembered that irregular watering could also cause the disaster. People just didn't get enough help, he thought angrily. Poor Eric Dobson was carrying the burden of responsibility, whereas the Association staff such as Jonathan just didn't seem to care.

Three

The day was approaching. Their first glasshouse crop of lettuce was almost mature. Eighteen weeks after moving south the maiden crop stretched out in front of them like a patterned carpet. More experienced growers might notice the patches of creeping thistle which spiked through and smothered the lettuce in places, or the gaps where a mature plant had suddenly collapsed and died. But to Karen and Steve this crop was their pride and joy. It had been watched and fussed over like a firstborn child and it represented their horticultural credibility, of which they were by no means sure. More importantly it was money, eight hundred boxes at an estimated two pounds fifty a box, their first income this year. They were itching to cut it.

Flatpack boxes were assembled, ready and waiting in the shed, a massive great tower of them. 10,000 plastic bags had been purchased from The Stores too. As soon as most of the lettuce had reached six ounces in weight they could be cut and sent as class one produce, but of course a watched pot never boils. Karen had created a small clearing near the door in her impatience, for alas a lettuce cannot be weighed without being cut first. At last they had definitely made the grade, and Steve was about to prove it to Jonathan, the Land Settlement Association Fieldsman, whose job it was to say yea or nay.

As the wind whipped and whistled and the rain lashed intermittently on the glass, Steve cut yet another specimen and handed it to Jonathan. He took it, speared it and hung it from his pocket scales as a fisherman might a fish. The twins,

Mandy and Trudy, red-nosed but snug in their duffle-coats, collected loose leaves and dug holes in the soil at his feet. The fieldsman eyed them with irritation, but Karen didn't care. She'd no choice but to bring them out with her, and she'd taught them not to damage the lettuce. And teaching that to three year old city kids was no mean feat.

'Yes, six and a half ounces,' he said, handing the lettuce back to Steve. 'But we don't want 'em. You might as well have it for your tea tonight. They're not making much at the minute, we'll leave them till next week. In fact if this lousy weather keeps up they'll stand for a fortnight.'

Steve glanced at Karen, and then to Jonathan, who seemed oblivious to their disappointment.

'You're joking!' said Steve. 'You said we'd have 'em all cleared a week next Monday!'

Jonathan shrugged, and turned to go. 'You've waited long enough already. What's another couple of weeks? The price will improve by then. Don't be impatient, take a break, relax. Go and see Dennis, learn how he does things.'

'Can't we just send a few?' said Karen. 'To get the hang of it?' Pleading didn't come naturally. She pushed the words out from her throat.

'No, I'm sorry, we just don't need them. Can't sell 'em. Probably couldn't give them away.' He opened the door, pushing against the force of the wind. Luckily it had stopped raining briefly, he might reach the car without getting wet. 'You'll thank me later, when they get a better price.' And he ducked under the doorway and was gone.

Steve and Karen watched miserably as Jonathan picked a path carefully along the muddy roadway. A tall thin man of twenty-six, the same age as Karen, he always dressed smartly; black cords, black jumper and black leather jacket. Somehow he managed to keep as clean as if he worked only in the office when in fact he spent the bulk of his time out on the holdings. He even managed to keep his shoes presentable, for there was no way he was going to wear wellingtons. The only colour about Jonathan was his blond hair, gelled in place at the front, but curling around the nape of his neck. He was certainly the cool side of acceptable. Steve also wore black but the contrast between them couldn't have been greater. His clothing was biker gear and his tee-shirts were screen-printed with heavy metal images. And although they were the same height Steve had twice the girth.

Jonathan passed Eric the ADAS advisor at the gate. The big man wore a cagoule over the top of his bodywarmer. They had a brief conversation and then Eric strode up to the glasshouse, clocking the despair on the faces of the newcomers.

'Hello there!' he said, bending down to ruffle the hair of each of the twins. 'Jonathan's just filled me in. Crop's looking great. It *will* keep, you know, as long as you damp it down on bright days to keep it from tipburn.'

'Oh Eric,' said Karen. 'We were all ready. All geared up and ready to go, now we've got to wait. Apart from needing the money!'

'It's bloody frustrating, especially when they're ready. Instead, he told us to go and see how Dennis does it.' Steve said.

Eric walked carefully along a narrow pathway into the bulk of the crop, then bent down, squeezing lettuce hearts at random between his thumb and forefinger. 'There's plenty of room for growth. They'll be so weighty in a week you won't have to bother checking them.'

'We may as well have a brew, then,' said Steve, gloomily. 'D'you fancy a cuppa, Eric?'

'Please, but it'll have to be a quick one, I've got two more visits yet.'

Karen and Steve scooped up a twin each, and Eric latched the greenhouse door. A cold wind sliced into them. It was easy to see why lettuce weren't selling.

Eric had a thought. 'Have you met Jim and Janice?' he asked.

'Aye, I've met Jim in The Stores. Seems okay, has a witty way of talking. But I've not met his missus,' Steve said.

'No, you wouldn't have,' said Eric. 'She doesn't mix much. but they're good growers and a good team. It would make more sense for you to visit them, and they're busy cutting this week. They'll show you the ropes.' He realised that Dennis' huge operation would probably worry Steve and Karen, whereas Jim and Janice had a nursery they could aspire to. 'Janice will show you her livestock too, if you're interested in that sort of thing.'

℘ ℭ

What a difference the sun made. It dazzled, it sparkled and it banished the doom and gloom of yesterday, transforming this holding-to-aspire-to with a rosy glow. Karen and Steve, encumbered by the twins, were looking and learning as Jim and Janice showed them around. The glasshouses stood tamed and obedient either side of a concrete driveway, their crops perfect lines and geometric patterns. Some of the glass was old, but it was well cared for and Steve noticed all sorts of clever and practical inventions used by Jim to save money and time.

All the holdings had three original buildings which belonged to the Land Settlement Association, a large barn called the henhouse, a piggery and a small propagation house. The henhouse was a vast wooden shed, and Jim had cared for his. It was richly creosoted, had glass in all its high windows and the floor had been recently concreted. Karen and Steve's was not like that; their wood was weathered a bleached grey and deep cracks criss-crossed their fractured floor, collecting dust and harbouring spiders. Blue fertiliser bags were stapled across two of their windows. Most growers used these large barns as packing sheds and shelter for their rotovators, extinct cars and excess furniture. But the bulk of this one was uncluttered. You could hold a disco in it.

Karen was impressed, but irritated at how Jim addressed everything to do with growing to Steve alone. And he spoke in the first person as if Janice had nothing to do with any of it.

'My celery's nearly there,' he told Steve. 'I'm proud of this.' Picking his way into the crop, he took a knife from his pocket and harvested a stick. It cut with a crunch, so crisp was this celery. Jim's thick yellow hair fell forward as he stooped, and the crop was so wet it polished his wellingtons. Karen thought she'd be preparing celery for their tea, nutty little hearts in a jar ready to dip in salt, but back on the path Jim sliced it longways, demonstrating to Steve that it wasn't about to bolt. Steve looked suitably knowledgeable, as the twins ran circles through Karen's legs. Janice stood by quietly, leaning against the wall, her arms folded. She wore a black shellsuit, the trousers bunched into hefty wellingtons. Her dark hair was cropped and feathery. Her femininity and her past life were condensed into three gold chains and a pair of heavy hooped earrings which she wore all the time. Karen guessed she'd have a couple of sovereign rings she couldn't fit on any more, as her hands were raw and swollen with years of outdoor work.

'My four are about grown up now, the youngest's twelve,' she said. 'Don't seem long since they were running around like that.' She smiled fondly at the memories, a happy face with a healthy colour from the great outdoors. No blusher needed there, noted Karen.

'*Four?*' she said, thinking of the tiny house.

'Two of them live in that mobile home now,' she explained. Karen could see it, and could hear the beat of a bass.

'Why don't you show them the animals, Jan, and leave the growing talk to us men?' Jim smiled patronisingly. Karen watched the line of Steve's mouth carefully. She was about to protest when she noticed Janice's face.

'Yeah, come on, the kids'll love it,' Janice said. 'I've got Jacob's sheep, lop-eared rabbits, all sorts.'

As Karen followed her back towards the paddock she asked: 'Don't you get involved with the growing?'

'I sure do, been up since six this morning! There's not much Jim can do what I can't. He just won't admit it. That's men for you.'

'Are you happy here? On the Estate, and stuff?'

'Oh, I love the life. Wouldn't swap it. Mind you it breaks my heart how the Settlement's changed, in recent years. It's not what it used to be.' She was smiling as she said it, Karen noticed.

Breaks her heart, thought Karen. If she looks that content on it, it'll do for me.

෨ ඏ

Janice was suited to the outdoor life and appreciated the changing seasons equally. Even in the freezing weather, bitter cold and driving rain, she enjoyed the pioneering spirit of caring for her animals or harvesting the leeks. So long as she could see the warm glow from her living-room window she was happy. She was also a loner and rarely felt the need for close communication with her neighbours, but she had the security of knowing Maisie and George were there, their nursery sharing a fence with hers, or Nigel and Julie behind the line of tall dark green conifers the other side. She recognised everybody on the Estate by sight although she stayed a little aloof by choice. It wasn't through any misplaced snobbery, just a reluctance to make close friends. There were few women she felt she had much in common with although Karen, whom she'd met yesterday, had seemed interested in her animals, in fact she appeared quite down to earth and sensible. Janice felt Karen and Steve were the sort of people she would like to succeed on the Estate.

Janice was always looking to add to her livestock.

'I've been thinking,' she said to Jim, who was stretched out in the conservatory, a copy of the Wansbridge Gazette hiding his face. 'If we had a goat, it could eat some of the waste and we'd get free milk.'

This suggestion in one form or another was made regularly by Janice, and Jim always resisted because he knew that goats ate anything and he feared for his crops. This argument was faltering because Janice now had a secure chain-link fence around the animal paddock. Jim shifted his resistance as necessary. Now he snorted.

'I'd sooner drink one of Nicole's hippie teas!' he said referring to one of their neighbours. 'And that's saying summat!'

'They don't seem to do Simon any harm. Anyway, *you* don't have to drink it, we could sell it,' persisted Janice. 'It's good for eczema, so that would suit our Joanne. Any surplus, we could put a notice outside for the Sunday afternooners.' Legend was such about the Settlement that it had become a local sport for outsiders to cruise the Drift to observe the "Good Life".

'Huh,' grunted Jim, returning to his paper. He shifted his shoulders so his newspaper was shaded by a huge weeping fig and the print didn't dazzle his eyes. Janice watched her husband in the lull of the afternoon. He was a large-boned and square-jawed man, with a thick shock of bright hair which neither his age nor his dirty job were able to dull for long. Like many men of his time, he wore blue jeans, blue jeans and blue jeans. Didn't feel comfortable in anything else, not even black ones which his mother found to her cost when she bought him a pair last Christmas. Janice made sure he'd kept his narrow-legged suit from years ago should a funeral be forced upon them, or they be invited to a wedding. Their relationship would never set the world on fire but they co-existed pleasantly enough.

Suddenly Jim sat up straight, and squinted at his paper. An advertisement for some rusty relic had caught his eye. He had a weakness for old farm implements and already owned a heap of junk he intended to paint up one day and position on the front lawn in direct competition with his wife's shrubs.

'Bargain here,' he said briefly to Janice, who was now stroking a white cat, the one he called Cooking Fat and she called Snowy. Taking his paper with him he disappeared inside the house to telephone, and when he returned he was smiling sheepishly. He did elaborate, but had he not done so Janice probably wouldn't have asked. There wasn't much heat of the moment communication in this marriage. Ideas always went cold before they exchanged them.

'An old horse hoe. Only a tenner, *and* they'll deliver!'

Janice seized her chance, and snatching the paper pointed out an advert she'd seen earlier. It was for a Saanan nanny, at an address ten miles up the motorway. The goat came complete with a female kid.

'Okay, woman.' said Jim. He knew when he was beaten. 'I suppose you need your little hobbies. But on two conditions. First you do all the dealing, and second no way am I drinking its milk!'

      ℰ   ᘓ

They found the goat in a field unpleasantly close to the main carriageway. Parking the van in a lay-by just off the slip-road they climbed the metal fence and walked with difficulty across the grass tussocks. Too near the motorway to grow vegetables, thought Jim as they walked, and too small an area for arable. To a grower every vacant piece of ground is a potential crop, like every unattended space to a policeman is a possible crime scene. Now they could see an old woman being ambushed for food. The woman spotted them and waved with her free hand, for the other held a galvanised bucket. The roar of the traffic could still be heard and Janice thought how much nicer it would be for the goats in the sheltered peaceful pen back home than on this bleak exposed hillside bordering the motorway. Breathless and tasting the pollution, they reached the group.

'You found it then,' said the woman, head down as she stirred the meal with her hand.

'Yes, easy,' said Janice. 'Nice looking goats.'

The snowy-white nanny exuded serenity and better still she had a promising pink bag and two long fleshy teats. After patting her head, Janice stooped and knowledgeably massaged the half full sac, searching for signs of mastitis. She'd been told how to play it by Nigel, next door neighbour and goat keeper. Look as though you know what you're looking for, even if you don't, he'd advised. He had offered to take Janice but she knew Jim wouldn't hear of that. The nanny didn't seem at all perturbed at Janice's touch and the kid bleated aimlessly by her side.

'You'll not find anything amiss there,' the old woman said resentfully. 'Does that kid look undernourished to you?'

Currants spilled from the goat's rear end, as if to underline her displeasure.

'No, no!' said Janice, rubbing her hand gently along the ridge of the goat's spine. 'She's a fine specimen, they both are. It was thirty pounds, wasn't it?'

The deal was agreed upon, and Janice flushed with pleasure. Jim stood in the background, chewing on some gum, offering nothing in the way of conversation. This was his wife's little hobby, let her seal the deal.

'They're yours then,' said the old woman. Janice noticed she didn't call the animals by name and she seemed very eager to get rid of them. She felt a tinge of annoyance as the woman passed the nanny's chain over to Jim, who grasped it reluctantly.

Janice passed the woman three ten pound notes, and as she accepted them her cold bony fingers touched Janice's hand for a second. She stared hard at Janice, then her face clouded over and her eyes, already red-rimmed, appeared to water.

'I'm afraid I haven't been entirely honest with you,' she muttered, her old voice quaking. Her head dropped and she stared at the ground, Janice could see the pink parting sharply dividing her head of grey, scraped back hair. A fleshy pimple punctuated the straight line.

'Why, has it got a disease or something?' asked Janice, flashing a pleading glance at Jim. 'Because if it has, I'm sure we can..'

Jim relaxed his hold on the nanny's chain and raised his eyes to the sky before shaking his head. 'Oh no, Janice. Now if there's a problem...'

'Oh, it's nothing like that,' the woman lifted her pointed chin. It was trembling slightly. 'You see, it's not a one parent family.' She wrung her hands in despair, 'You see, there's a billy, and now he'll be left alone, and I doubt he can take it.' Her confession was a whisper.

Oh, I don't believe it, thought Jim. What a con. And now the damn woman's making it seem like child abuse.

Now everyone wants nannies and nobody wants billies. That's why care had been taken to establish the gender of the kid over the telephone. There are two reasons for this; one is the smell and the other is a billy's utter uselessness. Even in societies which eat goat meat (and many of the families on the Estate could be included in this) an old billy

26

is tough and gristly, and would mean endless stews and not much else.

'What will happen to him?' Janice's face had brightened, for this problem was hardly insurmountable. Jim put his head in his hands, he could already see the outcome. What was the use of arguing? The old woman was mumbling something about slaughter and cut throats, and then as if by act of God a girl appeared dragging a large bearded billy goat, his head down and horizontal pupils blazing.

'Is he to go as well, Bernadette?' the girl asked the old woman, apparently innocently.

Bernadette looked beseechingly into Jim's eyes. 'If you take Old Bill I'll throw in a milking stool as well,' she pleaded.

'Well *that's* an offer I can't refuse,' he said. 'Bloody hell, Jan, let's take the damn thing. Let's get out of here before she throws in her grand-daughter too.'

And so they returned down the bank with a family of Saanans, Janice leading the nanny with the kid skipping close, and Jim dragging an aggressive and reluctant billy as he cursed under his breath. The milking stool was tucked under his free arm.

They wondered later if Bernadette's grand-daughter had sprayed the billy with some odour neutraliser, because he didn't start smelling until he was in the confines of the van and they were heading back to the Estate.

'Bloody hell, what a stink!' gasped Jim. 'It's worse than rotting sprouts, Jan. Most women go out and buy perfume, but no, my missus has to go and buy a rotten stinking billy goat!'

'What could I do Jim?' She wound down the window further and peered into the back. She wanted to laugh but didn't feel she could risk it just yet. 'How could we leave him to have his throat slit?'

'She conned us all right, start to finish, but I couldn't say no neither,' said Jim, removing his hand from the steering wheel to pat her roughly on the knee. 'We can sell him, take him to the auction on Wednesday. Anyway our acres of airspace will easily soak up the stink. And when we get home, I'll show you what this milking lark is all about.'

Janice smiled, Jim had accepted the latest livestock and she had got her way once more. She had long since learnt that the best way to handle her husband was to stand back and treat him like another child, let him have the first go. Early in their marriage irritation with his overbearing manner had given way to amusement because she saw it as part of a pattern she could manipulate, or perhaps that is too strong a word, steer might be better. She therefore knew when he told her packing peppers was a tricky job, that in fact it was likely to be a plum one. And so it proved; the plump, firm, blocky fruit, satin to the touch, almost plastic, were a pleasure to pack. She just made sure she got amongst the bushy rows a day early.

છ ભ

Bernadette (she'd been named after the old woman) was producing more than enough milk for her offspring, and by six that evening the pink bag was swollen and bulging, the lilac veins stretched tight behind wispy hairs. Her teats, handles in goat-speak, were engorged and immensely squeezable. Jim whistled as he took the bucket and three-legged stool into the piggery.

He knew of course that you don't pull a goat's teats, but you fold your fingers around them and squeeze in a sort of spiral. But Bernadette moved away edgily as soon as contact occurred. She fidgeted, she turned and got in every possible awkward position the compact space would allow. Then she began to kick, and with each kick his annoyance increased, as did the goat's. It became a vicious circle of irritation.

'You're putting her off, standing there watchin'!' said Jim, shielding himself from yet another onslaught. 'Go on Janice, you're scaring her. Get out the way!'

Janice did just that and left the piggery, and after twenty minutes Jim stomped into the house as well, defeated. He slammed the empty bucket down on the conservatory floor.

'We've been done, woman! Not only have we got a bloody billy, the nanny's no damn use, neither.'

Janice had visions of a burst bag, and having wrestled unsuccessfully with breast feeding herself some years earlier now felt affinity with the goat.

'We can't just leave her!'

'Sod her.' He picked up the newspaper.

'Let me have a go!'

'Woman, what do you know about milking that I don't?' Jim was rolling up his jeans and inspecting his bruises. 'I suppose I could get Nigel,' he relented. 'He's kept goats for years.'

Some people said Nigel favoured them over his wife, and this rumour was not helped by his effeminate voice and apparently hairless body. The heavily greased hair on his head had receded at the front and dropped at the back leaving a shiny dome. His pink chin showed no hint of stubble, and when he rolled the sleeves of his polo necked jumpers to his elbows, his arms were chubby, pink and bare as an overgrown baby's. His corduroy trousers were always stuffed into green wellies prolonging speculation that his legs were equally smooth. Oddball he might be, but he was crucial now.

Twenty minutes later Nigel positioned himself on the vacant milking stool, face more red than pink on account of leaning down. He squeezed gently and competently and the milk swished and spurted into the pail in thin squirts. The level crept evenly up the enamel. Jim, disgusted, had disappeared. Janice watched intently. This milk was white.

It made cow's milk look milky. Nigel explained it is best used fresh the same day, but chilled in the refrigerator first. After a couple of days it would acquire a strong nutty flavour which most people had an aversion to. He was indeed a fountain of caprine knowledge.

'Hairs can get stuck in yer throat an' tickle yer tonsils for days,' he warned. The swishes became dribbles, and Nigel straightened up and patted the Saanan on her rump. Yet another shower of raisins narrowly missed the pail (or did they, Janice wondered).

Bernadette looked up at Nigel, gratitude showing in her strange eyes. They were weird, Janice thought. She'd never been close enough to a goat to notice how peculiar they were.

'She's a grand lass, and to produce all this milk after young'uns had her fill!' enthused Nigel. 'I'll come and help you tomorrow night,' he offered.

The relationship between Jim and Bernadette worsened gradually throughout the next day, until his very presence in the piggery disconcerted her. Both morning and evening Nigel was on hand to release the nectar. Eventually Janice took her chance, she considered she'd left it long enough.

'Go on lass, course you can have a go,' Nigel said. 'I took it as you didn't fancy it.'

Janice squatted on the straw, and gently touched the warm bag. She wrapped her fingers around the teats, clenching from the top downwards, as instructed. Thin squirts of milk hit the empty pail with a high pitched ring, the key dropping as they grew into full blown swishes. The rhythm took hold. Janice knew that sometime, in another life, she'd done this before. It felt so right.

'Tha's soft hands lass,' commented Nigel. 'You're a natural.'

Soft hands! So that was it. Jim had hard hands, full of calluses due partly to his way of life and partly to lack of care. Still squeezing, she glanced up to Nigel. 'What are your hands like?' she asked. She knew he worked just as hard as Jim, and in the same conditions. He proudly held out his fleshy pink fingers.

'I Vaseline 'em every night, to keep 'em soft for the goats.'

Could they be true, those rumours about the status of his wife?

Four

If Eric the ADAS advisor provided a link with all the growers, a similar connection was made by Jonathan Foster BSc hort., Land Settlement Association Fieldsman. Part of his elastic job description was to visit all growers, observe the quality and maturity of their crops and equipped with this information, match their production with the co-operative's requirements for the coming week. Any excess became the Packing Shed Manager's responsibility to intelligently dispose of through the wholesale markets, aiming always to gain the best price.

Throughout this apparently straightforward arrangement lurked numerous stumbling blocks and pitfalls and recently these obstacles had been increasing. In addition to changes in the weather which delayed or accelerated the harvest date, and the constant problems of pest infestations and disease, there was now the erratic flooding of the market by cheap foreign imports. Fearful for their own survival, the wholesalers were proving disloyal. Supermarkets were clamouring for contracts, but the detail had yet to be hammered out. The current situation had reached crisis point.

Due to a warm spell on the heels of a cold snap, the delayed lettuce crop had matured simultaneously with the one accelerated by warm weather, and both had coincided with the docking of huge container loads of lettuce from the continent. The market was inundated and none of the outlets had been able to take the Packing Shed's last consignment. The English climate then made a characteristic u-turn and cold winds lowered temperatures yet again, so the housewife reverted to hotpots and nobody wanted lettuce. The Land Settlement Association couldn't give it away.

Bearing this news and with no armour other than his natural resilience, Jonathan had to deal with the aftermath. At least there were few good relationships to be wrecked, he thought to himself, and this relieved the pressure slightly. Jonathan's honeymoon with the growers had been brief, mainly because he lacked the communication skills to match his university degree and in his youthful arrogance didn't have the grace to pay homage to their practical experience, a skill ADAS man Eric Dobson excelled in. Jonathan was impatient with their stories of past triumphs and irritated by their lack of foresight. In return, they treated him at best with ridicule and at worst with open hostility. Despite having so little to lose Jonathan didn't relish the next few days, as the growers discovered the truth that their lettuce had not been sold.

Now he accelerated his new Astra past number twenty-two so Mrs Clay could not detain and abuse him further. He caught a glimpse of her tanned face and precisely waved white hair, sinewy brown arms swinging boxes to the top of the stack like a twenty year old. With her smart sta-pressed slacks and crumple-free blouses she could walk out of the greenhouse and onto the High Street any time. Who would have thought she'd threatened to "hang him by his balls to the washing line" last time he'd been the bearer of bad news.

Deep in thought, he caught a flash of something silvery-white as it looped in front of him. Just in time he swerved to avoid it, and as the road was still slippery from recent rain, hit the kerb. The Afghan hound disappeared into somebody else's crop. Jonathan's stomach gave a lurch, panic quickly evaporating as he realised he hadn't burst a tyre. He couldn't have taken that humiliation, for telepathy would have grabbed the growers from their greenhouses and they'd have grouped around willing him to cock up the simple task of changing a wheel.

He restarted the engine and drove rapidly past holdings on both sides, some with loaded pallets outside and signs of activity, others still and quiet. He pulled off the road into the driveway of an empty house to collect his thoughts. It stood blank with its boarded windows and wild garden, Virginia creeper unchecked in three years smothering the whole of the east side of the house. The propagation greenhouse had lost much of its glass. A piece of wood nailed to the back door was stencilled: KEEP OUT – LSA PROPERTY. *"I shot J R"* was overwritten in red scrawl. Broken glass and weeds littered the gravel beyond where Jonathan had parked.

This house, identical to the others, had not been let to a grower in years. It had been a staff house, offered to Jonathan when he first accepted his job. That had been a crucial decision, he considered with a shudder, to live in Wansbridge instead. How he hated this job, and how he detested the growers. Well, most of them. Hazel was okay, flirting with him quietly when nobody was watching. Maybe she understood it wasn't his fault prices had reached rock bottom, and recognised that his was the job from hell. For Land Settlement Fieldsman, read go-between, scapegoat, fool on the front line.

He wondered if the postman had delivered to the growers yet. Unlike them, he already knew they would get a nil return for everything they sent in last week. Dennis, Nigel, old timers and excellent growers would receive the same as Steve would for his maiden crop, the same as the fly-ridden rubbish sent in by Terry Turner. Zero, de nada, nothing. That was the way of the Settlement; the prices were averaged across the board, the only differentiation being the grade. Terry always labelled his produce class one, and they were invariably downgraded. This time that action wasn't necessary, for there was a glut, the worst in anyone's experience. The produce would all be returned of course, but in the April warmth the lettuce were probably already decomposing, and the boxes would be unusable, with rancid patches of rotten leaves stuck fast to the cardboard.

For once Jonathan wondered what he'd do in their position. To hang on in there was probably the best option, he decided. Grow just enough to avoid being thrown off the Estate, and then take a part time job. Problem solved. Never mind that they lacked his degree in horticulture. There were plenty of jobs around if you looked hard enough. Soon this empathy merged into something else as he found himself imagining Hazel somewhere she shouldn't be, doing something she certainly shouldn't. He smiled as it lifted his mood.

He glanced at his clipboard with the list, issued by the Packhouse Manager, of those he had to visit. If they'd sent lettuce that fateful day, Paul the manager had marked a star in red biro. Even Jonathan was shocked at the extent of the list, and he scanned it to check for mad Josh, whose name fortunately wasn't there. He could phone many of them, but he'd have to visit a couple at least, and explain it face to face. The easy option would be to visit Steve and Karen. He did feel a certain responsibility towards them as newcomers, for during their first six months all new growers worked closely with the fieldsman, who taught them how to work out and adapt a cropping programme for their first year. In truth he didn't really know the best advice to give them, especially as he had another duty to the Land Settlement propagation department to sell as many seedlings as he could for them, splitting his loyalties. So he just continued to juggle virtual figures and luckily Steve and Karen didn't question him too much. In fact he had an especially rapt audience in them. Maybe they needed to diversify a little, interesting possibilities in Jonathan's mind were beefsteak tomatoes or chilli peppers. He hoped there would be a letter or three on his own doormat. He was applying for jobs in the private sector, and it should only be a matter of time with his qualifications. He checked in the mirror to see if the gel was still holding his blonde hair. He even gave himself a wry smile in recognition of his importance and his style. Satisfied, he turned the key and the diesel engine of the new Astra roared into life, and Jonathan was away.

80 cs

Jonathan could see he'd lost out to the postman when Steve opened his front door. The flushed scowling face and the sheaf of paper in his hand told all. The return for his first crop of lettuce had arrived. He didn't waste time with polite preliminaries.

'Hey Jonathan, there's summat wrong here!' he said thrusting the paper in the fieldsman's face and pointing to a typewritten figure in a column. He was a big man, and courtesy of his doorstep he loomed over Jonathan, who although pencil thin was by no means short. Not that size bothered Jonathan, he had the authority of the Land Settlement Association to protect him, and his ability to disassociate himself from individual grower's problems remained more or less constant. Now he merely raised his eyebrows at the big man. Steve was a gentle giant, always conscious his size might be threatening, and he disliked aggression. He backed away now and made an effort to control his voice.

'It's got a *nil* here. Nil. What's *nil*? Can't mean *nowt,* can it? When do we know how much they made?' he said, then quickly remembering his northern manners: 'Come on in and have a brew, while we talk about it.'

'I've just had a cup thanks, but we do need to have a chat,' said Jonathan, taking a deep breath as he entered the tiny hall. He glanced at the cheaply carpeted staircase which rose steeply in front of them, and Steve led him into the cramped lounge. Jonathan wondered what to say, and decided to wait until he read his cue. Having only been on the Estate four or five months, Steve and his wife Karen were still an unknown quantity. She was nowhere to be seen, which was a pity.

The fieldsman sank unevenly into a poorly sprung armchair and Steve passed him the paper. He flicked his eyes over it, and the bad news was there in black and white. *500 boxes of class one lettuce @ 0.00p.* Subheadings, totals and "brought forwards" all told the same story: 0.00p. It was the sort of statement you dreamed of getting from the electric board but dreaded from the bank. Out of the corner of his eye Jonathan saw Steve staring expectantly at him, willing him to say it was a typing error.

'No, it's for real, it's not a joke,' said Jonathan. He felt saddened; he remembered they'd been plump heavy lettuce, very good quality especially for a first crop, and he recalled how the couple had stacked the pallet at the gate with such pride after he had delayed the harvest in the hope that prices would pick up. How was he to know that they'd crash like this?

'I don't know how it happened,' he continued. 'All I can say is there is some sort of horrendous glut, worse than I've ever experienced. I've heard the price has picked up now, though.'

Steve was tense with anger, but reluctant to place it on the wrong shoulders. He could tell how bothered Jonathan was by the look on his face. 'So I might as well have sprayed the lot with Gramoxone, then,' he said, bitterly.

'It would have been better had you done that, I suppose, in hindsight.' Jonathan agreed. 'But I'm sure things will pick up. It cannot go on like this.' He suddenly caught sight of the Afghan, as it wandered in the room and straight to Steve. It placed its pointed nose gently upon Steve's thigh, and stared morosely from its large velvet-brown eyes. Jonathan remembered his other task, the one which would shift the blame neatly.

'And Steve,' he added, with a measured amount of harshness. 'You've got to do something about that dog! It's running wild everywhere, and I nearly ran over it today, I don't know how I missed it! It's just not fair to the other growers.'

The dog's liquid eyes moved to Jonathan, but they didn't melt him or the writing on the wall.

'I know,' Steve answered, more resentfully. 'He's right miserable here anyway. He wishes he'd stopped in Yorkshire, and right now that makes for the two of us!'

Five

Wednesday was market day in Wansbridge, the local town where Jonathan lived, and the pubs stayed open all day. More importantly for the growers it was the day of the auction, a huge affair of the sort once common in country towns. This one was held in a cluster of warehouses on the edge of town and its car park was a swampy field the other side of a cattle grid. Sometimes growers put a few boxes of excess produce into the fruit and vegetable sale. This provided ready cash tax free for them, when strictly speaking they were not supposed to sell anything to anyone other than the official marketing agent, which was the Land Settlement Association. The Association, though, turned a blind eye to this auction on the understanding that only class two and three produce was submitted, such as lettuce speckled with fly (dead of course), banana-shaped cucumbers and misshapen peppers. Better observed amongst the growers was the unspoken law that nobody should flood the market as this would spoil it for others.

The "selling outside" rule had been ignored on a far greater scale as soon as debts became unmanageable, despite the very real threat of being thrown off of the Estate and made homeless should the LSA find out. Growers furtively sent boxes of premium quality to London and Brighton, and any destination in between. Devious plans were concocted and hundreds of boxes were smuggled out under cover of darkness. Narcotics and firearms would seem simple at the side of their endeavours! Bigger risks were taken all the time, as is the nature of these things. But the Wansbridge

Country Auction was a place where the growers could relax and sell produce openly.

This particular Wednesday Steve and Karen were preparing for a family visit to the auction, hopeful of a good price for produce they'd sent in earlier. They were excited by this chance of making extra cash. Their main crop had been good, and the lettuce sent here were the dregs, stunted by cold draughts from around the doorways, or dark, leathery specimens from dry spots where the irrigation didn't quite reach. They had plenty of inferior lettuce because their glass was old, mostly "Dutch Light" glass with lots of gaps and rusted vents which didn't open properly. They had just one relatively modern greenhouse, a mediocre "Fenland" house. Compared with Dennis' aluminium multispans their glasshouses were like the third world. When gales swept across the flat open countryside the glass rattled and creaked in the wooden frames like a choir of sore throats. Eric from ADAS hinted some disaster ought to befall at least one of the houses, but this had yet to be initiated as there were times of the year when it was inadvisable to be waiting around for an insurance payout.

Once the girls were in the van Karen went to secure the Afghan to his outside kennel. Remembering the days when he was taken everywhere Sandy began to wail in misery, straining at the end of his long lead.

'Aw come on, let's take Sandy,' said Steve. He was aware the Afghan's existence had indeed become a bit of a dog's life since they'd moved. Back home, he'd been trusted to stay close to Steve, walking free in a crowded town centre. Sandy's only real weaknesses were rabbits and hares and as there's a dearth of them in High Streets, he was the dutiful town dog.

'I suppose so,' agreed Karen. 'Best bring the lead, though.' So the town dog returned to the town once more.

The weather had become unpredictable again, and a cold

blast shifted the rain clouds across the sky. The children, red-nosed and toggled tightly into their duffel coats sang tunelessly from the back. Spirits were high. This life was new and exciting and although the work had been hard the buzz of making some money lifted them higher still. Karen, who unlike her husband spent a lot of time considering things decided it was true, boredom is a catalyst to tiredness. Despite the long days and stiff backs they often didn't realise how tired they were until that late glass of hot milk or cup of cocoa. The nil return for their first crop of lettuce had been followed by a reasonable rate for the next six hundred boxes, so they'd begun to relax again.

Rain stung the windscreen as they drove along the country lanes but died back to a gentle drizzle as they reached the town, which was packed with people, hoods up, struggling against the cold wind.

The vegetable auction was in progress in a vast draughty warehouse, not that you could see much of the action on account of the crowd. The auctioneer was visible though, raised on his rostrum. Two strapping and tanned females stood one either side of him, each with a protective hand on the edge of the rostrum, waiting for him to step down so they could drag it to another location. As he gave his customary tirade they stared blankly ahead like two Egyptian cats, occasionally throwing him adoring and possessive looks. To Karen, they looked like minders, for although they didn't outwardly respond when buyers appeared to scrap over a box of beetroot, and just stared blankly through black mascara, Karen guessed their long nails would soon be drawn if anyone physically attacked their master. He appeared to know everybody by name; "two boxes to Mr Ward, seven to Mr Smith...." She wondered what would happen if she or Steve bid; "six boxes to the complete stranger over there"?

The twins tugged at Steve's jeans and pulled at the hem

of Karen's coat.

'Pick us up!'

'Mam, we can't see!'

Steve hoisted each one up in turn. Karen wouldn't have been much use, she was having difficulty seeing herself, straining on tip-toe. The girls had soon seen enough and found a vacant corner, improvising a game with a stray turnip. Karen's neck swivelled back and forth, keeping an eye on them, and watching proceedings.

It was a stage show, with the auctioneer as compere. Now he roared: 'Who will give me two pound for this lovely box of rhubarb?' This was met with a cautious silence. 'Okay – One pound ninety? One pound eighty? Seventy? What's wrong with you all today – cat got your tongues? As I'm feeling generous, one pound sixty – fifty – forty? Do you want me to *give* it to you? All right, one pound and that's giving it away.. eighty pence and I'm not going lower than that. I'd rather chuck it in the River Wan. Come on, eighty pence. No?' There was no response so he shook his head and banged his hand down on his book in disgust, saying: 'Well they'll stay right here then.' His harem shook their scragged-back ponytails in mock outrage.

Then he sighed deeply and said: 'Alright, alright, We'll give it another go, then, just till you get warmed up. Who'll start the bidding at one pound seventy five for this lovely pink rhubarb?' At this the bidding commenced, and the original boxes sold for three pounds each.

Karen and Steve watched entranced as the trio scraped the rostrum up and down the rows of produce, and the crowd shuffled and pushed and edged their way behind them. Each time a lot was sold, usually a couple of boxes at a time, the buyers snatched their purchase away to the side of the hall, trying to grab the best box. There were plenty of scuffles and arguments, but they all seemed to resolve themselves quickly. As Karen and Steve began to pick out a few growers they recognised in the crowd, the twins wandered around, getting under people's feet. A lot of the buyers were elderly country folk; they looked like somebody's grandparents which they likely were, rather than wheelers and dealers which they doubtless were too. One old man stood out in the crowd, probably because the crush gave way around him on account of his smell. He had a tatty greatcoat fastened with a bit of plastic coated string and seemed to be buying quite a lot. Steve and Karen later learned he was a millionaire.

Once the sale was under way everything happened with such speed, and Karen imagined the auctioneer would sell one of the crowd if he laid down and curled up with the produce. It looked as if their lettuce had been sold because there was now a space where their row had been.

'Come on, let's see if we're rich,' said Steve, and they crossed the yard to the Sales Office to see what price their lettuce had made, as they hadn't been able to get close enough to see at the time. In fact the price compared favourably with the return for the class one produce through the official channel, and better still it was paid cash on the day. Now they had some spending money. They queued up and bought ice-creams.

In another large room a different auctioneer was selling plants and dairy produce. They looked at the trays of eggs, stacked in pillars. Steve showed the girls the different kinds and let them touch gently the blue-green duck eggs and the large white goose eggs. There were deep brown and speckled hen's eggs and tiny quail eggs. Then they caught sight of the poultry, newly dead and hanging like exotic jumpers from a rack.

'Ugh,' said Karen, turning away quickly. She was still struggling with her city squeamishness.

'These city folk,' said Steve. 'They don't mind eating it but they can't cope with how it's got on their plate! Listen to your mam, a right townie, just like our Sandy.' The dog was waiting outside, just as well, considering what they'd just seen.

The girls decided to side with their dad and be cool, so Karen left them and went to look in the furniture auction. Furniture was a broad criteria. If you couldn't eat it and it didn't move, then it might be found here. The produce auctioneer and his women had moved in and were surrounded by a crowd at the far end.

Karen raked through the lots. Desperate urges to buy something kept hitting her, anything, even if she didn't really want it, just because she had the cash. She stroked a handsome milk jug that wouldn't fit into her fridge and that she might just put out on Christmas Day, and daydreamed about her family resisting the pull of the television and eating meals on this beautifully polished table. She flicked through LPs, recognising one she used to have in her collection which Steve had accidentally left in a phonebox, the long-haired faces on the cover now looked jaded and distant. There was everything from fridges and freezers to bone china tea-sets. These were the days before car boot mania, and she was desperate to find a bargain, but she couldn't decide on which lot to stand and wait for.

'You're not going to spend your money in this old dump are you?'

Karen turned around to see Hazel from further along the Drift, who she'd met briefly through the children a few weeks earlier. About Karen's age, Hazel wore tight jeans and a bright red top. Her fair hair was tied back loosely and her lipstick emphasised her cheeky grin. She looked like a poppy in a radish patch, thought Karen, wishing she'd made more of an effort herself. It was easy to get into the habit of not dressing up on the holding, but then again Hazel was a bit over the top in her red high heels.

'I think I'm just desperate to buy something,' admitted

Karen. The bric-a-brac was losing its glamour before her eyes.

'I know, you get withdrawal symptoms when you haven't been shopping for a while, least, I do. Eddie, he has his flippin' crops but me – just give me a bit of retail therapy now and then. Come to the town with me? Eddie's chatting to your husband, I've just seen them.'

'What about the kids? Are yours here?'

'Just the youngest two. Nathan's at school, so I have to be back in time for the school bus. Daisy and Sam are here, so Eddie can watch yours while he minds them,' she said. 'He does a good line in bribery. It won't hurt them to mind the kids while we nip off for an hour or so. There's a couple of boutiques which are okay, but most of the shops are crap. Thank God for my catalogue.'

Now she had a partner in crime Karen was eager to go shopping for clothes in the town. They split the wads of money and dumped the children on the menfolk and headed off, leaving the heaving market with its wet donkey jackets and decomposing vegetables.

Sandy the Afghan lay close to Steve, but far enough away not to get trampled on. He observed the chaos through his soft brown eyes which had brightened up considerably. Sandy had "town dog" written right through him like Blackpool rock.

The auction eventually wound up in the outside yard where anything too large or too late to get in the saleroom had been lined up and numbered. Sometimes there were cars, but not this afternoon. Amongst today's bargains were a couple of dismantled garden sheds and a stack of greenhouse glass lay propped against the wall. But Steve only had eyes for a ride-on mower. There were plenty of push mowers, but he realised a ride-on one would be ideal for the huge area of grass around their house. When you're struggling with rotovators, mowing the grass should be more of a pleasure, he reasoned. He bid on it while Eddie watched both sets of kids, but it didn't make the reserve price, and he needed to save some money for the pub opposite, having promised the children orange juice and crisps as well. Fascinated, though, he wanted to see the auction through to the very end. When he remembered he glanced over to the girls, checking they were still with Eddie.

Ten minutes later the auction was drawing to a close and the mower still remained, forlorn and waiting for a buyer, a coat of paint and some tender loving care. Steve eyed it sadly, Sandy still at his side. A middle-aged man noticed this and approached him. He was wearing a checked gaudy shirt and had dark curly sideburns. He was apparently the owner.

'I suppose I'll 'ave to take the bugger home with me again,' he said, tapping it fondly on its flaky wheel arch. His eye caught Sandy, and he rubbed the dog affectionately with a large dark hand. Sandy stared back, and then gave a lick of approval. 'Nice dog,' the man said.

Steve was used to people stopping and commenting, Sandy got you that way. They either loved him or hated him, some thinking him too boney for their taste. But once or twice Steve had been offered money. He was a handsome dog despite the clear evidence that he had no pedigree.

'Aye,' agreed Steve. 'He is that.' The sun slid out from a bank of cloud, slanting sunlight across the yard. The wet tarmac gleamed in the bright light.

'I watched you bidding,' the man said. He tapped his chin in concentration. 'It's mine, this. Didn't make the reserve. Shame, 'cos I got the feelin' you was taken.'

'Aye, I was, but I was thirty quid short,' said Steve. 'Mebbe next week?'

The man shook his head. 'No can do, I'm away down the coast next week. I really wanted to get shut o' this by then. She's a lovely mower. You got much grass?'

'Too much. The wife wants a good lawn for the kids.

This would've been just the thing.'

The man wiped the wet from the metal seat with his cuff, climbed on and turned the key. The engine purred to life with the necessary cloud of blue smoke. Sandy moved aside to avoid the fumes, an action the man noticed. He liked a dog with common sense. Steve admitted the engine sounded good and was cheap at the price.

'Tell you what,' the man said, still aboard the machine. 'How about your highest bid plus the dog?'

'You what? No chance, pal. I love that dog. We all do. The family, I mean.' The man shrugged and climbed down, pretending to walk away. But he didn't get far, he deliberately hung close. Sandy continued to watch him with interest.

Steve thought for a moment. He knew in his heart that at some point they'd have to get rid of him. The Estate was no place for an Afghan. He needed exercise and to be able to run free, but all around were crops he could damage if led astray at the sight of a hare or even a bird. Only yesterday Jonathan had again warned him that other growers were complaining, and Dennis had been to see him already. They were surprisingly tolerant, but Steve knew their patience wouldn't hold out much longer. He glanced over to where the man still lingered hopefully.

'Hang about, mate.. How do I know you can give him a good home?'

The man took his time responding.

'Well you don't, of course. But I can tell you, I love dogs.' He strolled slowly and deliberately over to Sandy. 'But you'd just have to trust me, cos there's no-one here as can give me a character reference 'cos I ain't local.'

He petted the dog, and apparently passed the stringent canine test, because Sandy rolled onto his back. 'There, look, he's took to me already! Why don't you let 'im be the judge?'

Steve, known usually for his complete indecisiveness was hit by some impulse from afar. Go on, do it! The message in his head was plain. He heard his voice speak, and he kept his eyes clear of his dog.

'Okay, okay. To be honest he's a right problem where we live. He needs to run free. Can you give 'im that?'

'I surely can. I'm a traveller, 'spose you can guess that much. We have lurchers too. Dogs are me life, if you get what I mean.'

Steve felt a rush of relief, the man was saying all the right things. They shook hands and went into the office to inform the auction staff of the sale. Still buzzing from having struck a deal, Steve arranged to pick up the mower the next day, when he'd be minus his human cargo.

'Shall I leave you a minute so's you can say your goodbyes?'

'No, I'm not one for goodbyes.' However he did stoop and rub Sandy's head. But he kept his face averted and not once did he meet the dog's eye or even look back. Better that way, he thought.

As he crossed the yard to find Eddie and the children he began to sense the tiniest tinge of discomfort. Born in his belly, he battled to cast it aside. But in his heart he knew, whatever Karen might say, he had done the right thing.

                                   ৰ০   ଔ

As this dirty deal was taking place the two women were sitting in a cafe getting to know each other and planning other escapes. Karen was buzzing; she needed a friend. Steve didn't seem to need close friendship in the same way she did. Now she just knew that different as they were, she and Hazel would become close. Hazel knew all sorts of details and gossip about the other growers, and she related scandals, and not just those in the last four years since she and Eddie had arrived. Both were young and the responsibility of their lives weighed more heavily on their shoulders than they realised, but their giggles softened their worries at least for the time being. Karen looked at the pile of carrier bags on the cafe floor.

'Eddie don't mind you spending money on clothes?'

'No, he likes his woman to look good. Don't want me turning into some old frump like some of them I could mention! Steve won't mind, will he?'

'Naw, he'll be pleased for me,' she said. 'I just hope he's found something to buy. And we've got all that stuff for the kids.'

When they returned to the auction, both the yard and the warehouses were deserted but for a couple of men sweeping up with outsize brooms. Their laughter echoed across the empty shell of the saleroom, and their throaty coughs did too as they swallowed the dust they'd disturbed. Karen and Hazel crossed the road to the pub, and saw their kin huddled around a picnic table in the sunshine. Empty glasses and bottles littered the table as they sat hunched against the wind but obviously happy enough, the men drinking beer and the four children sucking on lollies, noses running with the cold. The two women squashed up on the benches as well. Steve had a pint of Guinness in his huge hand and Eddie went inside to fetch them a drink.

Suddenly Karen asked: 'Where's Sandy?' She guessed Steve had left him somewhere and forgotten him. He'd done this before, outside the corner shop back home, and in a snowstorm too.

Steve paled. He gestured a wild "not in front of the children" signal which Karen ignored. She sensed something, and wasn't to be put off easily.

'Just tell me,' she said bluntly. 'Where's the dog?'

Steve leaned nervously towards her. There was no dressing it up. 'Karen, you know we've got to get rid of him.

I've found him a good home, as part of a deal with a ride-on mower,' he whispered.

'Is this a joke?'

'Of course it 'int. Would I joke about summat like that?'

'A deal? You've sold our dog?' Karen hissed. 'And I haven't had a chance to say good-bye? How *could* you?'

The children caught on.

'DAD!' they wailed in unison, two pairs of red noses and chubby cupid lips. 'DAD'S SOLD SANDY!' Even Hazel and Eddie's children joined in.

'No I haven't' Steve protested. 'I exchanged...' his voice trailed off miserably.

'See what you've done! You bastard!' Karen said, in disbelief.

'You *know* we had to get rid of him,' he hissed. 'And this bloke – well Sandy took to him straight off.' Mandy, superficially more emotional than her twin, began to grizzle and his bravado vanished as he now felt as if he had sentenced the poor dog to death.

'Ooops,' said Hazel to Eddie.

Karen jumped up, knocking the table and spilling drinks. She raced across the road to search for the stranger and her dog, but they'd left. The yard was desolate, even the sweepers had gone and an indifferent employee was hauling a heavy chain across the entrance.

She stormed back across the road, tears pricking her eyelids. Furiously she snatched the van keys from the table and scooped up her children. 'Bloody well walk!' she spat to Steve.

'*You know we couldn't keep him!*'

But Karen didn't want to see it this way. She repeated her instruction.

'Yes bloody well walk!' echoed all the children.

Eddie turned expectantly to Hazel, and she shook her ponytail firmly from side to side.

'He can't come with us. Look how he's upset my friend!' she said, before Eddie could speak. Eddie mouthed a silent: "sorry, mate".

Oh, well, it's only four miles, thought Steve miserably.

Six

It was early May and the best sort of heatwave, for it heralded summer and the air was still free from dust. The sun warmed the cold earth and everything exploded into growth, from the crops Karen had been pot-watching to the lawn last cut a week ago. Just like a social life, she thought, nothing happens for months and then you're out night and day and can't cope. Nature softened the trees a pale green, and their colour darkened daily. You could almost *hear* the growth.

'Those birds are that noisy the council would've evicted 'em back home,' said Steve. The dawn chorus *was* outrageous, but then they'd got plenty of trees. Their fruit trees were old and craggy and ideal for tree-houses although the girls were a bit young yet. All the holdings came with an apple, a pear and a plum, planted when the houses were first built in the 1930s, and a previous tenant here had added rowan and silver birch.

There was no pollution haze as there sometimes was in the city. The sky was blue and the world sparkled and best of all it was a Saturday, which meant there was no produce collection, just the usual chores. Karen could pause and take stock of her new life. There was so much to learn and she was struggling to achieve competence. Now sitting in Hazel's car outside the supermarket, Karen decided she could be trusted. It happened like this.

'Can you spray for mildew at the same time as you spray insecticide?' she asked.

Hazel looked at her through a frown. 'Come again?'

'You know, as a cocktail, like?'

'How the hell should I know? Eddie does all of that stuff.'

'I must ask Eric, next time I see him.'

'That's for Steve to worry about,' said Hazel. 'Why bother yourself?'

'Trouble is, I don't think he does know. I don't want him to ruin a crop, just because he don't know what to do.'

'Of course he knows all that stuff. Let him get on with it, we've our mascara to consider!'

Despite recognising Hazel's flippancy, Karen was reminded that wearing make-up like reading newspapers was a habit she seemed to have left in Yorkshire. She ploughed on.

'He don't, though. He knows nowt about growing. Me neither, as it happens.' There, she'd said it.

'Of course he does, else how would he have got in here?' Hazel assumed he had some kind of experience Karen wasn't aware of.

'Aye, well, we wrote the reference ourselves – well I did. Made it all up. He worked down t'pit, didn't see a lot of daylight, never mind fresh air. Hey, promise you'll not tell anyone?' she added, suddenly worried. They'd managed to bluff it thus far and she wondered why she was spilling the beans now, although she was already experiencing a sense of relief.

Hazel pretended to look shocked, then her face lit up with a big smile.

'You never! So Steve hasn't got any horticultural experience? But you, you seem to know about all sorts of stuff! I mean, listen to you. To me, a cocktail's a Bloody Mary.'

'We did have an allotment,' Karen said defensively.

'Oh well *that* makes a difference!' said Hazel. 'My uncle had one of them. All he did was hide from my aunt Julie all

53

day and get pissed!'

Karen folded her arms and sat up straight. My big gob, she thought. 'We had thirty tomato plants last year. And beetroot and.....' She saw the funny side and began to giggle.

'So what *was* your job?'

'I did work in a nursery. The children's sort, mind. You know what really made us want to live off the land?'

'I don't know, not that stupid TV programme with those two couples?'

'No, it was much more romantic than that,' Karen confided. 'You remember the Gerry Rafferty song *Baker Street*?'

'Yep?'

'Well there's a line in it about buying some land..'

'Yeah I remember.' Hazel immediately broke into song. Years of listening to music radio had given her an extensive repertoire. '*I got this dream about buying some land..... Gonna give up the booze and the one night stands......Then settle down, in a quiet little town......and forget about everything!*'

Karen joined in loudly with the chorus: '*Used to think that it was so easy.... Used to say that it was so easy...But you're tryin'....You're tryin' now.....*'

'Hey, we're not bad! And here's me thinking you were some sort of gardening expert! You're into it much more than me, all this horticulture crap. To be honest I only like this sort of work 'cos you're outside and you get a good suntan. But as for all that growing lark, well I just leave all that to Eddie.. or Jonathan.' She cast a little smile sideways as she said this.

'I've noticed most folk don't like Jonathan,' said Karen, ignoring the smile.

'Aw well, they're just jealous.'

'What of – his education?'

Hazel smiled. Her blues eyes were shining with

mischief. Karen noticed again how pretty she was. 'No – of his tight little bum!'

'You *fancy* him,' said Karen. 'You fancy the fieldsman!' Takes all sorts, she thought.

'Might do,' laughed her friend. 'You've got to find your own excitement here. Lettuce and tomatoes don't turn me on like they seem to do you, Mrs Allotment Grower. Come on, let's get our shopping or people'll think we're weird!'

But Karen needed to tie all loose ends; after all they hadn't known each other for long.

'You'll not tell anyone about what I told you, will you?' Her face felt tight.

Hazel slapped her on the shoulder. 'Don't be stupid. And anyway lots of people only have like, *sort of* experience. And I'm glad you're not some stuffy horticulturist. Your secret's safe with me – and I don't care if my secret's safe or not – 'cos I'd only deny it anyway.' She jumped out and slammed the car door. 'Last one out pays the parking ticket!'

But I want to be a stuffy horticulturist, thought Karen, but of course she didn't say it.

      ॐ   ॐ

Early Sunday morning, with the twins still in bed, Karen carried wet washing outside. She felt the cool air on her bare arms, the sun only just clearing the ridge of the greenhouse. The shadows were still long and sharp and the dew on the grass soaked through her slippers. Her washing line was a mile long, no need to double-peg here. Taking her time with the task, she let her mind drift.

She felt no guilt at having lied on the application form. The Estate was originally built to relocate workers from the north and other industrial areas, who'd returned home from the Great War to the insult of unemployment. She wondered if they'd appreciated the colours and the fresh country air as she did now, and if any of the neighbours were their direct descendants. And what horticultural pitfalls had befallen them?

She looked across her land with satisfaction; at the children's swing in the crab-apple tree and their paddling pool, an old galvanised bath. Janice had given her two young ducklings and now they teetered across the lawn. Karen planned to get more, she liked ducks, but she didn't really want "table" birds. She'd been put off when Hazel showed her their lambs, their children were bottle-feeding them and Eddie said it made a nice round robin of the food chain. Karen hadn't quite got used to the idea of playing with your future dinner. Most of the smallholders seemed to take this carnage in their stride, but she wasn't ready for that. She'd been traumatised enough when she'd accidentally caught a frog in a mousetrap and more confused when Steve asked if it would've been okay in a frogtrap.

The lawn, which probably had less actual grass in it than Hazel's lambs had hope of old age, was looking lush, and Karen had to admit the ride-on mower had been a good buy. She still missed Sandy, even though she accepted they'd never have been able to keep him. She'd wanted to get used to the idea before getting rid, and whenever she thought about it she was filled with anger towards Steve.

Quickly looking for the positive again she noted the pond she and Steve had made was still holding water. Yes, here there was hope, a future for their kids, a prospect of a pleasant old age for them both. Her mind slid through decades like a knife through butter, for she couldn't imagine ever wanting to leave, to move on. Because here was community spirit, probably one of the strongest pockets in the land. Hadn't lots of people turned out last week to help clad their plastic tunnels? As the huge sheet of polythene had been draped over the metal hoops, all sixty foot of it, helping hands along its length, and the first sods of earth stamped into the trench to secure it, hadn't she been reminded of the tales of life down the pits, or even more relevant the barn-raising scene in *Oklahoma*?

Although Karen was competent at housework she'd never especially enjoyed it and here it came second in importance to the land. When harvesting, the pick-up was most important, and sometimes even Hazel didn't manage to get her make-up on before that arrived. Children would miss the school bus, because nobody had the time to direct them. The produce was all important. Too busy by day, people chatted at dusk but they didn't communicate in kitchens. Social interaction took place in piggeries, leaning and looking at a mother sow with her pea-line of piglets, or in a plastic tunnel watching a crop melt into darkness. There was plenty of home-brewed wine and beer but not much visiting the pub during the summer months. Did men and women seem more equal in this environment? Or was it just different? Karen wasn't sure.

She finished pegging out, aware of the space surrounding her. Nobody peeping from across the back, counting your knickers on the line, or criticising you to others, saying you "hung out like a gypsy." Anyway, she'd taken so long to do it, today her washing would grace the grounds of Buckingham Palace. Taking her empty basket and squinting against the bright sunlight, she walked back to the house, humming the introduction to that life-changing song. She was surprised to see Jonathan there.

'Working on a Sunday?' she asked in surprise.

He was sitting on their settee, his clipboard and calculator set out on the frayed arm. Steve was waiting for the kettle to boil, his back to him.

'Double time,' said Jonathan, throwing her a wink and leaning forward to pat the pocket of his black cords, ASDA style. 'I've seen your celery, it's looking good, plumped out nicely. I'm booking it in for collection next week. Looking at the weather, it should make a good price. Should at least get you over the disappointment of that first lettuce return.'

Steve said: 'Disappointment? Disaster, more like.' He bent and plonked two cups of tea on the carpet. 'Kettle's still hot, Karen.'

'Come on mate,' said Jonathan. 'We aren't dealing in plastic buckets, you knew that when you came here. It's supply and demand, a balance between the weather and the hungry housewife.' He liked that, the hungry housewife. It conjured an interesting picture in his head. Steve looked less impressed.

'Seems like we could be bankrupt before we start,' he said gloomily.

Karen cut in irritably. 'Oh Steve, give over. Gluts happen.'

'Gluts happen,' echoed Jonathan. 'Shit happens. Fact of life. You just keep on producing the quality and the quantity and we'll worry about the quids.' The salesman in him just took over, he was a natural. His father used to say he could sell knickers in a brothel. He felt he'd convinced Karen, and he knew that was what mattered.

When he'd gone, Karen turned on Steve.

'Why d'you have to be so maungy to him? What's he goin' to think of us?'

'D'you think I'm bothered what he thinks? Anyway, there's trouble a't mill, as they say. Not sure what exactly, but there's folk round here who'll not let it lie.'

'He's trying his best,' said Karen, thinking bloody hell, it's the pit all over again.

'He's a twat. And his best just in't good enough.'

૪૭ ૦ર

The Land Settlement Association had a sundries outlet, the

growers called it The Stores. It wasn't particularly good value, in fact the Farmers Supplies in Wansbridge was probably cheaper but The Stores had a distinct advantage, you could buy on tick. In there neither money nor chequebook saw the light of day, you just signed a chitty and it was added to your account. There were no deadlines for payment, just a bottomless credit card. The opening hours were limited, so The Stores was generally busy and a meeting place for growers and today was no exception. Rain pounded the flat roof and customers hung loose around the counter, chatting. There was nothing to browse as all the wares were somewhere in the depths of the building, like in Argos.

Steve, waiting to buy pesticide, looked around him. He recognised nobody, but they obviously knew who he was, as several nodded and asked if he'd settled in all right. An elderly man moved closer and struck up a conversation.

'It's to be hoped you like gam'blin, laddie,' he said turning towards him.

'Well no, not 'specially,' Steve said, hoping he'd not misheard and the old man was talking about something horticultural. 'Only the St Ledger, mebbe the National...'

'Well you's come to the wrong place if you divvent.' The old man had a bald shiny head the exact same ruddy purple as the rest of his face. Only his huge bulbous nose was slightly redder. Despite this, his blue eyes shone clear and bright, and the deep wrinkles around his eyes were the crinkles of years of contentment. His life may have been hard, but his face didn't suggest it had been one of misery as well. In his hand he held his corduroy cap which he always removed when he entered a building.

Half a dozen other growers trapped by the queue tuned in. Unsure, Steve didn't reply, and Vic paused for effect before wagging his finger and launching into his monologue.

'Our Davy,' he began and the peripheral attention died

away as they recognised his well worn tale. 'Mi brother, like, now he got addicted t' the hosses. He had some canny wins, mind, but soon he lost more, and he started giving short to the housekeeping. His missus, like, mi sister-in-law says: "Vic, bonny lad, it's you he listens to. This gam'blin is ruining wor lives. Will ye have a word wi' him." I did, though I suppose mebbes I shouldn't 'ave really.' The jowls were trembling slightly with concentration, and Steve clocked the work of years of sunshine and inclement weather on the old face. 'Can ye guess what he said?'

Conversation had returned to previous pitch, only Steve was listening. 'No. What?'

'He said "Vic, you're mi older brother and you oughta be wiser 'n me. But you can'n't be. How's it ye tell me about gam'blin, when ye risk not only a few pund but your whole livelihood ever' time ye plant one of them crops of yours?" Well, now, Davy, that's his name, like, he kept on wi' his gam'blin, retired now, he is. A cottage at Whitley Bay, bought an' paid for. I hope you's got the stomach for a risk, boy, 'cause it's yer bread n' butter now!' The wrinkles deepened on his face as it broke into a self-satisfied smile.

Steve retold the tale to Karen as they lay in bed. She listened silently, but Steve could tell she wasn't asleep.

'What you thinkin' about?' he asked.

'Nowt. I'm watching a star. It's so bright if we'd seen it back home we'd have thought it a UFO.' Karen never closed the curtains in the bedroom window. Recessed into the roof, they gave an angle of the sky and she loved to watch the moving picture.

'Don't it bother you?' he asked her. 'That we might lose everything, be even worse off than we wa' before?'

'Then we'll just have to make sure we don't go under, won't we?' Karen replied fiercely, putting her cold feet on his warm leg. He pushed her off.

'Giv' over. We 'ave done well, though, how we've

adapted? And I love having me own land, usin' me skills for us and not some bugger else. And we're not outsiders, neither. Seems like everyone's an outsider, the old guy, I reckon he's a Geordie.'

'Aye, it's good, that,' Karen agreed. 'It'd have been more difficult for us if they'd all been locals. Somehow it helps, that and having a common interest.'

'So long as we can keep it. I'd hate to go back home wi' me tail between me legs.'

'Things'll pick up,' she answered, snatching the quilt and pulling it over her head as she turned away from him. 'And if not, you can no doubt sell me like you sold poor Sandy!'

Steve winced, but the tone of her voice wasn't bitter, so he dug her in the ribs and said: 'Aye, but I'd probably have to pay them to take you!'

Seven

The growers' meeting was held monthly in the community hall. This was a large weatherboard structure built by the Land Settlement Association for the whole village at the same time and probably with the same consignment of timber as the hen-houses. The hall held the Women's Institute meetings and the children's Christmas party. It housed the cup presentation at the children's Sports Day, and if anybody wanted to throw a party which was too special to take place in a henhouse, then it could be hired for that purpose too.

Of late, the Growers' meetings had been increasingly rowdy, and they had never been known for their politeness or their attention to procedure. This was partly due to the spreading discontent which they all laid firmly and conclusively at the Land Settlement Association's door.

There was no automatic right for the Settlement staff to attend these meetings although they were occasionally invited. Usually this had a calming effect on the attitude of most of the men and the few women present, as you might expect, considering the precarious position of a tied tenant.

The first meeting after the "lettuce of nil return" was a memorable affair. The two representatives, George Farmer and Tim James sat behind a large trestle table at the front of the hall; the same table which on Wednesday evening would be draped in a green cloth and reverberating to Jerusalem. Not surprisingly, no staff had been invited this month.

The two leaders sat with heads close together consulting a bunch of papers. These included pink carbon copies which the men, slouched and questioning in the rows of chairs facing them, recognised immediately as produce returns. George, the older and broader of the two officials had changed into a fresh checked shirt, and clean trousers held loosely by narrow braces replaced his working dungarees. Tim, lean and unshaven, hadn't bothered at all and his jeans were caked with the morning's mud, his jumper faded and scruffy.

Tim thumped the table, and the babble died away leaving an aggressive and expectant silence.

'I do not wish to waste time with niceties, gentlemen and er.. ladies', he added as he spotted the upright frame of Vera Clay, permed white hair topped yellow as the evening sun slanted through a gap in the flowery curtains. 'I know what you're all bothered about, and I think I'm right in saying that it's the first time in our history that we have had a nil return for class one produce. We have done some research, and the numbers amount to – er,' he bent his head and checked a scrap of paper – 'Um – to 18,460 boxes, at zero return.' Angry murmurs punctuated his pauses and discontent buzzed round the room.

'Bring that idiot Jonathan! Let him answer for this!' a voice rang out from the back.

'Fetch the bloody lot of 'em!'

Shouts continued in a similar vein.

Tim cleared his throat and raised his voice to resume control. 'We have to remember that they are not totally to blame,' he began, but he was shouted down with jeers and false laughter. George in his turn, hammered the table with his fist. The noise abated. George was well respected. He was a good grower and had served enough years as a representative to gain the respect of the bulk of them.

'If you won't listen, *gentlemen*,' he said, straining his voice to its limit, and ignoring Vera, but it wasn't meant as a snub. Everyone knew George wouldn't know how to deliver a snub. He spoke quietly into the returning silence. 'We 'ave to sort this problem out, and find jus' how much of it's down to the Settlement. We know about the glut and those Dutch flooding the market here! We know as they get a subsidy, and we know Maggie Thatcher ain't gonna give *us* one!'

'I'm sorry, George, but it's an excuse. There's always been gluts but we ain't never got *nothing* for produce before! An' I *did* have me hand up,' the voice told his fellow growers.

George waved down a few more hands. 'Yes, yes, we know there's been some damn stupid decisions in the Main Packhouse, I'm the first to say – but we also know that some wholesalers have been refusin' English produce favourin' Dutch. In a way you can't blame 'em! No, hear me out, let me speak. We *know* they may well be heavier and better quality, 'cos they got *advantages*. That's not saying ours are bad. We gotta get the Estate sellin' to supermarkets in a big way. That'll help us because it'll be under contract and they'll supply packaging which means less costs for us.'

Heckles floated across the hall, dingy now as the light faded.

'English stuff's got more flavour!'

'Foreign muck's shite!'

'Bloody foreign lettuce's tasteless!'

Steve and Eddie were sitting together at the back, and Eddie nudged Steve. 'Listen to the dickheads. If they gave half as much energy to hard graft as they do to moaning, they wouldn't do half as bad!' Eddie, although polite to their faces, considered many growers to be whingers. He also supported Margaret Thatcher, and he was just as isolated in this. Steve felt confused, didn't know what to believe. He hadn't met a Maggie supporter up until now.

'Well I know it's true about farmers, not happy unless they're moaning,' he whispered back. This was in the days before BSE and the return of foot and mouth.

'Never mind farmers, mate, this lot are twats.'

Somebody stood up at the back, a tall man with an educated voice. 'That's true what you say, George, about the supermarkets. But let's not forget they don't pay straight away. And once you're committed, who's to say they won't back down on the agreement?'

Again the noise level rose. Vera Clay stood up. Her back was straight and her voice clear.

'We lost 800 boxes of good quality lettuce. Jonathan said send them this particular week, but they might 'ave held over til next. As it is, they came back five days later, all stuck to the boxes where they'd rotted in the heat. That's boxes, bags, fertiliser, seed, heat for propagating the seedlings, wages for casual staff and all for nothing! How much have we lost?! I say we take it no more! No more, I say!' And she sat down to applause and shouts of approval as if she'd beaten the substance out of the problem.

'Perhaps we shouldn't be growing lettuce at this time of year?' shouted Tim. 'Maybe the days of early lettuce makin' good prices have gone forever?'

Tim's words fell on deaf ears, nobody was listening. They wanted blood, they needed someone to blame. Chaos reigned, George and Tim didn't bother to try and officiate. They couldn't argue with Vera that the boxes should have been returned sooner so they could have been reused. They knew the marketing organisation needed to change its policy to fight this new competition. They knew there was no means of holding this meeting in this mood. Only the loudest voices could be heard.

'Spray the whole lot of 'em with the DDT!'

'Send 'em to bloody Holland. They're in their pockets already!'

Eddie shook his head. 'See what I mean? They don't deserve to live here,' he said.

Vera stood up again. She commanded attention, and not just because of her gender.

'I have a plan!' she announced shrilly, permed head thrown back, pointed chin thrust forward. The last of the sun had disappeared and someone switched the electric lights on, emphasising the expectant faces. And she described her plan, which was met first with disappointment and then with enthusiasm. Indeed a positive roar went up as she finished. The two officials sorted their papers and prepared to leave, George tight-lipped and Tim shaking his head. Just one question was audible above the hysteria.

'When?'

Vera even had an answer for this. Preconceived or what, thought Tim.

'Friday night. We've got four days. To get 'em off the compost heap. That's the busiest time on that road,' she shouted.

Eddie stood up in disgust. 'Come on mate,' he said to Steve. 'They're just as bad as the bloody dockers. Things don't go right for 'em and they throw teddy out. We're self-employed, you stupid arseholes!'

Steve, also rising to his feet, looked around apprehensively. Fortunately the uproar was such that nobody had heard his friend. But he'd heard him himself and a distance was forged between them.

෴   ඐ

It was five o'clock on Friday evening. A young man blew air out through pursed lips and tapped impatiently on the steering wheel of his Ford Capri. His name was Barry, but that's not important. In the passenger seat his girlfriend Sophie rechecked her make-up in the vanity mirror. They still had more than forty miles to go, and had not expected this hold-up, especially on a usually clear stretch of dual carriageway. The evening was warm and bright and the sinking sun glinted on the shiny queue of vehicles. The road was choked with lorries and cars and even motorbikes were finding it difficult to snake a way through. Barry wound his window down fully, straining his neck to establish the cause of the delay which was cutting into their weekend.

'Is it an accident?' asked Sophie, 'because if it is, I don't want to look.'

'I can't see,' said Barry, squinting into the distance. 'Hang on, yes – I think it's a bloody demonstration! I can just see some placards up there. I thought those days were gone!'

The traffic was now at a complete standstill, and Barry swore under his breath and switched the key. Other vehicles stopped too, he could see shuddering exhausts rattle to a halt in front of him. Now most of the engines were stilled, they could hear angry exchanges and blasting of horns.

Sophie squeezed Barry's hand. She wasn't going to get irritated; they were alone together and traffic jam or slow boat to China, she didn't care. Barry though, was tired and hungry, and he disapproved strongly of demonstrations.

He spotted a middle-aged man with a ruddy face walking along the hard shoulder, distributing leaflets through open windows to angry outstretched hands. Some of them were being ripped up and thrown confetti-like back onto the road. The man was repeating something in a robotic manner, which Barry eventually managed to decipher: 'We're very sorry for any inconvenience caused'.

'Well it had bloody well better not be long!' Barry said as he snatched the duplicated sheet. He scanned it quickly and handed it to Sophie, who read it more thoroughly. 'I'm getting out,' he announced. 'You stop here. I'm going to give them a piece of my mind.'

He marched purposefully along the hard shoulder, leaving his jacket hanging neatly over the back seat. Sophie screwed the leaflet into a ball, watching the ring on her slender finger sparkle as she did so. She wondered vaguely where the salad her mother always presented so neatly on her plate came from, but the thought faded and was replaced with apprehension as she watched her boyfriend strut along the grass verge with such aggression. She caught sight of the tip of his tie as it swung to and fro and the low sunlight coloured his white shirt a pastel peach.

Approaching the hub he deciphered the chants, something about Dutch produce. He saw a rowdy bunch of countryfolk, about twenty in all, of varying ages. They were waving homemade banners. The road was blocked with tractors and trucks, and tipped right in the middle was a monstrous heap of what looked like bags of rotten lettuce. Some of the lettuce had lost their bags and slimy leaves were scattered around the base of the heap. Lorry drivers were swinging down from their cabs and doors were slamming as drivers and passengers clambered out to join the fray. A petite figure stood high on a box and was holding forth in a shrill voice. Several people were shouting her down, but she just upped her tone to a more piercing pitch.

A man of Barry's age was aggressively swinging a placard which stated "Don't eat Dutch". He came over and began addressing him personally.

'Do *you* eat fruit and vegetables from Holland mate?' He moved forward as if he was going to grab Barry's arm. Barry backed away instinctively.

'I don't know,' he answered. 'I haven't really thought about it. What I do know though, is you're making me late with your bloody selfishness!'

'Well maybe you should think about it!' The board listed and hovered dangerously above his head. 'Because foreign produce is putting us out of business.'

'And you're putting us out of business!' roared a lorry driver, and the crowd shouted agreement.

'What can we do about it?' said Barry. 'I can't see what it's got to do with us if you can't compete with Europe.'

'Boycott foreign vegetables. Only buy English tomatoes. Ask your supermarket where they get their produce from!' Came the united reply, and the growers took up the chant. 'Support British produce. Don't buy Dutch!'

'I shall *never* buy British again. I'm going to miss my ferry thanks to you lot of Worzel Gummidges!' another driver shouted, and he held his hand down on his horn, blasting out the chants.

An emergency siren became audible above the din, as a panda car sped up the verge past the traffic and two officers jumped out.

Barry shouted loudly assuming authority: 'Arrest these men. They're blocking the road!' The crowd shouted and the demonstrators swirled their placards with meaning.

One policemen shouted 'Right, everybody back to their cars. We'll have the road open in no time.'

'Aren't you going to arrest this scum?' Barry persisted. Another policeman said to him:

'Just return to your car, sir, okay.'

Everyone else had returned to their vehicles but Barry insisted: 'Officer, do your duty. Arrest these men. These yokels with their tat have cost lots of people time and money!'

The policeman became irritated. 'My duty sir, will be to arrest *you* if you don't return to your vehicle!'

Furiously Barry turned and walked back to his car. The policeman, turning to one of the older growers, said: 'Look, you've made your point. But we've got better things to do, villains to catch! Just get this lot cleared and be on your way, and we won't have to take it any further.'

Eight

Karen had increased her waterfowl. She'd been introduced to soft-hands Nigel, the goat expert, a grower who used much of his smallholding to keep animals and birds, and paid lip service to the Land Settlement by growing the minimum amount of crops. What he did grow, though, was always top quality. He'd been on the Estate for years, arriving chubby and pink-faced straight from college. Now The Stores had run out of lettuce bags and Eric suggested Karen borrow some from Nigel.

'Take a look at his crops while you're there,' the advisor suggested. 'He's a little eccentric and doesn't produce much but what he does grow is better than most.'

Walking up Nigel's roadway in search of him she noticed the cleanliness and tidiness. No stray weeds, no discarded packaging rotting in the long grass. When she peered into his plastic tunnels the crops were even and lush. As there was no sign of him, she followed the mandarin duck calls – nih nih nih nih nih, plaintive cries, ringing out eerily from where the sky now glowed red, silhouetting the boundary hedge. She spotted him beyond the greenhouses where he'd created more of a lake than a pond. He was feeding his ducks from a metal container and Karen watched as latecomers skidded to a halt across the water.

'These are great!' enthused Karen, shouting above the din. 'Where can I get some from?'

'Shouldn't 'a thought you want t' mess about with these,' said Nigel. 'Reckon you've more than enough growing all them crops for Jonathan. I was speakin' to

Robert up the far end. He said if he'd ave planted all the lettuce that idiot had planned for 'im, his land would've had to stretch reet up the arterial!'

'Oh, he's been right with us.' Karen dismissed his comments. She didn't want to get involved in this. 'I'd love to have all sorts of ducks and things. What's the point in living somewhere like this if you can't enjoy it?'

'Aye, well, you've a point there lass,' he conceded. 'At least waterfowl i'n't that labour intensive.' Karen noticed how jargon spilled over into the growers' casual conversation. She watched as Nigel finished the feed, and then walked back with him to his packing shed, skipping to keep up with his long strides.

'I know a good rare breed show where they sell 'em,' Nigel was saying in his soft squeaky voice. 'But it's not while September. I could tek you wi' me to t'cattle market in Cranesbury, one Saturday morning. There you choose your duck or goose, and the man 'as its neck between 'is thumb and forefinger. Asks if you want it dead or alive.'

Karen glanced up to see if he was joking, but the podgy face just showed the slightest of smiles which was always present, as if painted on his lips.

'You're not serious!' said Karen, in horror. The dying sun bounced back at them from the greenhouses as they walked eastwards.

Nigel shrugged. 'Aye, o' course. Then t'buyer knows it wa'nt found dead, and it's fresh, important if it's for t'table.'

Karen imagined irrationally buying up all the waterfowl purely for rescue purposes. 'How horrible!' she said with feeling.

They turned into the shed, and Nigel switched on a fluorescent light. It lit up a bright, clean space, orderly as a pharmacy, the wooden walls, shelves and everything painted white. She even spotted a feather duster on a hook. She watched as he opened a large cardboard box with surgical precision, and took out 2 x 500 lettuce bags, strung together with a strong wire. He ran his thumb fondly along the bags as you might the edges of a paperback.

'You'd 'ave been a lot o' use when this Estate still had animals. How d'you think we slaughtered 'em – firing squad? Do I tek it from that as you'll pass on t' market?'

Karen took the bags. She held them aloft with her strong, thin wrists. She didn't want to bend the wire or spoil them, she'd learnt that spelt bother when cutting lettuce under pressure.

'No way. I couldn't,' she said emphatically. She hesitated, then asked: 'You couldn't get them for me, if I give you the money?'

So that is what Nigel did, and Karen increased her waterfowl without the anguish of having to leave some behind to be killed.

℘ ℛ

The hot May days continued, the sunshine drenching the Estate and sweltering those at work under glass. In the older greenhouses the vents were forced wide on the bottom notch of their rusted latches, in fact whole sections could easily be removed temporarily to let in the cooler early morning air. The newer aluminium glasshouses had better ventilation and some houses like Dennis' had automatic systems, creaking and shuddering above the workers as the morning wore on and sweat stained their tee-shirts.

Celery was being cut all over the Estate; the glass first, followed closely by the plastic tunnels where heat loss was greater at night. Tunnels had advantages though; the humidity was higher and celery like peppers enjoy moist air. They had to be planted slightly later when the sun had had a chance to warm the soil through.

Using a claw hammer, Steve lowered the plastic doors to

72

his polytunnels each morning and the rush of hot air from within steamed his glasses. He was proud of his own design; each door had a series of slots for nails to be fixed, giving varying amounts of ventilation. In these simple tunnels the doorways were the only source of air flow. Only a few growers had highly expensive plastic multi-spans which could be gapped along the sides. These super-structures were greatly aspired to.

Previously a little overweight, Steve had slimmed down thanks to hard work and heat. His black tee-shirts weren't stretched as tight across his belly any more. He still wore his black leather waistcoat unless it became too hot and he kept to his leather boots in preference to wellingtons, but they were starting to come adrift and the heels were trodden down unevenly. He was basically happy; he enjoyed the challenge of building and creating, and felt a sense of pride as it certainly helped to be practical in this occupation. He knew how the growers mocked Simon, the young intellectual turned grower who had a law degree but had to get help to fix the PTO to his tractor. Simon took all the mocking good-naturedly and exaggerated his practical shortcomings to increase the amusement, such was his confidence in his academic abilities. He unashamedly admitted that it was the atmosphere of the Estate that attracted him and the way of life for his children, should he and Nicole have any.

Prices were rumoured to be high this week and most celery crops had made the size. This lifted spirits and the recent lettuce fiasco was forgotten in a rush of activity and bright sunlight. Casual workers swelled the numbers as harvesting celery was very labour intensive. The cutter had the worst job, right in the heart of the heat. Once the sticks had been bagged, the sorting, weighing and packing could be done in the shed, or on a temporary table set up in the sunshine if a suntan was part of your agenda.

It was certainly part of Hazel's, and she sorted and weighed in the fresh air wearing just her candy striped bikini and singing along to the radio. Having lost the bulk of their greenhouse crop when it bolted, their plastic tunnels were producing beautiful creamy-white specimens. Hazel had cartons for the different sizes fanned out ready, and she soon learnt how to build up speed, spinning the sticks across the Avery scales and thence in all directions. Jenny, a local girl home on exam leave counted the sticks, sealed the boxes and sorted them to different pallets. Hazel and Eddie's two youngest children played with empty boxes a few yards away. Nathan, their six year old, was out building dens with his friend a little further up the Drift.

Eric pulled up in his car, Hazel hadn't heard him over the loud music. Her jumper and jeans were nowhere to be seen, Oh what the hell, she thought.

'Hi,' she shouted, pleased to have an excuse to stop, and sent Jenny for drinks. Eddie emerged from the heat, his face red and dripping with sweat. In just his swimming trunks his body was white against his flushed face and the red V of his neckline. His curly brown hair was plastered flat with perspiration, which also glistened on his chest. He went to pick up Hazel's tee-shirt, caught her eye, and wiped his brow with his own instead.

'How are they turning out?' asked Eric, entering the tunnel and walking across the flat bed of cut leaves which were browning rapidly with the heat. The smell was unmistakably celery but overlain with the sickly odour of decay as the cut leaves sweated in the sun. Eric wondered as soon as he said it why he'd asked, for according to Eddie every crop he grew was a cracker, even that disastrous early one.

'Magnificent. See for yourself,' said Eddie. 'You know Eric, if that bloody lot took more trouble growin' and less moanin' they'd all have a crop like this.'

'Well congratulations on these, after the disaster that befell your glasshouse crop,' Eric replied pointedly. He bent down and examined the standing sticks. 'Yes, not bad,' he agreed, wiping beads of sweat from his forehead as he rejoined them, lowering himself carefully on to the grass in the manner of one who suffered bad backs. Hazel lay on her back in order to bronze her front. She chewed a blade of grass.

'Haze, give Eric a stick to take home for his tea, a good big'un,' said Eddie, swigging from a warm bottle of pop.

'Thanks, but just a small one, there's only Marie and I, my daughter's moved to London.'

'London,' said Eddie. 'Ugh. Have a big stick and it'll last a while.'

'Oh, I'll be back, to check if any disasters have befallen you.'

'Oh we're in the clear now,' said Eric. 'Aren't we, gel?'

His "gel" had her eyes shut, face tilted to the sun. 'Mmm,' she said.

Jenny appeared with beakers of lemonade and lollies for the kids. After asking the time yet again, she sat down with the little ones. As they chatted idly, Eddie squeezed at a red patch on his belly, the discolouration standing slightly proud on a roll of white fat.

'What's that?' asked Eric.

'He's dropping to bits,' said Hazel, stretching a long brown leg out and scrutinising it. 'He's got blisters on his hands, but he won't wear gloves, don't want to be a pouf.' She flashed Eric a smile through her long dark lashes.

'It's nothing, woman,' said Eddie. 'Stop your whining. A bit of Savlon will soon clear that up. I reckon in the town they'd have a week on the sick with this. Or the miners, or the car workers – now they'd probably strike!'

'Yes, well, if it's celery rash you'll know about it,' Eric glanced at his watch and once again avoided Hazel's cleavage as he drained his cup. 'I must go. Thanks for the drink, and the celery.'

The big man opened the door to his Volvo, letting the heat out for a moment before climbing in, and tucking the celery under the passenger seat out of the sun. He slammed the car door, fired the engine and reversed up the narrow roadway, right onto the Drift. It struck him how well he reversed, all that practice, day after day. Kept his neck muscles supple.

Now the growers had to pay for his services, his workload from this Estate had been cut by eighty percent. They were currently on about the same level of call out as farmers and growers from outside the Settlement. This visit had been a paternal one, he'd wanted to make sure they had recovered from the early disaster of their greenhouse crop. Satisfied, he drove up the road. His next call, to Tim, was a scheduled one.

ഈ   ശ

Two British bikes roared up the Drift and pulled into Steve and Karen's driveway. Long standing friends of Steve, they arrived out of the blue en route to a rally on the coast. Steve was pleased to see them, and like many others, they'd promised to visit but he never expected them to get it together and actually do so. Karen was less happy, she was afraid their presence might remind Steve of his past and nights on the town he was missing.

However, it was good to have visitors and she liked showing off what they'd achieved. The big lads seemed fascinated by the Estate, the crops, the people, in fact everything that was so totally different to their life. That Steve was now a shit kicker they felt was down to Karen who'd never seemed right as a biker's moll. They were both quite wary of her. They came to lend a hand for a few days, big, strong, cheerful – everything you needed in a labourer but they wouldn't have the necessary application for more than a week at most. Perfect for a few days, though.

'Eh up, cucumbers! I never knew as they grew like that,' Mark said peering through the glass at the lush plants already reaching the roof of the small prop house. Steve had managed to coax the old boiler to work, and they'd cultivated a few plants as an experiment. Unfortunately it hadn't been possible to grow them on a larger scale as they couldn't afford the heat to start them off back in April. Karen had been amazed how quickly they grew. Cucumbers were forming thick and fast, the bottom ones forced to curl but the rest long and sleek. How she wished she had a proper crop of these, for the price was still sky high. They had a late crop planned, but no doubt the price would have slumped by then.

'Well how did you think they grew then?' Karen asked, a little sharply. 'Under the ground like carrots?'

'Come on, peanuts do,' Mark replied, wounded. 'It was on't telly last week. Anyway Mrs-I-was-born-on-the-land-Turnip, how long have *you* been the expert in all this?'

'I'm sorry Mark,' she said hastily. 'We're so grateful to have your help, you know that.' She always seemed to get it wrong. She had in the past too, never really forming a relationship with them, too fearful their lifestyle might be irresistible to Steve. She felt sorry and resolved to try harder.

Mark grinned. 'You jus' keep feedin' us meat like you did last neet, and we'll be raight while next Saturday.'

Both men enjoyed the good food, compared to the cheap meals they ate at home to finance nights of heavy drinking. They were ready for the challenge of hard work, and set to in the celery with their fresh energy. So long as in return they could drive the tractor and play daft games using the twins as their excuse.

One morning they were hoeing the outdoor lettuce in the shelter of the top greenhouse, when they heard a sharp crack above them, and a pheasant dropped dead at their feet. Tricked by the glass it had flown into the greenhouse and broken its neck. Phil who was nearest touched its floppy green head gingerly with his steel-tipped boot. They both stared at it. You don't get many pheasants in the city, and they couldn't believe their luck. A gift from God, for sure.

'Is it dead?' asked Mark, leaning on his hoe.

'Aye, course it is,' said Phil. 'Look, its neck's at right angles. Poor bastard! Bit like hittin' a lorry full on. Ever 'ad pheasant?'

'Not cooked,' joked Mark. 'But I reckon we will toneet.'

'Pick it up then!'

'Nay, it's yours,' said Mark. 'You saw it first.'

The brave bikers deliberated over the dead bird for a few moments more, then Phil spotted an empty lettuce tray. He tilted it and rolled the pheasant into it. Then they proudly carried their limp prize to Karen.

She was beating Yorkshire pudding mix in preparation for a Sunday dinner in honour of the guests.

'Ugh,' she squealed. 'Get it out!'

'It's free food, woman! Never turn down free food,' said Phil. Squeezing past her he plonked the tray on the table in the dining room.

'So Lady Muck 'as 'er limits then,' teased Mark.

Fortunately Hazel came in. She'd come to ask Karen for some antiseptic cream for the strange red patches on Eddie's belly, which were worsening. Karen passed her some and slipping the tube into the pocket of her hot-pants she turned her attention to the scene.

'Pheasant plucking? No problem, give it here!' And she expertly plucked it there and then, while still warm.

The two bikers sat and drooled as she deftly stripped the bird, deliberately emphasising the movement of her body as she swung sexily around the table. And it was difficult to swing around that table. They watched, spellbound.

'Of course, this isn't how we do this in the country, but you townies wouldn't know that,' Hazel said as she plucked, fingers a cloud of feathers.

'''Ow d'you mean?' asked Steve.

'We hang pheasants up for a few days, 'til they smell rank and get all maggoty. *Then* we pluck 'em. Helps the taste.'

Karen shivered in disgust. This matched with something she'd once read in the *Allotment Gazette*.

'Sounds good to me,' said Phil.

'Aye, bit like your stews,' said Mark.

'And of course you do know it's an aphrodisiac?' She looked up from her task to make fleeting eye contact with Mark.

'Well, I 'ad heard,' he lied. 'But I like to test me aphrodisiacs out, mind. I tek it you'll be joinin' us for tea?'

'Is she married?' whispered Phil to Karen, impressed.

'She is!' said Karen, shaking her head.

'Is he big?' asked Mark. They were now stopping till Tuesday and he was doubly glad.

⁊ ☙

Karen decided to keep the pheasant for the next day, as she'd all but prepared Sunday lunch. That way it could be barbecued, Steve would cook and she wouldn't have to touch it until it was officially meat.

Now they lounged on the lawn as the evening cooled and the sun bloodied the glasshouses. The twins played close by, in amongst the branches of the apple tree, then chasing each other in a circuit around the sheds. Their shouts echoed and bounced off the glass, and the sound of Nigel's Mandarin ducks drifted across as they cried for food. A plane droned somewhere lost in the expanse of sky, and the hens clucked and rooted for food at their feet.

'Eh lad, this is the life,' said Mark, leaning back on two legs of his chair, as the bird sizzled gently on the fire. Bats darted crazily just above their heads.

Karen had supplemented the pheasant with home made beefburgers, something she'd never cooked here. She'd mixed the minced beef with fresh breadcrumbs and grated onion (risky on your fingertips) and herbs. The burgers were a bit crumbly, so she'd cheated and part-fried them in the pan first. The aroma from these overpowered the pheasant. She served a big dish of Yorkshire scallops, potatoes cut one way into flat circles and deep fried in batter. She didn't make these often either; they ruined your chip pan before doing a slower job on your arteries. But they were always delicious. She'd taken trouble with the salad too, mostly bought from the auction, apart from the lettuce and cucumbers which she'd sliced really fancy on account of her pride in them. There were little scally onions and french breakfast radish, the hot ones which catch your throat. The pheasant, so tiny, had been carved up between the men and they ate it in sandwiches smothered in brown sauce. Karen and the girls wouldn't touch it. A crate of Newcastle Brown Ale was steadily filling with empties.

'Ow d'you cope with no offie?' asked Phil. They'd had to drive to the local pub a mile or so away to buy beer at the outsales. 'It's grand, all this,' he waved his arm towards the holding, 'but it wouldn't mean owt if I couldn't top up the ale wi'out gettin' breathalysed.'

'We walk. It don't tek long. I don't feel the need to get pissed every neet any more. I've right enjoyed this week, mind.'

'No hope for you then, pal,' said Mark. 'Mind you, give me a chance wi' that Hazel and I'd win 'er round right soon and set up on the farm next door.'

They all laughed.

'No, I mean it,' said Mark. 'Another time, another set o'

circumstances, who knows? I might even come t' terms wi' no offie.'

The girls had homed in and were climbing over Steve, who was feeding them crunchy bits left over from the scallops. Karen noticed that their hair, already blond, was now bleached almost white by the sun. She supposed it would eventually go mouse and then dark, like both her's and Steve's. Steve tickled Trudy, who squealed, and then Mandy. That's the thing with twins, you have to do everything twice.

As they lounged on the grass with full bellies, plenty of booze, and the aroma of the barbecue still lingering it did seem like a slice of paradise. Karen was happy; the lads had enjoyed it, they understood to a degree and Steve had stood his ground; he wasn't going to be tempted back home, she knew that now.

'You wouldn't stand it,' said Steve. 'It i'nt always like this, you know. Mostly it's just hard graft. If you hadn't come and helped us I don't think we'd have got all that celery out.'

'Aye, got to admit when we 'eard what you were doing we decided to come through an' tek the piss.' said Phil. 'Happen I'm getting old or mebbe drunk too much, but I reckon it suits you.'

Mark said: 'Anytime, pal. You just ring for us. Celery Hit Squad.'

It was cool having friends in the countryside but a few days visit was plenty. Any responsibility beyond bike care was just putting your head in a noose.

Next morning their bikes blasted down the Drift towards the seaside. Midge the landlord of the Red Cow heard them roar past his window. It had been a fair week for him, too.

Nine

Jim and Janice had agreed to take part in a cherry tomato trial for the supermarkets. Cherry tomatoes were a relatively new crop in 1981. Janice had seen them in her local Sainsbury's, tempting in their transparent punnets, shining like large plastic beads. Way back in February the decision had been made...

'They may look nice, but they'd be a pain to pick, Jan,' said Jim. 'We'd have to get the kids on it, or have me ma to stay.'

Oh no, thought Janice. Not his ma. 'We'd manage,' she said. 'And if you're sure Sainsbury's will want them, then it'll be a good price.' The LSA had already established that produce sent to the supermarkets would be in a separate pool.

'Well they'll take 'em if they're sweet enough. If not, they'll reject 'em,' said Jim. 'And then where would we be?'

They were both leaning on the fence, watching the bantams scratting around the magnificent cock bird, leader of the group. He strutted his stuff, the other males could only stand and watch. If he disappeared, another one would grow in confidence and majesty overnight to take his place. Only room for one cock bird, thought Jim. And although Janice worked as hard as he did, and was just as knowledgeable, there was only one boss, and that was him, or so he thought.

'Well it'll be too late, by the time they're sold and a family finds them sour. Can't take them back like you can a pair of pants!' Janice spoke casually, didn't want to appear too keen.

'Oh, Sainsbury's are ahead of the game there. A mechanical taster, would you believe, tastes some of every batch as soon as they reach the depot. Plenty of time to kick 'em back at you!' The lines around his mouth fell easily into a wide grin and his eyes lit up with fun.

'Now you're pulling my leg,' said Janice. She might have been married to him for eighteen years, but she still wasn't sure when he was kidding.

'No, straight up, they test the sugar content. Sweetness scale, they call it. ADAS's getting us one, so we can test 'em in the packing shed.'

'Whatever will they think of next? But if the Ministry's advice is good, they should be ok anyway. D'you think it might just be worth it, messing around like that? Nothing ventured, nothing gained, isn't that what they say?'

'Well, the price is already rock bottom for normal tommies, and it's still the heated crop. By the time our cold crop's ready, there'll be an armada of 'em coming across from the Canaries. When Spain joins the bloody Common Market that'll be the finish of us. Got to try something else, Jan, I reckon. Keep ahead of the game.'

Yes, thought Janice. Result.

ঙ   છ

Today, five months later, Eric the advisor was responding to a call regarding the "sweetness scale." Jim was worried the drip feed he was giving his young plants was too high in potash, and as the Settlement were paying the ADAS costs in this trial, he wanted Eric's additional reassurance about how the fruit was setting on the truss.

So as not to disturb Janice's livestock, Eric drove gently up their concrete roadway towards the top glasshouse. The area around the house was completely fenced off from the nursery and reminded him of one of the new Pet Zoos which didn't have wild beasts but concentrated on unusual fowl and the occasional wallaby. Two fat turkeys sat on a wooden perch next to the roadway and toppled off in surprise as his car approached. They fell like stones, then picked themselves up in a heap of gobbling and feathers. This happened every time a car passed. By the time the next one came along the poor brainless birds had forgotten the experience. This reminded Eric of a fishtank in his local takeaway, the goldfish bumped the sides every time.

The roadway narrowed as the glasshouses and tunnels closed in; an impressive sight. Since joining the Land Settlement Association Jim had gained a reputation for being an excellent grower. Somewhere between the dream of owning their very own market garden, which hadn't been realised yet, and the memory of his father at his age, Jim made the most of this way of life. Towards the dream he and Janice had accumulated an acre and a half of cover, and both sides of their roadway were lined with greenhouses and polytunnels.

The cherry trial was in their best house, an aluminium one. Jim had travelled to the Lea Valley to dismantle it last winter with the help of a couple of his neighbours. His holding totalled five acres and with the large water tank and pump shed, which was an expensive necessity for all growers if they wanted water pressure to reach the top of their land, Jim didn't have much open ground left. He'd abandoned the risky cultivation of outdoor lettuce some years ago. In the middle of this empty space, ploughed last winter but now flattened by weather and breaking out with weeds, stood the billygoat. He was roped to an iron pole driven deep in the ground and was chomping his way through a heap of gaudy titbits. His thirst was catered for in an old porcelain sink, and a galvanised bowl with side-handles contained his meal. He raised his head and glowered at the visitor climbing out of his Volvo.

Jim appeared from behind the compost heap at the very top of the holding. Beyond him a hawthorn hedge marked the extent of his plot, the other side of which stretched the prairie-like expanse of a farmer's field, vast and green right now with unripe wheat. He rattled towards Eric on his jack-truck, his powerful body arched and his legs astride the bars. Amazingly Jim's whistling, something he did continuously, still carried patchily over the noise of the engine. Throttle on full, Jim drove up deliberately skimming the wing of the Volvo, laughing at Eric's worried face.

'Nearly did you a favour!' laughed Jim. 'About time the government bought you a Land Rover!' Eric couldn't hear him but he guessed the gist.

'I see the old billy is still in solitary,' Eric shouted over the chug of the engine, which eventually rattled to a stop. Jim jumped off. He looked strong and healthy and his rolled-up sleeves and open-necked shirt revealed a deep tan which on closer examination proved to be a merger of freckles. This life suited him as much as it suited his wife and he was determined to keep it going.

'Huh,' grunted Jim with mock annoyance. 'I thought I'd found it a home last week. Some Italians wanted it. Then they asked if they could kill him up here on the field because they didn't have the space where they lived. Janice chased them down the street. Shame they didn't come while she was out!' Jim tossed his head back and laughed, a giggly laugh which didn't fit with his body strength. He never stayed serious for long. Eric wondered if he would have had the same cheerful disposition had fate treated him differently and he'd followed his father onto the tobacco assembly line. Ironically Jim's teeth were the only visible scar of a tough childhood and they only showed when he laughed.

Eric smiled. 'You'll have to do it on the quiet, then she

won't know till it's in a bolognese.'

'The way she is about her goats I'd be silent as an angel's fart, and she'd still suss it.'

Both men fell silent, watching the billy, scuffling and foraging. Jim was thinking fondly of his wife, he considered himself indulgent with regards to her animals. Better that than chasing men like his first wife, who'd left him for another. She'd done it in style too, fornicating with her driving instructor and poor Jim ignorantly signing the cheques. Over the years Janice had climbed slowly up his ladder of trust, but she couldn't reach the top, for in pride of place sat his mother, cross legged and chain smoking. Eric was pondering on the utter uselessness of a billy; no milk, tough meat and a penchant for vegetables. A real liability in a place like this.

'What *are* you going to do with him Jim? Advertise? Or sell him to one of your neighbours?'

'More chance of plaiting piss on a foggy night,' said Jim, gloomily. Eric wondered whether he'd had a flair for English in school and thought if he had, it probably hadn't been picked up on. 'He smells too rank. Lucky the wind's the other way, or you'd catch a drift. Anyway, mate, I hope you've fetched those specifications?'

Eric stooped to reach through the open car window and pulled out a clipboard. He detached a bunch of papers from it. Both men studied the sheets.

'See, this chart, it guides you, tells you how much to increase food levels each week,' the advisor squinted. He'd soon need reading glasses. He already used them for reading in the house. 'What week are these?'

Jim pulled a Christmas stocking diary from his jeans and the two men discussed the figures, matching them with the levels and dates suggested in the information. Two men of about the same age; one had the benefit of education and a salaried job but they had an interest in common. This probably wouldn't have been sufficient to sustain a social relationship, though. There was something missing. Eric couldn't put his finger on it; this man was always cheerful, pleasant, apparently happy go lucky. He was handsome in an average sort of way. But he was boring. Even his colourful use of language seemed to Eric like the rich satin skin of a tasteless fruit. Whatever this industry threw at him, and it threw plenty, Jim just responded with dogged determination. Other growers were angry, upset, vengeful. They could be arrogant, naive, idiotic. But at least they were something. Jim was just Jim, nothing seemed to touch him. Even his wife had turned to her goats for solace. Professionally, Eric liked his dealings with Jim, who seemed to take more responsibility for his lifestyle than most. But spend a long time with him? No way.

Now the grower scratched his head, tomato stained fingers disturbing the yellow thatch which his kids were thankful they'd avoided. 'I think I may have been a bit low, and in any case how do I know my diluter's accurate? I'm beginning to wish I hadn't agreed to this, Eric. But what else can you do?'

'There's bound to be a decent leeway,' Eric reassured him. 'I'm still waiting for the sugar testing equipment to arrive. Not that we can test until the fruit starts to ripen anyway. Have you ordered the punnets?'

'They came the other day. Who'd have thought old Joe would have people eating chats, by design!'

Eric looked puzzled. 'You've lost me. Do I know a grower called Joe?'

'No – Joe Sainsbury,' he said, chuckling to himself.

The tiny unfertilised chats were translucent and often misshapen, and there was no market for them. Jim's mother liked to eat them when she came to stay, popping them into her mouth like sweets and rejecting his warning of "Ma, wash them first!" Ironically she'd always called them cherries; "Save me the cherries, duck." And he would. Of course this new crop was nothing like them really. Eric placed the papers neatly on the back of the jack-truck and trapped them from the breeze with a large stone.

'I'll leave these with you, you can copy the details. But I want them back, mind. I mean it, Jim, I must have them back. Ted Challis over at Dayton is running a trial too.'

'You pen pushers love your bits of paper as much as our Janice loves her animals. This is all I need!' He patted the pocket of his jeans. Eric was used to Jim teasing him this way, thinking him pernickety. But he had good reason, Jim never returned things. If he'd ever joined a library, Eric was sure he'd be barred.

'You'll have to get a computer, Jim. That's the way forward.'

Jim chuckled. 'I'd rather walk the Chinese wall. And you know I'm scared of flying!'

The men went into the tall airy greenhouse. The plants were in double rows, with single lines running along the edge, all reaching to shoulder height. The trusses stretched out like bony hands with multiple fingers. Eric enthused about the number of fruit.

'Well, Jim, these are looking lovely,' he said as he held a particularly well-laden truss up to count. The small fruit were green jewels, smudged darker around the calyx. 'Thirty-five! That's grand. And there's minimum space between each truss, too.'

Jim felt proud. Eric was the expert. It was like Gary Lineker leaning over the school fence as you headed into the top corner. But like all growers he was wary of counting his chickens. He merely asked: 'Is the size okay?'

The bottom trusses were fully developed, the green cherry tomatoes the size of large marbles. Before replying, Eric moved about the house taking readings from several plants. He noted them down in his diary.

'Size looks fine to me, but the exact specification is on the truck outside.' Eric took a ruler from his cotton body-warmer and measured the diameter of an average fruit. The men moved out of the house and were immediately aware of a scuffling noise.

Something which looked like a dog on hind legs was rooting in the back of the jack-truck.

Oh no, thought Jim. Not his precious papers!

'Bloody hell!'

'That bloody BILLY!'

Both men ran to the truck and the billy hastily clacked his front hooves back down onto the concrete. His jaw was grinding in a circular movement, his shaggy beard shuffling from side to side as he chewed. His chain clanked loosely on the concrete and the last triangle of paper disappeared behind his thick lips. A musty odour engulfed the scene. Although the horizontal pupils blazed defiantly, he made no effort to escape. His purpose had been served, and the cherry tomato recommendations would be ruminated upon for the rest of the day. Jim was doubled up, hands over his mouth, unable to trust himself to speak. Eric was less amused. Looking over to where the billy had been secured, the men saw that the metal stake now gave an angle of twenty degrees to the ground, listing forlornly above the heap of food, the white sink, and the galvanised bowl.

Ten

George the Chairman of the Grower's Association sat in his cramped dining room enjoying his tea-break. While his drink was cooling, he knocked out the dottle from his pipe into a heavy glass ashtray. At the same time, he studied a glossy trade magazine. It was brightly illustrated and was all about pelargoniums – regal ones, zonal ones, miniatures and scented ones. His wife Maisie was a spit away through an archway in the galley kitchen. Maisie hummed to Radio Two as she chopped onions, mushrooms and then some rashers of pre-cooked fatty bacon. A plastic jug contained the already beaten eggs, for Maisie was making an egg and bacon flan. Some of the others at the Women's Institute would call it a quiche, she considered as she chopped. I'm not French, so it's an egg and bacon flan, like my mother and grandmother made before me.

She stirred in the eggs. It was the monthly meet of the WI tonight. A lot of Estate women attended, even the younger ones, probably because there wasn't much else socially for them to do. Maisie didn't mind, it was good to get new blood into the Institute and according to what she had read in women's magazines, sadly this was not the case countrywide. Last month though, that Hazel and her new friend with the dog had giggled the whole way through the talk, about life on an Antarctic Survey Outpost. Far from being put out, the young speaker had flirted madly with the two girls during the interval and couldn't take his eyes off them in the second half. It had spoilt it a bit for everyone else, because he kept forgetting his gist mid-sentence. Still, she couldn't blame the girls, she thought with a chuckle, he was rather a dish.

The front room clock chimed the hour, and Maisie switched over to Radio One in time to catch Simon Bates and "Our Tune". She always listened to that and after her emotions had been either lifted or saddened by the unbelievable experiences people shared with the world, she turned right back to Radio Two. Maisie preferred George to be elsewhere during "Our Tune", because he sometimes teased her, especially if the tale brought a tear to her eye. She glanced into the dining room, and today he made no attempt to move. He kept peering out of the window towards the Drift. He was probably waiting for the postman.

As if by arrangement with her, the red post van drew up. Kevin the tattooed postman, always in a rush, jumped out and raced to the door. He banged the knocker with the speed of a relay runner, dropped a large parcel on the doorstep and was back in his van and away in a cloud of diesel before George could reach the front door.

It was a box, the size of a large hamper, with "fragile" printed a fierce red against the brown. George knew what it contained.

'I've got me new varieties, Maisie love,' he said, clouting her affectionately on her large rump as he squeezed past her on his way to the back door. He would have to go out around the house to retrieve the box as it was too bulky to fetch through.

He carried his parcel carefully into his propagation greenhouse instead. Built at the same time as the house, it was an old type structure with a brick wall up to waist height and narrow white glazing bars above. Ancient layers of white paint ringed the small panes, and where they overlapped, velvety green moss clung to the gaps. Redundant water pipes traced the interior walls; in winter George now lit paraffin heaters beneath the staging. This method was much cheaper.

The staging was filled with young geranium plants, mostly just-rooted cuttings. The leaves varied from plain green, through yellow to patterned, and their shapes from regular to ivy-leafed to miniature. Those which weren't potted up were crowded into white plastic "multi-pots" to help them develop a root system. Each different variety was meticulously labelled. Further along the bench, plants in three-and-a-half inch pots were spaced so they could spread out and those large enough to be flowering already made an impressive show.

George slit the cardboard with his penknife revealing the polystyrene used for protecting the tiny rooted cuttings in transit. On top of this lay a folded sheet of paper with the printed names of each variety in columns. He smoothed the sheet open carefully and examined it as he puffed on his pipe. George never rushed anything; each of these little tasks was part of the whole pleasurable experience. Scanning the checklist, he laid each new cutting out carefully, matching its label with the name on the sheet. He handled each tiny piece of plant life gently between his large thumb and forefinger, taking care not to squeeze too tightly or to knock off the fragile fragment of root.

When he had satisfied himself that all was present and correct, he shook the loose soil into a bin and carefully stowed the container below the bench. This could be re-used, he thought. The collection which he had bought was called Dark Dazzlers and each individual name was black something; Black Imp, Black Vesuvius, Black Torch. They were quite unusual and the brochure had boasted that the bright flowers would glow against the dark leaves giving a blaze of colour in the border. Once ignited they would flower and flower in the manner of a battling winter pansy.

George's potting trough was heaped ready with a rich loamy compost, and he had potted up most of them when he was startled by a scraping sound followed by an abrupt opening of the door.

'Well, George, no wonder we don't get much lettuce from you.'

Jonathan leaned smiling, or smirking, thought George, against the white doorpost of the greenhouse. The thumbs of each hand were tucked in a pocket of his narrow black jeans, and his right leg crossed the left at ankle height. All in black he put George in mind of a pernicious insect, resting briefly on his woodwork before alighting on, and devouring, his crops.

'I didn't send for you,' George commented, barely looking up, voice level, neither friendly nor hostile. He continued with his potting, scooping the compost up expertly and firming a dusky cutting centrally in its pot.

'Well, that's a nice greeting from the Chairman of the Growers,' said Jonathan. 'Are these geraniums too?' He bent and examined them. In truth, he had difficulty telling a geranium from a fuchsia.

'They're miniatures.' George finished the last one and patted the top of the remaining soil. 'What can I do you for?'

He took his tobacco tin from the deep roomy pocket in the bib of his dungarees. George often wondered how men managed without them these days. He knew he couldn't wear those tight jeans like Jim or Josh, squeezing their stomachs as they bent up and down at their work. They must have very different digestive systems to him, he thought. But then their guts didn't have to contend with Maisie's delicious fried breakfasts. Jim he knew ate cereal and Josh had told him he greeted each morning with a cigarette, another cigarette and a cup of coffee, and in that order too. Jonathan wore tight jeans but, thought George, the furthest he likely bends is to get into that new Astra. He concentrated with difficulty on what the fieldsman was saying now.

'Two things, George, firstly how is your outdoor lettuce coming on? Can it be cut for the weekend?'

This was a surprise. The glut must be over if the Packhouse wanted lettuce early.

George said: 'It ain't properly ready, mate, I doubt it'll make the weight yet.' Six ounces was the minimum, any less and they would have to go second class.

Jonathan admitted: 'George, we're *desperate* for lettuce, and if a few don't quite make six ounces nobody will bother just this once.' He picked a wedge of emerald moss from the pane of glass nearest to him, then flicked it to the side.

I wish they'd make their bloody minds up, the older man thought to himself. Keep on moving the goalposts! Still, despite his annoyance at the unwelcome visitor, he was relieved to hear this because he had been anticipating ploughing them in. It wouldn't have been the first time he'd had to do this with a crop out on the field.

'So what's the second thing?' he asked warily. He was sure Jonathan was snooping, trying to discover the extent of his pot plant business. The Marketing Agency didn't deal in pot plants, so it was perfectly legitimate to sell them elsewhere. But George had a couple of houses full of geraniums and bedding plants, although they would be planted up with tomatoes later. He knew he was skating on thin ice at present and was reluctant for Jonathan to study his nursery too closely. He felt a rising sense of annoyance that he wasn't a free man.

Jonathan fell into officialese. 'We want all the growers to attend a meeting, about diversifying. We want to suggest new crops, like beefsteak tomatoes, chillies. Geraniums won't be among them,' he added, and George was unable to guess if he was mocking him or not. 'ADAS will be there, of course. And Ted somebody who used to live here will be giving a talk on cherry tomatoes. Two o'clock tomorrow afternoon. Can we count on you?' He smiled affably. Yes,

Jonathan was definitely making the effort to be pleasant.

'I'm sure as I don't know why you never phoned,' George persisted with his mistrust. 'Could've saved yerself a journey.'

'We wanted to give you a personal invitation, because we know the influence you have over the other growers.'

That bloody "royal we" again, thought George.

Jonathan made a move to go. 'And because we know that you are wise enough to see the dangers in relying too much on lettuce and tomatoes.' He could have added: you've obviously recognised this and are acting accordingly with your geraniums, but he didn't, he let the compliment lay feeling reassured that he would see not just George but other growers too at the meeting the following afternoon.

∾ ℚ

The meeting as usual took place in the hall and this time two trestle tables were pushed together to accommodate the Estate Manager Jack Ball, Adam Burton representing the Packhouse and an unfamiliar figure from ADAS, an expert in "diversification".

The growers faced the group with hostility. There wasn't a high turn out, and Jonathan noticed that a lot of the established growers such as Dennis and Tim had deliberately stayed away, as had Eddie, Vic and Sammy.

'If I decide to grow cherry tomatoes, I'll use my common sense!' Eddie had told Hazel. 'You go. If I'd 'ave wanted to go to meetings, I'd 'ave been a bleeding solicitor!'

Steve had also told Karen: 'You go, you're the growing brains, and I'm the brawn.'

So Hazel and Karen attended their first meeting. There were several women this time, amongst them of course "Red Vera". George was present, Jonathan noted with satisfaction.

When it was apparent no more were coming, Jack Ball stood up, cleared his throat meaningfully and addressed the meeting. A larger than life character with a big chin, he had removed his suit jacket and a wide gaudy tie hung adrift of his button line. He referred only indirectly to the lettuce fiasco, cleverly diverting any chance for any of the growers to raise objections or arguments. Instead, he handed over to the ADAS man, a thin, bespectacled fellow with a quiet voice who looked as if he hadn't ventured out of doors since January.

The growers leaned back, crossing their legs, stretching and yawning outrageously and generally presenting the appearance of bored recipients at a school speech day. Only George, out of politeness, and Karen appeared attentive. The man droned on about possible new crops like beefsteak tomatoes and aubergines and indicated a bunch of leaflets on a side table. When he had talked himself to a halt, Vera, not leaving a decent enough interval, cut in quickly and discourteously:

'All this is a damn waste of time,' she pointed vaguely to the Chair, 'because *they* won't be able to sell it!'

'Here we go again,' Hazel nudged Karen. 'Silly cow. Look at Jonathan – she don't worry him.'

They turned to look at Jonathan, who was leaning back in his seat, stick legs stretched open diagonally. A smart shoe rested on a chair in the row in front. His mouth was a thin line, and his eyebrows just might be showing surprise. Karen had to admit he didn't look particularly concerned, in fact he seemed barely awake, but he caught Hazel's eye and winked.

Hazel elbowed Karen. 'Did you see that?'

'What? Shut up!'

There were cries of approval for Vera from the floor but George turned and delivered a general glare. He didn't want this to collapse into chaos, at least the LSA were making some sort of effort and he hoped it wasn't purely cosmetic.

Jack Ball cleared his throat and stretched his ruddy bull neck. His whiskers twitched authoritatively. Somehow he had knocked his tie even more askew and now he tossed it irritably over his shoulder.

'Madam, Madam' he said. 'Have we not arranged this meeting so that we can salvage the situation? *Salvage* the situation? Of course, if you are not interested in pulling the situation around and making the LSA a success again, then please feel free to leave.' He paused and added in a more conciliatory tone: 'Now if you are quite ready I would like to hand over to an ex-Settlement grower, Mr. Ted Challis.'

The audience grumbled and then clapped obediently. A few of the older growers remembered him. He stood up, casting his eyes about in bewilderment. This aggression was alien to him. When he had left the Settlement several years before there'd been harmony and friendship between growers and staff. He had heard rumours of course, he didn't live that far away, but he hadn't anticipated raw rudeness like this. He began to describe in detail the cultivation of cherry tomatoes in a flatter voice than he'd intended but at least Jim was listening carefully.

Eric, observing at the rear of the hall, had the feeling this was the start of changes which could see the end of the wonderful system which had been the first step on the farming ladder. As somebody who still believed in the sociology of the scheme, he felt a surge of sadness.

Eleven

Eddie believed most illnesses to be in the mind and you should either fight through them or work off the symptoms. He considered the local Health Centre to exist mostly for pregnant and nursing mothers, a club where they could receive and share tips on childrearing. Of course serious illness needed medical attention and this would be better served if doctors didn't have their surgeries cluttered with malingerers. In all aspects of his life, everything was black and white, greys just didn't come into the picture. Even in his relationship with Hazel he felt their feelings had been set in stone when they married. That any minor adjustments might be needed as circumstances changed was not a consideration to him. On the subject of illness, he had been impressed with old Vic. Asked when he last saw a doctor, Vic replied proudly: '1945, and that was to check on something the day before my wedding!' He'd winked, and Eddie thought the advice or potion must have been worth it because Vic and Ruby had reared seven sons and two daughters, half of them spread across the world, no doubt enriching the population with more of the same healthy stock. He hoped to follow Vic's example, but now, bang in the busy season, he needed to go to the quack.

The red patches which first appeared a week ago on his belly had spread to his hands, his arms and his legs and then erupted into dozens of watery blisters. Still he continued slicing the celery, but now he covered up like a worker in a nuclear plant and the juice splattered onto his cotton shirt and his once smart trousers. He even wore gloves and he cursed his wife, the Settlement, the celery and the heat in that order. The blisters didn't go away and each time he undressed after work more had bubbled up. Then they began to itch.

'It's the bloody Nitram,' he grumbled, blaming the fertiliser. 'I'm being poisoned! And we've still got two tunnels to cut.'

'Why's it only you then?' asked Hazel. 'Perhaps you got the quantities wrong!'

So again Eric was summoned, and he was able to confirm his earlier suspicions. The two men were sitting at the dining room table as Hazel cooked breakfast and made a cup of tea for the advisor.

'You must come out of the celery,' Eric announced. 'You and celery are finished. You have a severe allergy and you *must* go to the doctor. Otherwise you will end up with blood poisoning.'

'How can I,' said Eddie. 'Who's going to cut the other two tunnels?'

They both looked at Hazel who in her shorts and tank-top was removing fried eggs from the pan with a fish slice and placing them on buttered toast. She turned around in alarm.

'Sorry, no can do,' she said firmly. Eric had a vision of the lovely bronze legs disfigured with pustules. They fell silent, each away in their own thoughts. Then the voice of Elvis came over the radio, belting out *'Return to Sender.'*

Eddie brightened. He twisted the knob on the radiogram, upping the volume. 'The King,' he said, rocking and tapping his foot. 'Can't beat *'im!'*

Hazel slapped his plate of eggs on toast in front of him. She reached over and squirted an arc of tomato sauce across the yellow. Eric winced.

'The Dead Greats,' she said. 'He loves them all, Eric. Not interested in anything else. They have to be dead. He's like a flipping dinosaur himself.'

Eddie squashed the bloodied yolks with his fork. Then he poured salt liberally on top.

'I like Chuck Berry and I don't think he's dead! I can't be like you and listen to all that smoochy Motown crap. They were proper musicians in them days. An' there's been nobody yet to touch Elvis!'

In fact Eddie's taste was about to embrace Bruce Springsteen, but at that time he hadn't heard of the Boss.

'What about you?' Hazel turned to Eric. She liked her eggs fried solid, and she sliced through one neatly, and speared it with her fork.

Eric must have been considering this, as he answered straight away. 'Folk – and Blues for me. Bob Dylan, Joni Mitchell,' he leaned forward enthusiastically, 'and I like anything live.'

'*Folk*?' said Eddie, in genuine shock. 'Not that finger in your ear stuff? I'm surprised at you, Eric!'

So sure he's right, thought Eric. Good job he's not President of the United States.

Hazel finished her egg and laid down her knife and fork neatly. 'So, Mr Clever,' she said to her husband. 'Just how are we going to get our celery out?'

'Unless I do it, I don't have a clue,' said Eddie, picking at a blister through the gap between his button holes.

'Well, if you're not too scathing of them,' said Eric, reaching in his pocket. 'You could ask your neighbours for help.'

He leafed through his diary, its pages stiff with stains and dirt, and still half the year to go. Charted there was the overview of who would be hopelessly busy and who could spare some time to help a friend in need. Before he disappeared Eric whispered to Hazel that it was crucial she made Eddie an appointment with the doctor, an emergency one. Blood poisoning, if allowed to take hold, would create a situation which would be beyond the help of his fellow growers.

⁞ ⁞

Next morning as Jim, Steve and Sammy Dove made short work of his remaining celery, Eddie walked out of the Health Centre, head spinning and prescription in hand.

The doctor was familiar with the condition and confirmed Eric's diagnosis. Celery would be no more on their cropping programme and he would have to rest until the allergy was under control. His hands had begun to swell and this was a bad sign. The strong dose of antihistamine would hopefully prevent blood poisoning, but there was little that could be done to stop the itching which now encompassed most of his body. He could try children's chickenpox remedies, such as calamine lotion, but really he would just have to keep cool and be *patient*. First the noun, and now the verb, each as alien to someone like Eddie.

Keep cool? The temperatures were in the eighties and the sun blazing down on the old Cortina had made it an inferno. Eddie had to pace around the car for five minutes with the doors open wide before he risked getting in. The steering wheel was hot and sticky and the toffee bars his children had left on the dashboard had oozed and stuck to the plastic. Gloomily he headed towards home, his discomfort too great to even consider that the prime cash crop was no longer an option.

As he drove the couple of miles along the back road he shuffled and shifted his bottom, wriggling so the cloth of his trousers rubbed against his itching body. He didn't notice the speckly white flowers of the Queen Anne's Lace along the roadside, or the fresh new green of the hawthorn hedges beyond. He didn't observe the wet patches on the road ahead which faded as you approached, the mirage effect of a really hot day. All he thought of was the ice cold bath he planned to plunge into when he got home.

        ℘   ℞

Simon and Eric were drinking raspberry tea in Simon's conservatory. It was Eric's first fruit tea and he thought probably his last, but he was a sociable fellow and would give most things a try. Fortunately Simon hadn't offered him a joint, that might have placed him in a difficult position. He could smell the unmistakably pleasant aroma of cannabis, but there was nothing more concrete in evidence. No tubular cardboard roach in the ashtray, just squashed to death roll-up butts. Nicole hovered in the background, long wrap-around skirt flowing below a tight tie-dye tee-shirt. She was busy measuring pieces of string for something she was making indoors. Eric often wondered how she spent her day and guessed it was doing something terribly creative and artistic.

Nicole was an enigma to most people on the Estate. She could be seen cycling up the concrete road, skirt hitched up above the greasy chain, sketch book under her arm. Her dark hair had a fringe but that was the only constant. Sometimes she had a handful of tiny plaits, sometimes her hair was pinned back in a wispy bun. She had no routine, and the seasons and crops which determined most people's lives had no effect on her, but in contrast to Sylvia she existed amongst it all. She smiled and waved at everybody, and they waved back. She was so pretty and pleasant, what else would they do? Uncertain, they kept a cautious distance though, and this was appreciated by Nicole in turn.

Physically Simon reminded Eric of the stereotypical Australian male tourist, all muscle and hairy legs, crammed on the Tube with an outsize rucksack, indeed just like the specimens he'd observed last time he was in the capital for a seminar. They looked like they ran a daily half-marathon but Eric suspected the furthest they'd hiked in the last month was from underground station to pub. All indications were that Simon's physical exertion was minimal also. They were a strange pair. Few people gained access to their house but those like Eric who did, told tales of cushions and futons instead of lounge furniture, and of dreamcatchers and mobiles swaying softly in a house of mystery.

How the couple survived, Eric wasn't sure. Maybe there was money from a family in Hampstead or somewhere. He remembered searching for Simon one morning in his glasshouse, and finding only a trail of bagged lettuce, turned white with condensation and useless because they'd been left too long in the heat. He eventually found him in his conservatory, poring over a book and researching a point of law which occurred to him as he harvested. He'd become so involved he'd forgotten the time. Damn, he'd said, are they salvageable? When Eric confirmed they weren't he'd grinned and said they probably wouldn't have made much anyway. Eric wondered how Simon kept the Land Settlement off his back with such a meagre throughput. He could only assume his accounts were straight and all debts attended to regularly.

Today, though, it was Nicole he wanted to see. He had questioned her previously about the spiky succulents which were crammed on every available ledge of the conservatory. They were too ordinary for anybody to want more than a token one or two. The flower was an insignificant affair on a stalk and although the herring-bone arrangement of the fleshy leaves was interesting to a botanist he would have expected Nicole to collect something more flamboyant; orchids, perhaps. She had told him she was into herbal medicine and natural treatments, and that the succulents had healing qualities.

She left her string and sat at his feet, cross-legged and attentive. She looked up at him with cow eyes, like an infant on the school story mat.

'Don't tell me what you want, Eric. Let me guess. I'm honing my skills,' she said, squeezing her eyes shut.

'Oh, bloody hell, Nicole,' said Simon, 'don't be so tiresome! Eric's busy, he has schedules and timescales, things you've never heard of.' But he said it with affection, from behind a copy of *Private Eye*.

'Can I at least guess your star sign?'

'You may.'

'I think Virgo. Yes, Virgo. Am I right?'

'No, afraid not,' said Eric quickly; he classified astrology with conceptual art. 'And it's your herbalist skills I'm interested in today.'

ဆာ ಲ

It was four in the morning and beginning to get light. Eddie rose from the bed which Hazel had abandoned two hours earlier in favour of the settee. She couldn't stand him tossing and turning and the last straw came when he told her the blisters were beginning to burst. Disgusted, she'd swung her legs over the side and was gone in a flash. She'd taken the best pillow. Now he was considering yet another cold bath. He didn't think he could take much more of this infernal itching.

In the pale grey light of dawn he stood by the window and examined his midriff, oblivious to the uproar of the dawn chorus. The small blisters had merged into several large ones, the biggest stretching a full three inches across. Negative speculation, so unfamiliar to him, began to creep into his mind. Perhaps he would die from this, the medication having been too late. He had not slept for four days and four nights, and he felt strangely drunk and aware at the same time. He was now ready to make the transition from cynic to hypochondriac, maybe he should ring the clinic at eight-thirty and arrange a home visit. The heat of panic flooded over him.

Back on the bed he threw off the white sheet, the material irritated too much. He felt he must have drifted off because... because...

'You've got a visitor,' announced Hazel, bending over him. 'Just make yourself decent!' She rummaged in the drawer for clean Y fronts and his faded cotton shorts. They hit him with a thud.

'The doctor?' This would save him the humiliation of ringing the surgery himself. He could protest, just enough.

'I suppose you could say that,' Hazel smiled. 'It's Simon's wife.'

'That crazy bird?' He jumped up in alarm. 'You can tell her where to get off. It's probably witchcraft or voodoo. *Hazel!* His sleep deprived eyes pleaded with her.

'She has something to soothe the itching, and I've had enough of you. So come on down! Sorry I can't stop. I'm off into town with Karen.'

ℰℴ ℭℛ

The potion worked almost immediately, soothing and cooling and providing relief. He felt his body relaxing. Nicole let Eddie smooth the gel over the blisters himself, despite his rough red fingers. She watched, though. She wanted to make sure it had the desired effect. Last week this would have been inconceivable; he, down-to-earth Eddie at the mercy of a crazy hippy. Now there was no embarrassment as he relaxed in the gaze of her soft brown eyes. Her long dark hair curled about her face, how could he have judged this ministering angel a witch?

'You look so tired,' she whispered in a soft voice he believed to be extinct from Hazel's repertoire.

'I am,' gasped Eddie. 'I haven't slept in nights.'

'Would you like me to give you a reflexology treatment.. treatment...treatment..' The words seemed to echo around his head. 'I massage your feet, and you will relax and fall into a deep sleep...deep sleep...deep sleep...'

The last thing Eddie was aware of was her gentle fingers working their way over his feet. They massaged the balls of his feet, and separated his toes...

Hours later Eddie awoke, the experience still sketchy in his head. Unconsciously his hand moved to his shorts. They were still in place.

Twelve

Adam Burton, Estate Packhouse Manager, was talking on the phone in his office, handset balanced between his shoulder and his neck. There was a problem somewhere because he was drumming his fingers on his desk and a pen was poised in his other hand.

'I'll try my best, Ben. What am I supposed to do? The poor bastards lost thousands six weeks ago, they even dumped it on the Arterial. Didn't you see it on the telly? Now you tell me you want anything, so long as it's made a heart.' He spotted Jonathan out in the yard, chatting to a lorry driver. He stretched the cable just enough so he could stand up to knock on the window. Jonathan looked up and Adam beckoned him inside. 'I'll ring you back when I've spoken to Jonathan. He's the guy in the know.'

Jonathan stuck his head through the doorway. He was smiling. He'd secured a date with a girl he'd been stalking for months. He had feigned disinterest, rained her with innuendoes, smothered her in compliments and finally given up. This must have been the successful tactic, coldness to the point of rudeness. Suddenly she was all his. Nothing was going to spoil his day, for he was determined to be fresh after work, not tense or stressed.

'Everyone's wanting lettuce,' Adam told him, playing with figures on his electric calculator. 'We need to find 600 boxes from somewhere for tomorrow, in addition to what's already booked in.'

Jonathan was trying to remember which lay-by he had taken some girl last summer. It was more of a pull-in, surrounded by woods, hidden from view by over hanging branches. He found he couldn't even recall her name, let alone the location. Too much pressure from this shite job, with all the crops to be noted mentally, as well as their optimum harvest dates. He remembered how she'd slid across him in the back seat, though. His eyes gave in to the smile.

'JONATHAN. You haven't heard a bloody word. What is it with you? No wonder they get so irritated with you!'

There had been a time when Adam had good relationships himself with some of the older growers, when there'd been mutual respect. And now he could understand their resentment towards this skinny youth, who pretended such knowledge and insight. For all his twenty-six years that's what he is, just a bloody kid, thought Adam. Now we have a real problem and I bet he's day dreaming about his love life.

The youth read the older man and cut dead the smile and the daydream. There were rumours in the yard that the price had shot through the roof and lettuce he knew was in short supply. The recent hot weather had brought the harvest date forward, and much of the early outdoor crop had been cut or ploughed in last week.

'There's none. I'm scraping the barrel as it is. Tim's cutting half an acre of immature; luckily they're quality so they should make the weight. Steve's have tipburn, but if you're that desperate they'll pass as class one. What's happened to all the foreign stuff?'

'Who knows?' Adam sighed and stood up. He was short and stocky and his belly flopped over his belt. This was due to his job, continually static, all his contact with people taking place on the telephone. The blower, they termed it. Well it had certainly blown him up. 'I'll come with you. I'll take a bet that Sammy Dove has a crop of lettuce somewhere!'

Jonathan was surprised. 'Sure you still remember the way?'

Adam hadn't abandoned his desk in favour of the field for a good twelve months, since the last purge on "selling outside". Then all the holdings had been visited without warning and their crops listed. This action had resulted in an awful lot of bad feeling, with one blatant offender being evicted along with his pregnant wife. The growers had banded together, and there had been uproar, but the Association had taken the only possible route in dealing with a man so openly defiant. In an act of unprecedented arrogance, he'd sailed past the office in an open truck stuffed with boxes painted in alien colours and logos, gesturing a "Harvey Smith" at the window. In broad daylight too.

Both men knew many of the growers still sold outside and they both suspected Sammy Dove to be a prime culprit. Although Adam sympathised with the growers' predicament it made his job difficult. He was convinced Sammy would have lettuce, he'd always been a big outdoor grower. Adam was equally sure the Packhouse would not be seeing any of it. But Sammy was wily. He did not want to lose his holding and be forced to return to his job as a greenhouse dismantler and erector. No official got near to Sammy's produce, at least until it was cut and boxed. Telephone enquiries received only vague replies, numbers of boxes were impossibly approximated. "Ask the missus, I've no head for figures" was invariably the reply. And his wife Maureen was elusiveness itself. God knows what he grew on that holding, mused Jonathan. If white poppies could stand the temperate climate it could easily be heroin.

Adam said as he struggled into the passenger seat of the Astra: 'Has he still got those dogs? Huh, course he has. That man is always doing something illegal. From the dinner on his plate to the diesel in his Land Rover, I can guarantee nothing's paid for honestly. Old Mike opposite, he says he hears all sorts of goings-on at night. He daren't go and investigate, though. He hears shots, reckons they're from Sammy's twelve bore. Don't suppose he has a license for that, either.'

Jonathan drove with more care than usual; he didn't want one of his bosses thinking he was the cause of those hefty garage bills last month. Colour, mainly green, flashed by in the glasshouses; tomatoes, cucumbers, peppers, all recognisable in a blur to the trained eye of a Packhouse Manager. Halfway along the Drift another roadway cut in at right angles, and Sammy's holding was the fourth along there. Quick growing trees, silver birch, poplar and rowan surrounded it and the gaps were crammed with wood and junk of all shapes and sizes. It looked more like a gypsy camp, all that was missing was draped washing. Broken-down vehicles butted up to the verge. Twenty years of wheeling and dealing had been squashed tightly into the confines of the plot and were now overflowing and polluting the roadway. Opposite, Mike Taylor's sternly clipped laurel hedge contrasted sharply. His house stood raw and isolated in a bare square of lawn. There was no nursery behind, this was a staff house and would be his until he retired completely from his tractor driving job. A council bungalow in the nearby village of Market Bolton would await him then.

Jonathan pulled up outside Sammy's heavy wrought iron gates which looked ridiculously overstated. They afforded no view to the house because Sammy had curved his driveway in the manner of a large suburban detached. Two hungry Alsatians, one an unusual large white known as Sabre, growled and paced the other side of the gate. Normal barking was too tame for them.

'Sammy!' shouted Adam. They waited. Nothing could be heard but the birds and low throaty moans from the dogs. 'SAMMY!'

'Lazy bastard,' said Jonathan. 'Bet he's still in bed.'

A cuckoo repeated its call. If became a jeer.

Eventually somebody approached, whistling lightly to the dogs. They turned like teddy bears and padded softly in the other direction. Michelle Dove, small and fair, aged about sixteen, unlocked the huge gates and told the two men to wait there while she fetched her father. The gates clunked back together with the Settlement staff inside of them.

'I'll shut the dogs up.' she said and Jonathan stifled a leer. 'You wait here.'

Sammy could see the two men but they couldn't see him. He was watching from his packing-shed window.

'I think I'll just stay 'ere and observe a bit!' he said to his wife Maureen. 'The fun should start happening in a bit.' He rolled a cigarette so he could enjoy the approaching action.

The men stood, one gangly and tall, one short and stocky, both with pocketed hands and swivelling necks, trying to take in the scene. Scrapyard, junkyard, call it what you like but there was no obvious evidence that this was a productive market garden. There could have been glasshouses behind the stacks of clutter, but then again there could have been a couple of rhinoceroses. The house was gripped by ivy to roof height, windows and doors just about holding their own. The maintenance department must have given up years ago...

Jonathan saw it coming before Adam, its head down, beak out, long neck moving along like a self-automated vacuum cleaner. It hissed as it approached Adam's leg.

'Quick! Grab its neck!' shouted Jonathan, more streetwise in dealing with fur and feathers than his office-bound companion, but his directive was too late. The goose had clamped its beak around Adam's turn-ups. It flapped its wings, snorting through its beak as it increased its grip.

'GET IT OFF!' screamed Adam in panic. He disliked flapping fowl, it was a phobia passed on by his mother.

Jonathan tried to grab the goose, but it flapped and thrashed with such verve he was unable to decide what to do. He snatched uselessly at the air as the ferocious bird outwitted him.

'Get its bloody NECK!' shouted Adam, but as Jonathan stretched his hand out to do this the goose loosened its hold on the material, snapped at his hand and then grabbed Adam again, this time securing the flesh of his ankle.

'YOU BASTARD!' shouted Jonathan, 'It's drawn blood!' He concentrated on sucking his hand. Adam hopped desperately round in circles, dragging the goose with him, a bobbin trying to spin off a piece of raw cotton.

'OH! OH! OH!' was all he could verbalise now.

Sammy came racing over from the shed with a stick and the goose released its hold at once. To his credit, he wasn't laughing. That could wait until he had a audience and a few beers in the Red Cow later.

Jonathan recognised the goose, it was the same lettuce grazer that had cost Simon so dear in compensation. It looked like a regular greylag, but the red eyes gave it away. Steer clear when its eyes turn to red, Simon had told him. That means it's losing its rag. Happens when it's pre-menstrual, he'd joked.

'Is this Simon's goose?' asked Jonathan, angrily. 'It wants to be bloody destroyed. It's worse than those hounds of yours. It *is* Simon's, isn't it?'

'Yeah, the very same. Likes lettuce, see. Can't resist the stuff. Simon reckons it'd swim the ocean if it got a whiff of lettuce from across the other side. I'm looking after it 'cos we ain't got none here, so it ain't goin' to be tempted. Sorry mate,' he said to Adam, who was dabbing at the blood on his rapidly swelling ankle with his monogrammed handkerchief. Sammy's large bearded face was a picture of commiseration. 'I didn't know it was vicious, like! I'd 'ave a word with Simon about this if I was you, guvnor. Anyhow, what was it you was after, mate?'

'Don't bother. Nothing,' Adam muttered through clenched teeth. 'Come on Jonathan.' He hobbled away to the Astra, Jonathan at his heels. Only when Sammy heard the car squeal round the corner did he allow himself to break into laughter.

'You cannot help these people,' Adam said as he struggled to reach his ankle over a roll of fleshy stomach. 'They won't co-operate, they expect you to work magic with the markets. They refuse to understand about supply and demand, and to top it all they set their livestock on you! Sammy Dove, I'll get to the bottom of your lawless lifestyle. See if I don't!'

Never mind him, thought Jonathan, just get me away from all this.

Thirteen

Karen and Steve were struggling with their first tomato crop. They had a thousand plants, against a couple of dozen last year on their allotment, hardly comparable, of course. The plants had been ordered by Jonathan and now waited in trays to be planted. Back in February the three of them had decided on the cropping programme for their first year, Jonathan feeding figures into his calculator with something called a profit margin cosily displayed on the screen. It all seemed so easy then. Jonathan had allowed two weeks to prepare the greenhouse for tomatoes. He'd marked diagonal stripes in black felt-tip across that fortnight on their LSA planning chart, the one pinned to the dining room wall. Plenty of time.

Now they were halfway through the fortnight and debris from the last crop still remained.

'Can we not just plough all this rubbish in, like farmers do?' said Steve. 'It'd soon break down in the soil, surely.'

Eric looked at him in surprise, and then back to the rotting leaves and slimy hearts and the trodden down soil.

'Not that I'm lazy,' Steve added, second guessing the advisor's thoughts, and wrongly, as it happened. 'Just the time factor. We've had the plants ready to plant for a while now.'

'Not a good idea. This house hasn't been sterilised recently, and the risk of disease will multiply. It's different outside in the elements. What base are you putting on?'

'Er, what do you suggest? Does it need owt after we put all that on for the lettuce?'

Catching Eric's expression, Steve pulled his mouth into a line which admitted his ignorance. He knew Karen would never do that, if she didn't know she found out by asking clever roundabout questions. But that wasn't Steve's way, and his wife was nowhere to be seen.

Eric poked at a lettuce stump with his worn but highly expensive suede boots. 'Steve, what *did* you do before you came here?' he asked gently.

' 'Ave you sussed me, Eric? I was pit deputy, but we did have an allotment, but I never had much time for it, always too knackered when I got home,' he admitted with a sheepish smile. 'But don't tell our lass I've told you, she'll go mad.'

The ADAS man shook his head. 'I thought as much,' he said. 'You were less than truthful on the application form.'

'Aye, we lied. Swotted up though, well Karen did, for the interview, like. We wa' that desperate for a new life. So now the cat's out the bag, and that's why we need so much help. But it's just between me and thee mind, Eric.' How's he going to take that, wondered Steve.

'We-ell,' said the older man, rubbing his beard. It was so quiet you could hear the bristles rasp. 'As things are, I don't suppose it much matters. And I think if you were that keen to come, you'll give it your best shot. Mind you, I still think honesty's the best policy, myself.'

'That's why I'm telling you!' laughed Steve. 'It's our lass who's not so honest! So, it's cart all these to t' top't field, is it?'

'Fraid so,' said Eric. 'I'll write your fertiliser amounts down if you find me a scrap of paper.'

Eric thought all this could make an interesting article for his daughter, not that he'd pass it on, he valued people's privacy too much. Then he wondered would Marie have come round sooner if Gail had lied about Colin's ex-wives? He thought she just might have.

Karen and Steve decided to pay for the Land Settlement cultivation service and were now impressed by the satin finish to the soil. The tractor driver was expert at negotiating the rickety struts of their oldest greenhouse. The machine spread the soil beautifully, transforming it into silky dark-brown sand, the surface disturbed only by the swirls the back-flap left behind as it swerved around the supports. Karen knelt down and let the grains fall through her fingers. Wouldn't her fellow allotment holders have killed to plant their vegetables in a topsoil such as this?

Steve had shrewdly purchased some irrigation pipe second-hand. It arrived in a jumbled heap, lots of different sized reels and disjointed lengths of varying diameters. In addition to the nipples and the reels, there were lots of bags of spares. The vendor had thrown in "bits and bats, buckshee", which he said would be useful, but which now seemed to be part of a different system and a distant decade. The tangled mess took an age to sort out and then the lengths had to be cut to fit their glasshouse and the inevitable leaks had to be patched. The two weeks allocated so boldly were soon eaten away.

A thousand tomato plants in turquoise LSA trays now covered the lawn near the front gateway, just where the driver had unloaded them. Karen and Steve had so many other jobs to do they left them there, smothering the grass and having to be hand watered daily.

The peppers would be arriving soon. The celery had been harvested, and the field of outdoor lettuce would be next, if there were any that hadn't been choked by weeds. Mid-June would see one of the celery houses replanted with late cucumbers. Each crop was now a separate monkey on their backs.

"Diversify, that is the key", Jonathan had urged them,

116

way back when, a natty little catchphrase. They'd begun to think it good advice after the lettuce glut. Now they weren't quite so sure, so many crops all needing different care.

They were nervous about employing any labour, the lettuce-of-nil-return having left them shaken. Somehow they managed to keep up, just. The children must be suffering, thought Karen, but they seemed to enjoy the freedom, and most of the time they were within her sight. By the middle of June though, despair was beginning to creep in as the work piled up.

They'd lost most of their outdoor lettuce because they never got around to weeding it, at least until the groundsel seeded leaving white fluff all over the hearts. The tomatoes were planted and the trickle feed was working but they had no time to tie the plants up to the wire, so consequently they straggled in all directions, stems zigzagging and tangling together. The celery was long gone and the peppers were planted, but they didn't have enough floor irrigation left so were watering them by overhead lines instead. The final house was nearly ready for the cucumbers which lay straggly and yellow in pots and trays exactly where the tomatoes had been a few weeks earlier. Karen wondered if they could ever be separated from each other. She doubted it. You couldn't see the trays now for the papery leaves and to make things worse golden flowers were appearing too. Full summer was upon them and there'd been no recent rain, but the skies were full of cloud, occasionally giving way to broken sunshine. Karen stood by the roadside with the hosepipe, squirting water at the yellowing tangle of cucumber plants.

The twins squatted on the verge, flicking plantain seed heads at passing cars, tractors and lorries. They'd been taught this by old Vic. "Here, I'll show ye somethin' which'll drive your mammy daft!" he'd said. Karen looked at them, plump and sun-tanned, muddy but content. You would never think they were town kids this time last year. Apparently one of the wives was setting up a playgroup. The details were inside, but she'd only had time to scan them as yet. She showered the girls with the hosepipe and they screamed and squealed in delight. She promised to let them play with it later.

Karen concentrated the spray away from her children and back to the leggy plants. Not only were the brittle hairy stems tangled, tendrils were beginning to explore and grasp their sisters by mistake. She wondered if this long watering job, which had to be repeated daily if the plants were to be soaked enough to survive, would turn out to be as pointless as attempting to weed the lettuce on the field had been.

As traffic passed, whether it was the occasional tractor, a lorry, or a moped, everyone raised a hand. This was something Karen really appreciated, she felt it showed the people of the Estate had really accepted them. Eventually, while still she watered, a battered car pulled up.

The driver hopped out and searched the road north and south like a criminal from *Keystone Cops*. Reassured, he ducked back inside and pulled out two bulging carrier bags.

'Hi Maurice.' Karen pretended to spray him.

'Don't you dare, you little bugger,' he grinned. 'Is he inside? Where shall I pop these?'

'Just stick 'em in the kitchen, Maurice, I've nearly finished here. Steve's up the holding. Then I'll make you a cuppa if you want.'

Maurice looked doubtful. He shook his head. 'You're not expecting a visit from that Jonathan are you? I'm sure he's on to me,' he added, hugging the shade of the shed. Karen smiled. Anyone would think he carried diamonds, not bacon and cheese.

'No, he's been already,' she reassured him. Maurice disappeared, and returned almost immediately, empty handed. Karen knew Jonathan was disliked but she wondered if he was aware of this back-handed respect.

'I hid 'em under the free paper, just in case,' he said. 'Must press on. More deliveries to make.' He waved as his engine spluttered into life.

Settling back to her watering, Karen reflected on how much lower the cost of living was on the Estate. If they hit lucky with a crop or too they'd be comfortable, if not rich. Gone was the weekly trauma of the supermarket, the bulking out with cheap brand baked beans to make the money stretch. Here, home baking, especially things like custard tarts and cheese flans, had been abandoned in favour of more pressing duties like feeding the chickens and opening the vents. As soon as they bought a chest freezer household management took on a new dimension.

Maurice provided many of the growers with 3lb slabs of medium cheddar at what can't have been much more than the wholesale price. She'd learnt that cheese could be frozen like most other things. Bacon too, came in huge plastic packs. It wasn't best back, more of a mix-up. Of course she didn't question Maurice as to his source; financial survival was too crucial for that. All he asked in return was to bring his old dad to sit in the lee of the wind in his wheelchair, cocooned in a tartan blanket, whenever the fancy took him. The old man liked to have a choice of small holdings. Maybe he pretended they belonged to him. She thought of her own invalid father before he died, and then of her mother, who wrote and telephoned regularly but refused to visit, as if it was the end of the earth.

It was strange, mused Karen, relaxing as the cucumber roots at last became impregnated with water, how the Estate seemed to exist in a vacuum, almost immune from the tedium of petty rules and regulations. As you entered the Drift, a sign stated: PRIVATE ROAD – SLOW – CHILDREN AT PLAY. To the growers it signified their haven, the outside world couldn't touch them here. It reminded Karen of passing through into the tax-free zone of an airport. On the private road, children sat eager on their fathers' knees, steering pick-ups and three-ton vans. Fourteen year olds practised in their parents' cars, and twelve year olds careered about on mopeds as they do on the continent. Whole families squashed onto the back of tractors, and animals moved between holdings secured on the back of jack-trucks like in some third world country. Growers who had livestock sold meat cuts to each other very cheaply, or more often they bartered; half a pig returning from the abattoir often contained much you didn't need yourself. Most of them grew a few extra vegetables in the corner of a glasshouse, for themselves and their families. If meat, cheese and vegetables were not enough for you, virtually all growers had a cash and carry card from Bookers in Wansbridge. I need a card, they would explain, because I have to provide toilet paper, Nescafe, first aid requisites etc. for my workers. And yes, of course I have a VAT number.

VAT, thought Karen in alarm. She still hadn't had time to attack the books. She knew it was down to her; accounting was beyond Steve's mathematical capabilities, or more likely his concentration. Gun to his head, she knew he could do it. He refused even to try, and this irritated her hugely. Luckily for the grower, VAT was all money back to them. There was an overflowing shoe-box of yellowing pieces of paper tucked well out of the children's reach, top shelf in the dining room. Even her brother was saving petrol receipts back in Doncaster, but Karen knew she wouldn't dare include those.

Another car pulled up.

'Eric! Eric!' shouted the children. Eric always had sweets. He got out and pulled both little girls into his huge arms, snug against his lumberjack shirt. He hadn't received any calls to see Karen and Steve lately and he thought he knew the reason why. He searched his pockets for the goodies, still gripping a wriggling child. He popped her down (was it Mandy or Trudy? He could never really tell), and handed her a paper bag of peardrops. Whichever one it was began organising, doling them out, for she was the boss of the pair. A bit like her mother, Eric thought. Karen definitely was in charge, despite her husband's ability to work and his natural practicality and of course his size. In contrast Karen was five foot nothing.

'It's Trudy, you tell by the dimple on Mandy's face, and Trudy's voice is higher,' Karen explained. To her it was always amazing people couldn't tell them apart, there were so many differences to see, expression in the eyes to name just one, how Trudy stood with her weight on one leg, for another. And that was without considering their personalities, with Trudy taking charge and Mandy apparantly much softer. Karen knew Trudy got just as hurt as her sister, but bottled it in. She'd have to watch that, she thought.

As the girls sat back on the grass with their sweets, Eric surveyed the sodden mass of vegetation at Karen's feet.

'What have we here, then?' He heard himself say, stupidly. What a thing to ask! It was all too obvious what they were.

'Have they had it, Eric?'

'Well, they look as if they'll have cues on them shaped like catherine wheels this time next week,' he said, following Karen as she walked over to turn off the tap. She smiled, despite her despair.

'We're losing it, Eric,' she said.

He looked up and studied the sky for a clue to the immediate weather, as he did most mornings, at this sky full of billowy clouds. As if giant hands were pulling at them, they parted here and there giving patches of gaudy blue. The ever present wind was rushing them across the sky and the sun glanced through whenever possible. The white clouds reflected sharply giving a bright harsh daylight. Distant dark clouds of charcoal grey would pass by if they came near at all. The prospect of rain seemed unlikely. It was a good job she'd watered them, he thought.

'Well, you are cutting it fine,' agreed Eric, bending down and doubtfully teasing a plant from its tray-mates. He pulled too harshly and the stem snapped. 'Sorry,' he said, shaking his head. 'I don't know, Karen. Is the ground ready?'

'Not quite. Steve's still got to sort the irrigation,' she said. 'But I mustn't keep you,' she urged, remembering the cost of a consultation. Eric read her thoughts. He pushed up his chequered sleeve to consult his watch.

'Well now, it must be tea-break time,' he said. 'Any chance of a cuppa?'

Inside, Eric sat down in the wicker chair. The floor of the conservatory was caked in mud and littered with children's toys, empty cups, discarded plates. The whole area was unkempt. The few pot plants on the ledges were dead or dying, making those cucumber plants look positively robust. Karen filled the kettle and stuffed the cheese and bacon in the freezer. There was no sign of Steve but she made him a cup anyway. She passed Eric his drink and then squatted on the floor. The advisor searched for suitable advice, which wasn't forthcoming in his mind. He felt she needed to talk about her problems, at least so she could prioritise them.

'Do you wish you'd stayed in Yorkshire?'

'God, no,' smiled Karen. From where she sat she could see the children, chasing chickens on the grass. 'As soon as our removal van arrived, and it turned out to be that scruffy old curtain-sided lorry I knew the going would be tough!'

Her thoughts sprang back to the present, the disorder throughout the house, the tangled mangle of cucumbers, the huge tomatoes plants fat with sideshoots and laying on their backs. She burst into tears.

Eric looked and felt alarmed. He wasn't good with tears, couldn't cope with his wife's. He gazed around, empathising with her predicament. What could he say? What should he do? Karen continued to sob, a blubbering heap on the floor, frail and small in her dirty jeans and grubby tee-shirt.

'Now, now,' Eric heard himself say. He scrabbled uselessly in his pocket for a handkerchief. He patted her nervously on the shoulder and she cleaned her face with her forearm and smiled through her tears. 'What's happened is you've taken on too much.'

Damn Jonathan and his cropping programmes, he thought to himself. 'Look, I've an idea. Leave this with me, and I'll be back later. All is not lost.' He patted her clumsily on the shoulder, drained his cup and hurried away.

Rejuvenated perhaps by the rush of emotion, Karen walked across the grass in search of Steve with a slightly lighter heart, his lukewarm cup of tea in her hand. Eric hadn't been specific about his plan, but she was quite overcome with his kindness, which in itself was almost sufficient.

∽   ∾

Upon leaving the nursery, Eric drove straight to the Land Settlement propagation department. Like all the office buildings and The Stores, it was situated across the main highway, right at the end of yet another straight concrete road. Mid-West America, he placed it suddenly. Same geometrical layout, same flat land, same merciless wind and the same despair. Except that this was the 1980's. The people he felt most sorry for in all this were the latest tenants, Karen and Steve, and Josh and Angie. Josh was beginning to suffer too. His tension was beginning to show in bursts of unpredictable temper.

Now Eric needed to persuade Colin the Propagation Manager to replace Steve's original order of cucumbers for a new one, young plants with just the hint of a shoot pushing past the cotyledon. This was no mean feat as cucumber plants were very expensive. Quite what he said to Colin was never public knowledge. The second part of his plan was to tell George and Maisie about the newest recruits' plight, with special reference to those out-of-control tomato plants. Maisie had every possible short-cut, every useful tip ever stumbled upon shoved somewhere up her bulging jumper. She'd be happy to pass on her secrets to Karen along with any scandal which came to mind.

Fourteen

Old Vic was semi-retired now. He didn't want to give up growing entirely, for that would force a move to a council bungalow in a nearby village. He had vowed to his wife Ruby that this would never happen, he would die with his boots on and she with a scarf on her head, sideshooting, packing or feeding the animals. Secretly Ruby yearned for a clean cul-de-sac, a through-lounge and a carpet you took your boots off to walk on. She knew she'd never get it, not unless Vic pegged out before she did, and he as strong as a creeping thistle. She conceded his home-brew might have something to do with this. He had told her it was packed with vitamins, minerals and other unpronounceable benefits. Everyone else termed it "Victor's paint remover", but not to his face. Although some hardened drinkers like Eddie and that new one Josh could drink it on an empty stomach, she had noticed most of the other men had to be already merry on Carlsberg or some other weaker canned beer before they could drink it.

Vic didn't only brew beer; in the autumn he made wine from authentic Sicilian grapes which he purchased by the box from an Italian acquaintance. Ruby liked the wine but she had to mix it with ginger beer to warm it up a little and make it palatable. Most of the other growers brewed too, although they used kits from Boots, cheating with tins of wine concentrate. Only Vic used hops or malt and Simon, with Nicole's help produced demijohns full of non-specific alcoholic concoctions based on pickings from the hedgerows. Home brew was drunk randomly, on the lawn on summer evenings or celebrating the end of the celery, for instance.

Occasionally though, events were planned. Vic's gambling school came under this category, taking place discreetly maybe once a month but never quite as predictably as that. Its summer venue was his henhouse and he had a fridge out there to cool the drinks. Women were not invited, and especially not Ruby, although she was expected to clear away after them next morning and she always prepared sandwiches beforehand, leaving them covered in cling film to protect them from flies and dust and heat curl.

Bad happenings transpired at these gatherings, rumour had it. Most of the older men refused to go any more. It was usually the greenhorns who attended, persevering until they knew better. This particular evening Vic had invited Eddie, Josh and for his maiden visit, Steve. All three took along their own beer to be consumed first in order to gain courage for the host's refreshment later which they wouldn't be able to refuse. Old Vic's pride would be injured beyond salvation if they did.

Tonight was no different. Luck oscillated around the table and the sandwiches were swilled down with fiery liquid. The men usually played cards until they were too drunk to continue, or one of them won outright. This time it was Eddie. The amount was not vast but Eddie was pleased with himself, nonetheless. His confidence boosted his mood until nothing presented a problem. Lady Diana could be his if he chose, engaged to Charles or not.

Josh, head propped just above table level, elbows slumped, peered at him across the cluttered table, eyes level with the empty bottles and full ashtrays. Some drink had been spilt on Ruby's paper tablecloth, causing it to disintegrate, dark stains added to the gaudy pattern. A bare 40 watt bulb dangling above the table poured soft light on the sorry scene.

'Have you got a pump yet, then Eddie, for your water tank?' Josh spoke, sounding as if his tongue had swollen up in his mouth.

Eddie shook his head and hiccuped. 'No, mate,' he sighed. 'Can't afford it now. It'll have to wait for another year.'

To get water pressure to the top of his land he needed a tank and pump. He had built the tank, and if he had a pump then he could grow an autumn crop of outdoor celery, which might possibly catch that gilt-edged market just after the Fenland crop had been exhausted. Autumn celery could stand a little bit of frost, though not a severe one, so there may well be a month of high prices. Despite his allergy, talk of a high monetary reward was enough to tempt Eddie, and he could always hire a youngster to cut it. As always, solvency was just a crop away.

'Suppose I said I knew where there's a pump for *free*?' All eyes turned slowly on Josh.

'Eh bonny lad,' Vic slurred slightly, and his old eyes bulged red in the shadowy light, his bald head reflecting like a full moon rising. 'I think I mebbes kna what's in yer mind.'

Everything was spoken with the deliberation of a wild west film. There was some protest, but not enough to count. Ten minutes later Eddie's tractor and trailer wove erratically up The Drift towards the main road, three drunken figures swaying perilously in the back of the trailer. The whole scene was silhouetted clearly by a large pale moon masked lightly with very thin cloud.

෨ ෬

Eddie awoke next morning to find Hazel already gone from the bed. Her corner of the duvet was turned tidily into a triangle and the curtains were pulled back aggressively and unevenly. He blinked at the harsh daylight. The jabbering of a Radio One dee-jay drifted through the floor boards, the high-pitched well-educated voice easily recognisable. The voice merged into music, the rhythm thumping into his head. He heard footsteps running up the stairs. Realising she was travelling too fast to be carrying a cup of tea Eddie pulled the sheet over his head.

With a swift movement, Hazel whipped it back again. 'Sit up!' she hissed. 'Whatever have you been up to? Why is the tractor blocking the driveway? And what's that thing in the back?'

Eddie shielded his face with his forearms. He groaned. He remembered all too easily why it was blocking the driveway. It was blocking the driveway because he'd been too drunk to negotiate the gap. Josh and Vic had tried. They had all been too pissed. Why hadn't Steve tried? Try as he would he couldn't remember. He didn't know when or where he had last seen Steve. Then the full gravity of the situation shook him with the force of a tornado. He jumped from the bed, pulling just his jeans on. 'What's the fucking time?' he gasped.

'Charming.' said Hazel. 'How dare you swear at me just because your head hurts!' She threw back her head, ponytail swinging dangerously.

'Hazel, I need your help,' Eddie said in a tone which she knew not to argue with. 'Go to the other gate. If you see Jonathan or any of the LSA staff, stop them. Keep them talking, and DON'T LET THEM ON THE NURSERY! I don't care what you do – get your tits out if that's what it takes!' And he was gone, slamming the door behind him.

Hazel positioned herself outside the first gate. She folded her arms in annoyance. She realised there was something dodgy in the trailer and she wondered what it was. Nothing would surprise her. She was just in time; she could see Jonathan's Astra approaching as he made his morning visits. It didn't appear like he was going to slow down or stop, but she couldn't be sure. As she flagged him down she was aware of the straining of the tractor engine as Eddie made too many panicky moves reversing it out of sight.

Jonathan stopped and wound down the window. He had scored last night, and now evidently the prettiest of the growers' wives was in distress. He squinted sexily through his sunglasses.

'Now then gorgeous,' he said smoothly. 'What's happened? It can't be that bad.'

'It's my cat, Matilda.' Hazel had seen her tortoiseshell moggy slink across the roadway and into the conifers opposite a moment earlier. 'We don't let her cross the road. I'm afraid she'll get run over.' It was weak, but it was all she could think of. She guessed rightly that cats didn't figure highly on Jonathan's scale of things, so he probably hadn't noticed that Matilda criss-crossed the road most days. 'Could you help me to catch her?'

Jonathan and his overpowering aftershave hopped jauntily out of the car. Together they walked across to the trees. Matilda was washing herself between the conifer trunks, leg raised, playing the violin.

'There it is,' he said, slightly wary of the strange situation despite the intoxicating closeness of Hazel's left breast. She bent down and scooped up the animal, which hung limp in her arms, resigned, waiting for the opportunity to escape. Hazel turned her face to his, lingering just enough over the eye contact to interest him, and gave a big smile.

'Thank you,' she whispered.

'I haven't done anything -' he whispered back, and she was sure she caught the word "yet". 'How about a coffee to celebrate catching your pussy?' The tart fancies me, he thought. It would explain her strange behaviour. Nothing succeeds like success!

Hazel could see past his head that all was clear. She

didn't want Jonathan near her house, or anywhere on her land. 'Not now, Eddie wouldn't like it,' she murmured. 'I'll see you sometime.' And she granted him a little wink, almost as subtle as his "yet".

Back in the house, she checked on the children and stuffed the wriggling cat into the front room, slamming the door. It wouldn't do for Matilda to be traversing the road again too soon. Then she ran up the garden and onto the nursery. Eddie was struggling to hide something with a piece of sacking; as he covered one side the other became exposed. The sky began to spit rain.

'What's that?' she demanded, angrily.

'Well it's a pump,' Eddie said through gritted teeth, tugging desperately at the sack.

'I can see that. Whose pump?'

Eddie didn't risk any more sarcasm. He couldn't waste time. He needed all his energy to plan. 'We stole it last night,' he admitted in a low tone. 'It's a new one, from the Prop. They were waiting to fit it. It's been lying around for a fortnight,' he added this as if it was a significant factor, one which would save him from prosecution. Except prosecution here looked like an easy option. What we are talking about here, thought Eddie, is eviction, disgrace, bankruptcy...

'That was bright,' Hazel said. 'One pump gone. Only useful to growers, especially only to growers who have a tank awaiting a *pump*! You stupid IDIOT!' and she turned to storm off. Suddenly she stopped and swung around. 'You know what you have to do of course?'

'Take it back?' asked Eddie miserably.

Hazel spoke to him as if she was telling an unintelligent dog what to do with its bone. 'Bury it, of course. Ring up your moronic friends and tell them to bring their spades.' The blonde ponytail bobbed into the distance. Eddie relaxed. His Hazel had taken control.

Fifteen

Maisie's quick fingers sped along the tomato plants, nipping the superfluous sideshoots which sprouted between the main stem and the leaf branches whenever they were allowed to. She even obliterated them before they had a chance to be recognised, wiping her fingers around the junctions just in case.

As she removed the more substantial ones, in this case those about an inch long, she didn't drop them to the floor because that was unhygienic and might lead to disease. She tucked them instead into a canvas pouch tied around her middle, an oversized market trader's money-bag. This was the only way to cope with sideshoots, she decided. Not like yesterday, when she and George had attacked those monsters in Karen and Steve's tomato house. She had been glad to help; it had given her a nice warm feeling.

The four of them had wrestled with each of the distorted stems. The sideshoots were so huge in some cases that it was impossible to tell what should be discarded and which was the crucial growing point. Once chosen, the offending bough had to be hacked off with a Stanley knife. Even with such a keen blade the shoots were sometimes so tough they didn't come off cleanly but left a hang-nail behind. However careful you tried to be, Stanley knives were lethal and she now had a sore thumb covered with hairline slits. There was no tucking *those* sideshoots into a pouch. Some of them were a foot and a half long, and bent as boomerangs. They had to be tossed into the pathway for the children to drag outside later. Once stripped of this energy-sapping and unnecessary growth each poor plant had to have string attached to its base and wound around its crooked body, taking care not to strangle it. Then the plant was wrenched upright and the string secured to a wire above by means of a slip-knot. Maisie thought they looked as if they were hanging from a noose, all bent and reluctant. Thank goodness there had been extra help. Dennis had sent round a couple of his girls. Maisie smiled to herself remembering some of the jokes they'd told. They were a bit vulgar, she admitted, but everyone had a laugh. Eventually the greenhouse had been transformed and you could even make out the pathways. The crop had been saved.

Karen had invited them all into the house for tea and toast. Maisie had seen how embarrassed the poor girl was over the neglected housework. It was obvious Karen was not like Maisie's next-door neighbour, another newcomer. Angie never let the state of the house depress her, no matter how dreadful it was. Her biggest source of unhappiness was her inability to conceive, although she didn't mention it often and Maisie steered clear of the subject. Karen had those lovely little twins, terrors despite being girls and Maisie wondered if she was finding it difficult to cope. She felt a bit sorry for them all. Life had been easier on the Estate years ago, certainly for the women, and she and George had made sure they didn't have children until they were established in business. Then they'd had five! Maisie laughed to herself, remembering how she used to chase them around the huge garden when they'd misbehaved. Now they were scattered around the country all with families of their own.

Now Karen had arrived here just when the twins needed her most, but she found it necessary to work alongside her husband all day as well. It wasn't as if they stood a good chance of survival, thought Maisie. Everything was set against them from the lack of capital to buy good equipment to the poor prices everyone was receiving recently. Maisie knew they shouldn't have been accepted onto the Estate, because it was obvious they knew little about growing. She chuckled to herself, remembering how Steve had been chopping sideshoots *and* growing tip off, until one of Dennis' girls had realised and intervened. Could you survive, the girl had asked him, with your bleeding head cut off? Yes, thought Maisie, Karen is obviously in charge and she's one of those people who grit their teeth and say okay, there's a problem, but I'll win through. Salt of the earth, them sort.

Maisie's reminiscences took place in silence, with just the rustle of the leaves as she disturbed them and the occasional rattle of the wind on the glass. She didn't listen to the radio in the greenhouse. She liked the peace, it made her think. When she was between the rows, all of them conforming and perfectly controlled, she felt relaxed. It was different in the evening when in the fading light the growing tips seemed to scrunch themselves up and become harsh and brittle. Then it was as if there were a thousand nodding heads all intent on the business of growing and the whole house took on a shadowy, sinister feel. No, Maisie did not work on the tomatoes at the end of the day. The next morning after a hard night's industry they seemed relaxed once more, stretching their scrunched heads out again towards the warm morning sunshine.

Suddenly her peace was disturbed by a rumpus, screaming and shouting to be precise. She couldn't make out any words but she recognised the two contrasting pitches well enough. She knew it would be Josh and Angie, having yet another argument. The shouting continued and was followed by the unmistakable tinkle of breaking glass. Maisie removed her waist bag and picked her way through the dense vegetation to the far side of the house. Using two tomato plants as her net curtain, she surveyed the scene.

This glasshouse formed part of the boundary between the holdings so she had a grandstand view. It was just like being at the cinema, and Maisie loved a good film. Josh was sitting up on the seat of his old grey Ferguson waving his arms expressively and Angie was shouting up at him, her hands on her hips, large bosom thrust forward defiantly. Shards of glass speckled the concrete; it looked as if Josh had thrown something through a greenhouse light. Maisie had to admire Angie. She was only about five foot two, voluptuous rather than dumpy but she was totally fearless of Josh. Angie had told her that he only broke things in temper. She was sure he would never hit her, although there had been a few near misses when she had inadvertently got in the line of fire. Maisie listened careful as the squabble continued.

'That's right! Smash the place up. Very clever!'

'I don't fucking care any more! Why should I? You don't, that's flamin' obvious!'

'Well if you carry on smashing things up you won't need anyone to work for you,' she yelled. 'Anyway, I'm off!'

Maisie watched as she clacked down the path in her tight jeans, shocking pink top and well worn high-heeled shoes. Josh searched fruitlessly for a missile which wouldn't cause him to dismount, and leaning on the steering wheel put his head in his hands. To an ignorant observer it might have appeared that Angie was leaving Josh, but Maisie had been privy to what was now occurring, for yesterday the girl had used her as a sounding board...

'Maisie, don't you ever get fed up, stuck here in this God forsaken hole?'

Maisie had been hanging her washing near to the boundary fence as she did once or twice a week. Angie was leaning on it and it rocked slightly. A little hurt by Angie's words, Maisie determined not to show it. She'd had plenty of experience of youths, and Angie in her early twenties was still young.

'Umm, I remember I did a little bit when I first come 'ere,' Maisie had admitted. 'I was jus' eighteen and new married. But I soon made friends, I did, and so'll you.'

'I've *got* friends,' Angie had said. Maisie looked at her bright red lipstick and her black eye makeup. Her frizzy dark hair framed her pretty face and pointed chin. 'It's workmates I need. Me and Josh, we can't work together, we get on each other's nerves.' Maisie knew the truth in this; they fought continually, like a couple of cock birds. She wondered how they had ever lived in a street. Or perhaps they were kicked out, a huge petition sent to the LSA by their neighbours, the admissions panel saying yes, they've got a garden, we'll take them..

'I heard Dennis Fensome is looking for more staff,' Angie told her. 'He pays well too. The money I bring in would be more use than what we lose here. And I'd have a laugh. It will probably save our marriage. What do you think, Maisie?'

Maisie had considered the matter. At least then there would be some point in her lathering on all that makeup. And she was right, it wasn't easy spending all day and night with your husband, joined at the hip. Over the years she and George had learnt to cope, but she would have loved to have had an outside world to report on across the tea-table. Now it was different. He had his separate world, a brightly coloured one full of geraniums. Maybe she should search for a hobby too.

'What will Josh say?' she'd asked cautiously. Maisie knew that George would never have accepted it if she had done the same, all those years ago. He would have seen it as abandonment. But then George and Josh were very different people and this was a new generation. Why, Josh didn't even look like a grower, with his thin face and longish black hair and he didn't even wear wellies! Angie told her he didn't own a pair. He trailed mud into their house continually on his Doc Marten boots which he couldn't be bothered to unlace, and Maisie knew this to a root cause of Angie's battle with the housework, a battle which she'd evidently lost.

'He'll shout and he'll smash something, and then he'll accept it and take on a teenager,' Angie had predicted.

Two out of three so far, Maisie grinned. She replaced the leaves across her spyhole and pushed carefully through the plants, straight as soldiers, to the doorway and hurried towards the house to telephone her grandson, Guy.

Sixteen

Jim's mother was sitting on a bench on an otherwise deserted platform at Wansbridge railway station. Had she arrived at either end of the day she'd probably have had to stand, caught amongst a whirlpool of commuters, but they would be in London now and the empty platform basked in the heat of the day. She was surrounded by cases too numerous and bulky for a woman of her age although Myra was stronger and tougher than her slight build suggested. She looked at her watch, opened her black patent leather handbag with the large brass clip and located and lit a Woodbine.

'Hey Nan, caught you!' said a voice behind her. Myra jumped guiltily and nipped it out with her knobbly fingers. She popped it back inside the packet and jumped up to give her grandson a big hug. She came to just past his waist. Standing back she surveyed him proudly, a tall and skinny long-haired youth.

'Look at you! You're *still* growing duck!' she cried. 'What a lovely surprise. Where's your dad?'

'He's busy,' said the boy, timing his moment of pride. He picked up most of the bags, leaving her with just a hold-all. 'Chauffeur's outside.'

They walked through the quiet station, Myra's metalled heels ringing out on the concrete as she tried to keep up with her striding grandson. They carried the bags through the gloomy ticket office and out into brilliant sunshine where short sharp shadows emphasised the newness of the afternoon. The street was quiet, just a long line of parked cars reflecting the sun and dazzling the youth and his grandmother.

Paul tossed the bags into the back of a rusty white pick-up, parked illegally just outside the entrance. 'Well, the driver's run off, Nan,' he said. 'I suppose we'll have to catch a bus. Or shall I drive you?' His freckled face broke into a grin.

'Oh Paul! You've passed your test! Well done, duck! First time was it?

'Yes. Mum taught me. I only needed five proper lessons to finish me off!' He climbed up into the driver's seat.

Myra ignored this. 'You take after your dad. I always said he was a natural driver.'

He leaned over and stretched a hand to pull her up into the cab, lacy petticoat showing against the dark seamed stockings. She gave him another hug, as he fired up the engine and swung the pickup around using excess throttle. He roared up the by-pass and turned sharply into a country lane. As his Nan bounced up and down in the cab, empty packets and bags of sweets bounced off the dashboard and into her lap. Bleached VAT receipts fluttered to the floor. She turned to him and said: 'If you're going to drive as fast as this you don't mind if I light up a ciggy, d'you duck?'

'No Nan, you go ahead.'

യ   ൽ

Back at the house, Janice was waiting for the visitor with less goodwill. Her mother-in-law came to stay every summer and she judged it a bit of an ordeal. Myra was overpowering and tended to take over, but it had to be admitted that she worked hard and the free labour was well appreciated. Janice was hurriedly preparing a room for her, a job she'd put off until the last minute.

Myra was to sleep in a room stuck to the back of the

house. All the houses on the Estate had been extended a decade ago, and in addition to a bathroom an extra room had been added, a flat-roofed square room with a plastic tiled floor. This room had neither nook nor cranny to sustain interest, it was a cell of a room. For years Janice's sons had slept in it, but now it was too cramped for the both of them. They now lived noisily and untidily in a caravan, just far enough from the house. Some growers used the extension for a study, especially if their children had grown up and left. They might have a desk and a couple of filing cabinets. It could be where they shelved their trade magazines and horticultural bibles. Some folk kept a chest freezer in there, as it was the only possible place inside the house.

Somehow Janice had made this room, as she had the rest of the house, like home. She'd taken care with the choosing of the curtains, and the selection of a warm paint for the walls. She'd cheered it all up with a patterned border, and pastel drawings of animals brightened it further. She'd even hung delicate nets to hide the ugly iron windows, each frame split into six smaller ones, with ill-fitting push-up handles to force them open. Rust ate through whatever you painted them with and they also let in draughts. When the LSA handymen painted the outside, they usually glossed an inch of glass around each metal strip as well. Janice couldn't blame them; she thought it would take a saint or certainly a bigger pay packet to do that job satisfactorily, day after day. The windows were indeed the worst feature of the house. Jutting out as the extension did, three of the walls were exterior ones making it chilly in winter. When and if the government sells them off you won't recognise ours, she thought.

Putting the finishing touches she gently tugged at the candlewick bedspread to free it from ripples, then she opened the window to let some fresh air in. Did Myra like goat's milk, she wondered. Bernadette was still giving a bucketful a day, but her kid had been sold to another grower at the far end of the Drift. A cloud of guilt descended immediately upon Janice, as she remembered the circumstances of that separation...

Nigel had told her: 'Tek the kid when she's not looking. She'll 'ave forgot in five minutes. Otherwise, lass, she'll drive you daft with 'er bleating for days on end, if she sees you do it.'

Taking his advice, Janice had distracted Bernadette who'd recently been enjoying enough false security to let the kid wander off on its own. On the fateful day, the kid had strayed over by the swing, and was under the Bramley apple tree licking experimentally at the bark. Bernadette was chomping titbits at the far side of the piggery. Janice had found her some hollow-stemmed sow thistles, a caprine delicacy, a Judas dinner, as it turned out. As Bernadette munched obliviously, her kid was being bundled into a truck before it had chance to bleat. Finishing her snack, the nanny casually wandered off looking for more. Such was her trust in the human race that she didn't discover the awful truth for a couple of hours. Janice had heard her contented voice change key as panic hit home. Bernadette cried solidly for five days, and Janice's guilt had lasted somewhat longer. How could she have taken a man's word about such a feminine issue as the bond between mother and kid?

There was a screech as *her* kid brought the pick-up to a halt in the drive. Taking a deep breath, Janice compelled herself to take up position of hostess, and to greet her forceful mother-in-law. She heard them enter the conservatory, and then the loud "dong dong dong" as Paul shook the metal cow-bell used to summon the family for mealtimes and special occasions. This was a special occasion in his eyes; like his brother and sisters he couldn't understand his mother's irritation, blatant and sometimes even bordering on hostility. He loved the old lady, admired her enthusiasm for living, and laughed at how she was full of excuses for him and his father. He led his Gran through the stiflingly hot conservatory, and into the cooler confines of the house.

Janice was pouring tea and tea was irritation number one; Myra liked loose tea in a pot and last year Janice had discovered the decadence of dropping a tea bag into a cup. She greeted her mother-in-law with as much warmth as she could muster, taking her coat from her.

Jim came in from the nursery, his hands coloured black from the tomato plants. It wasn't worth washing them for a cup of tea, and a quick rinse would only loosen the stain, leaving yellow dye everywhere. He joined the others at the table. He greeted his Mother with pleasure, but they didn't hug. That wasn't part of the etiquette of his family, at least not for grown adults. When they'd exchanged preliminaries the excitement subsided.

'Nice cuppa, duck,' said Myra to Janice, draining her cup thirstily. She got up to pour another. Myra wasn't one to have others wait on her. It was then she noticed the jug.

'Is this Longlife?' she asked suspiciously. Janice wasn't the type to bother with the niceties of unnecessary crockery. So the wily old girl lifted the striped milk jug to her face and sniffed hard.

Since Bernadette, Janice saw no reason to buy cow's milk any more. Nigel had been right in something; so long as you drank it fresh and refrigerated it the milk didn't develop that unsavoury nutty taste. The family still argued occasionally for cow's milk but Janice had saved a couple of glass bottles before she cancelled the milkman. These she filled every day, placing a Tupperware "easy-pour" cap on each. This seemed to satisfy everyone. When guests visited, they might say: "not that goat's milk, please Janice," and she was often able to trick them completely. There was always the risk of missing a coarse hair in the straining process but if this pitfall had been avoided, and they congratulated her on her brew, only then would she admit to the source of the milk. But some devil in her wanted Myra to discover the truth straight away.

With just a hint of malice, she now said: 'D'you like goat's milk then, Myra?'

The old girl slammed her cup down in alarm.

'Oh no Janice, not for me please, duck,' she said. Like many of her generation she remembered the threat of TB, back in the days before pasteurisation. 'It won't have been whatever it is-ised, and it'll be sure to give me indigestion.'

Along with peppers, mushrooms, sweetcorn, brown bread and anything with enough roughage to make your gut work, thought Janice. Here we go, six weeks of green sludge masquerading as vegetables. Still, she'd welcome the break from cooking.

'It's okay Ma,' Jim said quickly, getting up and fetching a bottle of milk with its plastic cap from the fridge. 'Here, have cow's milk. We still use that too.' Janice looked over to him, but there was no flicker of conspiracy in his face at all. I fooled him as well then, she thought in surprise.

Seventeen

Although the stolen pump had been buried Eddie's tribulations didn't end there. Firstly he had to carry his guilt, which was considerable. Secondly he had to deal with Hazel's contempt, and thirdly he'd developed a bad back. The latter was the greatest burden to him, as he'd had plenty of experience of the first two, and knew in time their intensity would wane. The last though, was quite the opposite. Back problems inconvenienced others, he'd always considered them an excuse for skivers, doubting they existed at all. Worse still, he couldn't show his symptoms to anybody who might partake in a little mathematics. This included both Jonathan, who was definitely suspicious anyway and had been using all sorts of excuses to pry, and Eric, for whom he had a lot of respect. He knew if the ADAS man found out he would not approve. Eddie would have come clean and confessed but he feared for his holding and his house. So when the two fieldsmen were in the vicinity, poor Eddie had to force his stiffened joints to move freely, and this caused him to sweat with pain.

'My back's getting worse,' he said to Hazel one evening. He was lying on the floor, flat on his back with knees up, yoga style. News at Ten droned on benignly; they were waiting for the local weather. The little ones were asleep, but Nathan at six was going through a "can't sleep" phase. He'd been downstairs five times through the course of the evening, and Hazel who had been sweet and motherly at first was now getting irritated. She hadn't forgiven her husband, but she saw the benefits of an Eddie restored to former vigour.

'You'd better go to the doctors,' she said. 'Unless – well, she cured you last time. I'll give Nicole a ring, see if she can come and sort you.'

'No, no,' said Eddie hurriedly. He couldn't explain it, but ever since she had cured his celery rash he'd had strange feelings about her. Lately he noticed her as she floated past on the roadway. It was as if they were partners in some connivance. This was especially peculiar as he knew he had absolutely nothing in common with her, she an airy fairy hippy and he down to earth and solid. She wasn't even the sort he fancied. He liked his women voluptuous and her tits were like fried eggs. 'It'll sort itself. Stop your meddling, woman.'

'That it will, I don't think,' Hazel swung her legs from the settee arm. She began gathering empty coffee cups with great purpose and said with an air of finality: 'I'm sick of you like this. All the sodding graft's falling on me. Well I'm phoning her tomorrow cos we can't carry on like this.'

'Mum! I still can't sleep!' Nathan's voice drifted through once more.

'If I have to come up those stairs again –' shouted Hazel. 'It's not fair, Eddie, I'm knackered!'

Well, what can you do, thought Eddie. And now I've missed the weather. And although his uneasiness persisted, he wasn't in a position to protest.

                                                           ৪০ ೞ

Next morning Eddie's back was worse. Again he lay on the front room carpet, unable to do a thing. His role was relegated to that of a baby-minding log, so ineffectual was he in his present position. Daisy and Sam, aged two and four respectively, crawled over him as they watched cartoons together, making him wince with pain.

Hazel had picked what few ripe tomatoes she could find, Eddie was convinced she hadn't done a proper job but wasn't up to a challenge. She was back in the house by nine-thirty. She went to get changed, vibrating the floor as she clattered back down the stairs. His irritation was tempered with pride for she was looking especially attractive in her jeans and a clean blouse, he thought. Her blonde hair hung loose tickling his face as she bent over to give him a quick kiss on the lips. Eddie could feel she was beginning to forgive him. She'd probably want them to make up tonight, he thought. Not that it would be possible in his present condition.

'Where're you off, then?'

'I told you! You never listen. I'm taking Sam to the new playgroup,' she said. 'As it's the first time, we have to stay with them, and it'll be nice for Daisy. Oh, that'll be Nicole at the door. Come on, you lot! Get a move on! See you at twelve, Eddie.' She hardly stopped for breath. Pity she don't shift as fast in the glasshouse, thought Eddie.

'Bye Daddy!' A little one tripped over his foot as she ran to the door. It jarred his back, and left him gasping with pain.

Help, thought Eddie. He felt very vulnerable. He heard his wife giving casual directions to Nicole, in the hallway.

'Do whatever necessary,' she was saying. 'It's driving me mad. I can't take much more of it. He's as much use as a chocolate fireguard.'

He heard the women laughing, and then Nicole's soft voice asking for a towel, to prevent a spillage of massage oils on the carpet, she said. She thought she would probably give him another reflexology treatment, if that was all right.

'Whatever,' Hazel said carelessly. 'He's all yours.' Then the back door slammed and Nicole came into the room. It was like a new scene in a film. The noise had gone and calm took over.

She looked ethnic as ever, thin brown arms against the turquoise of her silky flowing dress. Her sandalled feet were bare and she was carrying the towel Hazel had given her and her own flowery duffel bag. Eddie noticed for the first time that the curtain was closed, to keep the sun from the television screen. Again he had a sense of the bizarre. She seemed like some strange spectral being and he wasn't comfortable, but he was interested. He found her ghostly but attractive. A shiver passed through him.

'Hi, Nicole, open those curtains, can you please?' he asked.

She smiled, shook her head, and turned the television off instead.

He was unsure how to react now she'd ignored him. Hazel disobeyed him all the time of course, but not usually to a direct command.

'The kids closed them, and...' he began, but she put her finger to her lips.

'You will have to show me where it hurts,' she said.

Obediently Eddie struggled to roll over, and she pulled his shirt delicately up to his shoulders. Sharp pains shot through the base of his spine.

'Right there,' he indicated, realising his jeans were in the way.

'Well you'll have to undo them. Don't mind me, I'm a doctor.' He was ready to believe her. Now her slender fingers were easing them down a little. Eddie was grateful his face was buried in the carpet. Luckily the pain kept reminding him of the original purpose.

He was aware that she was removing jars and potions from her bag. Then he felt her squirt some cold gel on the hollow of his back. It made him jerk.

'Sorry,' she said, just audibly. Then he felt her soft sensual hands moving across the area of the pain, and he heard his own voice directing her. He felt warmth from the potion spreading across his stiff joints. Gradually he began to relax.

'This is a special gel,' he heard her say. 'It doesn't heat like Tiger's Balm, or any of those. All natural,' and he then felt her hands slide down over his buttocks as if to prove a point.

Oh shit, he thought. But he found himself both unable and unwilling to do much about it.

'Can you roll over for me, and I'll complete the treatment?' she was asking, her voice sounded faraway as before. Eddie kept his eyes shut, and found he could do so without much difficulty. It didn't seem to matter now that his jeans were undone. She was kneeling down beside him, and Eddie peering through slits in his eyes saw that she was distant, her dark eyes were looking at him but they seemed far away. He went to lift his head and shoulders and reach out for her, but a shaft of pain shot through his back, and she pushed him gently back to the floor again. This was her agenda now. She took his penis in her slender hands and began massaging it with her fingers.

As he came she lightly placed the towel over him, and said 'You'll be needing this,' and with a spin of her skirt she picked up her bag, tossed him a smile and was gone.

Eddie, light headed, stared at the closed door in disbelief. He lay for a minute experiencing a cocktail of horror and elation. What had he done? Well actually, he hadn't done anything. He reached down and wiped himself with the towel. Cautiously he fastened his trousers. His back was eighty percent better, he judged. A moment of panic seized him. What would he do with the towel? With shaky legs he eased himself cautiously to his feet and shoved the towel deep down in the laundry basket.

Eighteen

When you work on the land, you become an expert on the weather. You can't help it, it's unavoidable. You get to know, without having to lick your finger and hold it to the sky, which direction the wind is blowing from. You recognise which dark skies will lead to rain, and which ones will blow over. Without the aid of the Observer's Book of Clouds or being an expert of cumulo- strato- nimbo whatever, you understand which threaten to build into thunderstorms, and which herald a change in the weather. You then learn that however many times you may guess correctly there'll always be a time when you're hopelessly wrong, usually when you're furthest from shelter, or there's lots of expensive cardboard packing boxes strewn across your crop about to get soaked. It's crucial to know when to run, and a good grower's rule is when a tree a hundred yards away suddenly disappears take cover!

Long standing growers like George and Vic had their countryman's lore too, usually based on how the birds were behaving, or how thickly the hawthorn berries had set last autumn. They loved to talk about foul weather from the past; this was more memorable than clement weather. They reminisced about that winter in 1940 and those floods of '52. Of course the snow lay deeper and temperatures plunged lower with each year of added distance.

The weather affected everything the growers did, even or especially inside the glasshouses. The temperatures could beat the Sonoran Desert in there. When it was sunny and warm, the tomatoes ripened as they looked at them. They could pick a row, plucking everything with the slightest flush of orange, only to return an hour later to find many they'd apparently missed. Alternatively, if the skies were overcast and the temperature chilly, the colour hardly moved at all.

This summer so far had seen prolonged rain, followed by days of uninterrupted sunshine. Fortunately these had not lasted long enough to cause a drought. Perhaps the worst enemy was the wind, sweeping in from the west across the flat fields beyond, now pale with ripening wheat. Wind was rarely absent from the Estate, continually rattling the loose Dutch Light glass in the wooden frames and flapping the polythene tunnels which were always skinned tightly but soon expanded and loosened with the changing temperatures. This produced a background noise in the same way as living near a busy road. On a rare day of perfect calm they noticed something was amiss. The wind also dried out your land, setting it hard as rock. It tip-burnt the lettuce and the tomato plants near the doors dried out and wilted causing their fruit to split. Traditionally growers encircled their land with tall trees, but this Estate was supposed to be a stepping stone, so most hadn't bothered. Why spend out on somebody else's future?

Dennis was a grower who'd viewed this differently. Conifers, now twenty feet high, sheltered his holding and his wife's mini Kew from the wind. Today he emerged from his sanctuary onto the roadside with a barrow-load of empty LSA trays. As he began unloading them, a tractor pulled up a few yards from him. Nothing unusual about this, until Dennis noticed it was Josh. The two men had hardly spoken. Even though Josh's wife Angie now worked for him, this hadn't provided any introductions to her husband. From what he'd heard from her, Josh wasn't the sort of man Dennis wanted to know at all.

Now he looked in surprise at Josh's face, for it was

obvious from a glance that this wasn't going to be a courtesy call. Josh looked as if he'd been drinking. He staggered down from his seat, his face red, and addressed Dennis. His wild black hair was frizzed and matted, and his wide eyes were near enough now for Dennis to notice the dark pupils completely encircled by white. His baggy hand-knitted jumper danced unevenly about his knees.

'Hey! I suppose you think it's funny, do you? Having a laugh, are you? But you're not laughing now! Are you laughing now? Oi! are you *laughing* now?'

Dennis didn't get time to greet him. He watched in a daze as the man loomed so close to him it was impolite. Josh was pointing his finger, stabbing the air with it, and he looked furious. Dennis could smell the alcohol on Josh's breath as his face lurched nearer and the smell of stale cigarette smoke rose from his clothes. Dennis was much the shorter and Josh was using the discrepancy to full advantage.

'What? You what?'

'My *wife* that's what! *Luring* her away from me!'

He had to back away, or Josh would have poked him in the chest. Dennis felt revulsion surging inside him. Josh's reputation for being a drinker together with his aggressive nature and his foul tongue had spread through the Estate like potato blight. Angie, bright, sparkly-natured and hard working was a sharp contrast, and he'd been happy to employ her on just those grounds.

Then this fog of confusion suddenly cleared. Josh must think she was having an affair with him! He explained quickly:

'Look mate, you've got hold of the wrong end of the stick! She's only *working* for me, she hasn't moved in or anything!' His face lit up with a comprehending smile.

He was wrong though, that wasn't the problem. Josh's eyes only blazed more angrily. His thin angular face became more skull-like and he gazed at Dennis in total disbelief.

'Don't be fucking stupid, I know she wouldn't, not with *you*,' he said contemptuously, as if Dennis was aged a hundred with three heads. A bead of spittle hit him on the cheek. 'She's working for *you*, and where the fuck's that left *me*, eh, where's that left *me*?' The bony stubbly chin was only inches now from Dennis, who was pressed up against those protective conifers looking up the flare of his large nostrils. He felt totally helpless. He wasn't an aggressive person, any fighting he liked to do verbally. His eyes slid sideways for help, but the Drift was empty.

'Well sh-she said she'd okay'd it with you,' he said tamely, wondering now why he'd employed the wife of a madman. He felt a sharp stab in his sternum and he only stayed standing courtesy of his conifers.

'Of course she fucking did! Well it ain't!' and he leaned back with his right shoulder and swung a fist between Dennis's eyes.

Seeing stars, Dennis fell back in a heap, dropping awkwardly between two tree trunks, the thin feathery off-shoots closing behind him like a curtain, leaving just his feet sticking out. He could smell the unmistakably acrid stink of dog excrement too near for comfort. When he managed to scramble to his feet, he saw the rear of the tractor disappearing up the Drift with a tail of blue diesel smoke. The road was otherwise deserted.

∞ ℃

Karen, Steve and the children were returning from the Cash and Carry, the car stuffed with giant tins of coffee and enough toilet rolls to lay siege for a month. Among Karen's best buys were the catering sacks of pastry mix (just add water) and packets of what she called 'magic' custard. Each generation slipped a little further into decadence with regards to custard, Karen noticed. Her grandmother told of beating egg yolks and adding cornflour, her own mother mixed Bird's Powder with milk and put it back to boil, and would have no truck with Karen's even lazier custard. The trade outlet provided the commodities needed to prepare fresh meat and vegetables, and bulk buying suited the growers' cashflow. The irony for Karen was that back home she'd had a huge pantry, sparse apart from Christmas, and here she had a pokey kitchen with inadequate cupboard space, so much had to be stored on the stairs creating a regular obstacle course.

'Look Daddy, watch out – tractor!' said Trudy, who like her sister was standing up in the back in front of the groceries.

'Oh, that's only Josh!' said Steve, pipping his horn to warn him as he moved to overtake.

The grey Ferguson swerved to the side, and a red-faced dishevelled Josh waved and stuck his thumb up to Steve.

Steve put his hand up, and so did Karen, as they passed.

'That's Josh,' said Steve as if it explained all. Karen hadn't met him, but she'd seen him in passing and guessed who he was.

'Looks like a yeti,' she said.

'He'll be on his way back from the pub.'

'Lucky he's got the time,' said Karen.

೫   ೧

Meanwhile, Dennis retrieved his barrow and pushed it into the safety of his nursery. His legs shook. Normally so much in control, he'd been knocked off balance mentally as well as physically. He touched his nose, and found wet blood. He walked unsteadily towards the house, to survey the damage in the bathroom mirror. As luck would have it, Sylvia was away in London visiting her sister. She often took a week away alone, unable to detach him from the holding.

As habit and Sylvia dictated, Dennis pulled his wellingtons off at the door. The large conservatory, completed the summer before, was more of a parlour. It had geometrically patterned cushioned flooring and the curtains were swagged and tailed. A cane three-piece suite was arranged with care, and an artificial parlour palm stretched to the roof. Blood splattered a trail on the floor, and Dennis pulled a length of kitchen roll from a dispenser. Holding it tight to his wound, he crossed the thick lounge carpet to get some whisky as a stiff drink was necessary before facing the mirror. The house was silent apart from the muffled tick of the clock and shuffle of his clothes, and it felt strange. Dennis never entered the house in the day; he made drinks, used the toilet and washed his hands on the holding. This was Sylvia's domain, and he felt like a cat burglar.

He sat on the cane settee in the conservatory and sipped at his whisky. He was embarrassed, found it hard to re-run the incident. Despite his anger, he was man enough to admit to himself he'd handled the situation badly and maybe should have checked with Josh, for it was obvious she'd be needed at home. But she'd been so persuasive and Dennis believed a wife isn't just a chattel of the husband. Why, his own wife refused to work on his nursery. This had caused problems between them in the past, but now her reasonably prestigious position with salary to match, as well as sick leave and holiday pay, more than compensated. Angie had sold her case well; she told him the knowledge gained from working on his efficient unit would benefit both her and Josh. Reflecting now, Dennis could see there was as much comparison between his electrically-vented greenhouses complete with automated watering systems and Josh's run down draughty glass as there was between the Drift and London's Oxford Street. Perhaps also, he was forced to consider, he'd been influenced by a pretty face.

Whisky glass drained, he moved to the bathroom. The wound wasn't as bad as he'd feared, but the shock was a different one. Staring at his reflection in the mirror, yes, he saw the anxious face of a middle-aged man with a red and swelling nose, blood smeared across a cheek. But in contrast to the ridiculous flush inflicted by the blow, the rest of his face looked tired and grey. And it wasn't just his hair, still thick but shrinking backwards, it was his whole demeanour.

Good God, Dennis, he acknowledged to himself. Look at you. Once young and if not handsome, then certainly bright-eyed and bushy-tailed. Where had his vivacity gone? Probably somewhere flattened under the years of worry and responsibility. How come he hadn't noticed it before? He experimented with a smile, and his swelling nose stretched and hurt. Transformation was instant, though. Colour started to spread across his cheeks and his eyes began to lighten. How come he, most successful grower on the Estate, trapped here only by the rumours of opportunity to buy, looked like he had the world on his shoulders? No, he resolved, as determination leaked back into his brain. He'd keep Angie on, he wasn't going to be intimidated by that yob. He'd get even though, at some point.

'Dennis, old boy,' he actually spoke aloud. 'You need a bit of fun in life. Maybe you can teach the animal a lesson, and enjoy yourself at the same time.'

He decided against telling anybody, and set about concocting a story. He hoped Josh wouldn't speak of it to Angie.

Nineteen

One of the long standing problems on the Estate was the easy spread of pests and diseases. Because of the proximity of so many small units, crammed together all producing similar crops, natural resistance to chemicals soon built up. A grower would spray his outdoor lettuce against aphids for instance; some of the insects on the edge of the crop would get a lesser dose, and hop across the boundary to the neighbouring crop. Those which had already survived spray were now slightly immune and this resistance would breed true in their descendants.

To counteract this The Stores stocked everything necessary and plenty which wasn't, and by law the storeman had to keep a "Poisons Book". When growers bought anything toxic, they had to sign the book. Thus responsibility for safety passed to the grower, who was obliged to provide a locked container to keep nasty concoctions secure.

DDT had already been banned, and brushwood herbicides were about to be. Getting wind of this, many growers bought up herbicides before the deadline as housewives hoarded sugar a decade before. The longer established the grower, the more colourful and perilous his defence against the twin evils of pest and disease. Often chemicals hung around well past their expiry dates due to difficulty in disposing of them. Generally speaking the growers did not give these chemicals proper respect.

Eric was aware of this problem and worked with Jonathan to persuade growers and their wives to attend courses to appreciate more fully the dangers to themselves and their workers, and ultimately to the consumer. Both men suspected a tiny minority of growers ignored the safe harvest interval. This was called the "clearance time" and the length of clearance varied considerably. Some selective herbicides had a margin of six weeks but this wouldn't usually pose a problem because they were administered when the plants were small, and therefore months before harvest. The difficulty usually occurred when a crop was close to being cut and a disease or infestation hit just at the wrong time. Chemicals with a clearance date of a couple of days did exist for some things, but obviously they weren't as effective as the ones which barred you from harvesting for three weeks. A few growers chose to ignore these dates, and it was generally the same foolish ones who mixed up unendorsed cocktails. Again, the same irresponsible characters blended the concentrates in poorly ventilated conditions, splashing themselves and others, and didn't follow correct procedure of using breathing apparatus when applying the sprays despite the manufacturer's recommendations.

Simon and Nicole were the opposite extreme. They disliked chemicals of any sort, although they were forced to admit it was occasionally necessary to use something. Simon was continually searching for an alternative, studying all the literature on biological control he could lay his hands on. But he was in the minority and green was not cool to the growers, who mocked him as they charged up their sprayers.

₭ ℞

The postman delivered identical cardboard cartons to George and Simon. George stooped to pick up his box from the front step. Despite being the addressee he could see it wasn't for him, no ready-rooted stems in this one. The label showed the name of the firm, and the word *"Predators"* in red letters. George wondered had this intrigued the postman, had he kept the box next to his van door so he could eject it if there was a breakout?

'Parcel for you, my little Butterwort,' he called to Maisie. 'Your cannibals are 'ere! I reckon it's your fly eaters!'

'Ooh,' said Maisie.

She'd been taught about biological control by Eric and he'd given her an address. George was sceptical but who was he to argue with Maisie when she'd made her mind up. Yes, Eric had been the instigator, during a conversation a few weeks ago....

Eric guessed that George, having stayed alive and healthy on the nursery for so many years was naturally distrustful of the new advice currently being administered. Nothing had harmed him so far, so why should it start now? Nevertheless, Eric considered it his duty to make all growers aware of new and safer technology.

'There's something relatively new, called Biological Control,' he'd explained to them. 'An alternative to some of the chemicals. We're running a course on it at Jones's farm at Little Nogden, next Wednesday. Why don't you come along?'

'We'd love to, wouldn't we Maisie, but we're too busy.' George gave the automatic excuse of growers everywhere.

'I could go.' Maisie spoke quietly. They were sitting outside the main tomato house in the shade of the henhouse, on a couple of upturned bulk bins used regularly for tea-breaks. George choked on his pipe. When his coughing fit subsided he said:

'Well you ain't been to any courses for the last twenty five years, woman. Why in 'ell would yer wanna to start now?'

Maisie patted her huge chest. The bosom had dropped, and the scooped neckline revealed mottled red flesh.

'Because I've a notion that that Metasystox's affecting me tubes,' she said defiantly, referring to one of the most commonly used insecticides of the time. She jumped down heavily but capably and began looping her sideshooting bag around what had once been her waist. 'I'm sure it's them sprays, what keeps making me wheeze.'

Eric privately thought she was carrying too much weight. Her stretch slacks were pulled tight over her big backside, and bulges rose out of her knicker line. The distorted seams of the material wound irregularly up her large thighs.

'That Metasystox stuff. You can smell it a mile off. Ain't you noticed, Eric?'

Of course Eric had noticed. It had a foul penetrating odour. Unfortunately it was extremely effective. It couldn't be used once picking had commenced due to its three week clearance, so the growers gave everything a good blast whilst the fruit was still green as a matter of course.

'Well!' George spat some tobacco onto the concrete. Horrible habit, thought Eric. Good job it's dying out.

'See what you've bloody gone and done now Eric. She'll be wanting to go to bleedin' 'orticultural college next, she'll 'ave us going organic!'

Eric smiled. He knew what to say to appease George. George was easy. No great psychological knowledge was needed to handle him. Not like his volatile neighbour, Josh.

'This method is a lot cheaper, George. If you follow the instructions and hang the tag of predator insects in the right places, they will continue eating whitefly and greenfly all season and anyway the way the market's going I think you'll be seeing more revenue from organic crops in the next five years.'

George grunted in disgust, for he considered any talk of

organic farming to be unrealistic nonsense, but he didn't say so to Eric, who added just to hammer the point home: 'You're one of the best growers, George. You'd expect to be leading the way in this. And you know how ineffective the two-day insecticides are.'

The compliment paid off immediately. 'Dunno 'bout leadin' the way. Them days is gone. But you go, Maisie, but no chattin' up the men. She used to be a bugger for the men, you know Eric, when we first come 'ere. Why, there was 'im as used to be up at number 29....' Maisie cuffed him on the head with her sideshooting bag. It knocked the fire out of his pipe with a cloud of sparks. '*Hey woman! watch it!*'

Just then an engine coughed into life on the next holding, and the sweet sickly smell of chemical began to drift over. Eric shook his head. He doubted Josh ever measured the concentrate or took any notice of clearance dates. It wasn't that he was deliberately careless, just that any responsibility he had was well exhausted stretching to cover himself.

At least I have one possible convert, thought Eric, and a responsible one at that.

                                          ဢ   ၶ

So Maisie had attended the meeting and now she was unpacking her parcel. Each plastic tag held a green tobacco leaf sprinkled with black dots, like a myriad of fly dirts. These were the eggs timed to hatch once inside the warmth and humidity of the greenhouse environment. Each tag had a hook, enabling it to be hung strategically from the tomato wires. Eric had helped her work out how many were needed to produce enough predators to eat all the aphids.

At the meeting it had been explained to her that there had to be a few pests when the predators were introduced, in order to provide them with some food, but not a whole infestation. It was control more than a cure. The amount of food determined the rate of reproduction. Maisie liked the idea of the minuscule eggs hatching into an army of warriors, ready to descend on whole sticky communities of aphids. There was something honest and natural about them being eaten, much nicer than being slowly and jerkily poisoned to death by some horrible spray. Too often she'd seen the dead bodies lying thickly in the their sticky juice. There were also some predators present which would feed on red spider mite, should there be any lurking amongst the tomatoes.

She hurried into the glasshouse to distribute her predators, organise her warriors. George shook his head, chuckled to himself and disappeared to deadhead his geraniums.

ଧ ଔ

Simon was busy researching "malpractice" and the implications for the Estate. He took his carton and stuffed it unopened in the spare room. He'd deal with it later; this was much more important just now.

It was a month later when he remembered it. By then the consignment was past the sell by date and the eggs had hatched and were all dead.

Twenty

Towards the beginning of July, just as holiday resorts on the south coast twenty miles away were bracing themselves for this summer's lucrative pillaging, the English weather reminded everyone of its unpredictability once more. Jonathan peered out from the picture window of his terraced home and saw that the skies were dismal and grey. He paused for a moment listening to the radio and watching cars pass on the street. As the announcer began to predict where the rain would have spread to by lunchtime, he noticed some cars already had their wipers moving intermittently. A young girl in tee-shirt and short skirt glanced anxiously up at the sky as she waited for a number 27 bus. A boy on a BMX bike with an orange newspaper bag slung across his shoulders increased his pace as he raced home. Now the rain was falling in large spots, patterning the roadway and pavement below.

By the time Jonathan had washed and shaved, water was dripping from the gutters and splashing on the dustbin lids and he could hear the unmistakable swish of car tyres on the wet road. He looked at his alarm clock. It was ten to seven. He could almost hear Vic repeating the old saying: "Rain before seven, fine before eleven, else it will rain all day." The growers would be pleased if the rain really set in. It would save them from the monotonous task of shifting the outdoor irrigation.

He himself was less pleased. He would need his Barbour and his wellingtons and his sunglasses would remain in the car. It also meant he was less likely to see Hazel alone, as she and Eddie would be working together under glass. When it was sunny, Hazel worked outside, topping up her tan paying Marie from along the Drift to watch children's television with the little ones. She could be found alternate mornings out on the field, picking courgettes alone. Eddie couldn't go near courgettes now; his recent brush with blood poisoning seemed to have sensitised him to anything prickly. Hazel couldn't wear her shorts in the courgette field because their coarse hairs and prickly stems scratched her legs, but she could wear her bikini top under her teeshirt and when she bent over to grasp a courgette the sexual simile did not escape Jonathan, at least until she slashed it off at the base with a sharp knife. After that, he concentrated his attention on her tightly stretched jeans...

Yesterday he had tried to question her about the missing pump.

'Hello, gorgeous,' he said. She bobbed up in the row, perfectly sized courgette in her hand. 'Well, I've looked everywhere for the pump, apart from in your bedroom,' he added, smiling seductively. He'd already made several comments in front of Eddie about the missing piece of equipment. This had annoyed Eddie, and relations between the two men were deteriorating daily.

'Pump? What would I need one of them for?' and she smiled back, arms now folded, plumping her breasts out.

'I thought we might search your bedroom together,' Jonathan continued, keeping eye contact across the foliage. Then he squatted down on the grass verge and pretended to scrutinise a courgette leaf for bugs, for fungus, for mildew – the list was endless. A fieldsman can get away with almost anything, he thought to himself. Hazel picked her way through the prickly straggly rows of monstrous leaves and joined him on the grass.

'I'll suggest it to Eddie,' she said, leaning backwards and supporting her head with her arms, an action which raised the hem of her skimpy tee-shirt. Jonathan's eyes linked the sun-tanned skin which was stretched tightly over her collarbone, rose gently over the swell of her stomach and covered her slim ankles as they disappeared into her sun bleached canvas shoes. He had a sudden urge to peel away the clothes and expose her whole body as if de-shelling some shiny brown nut. Hazel smiled enticingly, well aware of the effect she was having on him. He offered her a cigarette, and as she leant towards his cupped hands to get a light she allowed her body to brush his. Glancing around, Jonathan reassured himself there was nobody watching. He grabbed her wrist and pulled her towards him. She didn't really resist as he bent to kiss her.

She allowed his tongue deep into her mouth. With one hand, she pulled his shirt free from his belt and placed her fingers on the flesh of his back. Then she seemed to change her mind.

'Get off!' she giggled, weakly attempting to push him away.

'You've got wonderful breasts,' whispered Jonathan, as his hands started to move across them, his fingers tightening around her nipple through the material, his cigarette still burning but discarded on the grass. Suddenly Hazel pushed him away, definite this time.

'That's enough, Eddie will see you!' she said. She was still laughing, he noticed...

He could wait. But it wouldn't be today, he knew now. He picked up his wallet and car keys, and slammed the door behind him. The air smelt fresh, and the rain fell steadily upon the footpath.

80   CR

Meanwhile the growers were also contemplating a change in routine due to the weather. Rain lashed down on Maisie's glasshouse, splashing the plants through the open vents. She decided to close them. She watched the water slide down the glass as she worked.

Nicole peeped out from behind the blind in her bedroom, and promptly climbed back onto her futon knocking the dreamcatcher as she did so. It spun for a while, twirling above her head, before gradually rocking to a stop. Simon was nowhere to be seen.

Sylvia applied her lipstick and then went to find a light mackintosh; the weather made little difference to her in the hermetically sealed world of the Bank. Dennis rushed out to rescue a pallet of boxes which he hadn't bothered to cover the day before. This was an uncharacteristic lapse, he must still be shaken by Josh's visit.

Janice finished milking Bernadette, then told her: 'You don't want to go out today, my beauty. You stay in here out of the damp.' She had to cover the pail with a sheet of cardboard as she hurried back to the house with the udder-warm milk. Myra was waiting, tortoise-necked on the doorstep, wondering if Jim had got a waterproof coat on. Should she go and check? Stupid old woman. The whole female race could die of rheumatism, arthritis and pneumonia, thought Janice, so long as the menfolk are kept dry and warm.

Eddie welcomed the rain. He liked the smell, he even liked the way summer rain ran down the back of your neck and didn't chill you. He pulled on his wellingtons and plodded up the pathway for no reason in particular. At least he wouldn't have to be bothered with the outside irrigation. That contraption complete with oscillating box which gradually filled with water and tossed the spray different distances could be still today. No matter how much you poured water on artificially, he mused, it still didn't have the same effect as a good penetrating rain. This would really make the courgettes grow. They were the only things making good money at the moment. Goodness knows who ate them; not normal working people, he was sure of that. Probably someone like Nicole....

Hazel wasn't bothered by the rain. She certainly wasn't going to pick courgettes and get her jeans all sodden. Her body was cooked nicely now, so she could live without the sun for a day or two. She could visit Karen and tell her how she'd wound up Jonathan the previous day.

Josh was lying in front of the television. Delia Smith was demonstrating how to make a venison pie, proper pastry and all. It would be nice to have a real pie, not venison but steak and kidney. He was sick of sausages and frozen chips and tinned peas. He watched as Angie brushed her black curls and then applied her lipstick and blusher, pointed chin raised to the mirror. She still didn't know her husband had hit her boss, they had both chosen not to mention it for different reasons. As he watched her preen herself, he was filled with a sudden softness for his wife.

'It's pissing down, girl,' he said. 'Stay at home with me today.'

She came over to the settee, bent and gave him a kiss, printing a red mark on his face in the same way she branded every cup and glass she drank from.

'I can't. Dennis is giving me a rise! He says I'm such a good worker he is putting me in charge.' This wasn't strictly true. Dennis had told her she was so good he was raising her money, but not to crow about it to the others, as he couldn't afford a universal increase. Josh tensed. Bloody interfering git, he thought. He would consider the implications of this later. Instead he said despondently:

'You could be the lady of the manor here.' Then he added, increasing the gloom, 'If things don't improve though there won't be a manor.'

Angie looked through the mirror at the shabby room with the ash-trays heaped with tab-ends, and empty Old

English Cider bottles littering the floor. Last night's dinner plates were still in evidence and one had slid part way under the settee where it might be lost for months. She said nothing though, and dealt with it for the time being the only way she knew how. Without bothering with a coat she banged the door, flounced down the path and climbed into their battered old beetle, a petite curvy figure in electric blue top and jeans. A bit of rain didn't bother her. The drops sparkled in her hair as she rechecked her makeup in the rear view mirror.

Steve sat in his dining room, Karen's accounts book open in front of him. He was scribbling on another sheet of paper. He reached for his calculator and pressed some buttons. Wearily he shook his head, and looked up at the window. He had promised Karen he would study her workings, but they just made his head spin. The wind was lashing a branch of sodden Cotoneaster against the window panes, and the rain poured down with increasing force. Outside in their run-down Dutch Light houses, the rain splashed through gaps onto the peppers, and some of them had been bent to the ground by the force. The same thing was happening in the tomato houses. Karen watched, cold draughts blowing on her neck, drips falling on her from places which she had previously thought were watertight. She desperately hoped the downpour wouldn't last long.

Old Vic would spend the day brewing beer in the henhouse as Ruby wouldn't allow him to boil the mash in the house. She always said: "That smell gets everywhere! What would the Vicar think?" As he stirred, sorted, sterilised and strained he surveyed with pride all the contraptions he had invented over the years, most now defunct and dust ridden but all with a tale to tell. Now he heard the clatter of two saucepan lids and he hurriedly turned off the heat as he knew Ruby would be standing ready on the doorstep in her pac-a-mac and see-through concertina rain hat, to be taken on her weekly shopping trip to Wansbridge.

George, crowned by a dripping sou'wester crept up to the rain streaked pane of glass where Maisie was sideshooting. As she looked up he pulled a face, ridiculously stretched mouth, forefingers pointed for ears, and as expected, she jumped.

She screeched. 'You stupid ol' bugger!'

George laughed. 'It's ten past eleven my little hydrangea,' he called above the rattle on the glass. 'I think it's going to rain all day!'

𐅟 &#x18;

Hazel and Karen were in Karen's bedroom, and the kids played in the room next door, or rioted on the stairs, occasionally charging through to them and getting sent packing straight away. The two giggled together, whispering so the children didn't catch the gist.

'I can't believe you snogged him!' said Karen. 'What if Eddie had seen you? Are you mad?'

'No fear of that,' said Hazel, carelessly. 'Them courgette leaves are massive. And anyway, he's obsessed, just like you are, with this growing lark. Once his head's down in them tomatoes. Just like you, Mrs Farmer Wife. You never know, Steve could be at it in the house and you've not noticed 'cos you can't see past your sideshooting!'

She ducked as Karen flung a pillow. 'Dirty bitch!'

'To be honest,' said Hazel, 'I don't really *really* fancy him, I certainly didn't hear no violins when we kissed. I just need a bit of excitement and *I* don't get it from lettuce.'

'Bit risky, though Haze,' said Karen, her mind still half on the rain and its potential problems.

Her friend continued to explain she had no intention of doing any more than flirting and the odd bit of groping, and although she didn't fancy him that much he was probably the best the Estate had to offer. Karen privately thought this was a bit unfair on Eddie, but she was enjoying the excitement despite or perhaps because of it being second-hand.

'I feel sorry for him though,' said Hazel, voice serious now. Karen thought at first she was talking of Eddie, but no. 'How they all hate him! He doesn't deserve it you know. He can't win, you know. I mean, he don't set the flipping tomato prices now does he?'

'What did he kiss like?' Karen wanted to know. Hazel giggled again.

'It was quite nice,' she said. 'They all kiss all right with me. I make sure of that!' and the girls rolled about laughing, Karen on the bed, Hazel curled up on the floor, as if they were fourth-formers at school without the complications of husbands, children and a precarious way of life.

෨   ଓ

Rain lashed the Estate for three solid days. Water gushed off greenhouse guttering into large irrigation tanks. Mud, always a feature of the downstairs living space in the winter but unusual in July became a problem once again. Just answering the telephone could be a domestic disaster, although Steve had got that sorted, by moving the phone to the kitchen window-sill, where it could be accessed from outside. No matter how carefully you changed your boots in the conservatory mud infiltrated somehow, little trails across the vinyl tiles from the hallway to the toilet, even in those houses where there weren't any children. Only Sylvia kept a pristine house in bad weather, but then Dennis ran his business from his office.

Steve, busy in his shed, heard the outside telephone bell. Was it his? Hard to tell, sometimes. Often he ran towards the house only to find it was his neighbour's, the chimes carried on the wind. Better answer it, though, just in case it was the Packhouse. He sploshed through the mud and the lawn they'd been so proud of a fortnight ago. The water was ankle deep across most of it. The holding looked a pitiful sight and that was without close inspection of the crops. He reached the kitchen window, metal frame stiffly ajar, and pulled it open wide. As he reached inside, his hand didn't grasp the phone properly, knocking it instead and there was a clunk and a splash as it hit the washing up bowl. The ringing stopped abruptly.

'Shit!' Steve wondered what else could happen to wreck his week and he went inside to retrieve the phone from the cold greasy water, trailing mud everywhere as he did so. Karen would go mad, he knew.

He pulled the telephone from its watery death bed, tilting it to let as much water as possible pour back out. To his surprise it rang again and it was Sammy, known locally as Scofflaw Sammy. They knew each other only from chance encounters at The Stores, or growers' meetings. He held the receiver, still wet and slimy with globules of grease, not quite to his ear.

'Hi Steve?' Sammy sounded bright, Sammy always did. A few days rain could easily be accommodated amongst his varied business interests. The line sounded crackly; no surprise there, thought Steve.

'Sammy? How do,' he answered.

'I've been speaking to Eddie, and he thought as you might be interested in a little device I've got. It ain't for common knowledge, you understand,' Sammy said, with a well cultivated air of conspiracy which was evident despite the fuzzy line.

Steve wondered what the device could possibly be, no doubt something illegal. He felt honoured that Sammy had decided he was worthy of being included in a shady deal, and more so that Eddie had recommended him.

'What is it, mate?' he asked, automatically glancing over his shoulder to make sure Karen wasn't about. Karen would view things differently. She was very straight. Sometimes Steve thought it was like having your very own policewoman in the house.

'Let's say it makes your electricity bills bearable. I'll pop up with it tonight mate, if that's all right with you.' Steve guessed it was a device for turning back the meter, highly illegal of course, but in the present climate of disasters, necessary. Even Karen might be persuaded on this one.

'Nice one, I'll get the ale in. See you tonight, then, mate.' He replaced the receiver. Scummy water was still trickling out from the bottom of the phone. Across the paddy field Steve could see Eric talking to Karen under the shelter of the corrugated roof of their old woodstore. They had summoned the ADAS man, thinking him the best one to turn to in this current crisis. His wife looked pale and worried, wet hair straggling about her face. Eric, big hands stuffed into his body warmer was in serious conversation with her. His large reassuring frame was stooped towards her, an old oak protecting a birch sapling.

He'll sort it out, thought Steve, confidently.

'I had to ring you,' Karen was explaining. 'Hang the expense, we're going to lose everything anyway. What are we going to do? Two of the houses are under water at one end. Fruit's already dropping off the peppers. What can we do?'

Oh dear, thought Eric. How can I help here? With their ramshackle glasshouses and lack of experience they'd be bankrupt anyway, without the help of the dubious marketing practices of the LSA and the rapid decline of the horticultural industry. They want me to wave a magic wand and drain the houses, replenish the leached out minerals and replace the boggy soil with the dry silky loam of before the rains. Not for the first time he imagined himself soaring over the rooftops with his cape floating out behind him, deciding where he was most needed first to save the future of this glass village. Instead he cleared his throat and said:

'Well, let's take a look. Maybe it's not as bad as it sounds.' Together they squelched through the mud into the pepper house. The smell of wet dank air hit them as they entered it. It was as bad, Eric realised. In fact it was worse. About an eighth of the greenhouse was under water, the crop peeping through looked like pond plants. Everywhere bobbed immature fruit, a shoal of green plastic corks. Elsewhere in the house the crop was fine, but wherever there was a gap, especially under the eaves, the plants stood forlornly in water.

'Right..... okay,' said Eric, pulling at his beard and biting his lower lip. 'Now let's see the tomatoes.'

The tomato house which stood alongside was flooded in much the same way. The plants were taller here, and only their bottom trusses trailed in the water and quite a few of those had already been picked. Much of the fruit was splashed with mud, though. Eric picked a tomato which had made full size and examined it carefully.

He said: 'Let's find some light to look at this,' and they left the gloom of the greenhouse to stand out in the drizzle. He held out the tomato between his square thumb and forefinger, and a hairline crack was just visible around part of the fruit as if someone had taken a very delicate cheese-wire to it.

'Hmmmm.... I'm afraid this is the danger,' he explained. 'Irregular watering on tomatoes leads to splitting. This faint crack will be a gaping great gash in a day or two. I would expect most of the full sized fruit where the flood has been to develop the same.'

Steve had joined them and had been observing silently. Now he spoke.

'Are we insured for things like this?' he asked, as they trudged back to the house for a cup of tea, a forlorn trio.

'Nope, comes under an Act of God, along with everything else they don't want to pay out on! Now remind me – what else are you harvesting at the moment?'

They reached the house, and all three dragged off their wellingtons. It seemed unusually quiet, Eric noticed. This house usually vibrated with children. There were only two of them but it always felt as if there were five.

'The twins are at the playgroup,' Karen said, reading his thoughts as she wearily set up the kettle. She noticed the dripping telephone, and guessed what had happened, but it just didn't seem worth mentioning, such were the problems of the moment. 'We've got courgettes, if it clears up we can pick them tomorrow. And we have some inside lettuce about two weeks away in the tunnels, and some outside too. We have the other tomato house, of course.' Their larger house was a much better prospect. There were fewer leaks and it was away from the low patch of land where the flood was.

'Well, my advice, such as it is,' said Eric, 'is to concentrate on your best house of tomatoes. As soon as the weather improves, pull out all the flood damaged peppers, and strip all the split fruit from the tomatoes. If you leave rotten fruit you'll invite botrytis and disease.'

Karen knew all about botrytis mould. Behind its furry coat it ate away at healthy tissue, until a truss or a leaf just disintegrated in your hand. She always felt a bit guilty too as it crept in where damage had been done previously, a lettuce hacked accidentally by a hoe, a sideshoot ripped off leaving a hangnail. It needed moist damp conditions as well, and could be controlled by spray. Botrytis was a general scourge of the Estate and discussed so regularly that one of the girls had developed a fear. Karen found her sobbing one day, and when she had asked her what the matter was the little girl had said that she was frightened that her cut finger would develop the dreaded fungus and drop off...

Karen woke up and Eric was still talking.

'You will have to water the peppers by hand with the hosepipe,' he was saying. 'You can't use the overheads until the wettest parts dry out a bit.'

Basically he had told them nothing that would really help the situation. All they could do was sit tight and wait for the weather to improve. Draining his cup, he looked out. Bright sunshine was struggling through the low cloud, lighting up the droplets of rain on the cotoneaster which framed the window. 'Keep at it! Rome wasn't built in a day.'

As he walked back to his car, his foolish cliché still ringing in his ear, he wondered what the eventual outcome would be for the Estate. After the April lettuce fiasco, prices had improved slightly but the tomato price was expected to drop soon. Good weather after bad always brought a glut as the fruit ripened quickly as if to catch up. He had heard rumours that the government were not letting any more holdings until they reviewed the situation of mounting grower debt. Two stood empty at the moment, and the excuse of awaiting repair was beginning to wear a bit thin with the more wily of the growers. They were beginning to grow suspicious, and rightly so.

Twenty-One

There was a mystery afoot. Guy, Maisie's grandson, who thanks to her now worked for Josh, noticed the problem first. He called his boss over to the courgette patch.

'Something's eating the courgettes, Josh,' he shouted, standing up straight and rubbing his back. He had waterproof leggings over his jeans because the huge leaves were still wet, despite the strong sunshine. Everything was steaming, it was like an equatorial forest there amongst the foliage.

'Probably slugs,' Josh said, slouching towards him, hands in his pocket. 'Shouldn't be though, I've put enough Drazas down.' These pellets were highly poisonous and Eric was forever reminding the growers to treat them with respect. He'd once seen a bird eat one and it fell over like a stone. Mostly the growers didn't heed his warnings though. Josh was equally blasé and would certainly have overdone the application if anything.

He examined a courgette now. It was covered with tiny dints, positioned regularly as on a fragment of dotted material. They weren't terribly disfiguring. Josh rolled the offending item between his thumb and forefinger.

'Not a slug,' he decided, shaking his head. 'They don't eat like that. More like a big chew mark, from a slug. No, this looks like some disease, and it's – *got you*!' He moved like a flash to shove it down Guy's neck.

'Get off!' shouted Guy, ploughing through the rows and trampling the straggly plants. Gaining a safe distance, he stopped and stooped down. 'Well if it's a disease, they ain't got it here.'

The area with the problem adjoined his granddad's land. George had some courgettes too, most people did, they'd made good money last year. People were just starting to catch the habit of chopping them into stir fries, or omelettes. He walked back to his bucket.

'What shall I do with them, Josh?'

Josh looked at him. 'I don't get you?'

'Shall I chuck 'em, or pack 'em as class twos?'

Josh caught on fast. 'You'll bloody pack them class ones! You'll mix 'em in and put the good ones on top. Didn't you learn nothing at school?'

Guy shrugged and returned to his picking. He liked to work for Josh, it was more like helping a mate. There was little organisation and he was never sent off to work alone for days, for Josh liked company too. They had a laugh and a beer with their lunch and his boss didn't care how loud Guy played the ghetto-blaster. He taught him the world according to Josh. To Guy who'd been raised with reason this was a new and interesting viewpoint, this was lifeskills with a capital L. Guy now knew when to keep quiet, because he'd learnt the profile of Josh's temper. So long as he picked his way around it, he knew he'd be all right.

When Guy had harvested all the courgettes, he loaded the jack-truck and took them into the shed to pack, and he disguised the measled ones at the bottom of each crate, as instructed. On the top he laid the shiny satiny perfect ones. In the field, he'd noticed there was no sign of the disease on those just developing on the plant, so hopefully the problem would soon disappear. Neither he nor his boss gave it another thought.

ജ ഇ

Two days later however, the scarring seemed just as bad on those ready to pick, as if it had grown with the courgettes, and the ones which had been tiny and hairy the day before were now showing all the signs of the spotted lurgy. Still, thank goodness, only on the one section of the field. As he walked back down to the house, Josh saw Jonathan pull up in the Astra. Nothing unusual, he regularly came onto the holding, and the knowledge that he couldn't stop him was a bitter pill for Josh to swallow. Jonathan's sunglasses glinted as he jumped out and walked briskly up the roadway.

'Josh, there's been a complaint," he said bluntly as he approached.

'What, about you mate? Who'd do that?' Josh answered, with a false smile. 'I'll stick up for you though, never caused me any trouble, you ain't – much!' He leaned a bony shoulder against the edge of the glasshouse and holding his tobacco pouch in one hand, began to roll a cigarette with the other, a trick he'd learnt years ago. Jonathan found himself addressing a frown of concentration, which was as insulting as if it had been a backside.

'Not against *me!* You, about *your* produce, *your* courgettes, your poor quality disease-ridden ones to be precise.'

Jonathan wasn't keen on any grower but he especially didn't like Josh. He didn't trust him and avoided him as much as possible. He knew it was typical of Josh to pull a trick like that, potentially giving the LSA a bad name at the expense of the conscientious growers. Added to this he was frustrated by Hazel's behaviour. She was still teasing like a she-cat, rubbing up against him and then backing off. He needed desperately to screw her. It didn't matter that he had a girlfriend who would give him sex on demand. He wanted this hussy. The image of the softly curved Hazel jarred against the sight of this angular man who completed his task and looked up with contempt.

'My produce is a good as anyone else's,' Josh said waving his arms, unlit cigarette bouncing on his bottom lip as he spoke. 'It's you bloody lot, leaving all the boxes standing in the heat in the midday sun. You do it deliberate, so's they can be returned to us, to excuse your lot because *you* can't damn well sell 'em!' His eyes blazed dangerously.

This was a standard argument, Jonathan knew, but usually it was hinted at, not levelled at him quite so blatantly. He thought he really could do without this today.

'Well, you're getting them returned,' he snarled back. 'As we speak they are probably being dumped back on your lawn. Fancy putting diseased ones at the bottom of the box. Don't you know we practice quality control? We're smart, we are, at the Packhouse. With some people's boxes we go straight to the bottom!'

Although the last sentence was spoken with sarcasm, he was already backing away down the drive. He knew this man was crazy when roused. He had no wish to be pushed face first through a glasshouse.

Josh mumbled something incomprehensible. He turned and kicked the tractor wheel with some force, hurting his foot. He just caught Jonathan's words:

'You'd better get ADAS Eric out to look at them, it might be foot and mouth disease!'

ဆ   ଔ

Meanwhile George had discovered the same problem on part of his crop. Of course he had more sense than to put them in for market, he saved them to give to Jim for Janice's animals. It was strange, he hadn't seen anything like this before. Every courgette with its silky green coat was affected. As the courgette grew in size, the larger the dints became. They weren't visible when the courgette was tiny and still hairy but they showed as soon as it reached about three inches in length. He noticed that on the latest fruit the spots were more spaced out than they had been a few days earlier on similar sized fruit. Two days of pondering later and the equivalent sized fruit only had a couple of spots. He didn't really think it was a disease, because the marks were dry and not infected and the courgettes were perfectly fine inside. He flagged Eric down on the roadside.

Eric was able to give an immediate diagnosis. It was all very satisfying, the sort of problem he could really give an answer to.

'It's hailstones,' he said without hesitation. 'I've seen this before. Hailstones are often localised. That's why it's not the whole expanse of your crop. I wouldn't be surprised if Josh has a problem too.'

George knew he had, through Guy. He puffed thoughtfully on his pipe, he loved a problem to wrestle with, and especially one of nature's making. He had the utmost respect for all things natural, and if he managed to understand just a tiny bit about the order of things that would do for him.

'So the tiny courgettes were damaged an' all, but I couldn't see because of them being hairy and smaller, they only had room for one or two hailstones to hit, where as the larger ones 'ad a bigger surface and so got more dots. Well I never!'

Suddenly the pop pop pop of Josh's jack-truck engine cut into the calm of their puzzle solving. Both men turned to look.

'HEY JOSH!' George shouted. Josh jumped off, and the engine faltered to a halt. He walked casually (with anyone else it would be nonchalantly) over to the boundary, joining the two men. His scruffy hair framed his face and his once white tee-shirt exposed the tattoos on his arms. Already too fuzzy to read, they were surely home-made.

'I've got a disease on me courgettes,' George said, face set serious. 'It's a sort o' pox. Can spread to humans, Eric tells me. Makes yer bits drop off if it ain't treated fast, like.'

Josh looked a bit doubtful, then turned and said with an open face: 'Well that's a bugger George. I hope it don't spread to mine.'

'As it 'appens I was joking mate,' said George. He held out a shiny courgette, just two little scars. 'No, it's hailstone damage, so Eric tells me.'

Josh looked interested, but not overly so. 'Well that's all right, then,' he said.

Twenty-Two

After the three days of torrential rain, summer returned to the Estate. But all that moisture had left a legacy. Each morning began with a clear blue sky, but by lunchtime clouds began to gather, darkening to bring a brief convectional downpour. Then warm sunshine returned to give a fine afternoon and evening.

This was Utopia for the growers because they didn't have to irrigate outside but the long hours of sunshine meant crops were growing steadily and fruit was ripening nicely. The air was cool and fresh first thing on a morning and the midday rain kept temperatures from becoming unbearable. Farming your own land wasn't such a bad prospect even these days, thought George, as he spooned tinned peaches and condensed milk into his mouth. Maisie's voice broke into his pleasant meditations.

'I'm 'aving a naughty knicker party Wednesday night,' she announced. 'So you might be wantin' to make yourself scarce.'

George dropped his spoon into his dish, and stared at his plump wife. He grinned broadly. 'Do they make crutchless knickers out of sailcloth then?'

Maisie laughed. She liked "proper" knickers, the sort that came right up over your belly and didn't twist up in the folds.

'Well, I thought as it'd make a change from Tupperware,' she said. 'It's a mate of Susan's that's running it.' Susan was their grown-up daughter. 'And,' she added, leaning across the table and smiling into his eyes, 'I take me commission in goods. So if there's anythin' you fancy, you know, leather jock strap, perhaps, or even one of them mechanical thingys..' her voice dropped to a whisper.

George looked alarmed. He ran his fingers through his still-thick grey hair. He picked up his reading glasses and put them on.

'You choose, my little amayrillis,' he said as he picked up the free paper. 'Somethin' frilly an' pretty for you'll be just fine!'

He made a mental note to be in the pub on Wednesday evening. He'd stay as late as possible too, which wouldn't be difficult as the landlord always served after time. He would only return when he was sure every last one of the giggling women had returned home to their beds.

Maisie filled out the invitations. The women on the Estate regularly held these parties, usually clothes or toys or books. It was an excuse for a night out, they always drank wine and had a good laugh. The envelopes were generally distributed by hand, often using Eric and Jonathan as carriers. She smiled to herself. She wouldn't tell those two what sort of party this was going to be.

℘   ℒ

George spotted Jim in the distance, setting up his sprayer. He called over to him.

'Jim, do you fancy goin' down the Cow Wednesday night?'

Jim came over. He didn't often go to the pub in summer.

'Maisie's holding some flippin' silly party for the women,' George explained. 'Your Janice and your Ma'll 'ave invites.' He lowered his voice. 'It's sexy underwear!'

Jim laughed loudly. He pushed his shock of yellow hair out of his eyes with his rubber gloved hands.

'Just the thing! Janice 'as been losing her touch lately.

Don't know if Ma'll go, though. She's funny about that sort o' thing. Tomato returns are holding up, aren't they?' Nothing could keep the men off the subject of growing for long. It seemed to envelope their world like some all consuming hobby.

'Well, they ain't quite as bad as last summer gone. But I was lookin' up some ol' figures from five year ago, we was gettin' the same price, and look how the cost of boxes's gone up!'

Although the tomatoes were collected from the holding in the bulk bins, they were graded and sorted by the packing shed staff. Once the tomatoes were sorted into sizes they were then packed into boxes, and the grower was billed for these and charged a flat handling rate. The system was open to abuse, and how the growers hated it. Often there were discrepancies over the gross weight, and then there was the question as to what happened to the three-quarters full box? Jonathan told them the system evened itself out, the return going to the grower who supplied the heaviest part of the box. The growers had suspicions that the LSA staff were lining their pockets, setting up stalls in their cul-de-sacs. They also saw the potential for muddling the bulk bins, as a carbon copied ticket stuffed into each bin was all that identified individual grower's produce. They weren't allowed to write on the actual bins, as they were "Association Property".

'I'm getting twice as much in Brighton,' Jim continued. 'Our Paul takes 'em for me. They're looking for more you know, if you want to send some.'

George shook his head. He was getting too old for the worry now. He had sold produce outside over the years and he'd had some close shaves too. His glass was paid for, and his children grown up, and Maisie was such a good manager she could make soup out of a stone. He didn't need the money in the same way that most of the other growers did, and the risk wasn't worth taking anymore.

'No thanks, mate,' he knocked his pipe out on the fence post. 'I appr'ciate the offer, an' I don't blame you. But I'm gettin' too old for that caper now.'

'Suit yourself,' replied Jim, without malice. He could understand George's reasoning. 'Offer's there if you change your mind.'

ℬ ℭ

Maisie caught Jonathan as he stopped to get produce estimates for the coming week. She waddled up the road waving something, bright full skirt billowing around bottle-shaped legs. On the days she went into town, Maisie wore enormous skirts which rivalled her husband's geraniums for gaudiness.

'Where yer off next?' She gasped as she reached his open car window. He was fiddling irritably with his two-way radio.

'Why?' he asked suspiciously. He disliked these people who so obviously had no time for him but were often unprincipled enough to ask him favours. When he realised it was Maisie he relented. Always pleasant, never nasty, nobody could object to her. He took the invitations disinterestedly, and Maisie thanked him. He shuffled the pile, checking there was one for Hazel.

He drove straight up the road to her holding, and pulled into the driveway. He spotted Eddie in the tomato house, and stuck his head through a low level vent. Eddie looked up from the trickle pipe he was mending, and glared.

'I told you lot yesterday,' he said in an unfriendly voice. 'I've nothing to send tomorrow, I sprayed last night. I did the courgettes too, they're getting powdery mildew.'

'Oh, I got that message, though I don't know how you people expect to make a living, no produce to send! Actually

I was looking for your better half, not you. I've got a letter for her,' said Jonathan.

Eddie disliked being lumped with the shirkier of the growers. He just wanted rid of Jonathan with his poncey black cords and polo-necked jumper, and his perfume which smelt like a tart's windowbox. If he wondered who the letter was from he didn't ask.

'She's in the house,' he said. 'Don't give it to me.' And he held up his hands, his stubby fingers blackish with tomato stain.

See? thought Jonathan. He hands it to me on a plate!

Hazel was hoovering the hallway, and she took her time switching off the machine. Then she snatched the envelope and wriggled it open with her finger. She smiled at Jonathan. 'You'll be interested in this,' she said.

Jonathan eyed her breasts. 'I'm more interested in your body,' he said honestly.

'Maisie's having a naughty knicker party,' she said. 'I think I shall buy a basque, Eddie will like that.' She tucked the letter down the front of her tee-shirt. Jonathan tried to retrieve it, but today he got a slap, when yesterday it might have been a kiss.

'When you've bought it you can come round to my house and show it to me,' he said. 'I can guarantee I'll appreciate it more than Eddie.' He visualised a scrap of Hazel's lingerie dangling from Eddie's stubby and stained fingers. How had he got her in the first place?

Hazel laughed. 'Dream on! You've no chance,' she said firmly but once again her eyes sent him a message to the contrary. 'You keep your quality control to salad stuff!'

෫   ෬

It was approaching eight o'clock on Wednesday evening and Maisie and Angie were busy in Maisie's kitchen. It was awash with sandwiches and sausage rolls, fairy cakes and cup cakes. They'd set up a table in the spare room and were laying the food out in the style of a buffet. Maisie lined the glasses up. She'd borrowed from her neighbours and now they glinted in sets, their stems casting spindly shadows in the late sunshine. The white fizzy wine was cooling in the fridge.

A long-legged woman of about thirty-five in a leather pelmet was "arranging things" on the lounge carpet. She knelt in one position but stretched her body in all directions as she spread her wares. Maisie eyed her curiously and thought she wouldn't last long in a tomato house, with long white hands and painted talons. She seemed pleasant enough though. Maisie thought the name Gloria suited her.

The women began to arrive, gossiping and giggling, voices bouncing off the glasshouses which for once were not rattling as there was no wind. Hazel arrived with Karen, both girls dressed for a night out, and the way they were behaving Maisie suspected the glass of white wine she greeted them with wouldn't be the first they'd drank tonight. They were sharing a babysitter, with the twins sleeping at Hazel's. They liked this because they liked Nathan, who was an easy going friendly boy who played better quality games.

Next came Janice and Myra, Myra complaining she didn't much go for this sort of thing.

'Well go home then!' said Janice, wearily. She'd tried to snatch a night away from her mother-in-law but Myra had seen her open the envelope.

'No, I'm allus up for an "Experience",' she said, lighting a new Woodbine from her still glowing tab-end. 'Though I don't reckon you can beat giving a man a hot dinner and warm slippers. All that sex lark, it don't stand the test of time!'

The house filled up and they all squashed into the

lounge, eager to be entertained. Sammy's wife Maureen was there with Kim the landlady from the Red Cow, as were their daughters, protesting they were only there to keep an eye on their mums. Vic's wife Ruby stuck her head into the kitchen.

'I thought I'd best come and keep you out o' mischief, Maisie,' she said with mock disapproval. 'To watch yer don't lower the tone round here!'

Most of the wives were there, even Nicole although she hung shyly around the doorway, unsure as a butterfly which has flown into a wrong environment. Angie had persuaded Sylvia to come too, and she was also feeling self conscious. Vera had returned her invitation saying 'I don't need any extras in that department thank you.' The women sat in twos and threes on the armchairs and settee, and the younger ones sat at their feet. The little lounge was fuller than a doctor's waiting room.

Maisie passed the wine around over people's heads as the room was gridlocked. and Gloria began her act by giving out paper and pencils, ignoring protests of 'we're not at bloody school now...'

'Hiya Nicole!' said Hazel. 'Are you gonna get something to liven up your Simon? It's the quiet ones that's the worst, you know. Still waters run deep!'

'Leave her be," hissed Karen. Nicole smiled awkwardly. She hovered close to the doorway.

"Quiet, please. Let's get started,' said Gloria.

When she did manage to get silence she launched into her icebreaker.

'Now put the paper on your heads, ladies,' she said, demonstrating herself, her red nails pressing the paper on her brassy hairdo with one hand, and gripping a pen in the other. They followed her example, from Ruby downwards. 'Now I want you all, without looking, to draw your husband's meat and two veg! And if you don't have a husband,' she had to cover all eventualities, 'the last meat and two veg you remember seeing and,' she leaned towards the two teenagers, 'or what you *hope* it's going to look like!' She didn't pause for breath, probably a sign she was getting bored of the routine. Raucous laughter obediently filled the pauses in Gloria's patter.

Nicole slipped silently and unnoticed from the room and into the warm June air and the hoots and screams echoed after her. She bunched her muslin skirt up and mounted her bike, pleased to be out in the open air. Fireflies sparked. It was a treat of a night. As she pedalled towards home, a voice called from the dark hedgerow.

'Oi! I don't suppose you've seen Angie, have you?'

'Yes, she's at the party next door.' Next door, but with the bulk of a quarter acre glasshouse in between. Nicole knew who it was, but they'd never spoken before.

'Thought as much. Didn't you reckon much to the party then?' Josh asked.

Nicole dismounted. She could see him now, slouched on the doorstep with a bottle tilted in his hand. He smiled but his general countenance was sad.

'No, it's not my scene,' Nicole answered. 'Why aren't you down the pub with the other men?' Simon had gone with Jim and Sammy, she knew that. Josh was reputedly a big boozer, of all the growers he was supposed to spend the most time languishing in the public bar of the Red Cow.

'I've been asleep,' he said, swigging at the bottle. 'What time's it now? Nobody called for me,' he added petulantly.

'Nine-thirty,' said Nicole. She didn't have a watch, she just made it up.

'I went to bed for an afternoon kip. Angie didn't bother to call me for my tea, an' I just woke up. Found a note saying my dinner's in the oven. It's all bloody baked up though,' he said bitterly. 'Had to sling it.'

Nicole didn't comment but she propped her bike up

against the hedge. 'Can I join you?' she asked.

'Eh? Oh, feel free,' said Josh in surprise. 'I'll fetch another bottle.' He got up to go in the house. He was glad of the company, he needed someone to talk to. He'd heard she was a bit weird but he wasn't fussy; any drinking partner would do. She wheeled her bike inside the gate, away from the road, propping it out of view.

'Can we sit outside?' Nicole asked, following him through the front door, clambering over clutter everywhere. She didn't fancy an evening surrounded by this chaos. And she didn't fancy sitting on the front doorstep with him either, like a pair of alkies. 'Out the back?'

'Whatever,' said Josh, passing her a bottle as he led the way through the kitchen. Lights blazed throughout the house, as they usually did, night and day. They reached the back door, and as an afterthought he turned and teased a glass from the tangle of crockery on the draining board. It was a tall one with yellow elephants around the top, the sort children drink orange juice from. He wiped a tidemark away with his thumb and passed it to her. Nicole was quite touched.

She chose a shadowy spot under the trees, soft and grassy and discrete in the failing light. Bats were whizzing crazily above their heads and a Little Owl shrieked from the shadows. Josh launched into a monologue. He told her about his miserable life, his scallywag of a wife, his money worries and his fears for the future, pausing periodically to pull another bottle from the crate. There was something about this strange woman which made him want to confide. When he got to the bit about how he had thumped Dennis he had his head in her lap and she was massaging his shoulders. By the time her hands began to move down over him, he was in a different world.

As he felt her lips and her tongue on his chest and then move further down his stomach he wondered vaguely whether he was supposed to do something to her, but the inclination passed. Still her lips moved downwards.

From where he lay, and through half-shut eyes, Josh could see the narrowest of crescent moons hanging below a crop of stars. The noise from the party sounded more distant than it actually was as the glasshouse between them diverted the sound. It all added to a sense of the unreal. He gripped Nicole's shoulders and relaxed into her soft mouth and moving tongue. He heard his own breath become gasps.

Afterwards, Nicole kissed him on the head and whispered in his ear:

'If you tell anyone about this I promise I'll deny it!' And she was gone, vanishing into the darkness.

Josh pinched himself. He sat up and struck a match. In its restricted glow he clocked the empty bottles and cigarette butts on the grass. Then he noticed the glass with the yellow elephants. He stood up, feeling dizzy. Shaking his head, he walked towards the light of the house, to make himself a strong black coffee. He replaced the glass on the cluttered draining board but it wasn't part of the heap anymore.

It can't have been a dream then, he thought.

Twenty-Three

The Red Cow was an old public house marking the edge of the village, about a mile from the top of the Drift. At one point in history the main London road must have passed through the hamlet, because the pub had a clutter of outbuildings around a big old courtyard suggesting its origin as a coaching inn. The barns were now junk stores and the enclosed yard a discreet car park. Outside, the old alehouse had recently been snowcemmed and the woodwork re-touched a shiny bubbled-up black, the top coat to a couple of centuries. The Inn was split into two bars, both of them dingy but one more deliberately so, the other brightened by copper and brass artefacts which cluttered the walls. The ceilings were beamed and the plaster-work between them stained tobacco-smoke brown, but subtle lighting soaked everything in a warm glow. Cold daylight never quite penetrated the inside of the pub enough to highlight the dust which furred every horizontal ledge outside of immediate reach. The punters' entrance was a heavy black door, the exterior of which was flanked by two old tyres, turned inside out and stuffed with compost, and now ablaze with bedding plants. Any attempt to improve the aesthetics of the pub stopped right there with these home-made planters. The Red Cow was a serious drinking hole and a reluctant provider of food. The plate above the door stated:

William Midgley, Licensed to sell Alcoholic Liquor
for consumption on or off the premises.

To all his punters he was Midge. He was usually alone behind his bar.

Midge had a wife and child the other side of the ceiling, but he rarely got to see them. He was always ready to serve, treading the two square metres between Lounge and Snug with the repetition of a caged bear. Although Midge was confined to his quarters by choice, any casual observer might have expected him to be chained by the leg.

It was a Wednesday evening and the pub was busier than usual, due to an influx of growers. Midge stood, elbows pressed on the bar, chin on his knuckles, surveying the scene. He could never understand them, those creatures of the land, slaving away in all weathers, their wives as well, and all for a pittance. They thought they were free, farming the land, but in his view they were nothing more than bondsmen to the Association. He heard them discussing the atrocious prices, the outlandish cost of packaging and the misery of their crop failures. He'd heard rumours too about debts which would make your hair fall out, but he noticed that when they did cross his threshold they always had ready cash. Not like some of those in the new Barratt homes in the village, who found it difficult to cough up the cost of a pint twice a week and then wanted him to cash a cheque for a tenner.

In winter, wet and red-knuckled after rebuilding a shed or repairing a glasshouse, the growers sought warmth and company and congregated around the Cow's fireplace with its huge log basket atop a slag-heap of ash. This ash glowed red and hissed and simmered constantly from October until March, swelling day by day, with heat retention Midge's excuse for never clearing it out. When the growers squashed around it on harsh winter nights Midge drew a chair up too. Summer was different; it was only the group of hardened drinkers who maintained regular attendance throughout the busy season. Then Midge was thankful for his other customers from the village.

For their part the growers often wondered at the grim life of the publican, the hell of being trapped in that small area, day after day, night after night with no fresh air, just the smoky atmosphere already passed around everybody's lungs. His occasional escapes to freedom were his cash and carry runs, and Thursdays when he played darts, but this getaway was only once a fortnight because each alternate fixture was played at home. Despite the contrasts the growers and the publican co-existed easily with a mutual but secret pity. Midge made real effort to commiserate over their misfortunes, and they in turn spent as hard as their cash flows allowed.

Midge was in the fortunate position of running the only alehouse this side of Wansbridge and his clientele was varied, the growers being just one group. His punters filled different slots throughout his day. The pensioners with their dominoes at lunchtime gave way early evening to the creatures who worked in the city, standing up at the bar like Londoners, calming down before they faced the wife. In their suits and ties, Midge pitied them beyond the growers. Mostly they just passed through briefly and then left for their evening meal but there were a couple of heavy boozers in this group, Midge knew the signs.

Women? Yes, there were women, even a group who came in regularly on a Thursday. And you could never tell what the passing trade might bring. Couples were becoming more common too, not only to play cards like the three pairs in the corner were doing now, but just to sit together and whisper unsociably, sipping at their drinks. It seemed a new craze. What was wrong with own their front rooms, wondered Midge. Then there were the Young Farmers, male and female, all of them rowdy, and the darts and skittles teams. There was overlap of course, and dotted amongst all of this were the determined drinkers, often solitary within the crowd.

Tonight the growers were crowded into the Snug. A group played cards, another dominoes. There was a pool table in the recess, and Eddie and Steve were competing as Sammy looked on and gave a running criticism on how they were hitting. Eddie and Steve were obviously irritated but seemed to be biting their tongues. That was when Midge noticed Josh was absent. This was a bit unusual, he could expect to see him on a lunchtime and again at night. Josh was a bit fiery, but he was pleasant enough most of the time. Strangely, Josh's wife Angie was the one he'd had to bar. Remembering the incident reminded him that the Women's Institute were due in next week, they always finished up their July meeting with a meal, and Midge didn't want them to arrange to go elsewhere. He reckoned that if you had to cook food to survive, then at least make it worth lighting the stove. He would have to ask Josh to invite her back, next time he saw him. It hadn't been anything terribly serious anyway. Midge re-ran the episode in his mind...

It happened on a Sunday and Josh had been drinking all day. Angie stormed into the bar around three o' clock. Josh hid in the toilet.

'Where is he?' Angie asked. Midge, forever loyal to his male customers said he hadn't seen him all day.

'Right!' Angie had said, disappearing only to return with a roast beef dinner, a hefty helping which was beginning to congeal on the plate. 'You say he's not here? So why's his bloody pickup in the car park?' And to the amusement of everyone she tilted the plate, until the meat and vegetables slid on a sludge of gravy onto the Lounge carpet. As she made for the door she'd said something which sounded like "you gutless wonder."

Midge had been outraged. 'You're BARRED!' he'd bawled at her retreating back. After all, she could have meant Josh, but she might have meant him! And the stain had never quite lifted from the carpet, despite Kim's efforts and the mixtures she'd scrubbed it with...

Now he looked at the growers, chatting and laughing, still talking about their crops. Take Sammy, still mouthing it, who seemed to be one step ahead of the Association, his shady deals forcing any horticultural interest into second place. Whatever you needed, from a part to fix your car to a side of cheap bacon, Sammy was your man. The publican had negotiated many a deal with Sammy. Midge watched him now, big and burly with a bushy beard speckled all sorts of colours. Sammy was a colourful man, loud and boisterous. When he laughed he roared with great guffaws. It was good to have someone like that in your bar, mused Midge. It helped to lift the atmosphere. Sammy seemed to be very pally with the newcomer, Steve. Now his visits to the pub had increased lately, and Midge guessed he could expect to see a lot of him during the winter. Good, he thought, every little counts now the supermarkets sell booze as if it were milk.

Simon, now he was strange one, but he liked his drink. Simon often came in at lunchtime and sat in the Lounge, uncommunicative with head down, stuck in a book. He was supposed to be very intelligent, Midge had been told, but he wasn't sure whether to believe this. How come he was living on the Land Settlement then? Simon had a wife who only drank red wine, of all things. Midge had to order it in specially. She only came in with Simon, though, and there was no sign of her tonight.

Now look at Eddie. Eddie would grow into another Vic, thought Midge. Vic had been talking all his life about getting off the Estate, but the only place he was headed now was a council bungalow. Eddie would be the same, unless of course his wife sorted things out. Eddie's expectations of life were simple and he was always cheerful, whatever the weather, whatever the prices. Mind you, thought Midge, who wouldn't be with a wife like Hazel? Then he remembered how she flirted with every man she saw no matter what the age, she even made eyes at pensioners and it really made their night. He supposed she'd make an ideal barmaid in that sort of pub, but that was not what Midge wanted for the Red Cow. In his experience overtly sexual barmaids only caused fights. Yes, this was a man's pub, Midge thought smugly, one of the few remaining. He didn't mind the odd girl decorating the place once in while, but that was all. He didn't even want his own wife Kim about too often. This suited Kim, who could pass each evening soaking up the soaps and game shows in peace. Perhaps this was why their relationship had lasted so long.

Midge paused in his reflections to serve a customer in the Lounge, and when he turned back Jim was waiting at the bar, getting a round in. It was nearly eleven o' clock.

'Well, it'll have to be last orders,' said Midge, banging the gong. 'I need my beauty sleep.'

'Should've gone to bed at lunchtime then!' laughed Jim, as Midge passed him the glasses, precious ale slopping down the sides.

Midge knew in reality it was going to be a late night. At twenty past eleven he tried a weak: "Haven't you got homes to go to?", sighed, stretched the faded curtains across the window and slotted the bolts, top and bottom, across the heavy door.

'Count me in, next game,' he said.

Twenty-Four

Steve was puzzling over his lettuce returns when Jonathan rapped on his dining room window. The fieldsman noted with dismay that the plastic tablecloth was strewn with bunches of produce returns released from their bulldog clips. This had the look of a post mortem, and Jonathan yawned at the thought of more conversation along those lines. God, he was so bored with this job. Steve looked up from heavy concentration, and removed and polished his glasses on the front flap of his shirt.

'Come in, mate,' he called. The door was open to the conservatory and the air was still warm, yesterday's heat trapped by a layer of thick cloud. 'We've a hundred boxes due to cut, but at these prices it don't seem worth it.' Steve made no attempt to move from the table.

Jonathan drew up a chair, gritting his teeth to hide his exasperation. 'Well, it's always like this in summer, the bottom falls out of the market. It's because so many people have salad stuff ready in their gardens. Should change in a week or two though, because there's so many slugs about since the rain they'll have chewed the garden crop to bits. Housewife don't want bits of meat in her lettuce, specially if the daughter's veggie! Summer produce, well it just keeps you ticking over, helps your cash flow.' Bloody hell, maybe I should produce a tape, and just keep playing it to them, he thought to himself. He kept it light in the hope of a cup of tea.

And keeps you bloody lot in a job, Steve considered silently but he couldn't be bothered to voice his opinion. Spawned by Sammy, Steve had now grasped this theory.

'See here, even peppers and cues are down,' he persisted, tracing his finger along the line of figures. 'And I can't remember seeing many of them in gardens back home.'

Jonathan tried to be patient. 'Well it only takes one gardener on an allotment,' he said. 'He can't eat them all, can he? He passes them all around his friends and neighbours! Now, those lettuce, let's see, shall I put you down for fifty tomorrow, and fifty Thursday?' His voice resumed a business-like briskness.

'Lettuce, cucumbers, peppers, tomatoes – what the fuck. All that graft for nowt! What's the point?' Steve gathered the paperwork carelessly and tucked it behind the tacky carriage clock on the mantleshelf. The bulldog clips lay benign on the tabletop. Jonathan thought how he preferred to deal with Karen, and how annoyed she'd be when she discovered her husband had muddled her paperwork. She was altogether more intelligent and optimistic. Now he hadn't even been offered a drink, and this was one of the last holdings he could usually guarantee one.

'Am I booking these in or not?' he repeated abruptly. 'No skin off my nose. After all, we've got to sell the damn things.' Usually Steve responded positively if Jonathan was sharp, but today he just stood up and said:

'Aye, what the hell, might as well.' What he didn't say but was evident in his body language, was leave me in peace and get off my nursery. Jonathan was still thirsty and now he had to drive two miles to the garage to buy a warm coke.

                                                         ॐ ॐ

Tomato picking was a favoured occupation, which was fortunate as the fruit ripened so quickly in the heat. No-one knew the return in advance, and since prices dived up and down like planes at a summer air display, they were unable to make a decision on whether to cut their losses. In any case they couldn't leave them to rot on the plant as it invited disease and stopped further fruit development, so they'd have to be harvested and then dumped. So they picked on. In the greenhouses, the plants were now very tall and provided the picker with plenty of shade. On reaching the roof, the growing point had to be nipped. A few growers still practised layering, which involved untying the heavily laden plant at the wire, and dropping the same plant so the previously stripped stem at the bottom could now be pegged down securely further along the ground and then retied on the wire in the manner of a carefully layered hedge. This would extend production for three or so trusses, but they needed to have had artificial heat early in the season for this to be viable. As a practice it was dying out amongst small growers as recent profit margins did not justify the additional cost of fuel. George was saddened by this because he was skilled in layering and took pride in the regimented result. Maisie meanwhile was too pleased with the biological control to worry about a thing of the past like layering. Her "tubes" still wheezed, but she figured they'd take time to clear.

Jim was less pleased with his cherry tomatoes. They were time consuming to pick and even more so to pack. His mother Myra was a Godsend, out on the nursery every morning at six, totally free labour, the downside being she missed so many.

'It's as if she has little blackouts,' said Jim fondly, as he handed his wife a truss of blood red marbles, too ripe to sell. Another tasty treat for Bernadette.

'More like she don't look properly.' Janice stripped the truss into a bucket.

'Come on, Jan, she's getting old! It's thanks to her that

goat's the best fed in the land. It's a wonder her milk don't run pink!'

Slip it in the conversation now girl, thought Janice. She said: 'Well, I bet all these cherries do help to make the milk rich. I've been reading up, you know, I'd love to sell goat's milk commercially, run a little sideline. There'd be the market, but of course I'd need more lactating nannies.'

'Lactating nannies! Ge' er off! If Ma wasn't here you wouldn't have time to piddle about with this. Lactating nannies, my arse!'

Janice left it for now. She disappeared, crushed, with her bucket. Jim checked the stack of punnets ready to be boxed and transferred them to a pallet. Lactating nannies, that's a good'un! Better than chasing men, mind.

Myra also had problems with these plastic punnets. She was able to sort the cherries well enough but she became "all fingers and thumbs" when she tried to separate punnets individually. Jim once counted five stuck together. No wonder she couldn't get the lid on.

One morning she was poking at some stubborn punnets with her nails, ash spilling from the Woodbine suspended in her mouth. Unfortunately Jonathan was behind her. Armed with his entitlement to quality control packing procedure, he was undertaking a spot check.

'What are you doing?' he asked. Myra jumped and the cherries tumbled from the punnet spilling onto the dusty floor like a broken string of beads.

'Oh, it's you, duck! These damn plastic thingies!' she cursed, as she scrabbled to pick them up from around Jonathan's shiny black shoes.

'You can't smoke in here!' he said in disbelief to the top of her dark permed hair. 'This is food you're dealing with! It's not hygienic!'

Myra stood up, confused, cigarette frozen in her mouth. Jim clattered the edge of the doorframe with his bucket as he entered, and he soon realised something was amiss.

'What's up Ma?' he asked as he poured a bucket of cherries into the sorting trough. 'And what are you doin' here?'

'I'm just telling her she can't smoke in here when she's handling food!' said Jonathan, stoutly. 'And I'm checking everyone's packing procedure, so don't get your knickers in a twist.'

'Well what the fuck's it to you? It's my packing shed. I'll do what I want. You'll be comin' into my bedroom soon, tellin' me I'm not doing that right!'

Oh, I don't believe this, thought Jonathan. Don't expect any common sense from this lot.

'We don't allow smoking in the Main Packhouse as you well know,' he said staring straight at the grower who couldn't return his gaze.

'Well that's there and this is here,' said poor Jim, realising in his heart he had no argument. He was not, after all, a free man.

Jonathan seized and scrutinised the punnet Myra had just put down.

'Look,' he said triumphantly. 'Some ash has fallen through onto the fruit!' He passed it to Jim, and sure enough, there were the telltale grey-white grains showing loud and clear against the shiny red. It just might have been dust from the floor, but either way it wasn't good.

'Bloody hell, Ma,' Jim said, slamming the offending article down.

'I'm sorry duck,' said Myra, squashing the Woodbine out on the edge of the bench and placing it with care on the window-ledge. She was used to bowing to authority, she'd done it all her life. 'I'm sorry Jonathan.' Myra the meek. Jonathan grunted and turned to go, then he recognised that she recognised his position. This wasn't a common experience.

He smiled pleasantly to her. 'That's okay Mrs Carter. I know you won't do it again.' And he left behind a waft of aftershave to battle it out with resentment, embarrassment and humiliation.

Myra resumed work, but Jim stood in the doorway like a roped-up rotweiller, seeing the fieldsman off of his land.

'You don't have to apologise to that twat, Ma!'

Jonathan hurried away down the path, and the turkeys gobbled at him from the fencetop as he passed.

₭ ℞

In all aspects, the grower's weren't really free, their lives were tightly managed. For the first five years on the Estate, they agreed a sum each year with the Land Settlement accountant to be drawn each month to live on. This money came out regardless of crop failures or bumper harvests, and the well of debt with the LSA just increased drip by drip, swollen by interest and purchases from The Stores and the propagation department. There was no automatic scheme for repayment. In theory crop income should do that – it had in the past. Long term growers had been able to clear all debt and used their current accounts regularly to pay the Land Settlement. The idea was to build up savings in order to move on, but lately even successful growers were dipping into these savings to survive.

They saw several ways out of this sorry state of affairs. One was compensation – some politically minded growers were gathering information in an attempt to prove mismanagement by the agency. Another was the dream that the government would soon sell the holdings off cheaply, so they might be able to get a bridging loan and re-sell, but they'd have to leave the life they loved. Another was to decide to accept bankruptcy should it come, and hope the state looked after them. After these strategies there was only really the football pools and hope of an inheritance.

In daily life it was possible to ignore the mounting debt, as they didn't receive threatening letters or have to meet repayment deadlines. If they needed ready cash they sold outside, and big expenses like new kitchens or exotic holidays just weren't part of their world. If they could ignore the statements from the Land Settlement office, happy they were doing everything in their power, life went on but the spectre of debt was all too real below the surface.

Twenty-Five

As July wore on the children of school age joined their younger brothers and sisters for six weeks of den-building and water-squirting. Young children had a wonderful life on the Estate, so much space to wander in, so many random building materials. While town kids draped blankets across up-turned chairs under mother's eye, the Land Settlement boys and girls used sheets of corrugated iron, planks of wood and fertiliser sacks, largely uninhibited. They had easy access to hammer and nails and heavy duty staple guns. After making sure the very young were fenced off from roads and that dangerous chemicals were well out of reach, the children were left to chase chickens and dig muddy holes with sticks. The older ones had to learn quickly to treat the roadway with respect and to be on the look out for lorries and tractors reversing, even on their own land. There was general encouragement for them to use tools as soon as they were capable of holding them, as most of the parents valued practical ability far beyond academic learning.

Eric worried at this lack of supervision, although he could appreciate the parents' predicament. He had seen little ones spreading sandwiches on a kitchen chair, the table being too high to reach, as their parents slashed at lettuce in the glasshouse. He knew that countrywide there were more children killed on farms than in any other situation. Luckily he hadn't seen anything too disastrous here, but last year a group of the Estate children had a lucky escape. Having built a den at the top of a holding, deep in the ditch bordering the farmer's field, they'd sneaked a box of matches into it. The dry branches inevitably caught alight, and fire whipped through the den. Fortunately the children had the presence of mind to realise the blaze was beyond their control and had run, ashen-faced and shaking, to tell their parents. The blaze quickly ate along the hedge and into the straw bales beyond. The fire brigade had eventually put it out. Eric had seen the charred remains of the den, the burnt tables and chairs and blackened metal buttons and clips of what had once been their coats. The children too had been shocked. They'd learnt a good lesson – at an average age of seven.

For the older children life was less sweet. Teenagers wanted more structured entertainment, and anyway as soon as they were able, they had to help on the nursery. There were no buses into Wansbridge, and it was too far for a comfortable walk. But as youngsters, the children had great fun. They roamed in groups from holding to holding, finding a new lean-to or a better trunk for a tree house, just as the mood took them. The villagers held a different view. Many considered the Estate children ran wild, and some would not allow their kids to play with these ragamuffins.

Life continued for the growers with little impact from the outside world, especially in summertime. A van did deliver newspapers; the driver steered down the middle of the road as best he could, slowing down and lobbing the rolled up paper, javelin-style, through his open window. Mostly the newspaper landed somewhere on the front verge. This was fine in summer when nobody had time to read it anyway, but it could become soggy and forgotten in winter. Most of the tenants subscribed to The Grower, a shiny trade magazine, but few bothered with a daily paper. There were, of course, some exceptions; Simon took the Guardian and George the Daily Mirror, Pot Plant World and Woman's Own for Maisie; Janice, Fur and Feather, which she saved and re-read in the winter. Sammy would usually drive to Wansbridge for his Exchange and Mart and Sylvia fetched home glossies for her coffee table, all of which husband Dennis was too busy or disinterested to read.

Most growers listened to music radio, and world news and events made little difference to their lives. It was a year which had seen the shootings of Ronald Reagan and Pope John Paul II already and was later to witness the assassination of Anwar Sadat. None of these events provoked much more than a passing comment, usually about a fortnight afterwards, instigated by Midge at the Red Cow. They talked vaguely of the summer riots which were rocking places with strange names like Brixton and Toxteth, and promptly counted their blessings. They were much more likely to know who Blondie was than the newly elected President Mitterand. Even sporting events passed most people by; they just didn't have the time. Dennis made sure he watched Steve Davis win the snooker, and Janice took time out during the first week of July and watched John McEnroe win Wimbledon. Old Vic still dreamed of one last visit to St. James' Park to see his beloved Toon. The one event which broke through the bubble was the Royal Wedding on 29th July.

Sylvia and Dennis were drinking an after-dinner cup of coffee. The dirty plates had been stacked in the dishwasher and she rejoined him at the table, where he'd spread the latest edition of the Grower on the white damask cloth.

'I thought we'd hold a garden party on Royal Wedding day,' said Sylvia, topping his cup from the jug.

'Umm,' Dennis said, enjoying the aroma of fresh coffee, absorbed in an article about hydroponics.

'I've invited several people from the Bank and you might want to..'

Dennis came back to earth with a bang. 'You've what?' He folded the Grower and paid full attention.

Sylvia was aware of the need to tread carefully. 'We've

such a lovely garden, and nobody gets to see it,' she wheedled. 'All the work I put in..'

'You know there's going to be a big do on here, everyone's watching the wedding at the Sports Day. Weren't we talking about it just the other day? We've always joined in with the Sports.' This was true; it benefited the children of the Estate and it was an unwritten rule that everyone helped for the sake of the next generation once their own children were grown up. It was simple to celebrate the wedding at the same time. They only had to shift the races to the morning and place televisions in the Hall.

'Oh, I know,' admitted Sylvia. 'We can invite some of the growers too, if you really want. But I hardly know them, and we are leaving a lot of them behind, I mean those who don't seem to know what they are doing and are in such debt.' She ran a finger with its lightly glazed nail around the raised pattern on her teacup.

'Don't talk like that,' said Dennis. 'Bad times can hit anyone. I don't know any of your fancy Bank friends. What would I talk to them about?' He stared miserably out of the window, a man caught between two worlds. It was true he had little in common with the growers these days; most he'd been friendly with had moved on. But he certainly felt awkward with Sylvia's cronies. There was also the nagging feeling of disappointment that he wouldn't now see Angie at the disco afterwards, but he refused to analyse this and put it from his mind. Sylvia had expertly allowed him a strategic silence and he ended it now.

'Well, I'm much too busy to mess about organising it,' he said. 'I'm up to my eyes in it.'

'Oh, darling, I knew you'd see sense!' She leaned over and pecked him on his cheek. He caught a whiff of Oil of Ulay. 'I know how worried you are about those silly old growers. But they're their own worst enemies, you've said so often enough. They're dragging us back.'

'Yes, but it's not their fault, at least it's not their fault if they're not astute businessmen...' Dennis felt a flush of pride which didn't escape his wife.

' We're a good team,' she said almost too connivingly. 'You just let me see to everything.'

∞ ∞

It seemed like the whole world had a holiday for this wedding, so there was no produce collection the day before. The Estate had caught the buzz, the weather was still co-operating and for once history was about to be made and the country was ready and waiting. Newspapers were bought for souvenirs and bunting was strung up all around, threaded behind the glasshouse guttering, zigzagging across the Drift. The sun sparkled on the greenhouses illuminating the coloured flags, transforming the glass village into a kaleidoscope of colour.

George marked out the running track, just as he'd done for years. As he wheeled the chalk along a string guide, he thought back to the days when his children were small, and instead of growing fruit and vegetables the tenants had run smallholdings in the proper sense of the word. They'd kept hens and geese and other birds until they'd been wiped out by fowlpest. Then they moved on to pigs, but swine fever put paid to them. Disease spread like spilt milk through the holdings. No amount of disinfectant protected them; if your neighbour had contamination there was little chance of escaping it, the units were too close. Both times, he'd had to dig a massive pit and burn the carcasses. George remembered his relief when the Land Settlement turned to tomatoes and lettuce. Whatever disaster might befall them, he knew it wouldn't be as heartrending as having to assist the wholesale slaughter of your livestock. To this very day a circle remained on his land which wouldn't grow anything substantial. Plants would sit there as seedlings quite comfortably until they began to send roots down past the top soil. Then they withered and died. Yes, the experience had scarred him like the death pit had soured his land and the memory prevented him from keeping any animals, even domestic ones. He wondered what the next u-turn would be, perhaps a move to pot plants? He hoped so, he'd be well ahead of the game.

Sammy was sorting through his discotheque equipment. Usually with parties he ran power from the generator on the PTO of his tractor, but tomorrow he would be running the disco in the Hall. He'd picked out the records, plenty of Status Quo, the growers liked spinning around to them. His daughter had insisted on the Police, (strange name for a successful pop group. Could he bring himself to play it?), Blondie and The Specials who were number one at the time.

Hazel asked Jonathan if he'd be at the disco.

'Why?'

'Cos I might just dance with you!'

But he replied moodily that he'd rather party with Idi Amin than a bevy of growers. There would be staff and their families there too but Jonathan felt no affinity with them. He repeated his request for Hazel to visit him at his house in Wansbridge.

'He seemed serious,' she told Karen as they cut up crepe paper for the children's Fancy Dress. 'I'll just have to find someone else to mess around with. No way am I going to his house. Now why would I go and do that?'

'You're leading him on. You be careful.'

'I'm safe and careful, Mrs. Market Gardener,' she said. Then she shouted: 'Nathan! Come and sort what you're going as!'

But Nathan wasn't keen. He stuck his head around the door. 'I'm not dressing up, Mum. No way.'

'He's shot up recently, hasn't he,' said Karen. They

looked at the boy, swinging against the door, wiry if you were being polite, skinny if you weren't. His lovely smile was missing, though, at the thought of being dressed up.

'Yeh, but look how thin he is, just like a washing line. Hey, that's it, that's the answer! Go fetch my peg basket!'

So Nathan stood with his arms stretched out and Hazel and Karen stuck pegs along them.

'He'd be better wearing something dark, jumper and trousers, to show the pegs off,' said Karen.

'Stand back,' said Hazel. 'You know I think he'll win!'

Nathan went to the bathroom to look and when he came back he was smiling. Problem solved.

᧞   ᧠

On the day of the Wedding, the older women prepared the food. They spread the sandwiches on site, but the desserts were prepared and fridged at home. They were scathing about the wedding dress. Too many creases! They wouldn't have it as a gift, and that dirty off-white colour too. What a good job she was so beautiful.

Midge arrived early at the hall to organise his bar. He wanted to watch his little boy in the Sports Day so he needed to complete as much setting up as possible. Struggling through the narrow side entrance with a crate of glasses, he bumped into Angie who was carrying a trifle in a curvy glass dish. It nestled against her blatant bosom.

'Oh, Angie,' he said nervously, fearful of the trifle hitting him full in the face. 'Did Josh give you the message, er, that you can come back in again? To the Pub, I mean?'

Angie hadn't received any message, she rarely saw Josh to talk to these days. As she stood aside to let Midge pass, she smiled sweetly at him, then quickly spun around again so he was trapped against the wall pinned partly by a large breast and partly by the trifle. Midge linked the colour of her tee-shirt with the colour of the custard. It even had a cherry in the middle. Standing on tip-toe she placed her face, still smiling, close towards his. If he twitched, Midge would have lipstick on his cheek.

'Well thank you sir,' Angie said sarcastically, and then added sweetly: 'If you ever tell me that pillock of a husband of mine is not in the pub when he is, I promise you I'll get you done for selling after time!'

With that her smile broadened and she disappeared into the kitchen with her trembling trifle. Midge was shaken, he thought that was some threat. Thirty percent of his takings came after the shutters were down and he'd had a police warning not that long since.

Steve and Eddie arrived next, each carrying a television. They needed to stack tables up to make height so everyone could see, and string out the extension cables. It would be necessary to black out the windows because the chintzy cotton curtains only really diffused the sun.

'How's them special plants, Steve?' asked Sammy, who was on his knees checking tone levels. Steve was waggling the aerial around on top of his television set rather unsuccessfully for the screen was a snowstorm and a buzzing one at that. He stabbed at a knob and secured a picture before he answered.

'They're doing great,' Steve said. Eddie and Midge both paused and listened. 'This weather suits 'em.'

Eddie guessed what Sammy meant because he'd had some of Sammy's plants last year, until Hazel had found out. He also knew that Sammy wasn't really interested in regular greenhouse plants. The other growers were all hooked on horticulture, it was very addictive. But not Sammy. Midge guessed because he knew Sammy and because he'd made a sport of listening. He listened like the others didn't know how. Purely for entertainment value, of course.

'You haven't Steve,' said Eddie. He lowered his voice so

Midge couldn't hear. 'You're a fool, especially with Jonathan sniffing round all the time.' He glanced at Sammy, busy with a screwdriver. The picture on Steve's screen slid upwards and round and round, you wouldn't be able to watch history in the making on that.

'Leave it out!' said Sammy in a whisper. 'They're well hidden, and he's only got a few. I've got ten times his.'

'Yeah, it's okay for you. Nobody dares go on to your land. It's like fucking Fort Knox, it is. Steve, you're an idiot. You'd be kicked out, you know. Does Karen know?'

Eddie thought back to last year, when Hazel had made him chuck his on the bonfire. He remembered how they'd sat around it, watching the flames dance and breathing in the aroma. Hazel hadn't been totally opposed, he remembered, just fearful of the consequences. And he feared for Steve now in the same way.

'Course she don't, because she don't ever go in the prop house. If she does, I'll just tell her they're a new sort of hedging.' Steve wasn't usually decisive, and now he was adamant. 'So leave off, mate. I know you mean well, but I need all the brass I can get me hands on.'

Eddie shook his head. 'I've been there. Remember my close shave with that sodding pump,' he whispered.

'It'll be right, I tell you. I know what I'm doing!' Steve whispered back. The rolling picture on his TV screen slid to a halt at three quarter position.

Sammy touched something live, and he dropped whatever he was holding with a shout. 'Bastard!' Then he grinned. 'You've got to sail close to the wind to survive on the LSA!'

ഏ ര

On the day the sun shone and people basked in its rays without the bother of sun creams. That was all in the future.

The children's sports were conducted with a lot of humour and not a great deal of authority and there were highs, lows and a few fights. The adults had their events too, which included the sack race and wellie throwing. Afterwards they crushed into the Hall to watch the marriage ceremony, old and young alike, although a few of the men grabbed the opportunity to "go and check on things." An anarchic group of them congregated outside the hut.

'Bloody monarchy,' said Midge. He'd had to shut his pub, but it didn't really matter because everyone was here anyway and he was running an outside bar. His wife Kim had insisted on watching the wedding in company, not stuck in an empty pub waiting for a customer to arrive who'd been living in a cave. 'Won't last two minutes. The papers talk about love, but there's no such thing as love and marriage for the likes of them. Look at all the money the country's lost, having a day off like this.'

'There's no such thing as love in marriage for the likes of us, neither,' said Jim, gloomily. 'Mind you if I were Charlie boy I wouldn't knock her out the four-poster.' There was general agreement on this.

Midge persisted. 'What d'you reckon, Vic, is it a ploy to keep the masses down? All this monarchy revival stuff?'

'Naw, Maggie does that single 'anded. We need t' get the socialists back in!'

'Socialists? Labour?' said Eddie. 'No chance, they're done for, mate. Thank God.'

'But we're part of a co-operative, man!'

'Co-operative?' said Eddie. 'The only co-operative I have's with Hazel! I do the hard graft and give her the housekeeping, and she co-operates in the bedroom. Sometimes she gets a bonus and then she really co-operates.'

The other men all laughed, personal reaction to this hidden beneath a blanket of chauvinism.

'I'm not interested in your sex life,' said Steve. 'But 'ow

the heck can you be a Tory? You're not a land owner. What's she ever done for you?'

'A sight more than those bastards what put us on a three day week..'

'Fuck off Eddie, you know nowt!' said Steve, anger twisting his face.

'You can't say as I ain't involved in private enterprise, now can you?' said Sammy. 'I'm a conservative.'

'Aye, they'll be glad of that,' said Vic. 'You's just what they's lookin' for. Mebbe's you should join the local branch. All I kna is this co-operative worked canny enough til that bitch got in!'

'Hey, Come on, come on,' said Midge, 'I never meant to open this can o' worms.'

'Ne bother, I'm never afeard to say how I think. Anyroad, you're set to do all reet out of this,' Vic said to Midge, in a skilled attempt to change course. 'You'll 'ave em four deep at that bar shortly. I should a' fetched some of mi brew, they could buy some off me as they're waiting for ye to serve 'em!'

The men laughed at this. 'We want to stay sober for the disco Vic!' said Jim. 'The world's changed, you know. Most folk aren't man enough for your ale!.'

'Simon's helping me behind the bar,' Midge told them. This was a surprise because he always refused offers of a hand. Still, he was going to be exceptionally busy.

'Simon?' They asked in unison, this band of men in their best clothes, which hung loose on them because it was summer, the season of graft. Come Christmas the same trousers would be straining at the waistbands. The publican, slight and swarthy in his light slacks stood his ground.

'Well yes,' said Midge. 'He's educated. He can add up.' They all looked at him but he wasn't smiling.

That means he thinks we can't, they thought.

Twenty-Six

In the days before the restrictions on stubble burning, the atmosphere in arable areas was hazy for much of August. At first the pollution was difficult to detect; its effect was insidious. Then growers were aware of a lack of brightness, a loss of the sparkle captured so well in some water-colours. The sun still burnt its way through the pall and Jonathan persisted with wearing his shades, but the clarity had gone from the air. Light winds only seemed to consolidate the smoke, and still there was no rain. The summer was tired, the leaves dusty and the clouds teased the growers daily with an empty threat of rain. Each afternoon isolated clouds built up into great banks and the growl of thunder could be heard, but whenever they bobbed up from their work to see how close the storm was, it had side-stepped them. Each afternoon the sky took on the gloom of approaching rain, but it never came and the mugginess continued unabated.

If they had a suitable piece of ground, growers were planting celery for autumn, a lean time of year. All lettuce and celery plants were placed on the soil in individual cubes of peat, called blocks. The trowel was obsolete. These blocks changed the grower's life like the cellphone has since changed the teenager's. Karen and Steve had been amazed when Jonathan told them you just set the block on the soil, no need to bury it. A little push in is all you need. In fact the growers all spoke of "setting" the seedlings, an expression which just fitted the job.

'Setting makes me think of jelly,' said Karen, 'or me mam's hair.'

'Oh, that word was used around here years before,' Eric told her. 'Funny word, set. Did you know there are more meanings for the word 'set' than any other in the English language?'

'Nope, but I do now.'

'And no dictionary mentions setting lettuce specifically. Shall I tell you the biggest enemy of 'set' lettuce?'

'Aye, you better had.'

'Female blackbirds. They toss the blocks over their shoulders, looking for worms to feed their young. They're most vulnerable before roots have pegged them down. By the way, only the females cause this havoc.'

The usual method of setting the celery was by planting machine. Steve had been advised to spend out on one during the summer, and this was the first time he and Karen had used it. It had a petrol engine and was very fumey. Sammy had found this particular model for him at a knock-down price and it was quite a contraption. At the back, two narrow slatted wooden seats were suspended above the bare ground, with a rack in the front, so several correx boards of blocks could be positioned like a music score. The two operators sat with legs apart and knees up, so they could pick a handful of blocks from the supply and pop them down between their legs into the imprints marked by the roller in front. It helped if there was a third person available to shuffle correx boards and stack trays to save the operators from having to swing around and do this, as panic and squashed plants was then a possibility. Or a probability, depending on your level of competence. Fortunately for novices, the machine had an adjustable throttle. There were electric and diesel versions, but electric could only really be used in a large greenhouse complex like Dennis'. A diesel, cheaper to run and cheaper to buy was only suitable for outside use. The obvious choice for Steve and Karen had been this petrol one, and now they were arguing fiercely above the noise of its motor.

It was moving so slowly the engine kept shuddering to a halt. Even so, there were spaces everywhere and the machine had obviously drifted off course.

'Bloody waste of money,' Karen said, as she swivelled around to replace a tray. When she lifted the correx board, the plants slid off and over the metal side of the machine to be trampled by the wheels. 'Fuck it. I can't get on with this! You'd best send it back.' She clawed her way out and Steve switched off the machine. It died painfully.

Karen was now very skilled at planting by hand, but she or rather her lack of height was the problem with this new machine. And as a pair they were incompatible, her so light and tiny and Steve so burly. He had to sit towards the middle or the machine see-sawed up on her side.

'Don't swear at it! It's you, you need to grow more!'

'Bloody sexist thing, it's made for men. You'll just have to learn to do double the work, you cause double the sodding trouble!'

'Your mate manages all right.'

Crossly she recalled Hazel's demonstration, long legs slipping over the metal bars, and she'd sped up the field managing two people's work.

'You'll get used to it,' she'd assured Karen. Jonathan had been watching, drooling from the path, Karen couldn't believe Eddie hadn't noticed. God, men were so stupid. And now she felt she was married to the king of fools. Discontent had been stirring in her chest for days. Now was as good a time as any to broach the subject which was bothering her.

'Have you hidden those boxes?' she asked, arms folded, the petulant Yorkshire wife, as Steve disentangled himself from the seat. He stood up and began digging for his cigarettes in his jeans pocket. Typical, she thought. If in doubt light a cig.

'Yes I have,' he said irritably, recognising her tone and her stance. 'Don't nag.'

'Oh. Where?' Her dark eyes blazed and her pointed chip stared up at him. She looked a waif usually, which belied her inner strength. But now it was there for all to see. She bristled like a cornered stoat.

'Keep ya hair on! Under the bench, covered wi' a tarpaulin.' Steve sat on the side bar of the planter and lit his cigarette. But this obviously wasn't the root of it. She was still jittery with anger.

'Why the heck is it that you have to get in with the only iffy character on the Estate? Why do they always hang around you like bees round a flippin' honeypot?'

Steve's voice was eerily quiet. 'You got what you wanted, didn't you? I'm miles from me mates, you know, the ones you disapproved of, the same ones as helped us out of a hole back in t'spring. If you want me to fuck off back up there then you just carry on like you're going.'

She checked her anger but it took a moment or two of silence to do it. A super-tanker turning round. They both glared into the distance as the birds sang on in total disregard.

Eventually she said in a controlled voice: 'How can I just stand back and watch us get kicked out?' Tears were near and only her clenched fists kept them back.

'You're over the top again, Karen. What you got against Sammy? At least he's in the real world. It's only him as can help us. Everything that bastard Jonathan and the rest of the LSA staff told us is all shite! "Welcome to the first rung of the farming ladder."' His voice was sour with sarcasm.

'I don't trust that Sammy,' she replied, 'that's all. I don't like his eyes, they're too close together. And I know he don't like me.' She had a point, the man made little effort to communicate with her, almost acting as if she didn't exist.

'Bloody hell woman! Here we are on the brink of

217

disaster, a guy offers practical help and you don't like him because his eyes are too close together!' He threw his tab-end down in mock despair.

'No, it's not just that!' Karen made a serious attempt at communication and her voice took on a tone of reasonable pleading. 'We know he's crooked. He survives on his shady deals. He sure as hell don't grow much produce, and what he does he sells outside. And yet he won't be the one who is kicked off, when it all comes out in the open! Dirt don't stick to the likes of him. It'll be someone like us as gets it. Jonathan was saying the other day he never goes near there, he's scared of the alsatians.'

'Huh! Scared of the alsatians? He's scared of Sammy, more like. Last time Jonathan went up there, Sammy said he had to take Adam the Packhouse Manager with him, the cowardly twat!'

The admiration in Steve's voice didn't go unnoticed. All the years she'd spent trying to wean him from his rough biker friends, only to find him looking up to a small time crook.

'Anyway you can talk.'

'What?'

'Well, what about your mate?'

'My mate? You mean Hazel?'

'Aye, Hazel. The lovely Hazel.'

'What d'you mean? I thought you liked her.'

'Oh aye, I like her, I mean who doesn't? I've watched her, I know her type. Eat dinner with you and shag your grandad for afters, let alone the fieldsman!'

Karen flushed. 'What are you on about?'

'Karen, d'you think I'm blind? Eddie might be, but not me. She's probably at it now, behind the courgettes with that pratt.'

'Don't be ridiculous! She's just a flirt, a prick teaser, that's all.'

'Just remember next time you go slagging my mates,

your friend i'nt the virgin Mary.'

'Oh it's not really Sammy,' she continued quickly. 'I feel we're living like criminals. We eat knocked off bacon and cheese, we're buying in second-hand boxes so's we can sneak our produce outside. We're cheating the l'ectric board and there's red diesel in our pick-up! And he's behind it all, like some – like some bloody Ronnie Biggs. And what was in the back of the van you had to drive to London for him? Did you ask him?'

Steve's voice became reasonable too, suspiciously so. 'Look, I don't know and no, I didn't ask, but you were happy enough to go to the cash and carry with the fifty quid w'an't you? And you were laughing at the weekend when we had to use all that leccy up?'

She had to smile at this even now. Steve had overdone the rewinding of the meter and they'd had to run every possible appliance to make the reading believable, as the meter man was due. In the baking heat they'd had the oven doors open and the rings blazed all weekend. It surprised them how little electricity it used, how slowly the meter crept back up.

'I know, but I'm worried. I think we're so, I don't know, so exposed. Jonathan keeps such a tight eye on us, being new. I think Sammy's using us as a sort of cover to his own shady deals. I do understand we've got to sell outside, we can't do owt else, but promise me you'll not drive anything else to London for him, will you?' Her voice now had the slightest hint of wheedling. This wasn't a technique she often used, and its scarcity confused Steve. 'Please.'

Steve put his arm around her and he spoke automatically. 'No, I promise I won't do that. I was a bit bothered miss'en, but it's done with now. I do think you've got Sammy wrong, though. He's a man's man, he don't talk to women much. He's a good lad, and he's just trying to help.' He stooped to give her a kiss on the cheek. 'Come on, it's nearly time to fetch the kids from playgroup. We'll try this flaming machine again later. Maybe I'll try and stretch your legs first!'

Karen felt a little better for having spoken her feelings. She found this difficult to do with Steve. Despite having absolutely no gay tendencies she sometimes thought how much more tranquil the world would be if women married women, and they just ventured across the other side for sex. Then it occurred to her the obverse of that solution might well reek enough havoc to blow the world to oblivion. Steve wasn't all bad, she knew. And he did care about her, and that was something in this world of insecurities. She covered the exposed plants with a large piece of cardboard to protect them from the sun. They walked happily up the pathway, nudging and pushing each other in friendly banter, the air cleared for the present. Then Karen stopped in her tracks.

'D'you know something? It wouldn't surprise me if that Sammy's growing dope,' she said suddenly. 'What d' you reckon?'

'Don't talk daft!' he answered.

Twenty-Seven

Myra was falling in love. After twenty years the dodo in her heart was fluttering again. Most of the time she squashed her feelings with good honest housework, but deep in the the tomato plants she had no such vigourous escape. Jim had barred her from the radio for concentration purposes, and with no distractions her feelings ripened along with the fruit. Fred had crossed a boundary, for he was cropping up in her night dreams and had caused her to struggle with the small print on her open return to Nottingham. She worried about sharing her bed with a man again, after so long. This wasn't just the fear of smelly feet or breaking wind – Fred was impeccably clean and didn't seem to have digestive troubles although of course it might be different when he lay down – and should there be "relations" she felt she could cope. It was more the shift in role sharing life with a man again might bring. For years she'd been content on her own, running around after Jim and her other sons when she saw them, vying with their wives, but with long breaks in between when she could secretly put herself first. Could she keep it up all the time? She wasn't sure, and she didn't know how to respond in any other way. It was a real worry.

'He's just a friend,' she said, in response to her grandchildren's teasing across the tea table. She'd met him on the night of the Royal Wedding, and he'd been calling round ever since.

'Fancy Gran being the only one to pull at that disco!' Jo laughed, helping herself to more salad. Everyone was crammed into the dining room, except for Jim who ate from the armchair next door, and Janice, perched on a stall, half in the kitchen, reading a magazine and shutting it all out.

'And why not, she was the best looking woman there, weren't you Gran?' said Paul as he heaped up his plate and surrounded it with chunks of homemade bread. His grandmother had begun to bake it herself. What a treat.

'Janice, will you mek 'em behave, please,' said Myra.

Janice either didn't hear or decided to ignore.

'Did you see the look in her eyes when he asked if he could see her again?'

'I saw 'em snogging.'

'Shut it now! Tell 'em, Janice, will yer.'

'Gran's gettin' married, gonna wed ol' Fred!'

'She loves him! She loves Fred! In bed with Fred!'

Myra felt herself blush. How ridiculous at her age. She got up from the table without finishing her pilchard salad, to make a cup of tea and mask her embarrassment.

'I keep telling you, are y'all deaf or summat? Fred's a friend,' she replied tartly. 'I can have pals can't I, why shouldn't I have someone who understands what it's like to be old and alone! You'll understand when you reach my age.'

'Oh Gran, you haven't finished your salad, it will get cold.' Jo couldn't imagine being Janice's age, let alone Myra's. 'Come on, we're only joking.'

Myra continued making the tea. She poured boiling water into the pot, stirred, replaced the lid and parcelled it all up in a crocheted tea-cosy, the one made by her own fair hand. And all the time facing the wall.

'Come on Gran, sit down.'

'No, duck, I've had enough, I'm full to the brim,' she said. In truth she was getting fed up with salad, salad every single night. It was a wonder they didn't all turn green, she thought. If wives these days ate a bit less salad and a bit more proper food they might be able to look after their

222

menfolk a sight better. And to serve a fully grown man rabbit food, without chips or mashed potato. How could he be expected to work in all weathers on that?

Another reason she'd discarded her dinner was her date with Fred; they were going to the pub. There was nothing clandestine in this, in fact he'd called a few times to take her for an early evening milk stout at the Red Cow. This time though, they were going for a meal, a substantial meat pie, chips and peas. He was treating her, but she didn't want to tell the family and lay herself open to more teasing.

Fred was a widower and lived in a village council house, not one on a vast estate like Myra's but in a rural string of ten such houses on the High Street. He'd kept it impeccably since his wife died and the same meticulous care was taken with his shiny green Morris Minor. Its paint and chrome work reflected and distorted his bulldog face when he polished it and the maroon leather seats shone too. There were no old batteries or jump leads on the floor of his passenger seat, waiting to snag your tights, and his dash was clear of any clutter, free from petrol receipts and ice cream wrappers. His glove compartment was empty apart from a car manual and an AA book. Myra welcomed the order and cleanliness. The general chaos which seemed to prevail over the whole of the Land Settlement, give or take a few holdings, Sylvia's for instance, was beginning to get her down. She was wearing out dishrags and scourers, polishing pads and dusters all to no avail. The nature of her family meant that mud and disorder kept springing back. She scraped her plate and then swilled it under the cold tap before going off to get washed and changed for her tryst.

She put on her twinset of palest blue above a black pleated skirt. She wore her usual dark tights, twisting round to see if the seams were straight, well as straight as possible, curving over the bumpy veins which hid under the surface of the skin like gnarled old roots. 'Character. That's what they are,' she told herself. She surveyed the overall shape of her legs with pride. Many a young woman would be proud of them. She was sure it was good honest hard work which had kept her ankles slim. As she flicked a comb through her chemically black hair, freshly and tightly permed, she heard the toot-toot of a car horn from the road.

'Lover boy's here,' shouted Marie. 'Have a good time, Gran. Don't do anything I wouldn't do.'

Myra thought that if *The Sun* was right about what girls of Marie's age got up to, she wouldn't know where to start. She waited in the front porch as Fred struggled to reverse into the gateway. He just made it, swishing the conifers with his rear wheel arch. Myra made a mental note never to accompany him when he'd had a few to drink. As she climbed carefully into the car, bottom in first, legs last, she saw Jim and Janice waving and laughing from inside the animal pen. The turkeys were poised on the fence, ready to keel over again.

ഛ �

Midge stood at his usual post struggling with the Mirror's two-way crossword, and as he glanced up he saw a green Morris Minor edge cautiously into his car park. Despite this it still managed to straddle two parking bays. Good job the car park's nearly empty, thought Midge. He watched as Fred heaved himself out, limped around the car and opened the passenger door with the flourish of a nineteenth century cavalier. The years had stiffened Fred's limbs and manual work had bent his back so it would be a good few minutes before they appeared in the bar. Midge knew most people's drinks but with Fred he was sometimes caught out, as the old man occasionally chose tonic water instead of a pint, and Myra was still a bit of an unknown quantity. So he didn't get the glasses ready as he tried to do with his regular customers, just incase. To Midge details like this were the mark of a capable host, as was removing the cellophane from cigarette packets before passing them across the bar. He didn't skimp on clean glasses, emptied ashtrays more than once a session and gossip reached the end of the line with him. He often wondered what mayhem he could cause, if he wished. He wasn't adverse to tickling a tale back to life, but he never fanned the fire or added fuel. All these things were in his mental manual "How to be a Good Landlord". Superficial pleasantries and false high spirits, however, were not included. If he felt like being a miserable git, then that was how he'd behave, and he expected his customers to respect that and not take it personally. This behaviour had been formed years ago observing a landlord who almost licked the bar-top, let alone your boots, every time you walked in. Midge had found this embarrassing, and ended up walking two miles in the other direction every night just to be treated normally. Like most people trying to avoid something he went over the top and the most versatile reaction in his repertoire was a sour grunt. This was an invaluable disguise and as he grunted to everyone as a matter of course his true feelings were difficult to read.

Fred and Myra arrived at the bar. He reached up and unhooked the old man's tankard, his retirement present after forty-five years driving a tractor. Most of the regulars had their own pots, and Midge, being small and slight, just managed to reach them. Very dark with a natty moustache, Midge would probably be addressed as a local in Spain or even Greece but as he never took a holiday this hadn't been tested.

'Usual. Fred? And I take it it's a milk stout for the lady?' They agreed this and El Midge ducked below for the bottle. His moustache twitched and hinted a smile; he was as pleasant as he got tonight.

There were two other customers in the Lounge, Mr. Ball

the Estate Manager and Adam the Packhouse Manager. They were deep in conversation, discussing new deals which were being proposed by the supermarkets. There was a great deal of head shaking, this was not an easy discussion, Midge could tell. As he pulled the pump handle, beer rose up Fred's tankard leaving a skimpy covering of froth on top. He placed it on the beer flannel next to Myra's drink and tossed the empty stout bottle in the crate.

'Not got much of an 'ead,' commented Myra. 'Typical southern beer. Where I come from beer 'as to have a certain amount a' head, or you get it thrown back at you! Think it might be regulations.'

Midge's sociable demeanour was obliterated in one swipe. He wasn't used to criticism of his ale, which he prided himself upon. No dirty pipework to his barrels, for he cleaned them religiously.

He grunted. 'Then it just shows they know nothing. Froth's only air, so they're losing out on beer.' He made no attempt to change it. Now he realised they were about to order food. Pity they hadn't been twenty minutes earlier and he could have cooked theirs along with the other order.

'You're doing food today, aren't you?' asked Myra, more out of politeness than anything else. Midge reluctantly agreed that he was.

'Hmm. Nothing fancy though,' Midge said. 'All we've got's meat pie, chips and peas. Yes or no?' They had known it was going to be meat pie. It always was. Midge hardly ever cooked anything else.

'Yes duck, lovely, fine,' said Myra.

Fred remembered Janice's billy. Myra had told him it had disappeared, and her daughter-in-law wouldn't tell her where to.

'Er..excuse me, but what kind of meat is it?' asked Fred, terribly politely. Fred's good manners were something Myra especially liked about him. She felt sure that if somebody pranged his precious car, he'd still manage to pull an "excuse me" from somewhere. Don't make 'em like that nowadays, she thought.

'Meat,' said Midge firmly, thinking why the bloody inquisition? I thought they were hungry. Then relenting a little he added: 'Look, it'll be nice and filling. Now do you want it or not?'

They went to sit down, not far from the two men who were still talking earnestly. Myra lit a Woodbine and Fred took out his pipe. He surveyed her fondly; all neat and tidy, deeply wrinkled neck disappearing into powder blue. Her legs were crossed over twice, at the knee and at the ankle, one patent black shoe peeping behind the other. She looked smart, he thought. Just above her pearl necklace however, there was smudge of white paint. It showed up sharp against her suntan. He leaned forward and wagged his forefinger at her.

'I reckon you've been painting!' Fred said triumphantly. He'd always wanted to be a policeman. He folded his arms on top of his large belly which was disguised by an enormous Marks and Spencers pullover. His pipe had gone out and it lay discarded on a beer mat. Myra was chain lighting another Woodbine.

'Ooh, 'ow do you know?' asked Myra. Her strong voice echoed across the room as any unfamiliar lilt does.

'You've still got some paint on your neck. What are you doing now, decorating Janice's parlour?'

'No, nowt like that, though it could surely do wi' a lick. No, I'm painting out the name on these boxes,' said Myra. 'So as we can use 'em again to put tomatoes in. Jim's got 'undreds of 'em. Took me all day it did.'

Midge, leaning on the bar while the chip pan warmed up, watched Jack Ball and Adam stop talking for a moment. He knew they'd heard what she'd said. Midge lifted the hatch in the bar and walked across to Fred and Myra with cutlery and serviettes. Fred felt pleased; they were usually just slapped upon the bar along with the plateful of food and a shout. Then he realised Midge had given this personal service for a reason.

'Mrs Carter, you need to watch what you say,' he whispered. 'They're LSA guv'nors over there. You'll get your Jim shot!'

Twenty-Eight

Sara, office junior in the Land Settlement Association Estate office, watched the big hand on the office clock drag its way towards three o'clock. It was Friday afternoon and at three she could leave her desk to deliver the weekly Land Settlement newsletter. She liked this job because it was a break from the daily routine and if she finished early she still got paid her usual hours.

Historically this newsletter had been revered by the growers, they'd christened it the "Bulletin". Now it focussed their discontent. Some still eagerly awaited its arrival and walked to the roadside to take it from her hand. Some like Josh and Sammy protested too much, they swore they never bothered reading it. Old Vic and George had Bulletins going back donkey's years, proof that the style remained much the same, despite five different Estate managers in George's time and seven in Vic's.

The present manager, Jack Ball, shared his duties between two estates like a modern day country vicar. The Bulletin communicated between Mr Ball's two estates and growers could advertise equipment and write open letters, although the threat of eviction affected quite how open those letters might be. It was also used to welcome new growers onto the estates and to wish well those who were leaving. The "Watch Out This Week" column gave details of current pest and disease risks and the two packing shed managers wrote a review, commenting on good quality produce or high incidence of fly as necessary. There was always a break down of prices from the previous week and the figures for the combined output of the two estates were published. Jack Ball usually wrote a few lines as well, often commenting on this output. Generally it was a bland paragraph that couldn't be fixed to any particular week but today it contained a warning. Sara had been instructed to type it in capitals.

She looked again at the clock, ten to three. All she had to do now was push a few late letters through the franking machine. Then she saw Jonathan and Mr Ball pass her open door and pause, deep in discussion, in reception. Sara was Jonathan's girlfriend, and very much in love with him although she was sometimes doubtful that he felt the same. He was five years older than her, and into this age gap, which she considered to be vast, she cast all her excuses for his shortcomings. He was a real man as opposed to the boys she'd dated before, he even had his own house in Wansbridge. Her dream was that they'd be married, and live in some anonymous little house chosen by both of them. She occasionally stayed at his house overnight, but if she had to live there she'd make lots of changes, brighten the place up, for a start. When she'd franked the letters, she moved towards the door, just to hear Jonathan's voice.

'Well, I know Jack,' her lover was saying.

She felt a shiver of pride that he spoke so familiarly to the Boss. That showed how important he was. She knew none of the growers referred to him as Jack.

'- and I have proof.' He lowered his voice and Sara crept nearer, pretending to rearrange some folders on a shelf. Her job was so tedious a bit of gossip helped lift the day, and try as she did to make him, Jonathan never told her anything, not even in bed. "Oh, shut up about that bloody place," he said. "I have it all week, and so do you. Let's forget it." Now she had live gossip.

'Proof?' Jack Ball was interested, his deep voice rose an octave.

'Well yes, as good as. On Tuesday I went to the bank, at lunchtime, you know, to get the petty cash. At the desk next to me was Fensome's wife, you know, the one that doesn't mix. Sylvia, I think she's called. Anyway she didn't notice me, she was serving one of her cronies. The woman was saying that she didn't know how people made a living on the LSA and Sylvia, said, and I quote, "we are doing very nicely thank you, Dennis sends most of his tomatoes to Brighton!". I think she was exaggerating a bit because she was obviously pissed off by the way the woman was patronising her, but there you have it. You wanted proof and I've got it for you.'

Jack Ball sucked air in through his teeth, his mouth stretched into a triangle. He was a bulky man, not fat but had obviously been very muscular in his younger days. Now the flesh laid thick as these muscles waned. About sixty years of age, his body would still shame many men half his age. He was ideal as a figurehead, but his social skills towards the growers were lacking. He tried to avoid them if at all possible, a task made easier by running two estates concurrently. Jonathan waited for his reply and eventually it came.

'Wrong tree, lad,' he said. 'You're barking up the wrong tree there, sonny Jim.'

'What?'

'Well, that's no good, now is it? Exposing our best grower, the cream of our crop. It may be true, but it wouldn't be clever, now would it?' He poked his tongue out over his yellowing teeth and Jonathan was reminded of an old nag.

'So you're letting him get away with it?' he asked in disbelief. 'Cheating the Packhouse like that? Anyway a premium grower like him should know better.' Deflation showed in his face, Jack must have noticed, for he said:.

'Well, it doesn't surprise me, and Dennis probably has

enough equity to move on soon. But I agree, it has to be stopped,' His voice rose strongly. 'No question, it has to be stopped. I'll not have growers cheating the Settlement. We will let them digest the warning in the newsletter, and then we'll pull out all the stops, I say pull out all the stops. And catch one of our losers, one of our waste of spaces. God knows we have enough of them. And you will be foremost in this operation, Jonathan, Paramount!'

Damn, thought Jonathan, I'm paramount in everything, but my wages don't seem to increase.

He said aloud: 'Jack, I shall need help, though. You know how these wasters stick together, that Sammy Dove, take him, now it's near impossible to get on his land. If you survive the mutts, he's got that crazy hippie's goose. Then there's head cases like Vera Clay and Josh. Nobody's safe around those two, I think they're both nutters. My pay doesn't include danger money, it certainly doesn't feel as if it does!' He had managed to squeeze in the smallest of digs. Sara, listening, felt a flush of pride for her man.

Jack Ball ignored this reference to money and demonstrating his management skills twisted Jonathan's outburst to his own advantage.

'You were chosen, Jonathan, from a long line of applicants *precisely* because we felt that in your interview you demonstrated an ability to deal with cantankerous characters like them. *I* certainly have no cause to doubt you on that count, so you must have more confidence in yourself!' He patted him on the shoulder.

Slippery old bastard, thought Jonathan. Anger prickled him. He was at a loss for what to say.

'Anyway,' continued Jack Ball, 'The growers will see, when they read the newsletter, that the supermarkets want to scrutinize the crop in the field. So that will help your cause, young man, I say that will surely help your cause! Now if you'll excuse me I'm due on the golf course in twenty minutes.'

Jonathan wished he could get interested in golf, he felt it might help his career. But the only sport which remotely interested him was pool, but he'd never ever play in the Red Cow where the growers frequented. Now both men left by the main exit and as Sara heard the unlatched door bang against the secured one, she went to the window to catch a glimpse of her boyfriend. She saw he'd taken a different direction across the yard from his boss, but through her rose-coloured glasses she failed to notice the droop of his head, the hunch of his shoulders or the absence of his sunglasses. She turned to look at the clock. It was two minutes past three. She hurried to fetch her shoulder bag and picked up the roneoed sheets from her desk. There were two pages for each grower, she'd stapled them herself. She turned and poked her head through to the next office, where Muriel rattled away on her typewriter at a hundred miles an hour.

'I'm off to deliver the newsletter, Muriel,' she said.

'Alright for some!' Muriel answered, her shoulders moving and the machine still vibrating. She had her back to Sara and didn't even look round.

'And then I'll go straight home,' she persisted. 'Jonathan's taking me to the pictures tonight.'

'OK.'

What a cow, thought Sara. No matter how she tried, she seemed unable to get this woman to chat, like people did in normal offices. Still, once she was married to Jonathan he'd save her from all this. She could stay at home and prepare his tea and give birth to his babies. She fetched her bicycle, swung her leg over the crossbar and pedalled across the road and out onto the Drift.

Sunshine was attempting to force through the thick haze but there was an extra heaviness in the atmosphere today. The noises from the Packhouse yard drifted across to her on the still air. Two lorry drivers were hosing their wagons. Friday afternoon was a quiet time for them, and the staff were clearing up. A lone fork-lift jerked a bin of rubbish across an empty section of yard, the operator taking less care then usual. Clanks, squeaks and the rattle of running water rang out eerily loud. Then the machinery fell silent and a wolf-whistle drifted through the chainlink fence, and she smiled to herself, keeping her head down as she pedalled past.

''Hello beautiful!'

'Hello darling!'

More whistles, and she flashed them the fleetest of smiles. It didn't occur to her to find them offensive, she wouldn't be burning her bra. They picked up on it, and the shouts increased.

'Whoa there! Anythin' in that bag for me?'

She pedalled harder, and the weak sunshine struggled through a little, reflecting on her fair hair. She hoped Jonathan had heard the attention she was getting. It wouldn't hurt him to see other men thought her attractive.

At first delivering the Bulletin had seemed a big task, but now she was used to it she generally completed it within the hour. She tried to catch as many growers as she could from the roadway to save her legs and keep her fingers from being nipped by the narrow letter boxes. She empathised with the postman when he had to deliver A4 envelopes, the metal covers of those letter boxes were so stiff and tight. At Scofflaw Sammy's she wouldn't attempt to go through his gate because of the dogs. She always tucked his Bulletin through an elaborate twist in his wrought iron gate.

As she reached Dennis's holding, a car slowed as it passed her and drew to a halt a few yards in front. The woman driver leaned over and beckoned to her through the open window. She was smartly dressed, and Sara recognised Sylvia, whom Jonathan had just been telling Mr Ball about.

'I'll take that, my dear,' the woman said. 'If it will help.'

'Cheers,' said Sara, astride her bike, reaching in the bag and passing her a newsletter. 'There's a warning in there,' she said. Some instinct had made her feel she should alert the woman, but she immediately wondered why she'd bothered.

'A warning?' said Sylvia, smiling patronisingly. 'Well I must admit that I never read the thing, I leave that to Mr. Fensome. But if it's got a warning, then I'm obviously missing out. I'll make sure I read it. Bye now!' And she was gone in a cloud of dust.

Next she managed a double whammy as Janice was talking to Nigel by the roadside. They were deep in conversation about goats, hardly registering her presence.

'Cheers, Sara,' said Janice. 'I mean take this thing.' She waved the Bulletin. 'We could advertise for other goatkeepers, there's bound to be some on our sister estate.'

'Aye, if they'd do it. What d'you think, luv,' he said to Sara. 'Could we put an advert in to do wi' goats?'

Sara knew the answer to this one. She remembered someone wanting to advertise day old chicks. The Bulletin had been all ready to print and she'd had to re-do a page. Mr Ball had intervened. 'No, you can't put nothing in what's not horticultural. It's not professional, you see.'

By now the pall of smoke had thickened again to totally block the afternoon sun, leaving a yellowish gloom. Sara could taste it now, and she realised the farmer was burning stubble on the huge field directly behind the holdings.

Josh was sitting on the grass verge with Guy, they were sharing a quart bottle of cider.

'Give it 'ere, darling, and the newsletter!' Josh called out, and she rode over to where they were sitting, stopping her bike at ninety degrees to them. 'Let's see what load o' crap's in it this week!'

Sara had dated Guy briefly when she was just fifteen, an

age ago it seemed, and it had ended in embarrassment. She avoided his eye now.

'It's not crap! I typed it myself,' she said to Josh, importantly.

'How's your boyfriend?' Guy's nerve was bolstered by Josh's presence.

'He's fine, thank you,' said Sara haughtily. He's better at kissing than you were, she thought.

'She goes out with Jonathan,' explained Guy to Josh.

Josh pretended to choke on his cider. 'With that dickhead? A pretty girl like you?'

Sara knew her boyfriend wasn't popular with the growers. 'At least he's not a pisshead like you.' She directed her comments very obviously towards Guy. 'It's only twenty past three!'

Guy said nothing, but Josh answered good naturedly: 'We've got to drink, to settle all this smoke. Otherwise we'll end up with bronchitis,' he said indicating Guy, 'and you'll have to rub his chest!'

'Dream on,' said Sara as she cycled off. What idiots, she thought, as their laughter chased her, easy on the heavy air.

She saw Maisie, tearing creeping weeds from her hedge. She was wheezing badly.

'There you go!' Sara said as she passed her a Bulletin.

'Ain't this smoke horrid, dear,' said Maisie wrinkling her nose, big chest heaving up and down. 'Have a nice weekend.' Maisie squinted at the Bulletin more from habit than anything else, and anyway she didn't have her reading glasses. She folded it carefully and put it in her pocket for George. Sara rode off into the gloom.

Then she saw nobody until Nicole and Simon, who were walking along the roadway together, obviously bothered by the smoke. Nicole took the Bulletin and eyed it curiously.

'Thank you. What is it?' she asked Sara.

What do you think it is, Scotch mist, thought Sara. It

was an expression Muriel in the office used.

Simon took the Bulletin from Nicole. 'Thank you very much,' he said to Sara. 'Just the weekly communication from our autocratic leader,' he told his wife.

What weirdoes, thought Sara. But that's another done.

One house she always tried to creep up on was Vera Clay's, although this was nearly impossible as Vera's timid husband Gerry knew to his cost every time he tried to sneak up the garden for a cigarette. Vera, unusual amongst the growers, was very precious about her front flower beds. She objected to Sara jumping the low hedge and skipping across her bedding plants, which must have been set with a lettuce planter, such was the precision of their spacing. To Vera, Sara, young and innocent as she was, represented the collective enemy of the LSA, and she never failed to shout something controversial at the poor girl if she got the chance.

Today the coast looked clear. Everything was ship-shape, the empty pallets were stacked neatly and the rotary clothes line sported only polythene bags. Nobody was to be seen. Sara slung her bike and leapt the neatly clipped box hedge. Her heel sunk into the corner of the bed and she squashed a french marigold flat. She shoved the Bulletin in the tight letter box with urgency but the door flung open at her push. Vera stood there, face dark and fierce under blue sculptured hair.

'Bloody useless the lot of you!' she shrieked, as she snatched the two sheets from the metal jaws. Sara retreated up the path and retrieved her bike. 'And this is a lot of useless rubbish!' She shook the papers angrily.

'You'd better read it, it's got a warning,' Sara called over her shoulder.

'Warning!' screeched Vera. 'It's you what needs a bloody warning! Courting that toerag Jonathan. Can't you do better than that? GERRY! Where are you? Fetch me glasses!'

'Old bat!' said Sara over her shoulder as she rode to safety.

It was just after four o'clock when she delivered the last one, and was free to cycle home, wash the dust and the smoke from her hair and make herself beautiful for Jonathan.

છ   ભ

It was not only the Bulletin which drew residents to the roadside on a Friday. Between six and seven in the evening children hung around waiting for the mobile fish and chip shop, listening out for its loud hailer. The van also sold bottles of Coke, Fanta and other drinks. It had various sweets on board too. This was presumably to pressurise families into buying a fish and chip supper by tempting the children, and fish and chips were relatively expensive. Karen found it hard to believe England's second national dish had once been a cheap alternative. Now it seemed an extravagance to her. If they'd had a successful afternoon at the auction there'd be money for this treat, but if not the children had to watch the van sail by.

Today there was money, and the family were ready and waiting. The chipped formica table was laid, the plates were warming, and the mushy peas bubbled in a saucepan. Buttered bread was cut in triangles and placed on a plate in the centre along with the vinegar bottle. Next to it was a squeezy over-ripe tomato, congealed sauce clinging to the centre of its green plastic calyx. Karen always made an effort for a fish and chip supper, although Steve would complain they tasted better straight from the paper, and the children would prefer to eat in front of the television as usual. He'd also say they weren't a patch on Yorkshire fish and chips, and then go on to pine for Dandelion and Burdock. She could see him developing into a regular ex-pat. She even made tea in a tea-pot so they could drink it with the meal and she wouldn't have to leap up from the table straight away.

Waiting for the van, Karen flicked idly through the Bulletin as the children fooled around on the verge nearby. Steve was busy somewhere. She snatched the chance to enjoy a few moments of peace. The capital letters soon caught her eye:

WARNING

WE HAVE REASON TO BELIEVE THAT SEVERAL GROWERS (CONTRARY TO REGULATIONS) ARE SELLING PRODUCE ELSEWHERE. I MUST WARN YOU THAT THIS IS AGAINST YOUR TENANCY AGREEMENT, AND THAT ACTION WILL BE TAKEN AGAINST ANYONE SO DOING. WE ARE AWARE OF THE CULPRITS AND THE MATTER WILL BE DEALT WITH AS IT HAS BEEN DEALT WITH IN THE PAST

J. Ball, Estate Manager

Karen shuddered; she'd heard described in detail how a man and his pregnant wife were dragged screaming from their house and into the oblivion of the outside world. Each time a different grower related the saga the poignancy of the tale increased. She had originally been under the impression that the pregnancy was their first child, but each time the tale was retold another infant was added, as if to make the authority's action even more heartless and wicked. Like all embroidered tales there was likely a good base of truth. She knew she was going to have to speak with Steve yet again, who under Sammy's influence was becoming more blasé about selling outside. But at least he'd kept his promise and declined any more driving jobs.

80 ᘒ

Maisie made a rare effort to cross the lawn and enter her husband's domain. George was puffing on his pipe and admiring his geraniums. The new miniature range with the inky leaves were now bushy plants, busting all over with blooms. The catalogue had been true, they were indeed little dazzlers.

'Look, Maisie,' he said as his wife entered, easing her bum carefully past the ivy leafed varieties which were cascading over the bench. 'What d'you reckon to these little beauties?' Maisie looked at them and pulled a face.

'You care what I think? I think as you think more o' these flippin' flowers than you do o' me. Just like that Nigel thinks more o' his goats than his missus.'

'Well that's 'cause they don't nag me, my little nasturtium,' George said, solemnly. 'Now if you wore yer lipstick this colour,' he pointed to a vivid orange, 'then I mebbe I might jus' fancy you again!' She pretended to be upset, and George put an arm around her fleshy shoulders. 'No, you'll be alright, gel,' he said. 'These, lovely as they are, won't keep me warm at night!'

Maisie handed him the Bulletin. She dropped straight out of roleplay and became serious.

'I remember as you'd look forward to this,' she said. 'Now I don't reckon you'd as much as pick it up if weren't for me showin' it you.'

George puffed hard on his pipe. 'Tell the truth, gel, I've 'ad enough lately. I feel there's somethin' in the air, summat up, y'now what I mean. Lately I been wondering whether we oughta be thinking of moving out from 'ere. I'll tell you summat else too, I ain't standin' for Grower's Rep this year. I reckon it's time for someone like young Tim to take over. Me 'eart just ain't in it any more, Maisie.'

Silence fell as they both digested the implications of this. Maisie cast her eye around the old greenhouse, and the spectacular display of pot plants. It looked more like a winning stand at the Chelsea Flower Show. She wouldn't make much comment until everything had been turned around in her mind.

'Umm, well,' Maisie said, eventually. 'I s'pose it's 'ere with these Pot Plants where your 'eart is, George.'

'Right my little marigold, what was it that you was bustin' to show me in this ole rag?' George asked, brightening again. She smoothed the bulletin on the bench and pointed in the weakening light to the sentence in upper case. George tilted his head back and held the page at arm's length. He'd left his reading glasses in the dining room.

'Hmm,' he said. 'I hope Jim takes note o' this.' His voice sounded concerned. 'In fact, I hope most of 'em take notice.'

'Well if everyone's at it they can't do nothin', can they?' Maisie asked logically.

'Oh, they're just looking for a scapegoat, you know, someone to pick out an example of,' he added when he saw her blank face. 'Then everyone'll behave, get in line again. It's what 'appened before when there was an eviction,' he said. 'Trouble is, I reckon as it's too late for some o' them poor devils, all the debt they got an' that. Not that the Settlement care, We've been lucky, Maisie, we've seen the best years and we mustn't forget that.' He tapped her fondly on the head with the bulletin which he'd now rolled up conclusively.

Maisie agreed that they mustn't.

೫ ೱ

Hazel, stretched out on the settee like a cat, was reading *The Thorn Birds*. Sam and Nathan were playing with Lego, Sam making simple guns as usual, Nathan something much more intricate and just as destructive. Bits of Lego spread right across the carpet to the walls. Eddie entered and stood at the door in his socks. He looked cross even before he stood on any. The television played loudly to itself and both boys set about shooting him.

'Didn't you hear me shouting? You must all be deaf.'

'*Bang.*'

'*Wheee! Bang!*'

'Umm?' said Hazel, peeping lazily from behind her paperback.

'Come on, gel, the van's almost due. I'm ready for me fish and chips.'

Oh sod it, thought Hazel. I don't fancy standing out there. No chance of seeing Jonathan this time of day.

'But I've got supper planned. I thought I'd bung some pies in the oven tonight, and we've got frozen chips.'

'You know I love me proper fish and chips. Being Catholic, it's law on a Friday.'

'So why can't you go?'

'You're the flaming cook. Why should I? I've been working all day while you've been reading some smutty love story.'

'Anyway, fish is all polluted now you know, something to do with some nuclear power station.'

'Cut the crap and I'll give you some extra housekeeping, if you'll go. How does fifteen quid sound?'

Hazel jumped up and *The Thorn Birds* bit the dust. She gave him a hug and a smack of a kiss on his lips.

'Ok, ok. That'll do. A cod and chips for me,' he said, pleased.

'You can have a whale if you want, you lovely man,' she said. Now she could buy that sexy top.

ℝ ℞

Myra saw the notice first, when she went in to make a cup of tea. She now relayed it just to Jim like it was a conspiracy between the two of them, much to Janice's annoyance. Old bitch, she thought.

'What'll we do, Jim?' Myra asked, as the three of them drank tea in the evening warmth of the conservatory. 'How many of them boxes I painted have you got left? That'll all be wasted time and money,' she said. Secretly she was concerned about her indiscretions in the Red Cow a week or so ago.

Jim dismissed the warning as an empty threat. His philosophy was to keep his head down, grow to the best of his ability and avoid gossip. He knew all about how depression spreads like rotten apples. Just now he was more bothered by the stubble burning in the farmer's field behind. Huge plumes of smoke were rolling across the top half of his land.

'Never mind that Ma – it's this bloody smoke – I wish this damn government would ban it,' he said. 'It's not necessary, and all that stuff about the carbon adding minerals to the soil is a load of old bull.'

'I suppose it's fair comment that it does get rid of pests and diseases,' said Janice. She had first hand knowledge of soil borne problems such as rhizoctonia and sclerotinia. Growers had to have their houses commercially and professionally sterilised by methyl bromide every couple of years or so. She understood that farmers were unable to do that.

Jim said: 'Well we don't get the problem outside, do we, and neither do they. And all the technology and money in the world is ploughed in on wheat and corn. Look at the selective herbicides and subsidies which are available to them. It's just an excuse, they're too bloody lazy to plough it in properly and too tight to pay someone to bale it.'

There were attempts by the Green lobby to persuade the government to ban stubble burning, especially as housing estates were creeping further and further into the countryside and the modern disinfectant-crazed housewife was less inclined to put up with the dust and dirt which the practice created each summer. It was a general inconvenience to everyday life, and people enjoying their gardens were choked out and forced back indoors. Regulations stating specified times for burning were imminent, declaring evening and weekends smoke free. But this hadn't happened yet.

'Well as usual, both of you ignore the real problem,' broke in Myra. 'What'll happen if you're kicked out from 'ere?'

'Don't you worry about that Ma,' said Jim. 'That bloody lot down there couldn't catch a fart in their underpants! You just concentrate on summat more important, like what's for me tea?'

'Fish supper!' said Myra, quickly, back in a world she understood. 'It's nearly time for the van. And I baked a lovely deep custard tart for afters. Your favourite, Jim.'

଄ ଓ

Sammy scanned his Bulletin as he walked up his path. He studied the return figures slightly more carefully, then grunted and ripped the communication in half. He tossed it at the rubbish bin as he walked into his house. It missed and he didn't bother to retrieve it.

'What a load of pillocks they are,' he laughed. 'I'd like to see them bring some poncey supermarket geezer round my nursery,' he added, 'Don't cook anything, Mo,' he said to his wife who was watching television with her feet up and didn't look as if the idea had entered her head. 'Let's have fish and chips tonight.'

Twenty-Nine

The next morning the weather had changed and the sky was flat and grey. When Janice went to milk Bernadette at six-thirty she felt a strong breeze fresh on her face, blowing her hair into her eyes. The greenhouses were rattling again and the top of the barn door was banging where it hadn't been properly secured the previous night. The warm wind was gusting around the sheds, bending the upper branches of the poplar trees. Their leaves, which fluttered even in the slightest breath of air were rustling noisily now, and the lower branches creaked loudly as they swayed.

Entering the piggery she fed the pigs in their troughs, giving them a special treat, milk left over from yesterday. She was careful not to let Bernadette see this. She didn't want to break confidence with the old goat yet again; the memory of the stolen kid was still prominent in Janice's mind. The pigs squealed and snuffled in delight. Janice thought it a happy reassuring sound. When she'd finished she took the enamel bucket and swilled it under the outside tap. The wind was so strong here it disrupted the run of the water, splashing her in the face. She returned to the shed with her clean pail.

She conversed as usual with Bernadette as she squeezed her plump handles (what a derogatory term, Janice always thought, but one recommended by the goat fraternity) and the milk swooshed into the pail. It was easy to confide aloud in a goat, she found. It wasn't like talking to a sheep or a pig, she felt that would be embarrassing. It had all started when she'd found it necessary to talk to Bernadette to relax her, and now the nanny would only stand still and co-operate fully when Janice spoke softly to encourage her.

Gradually their relationship strengthened, and before she realised it, Janice was voicing her feelings and opinions to the wise old Saanan. As long as she kept her tone soft and her fingers gentle, she could tell her anything. This was quite therapeutic because Janice had always found it difficult to confide in anyone. So Bernadette was honoured and the grateful goat often turned and looked at her in a special way with those strange horizontal pupils. She guessed it was a bit like having her own confessional, the goat the equivalent of a hidden priest, but without the inconvenience of Hail Mary's. Today she was dissing her mother-in-law, and finding it difficult to keep her voice calm or her fingers gentle.

'That woman, Bernadette, is already up and putting the washing on the line. I saw her as I swilled the pail, and she's doing it deliberately to make a point. She's out to make everyone think how good she is, at nearly seventy. And how bad I am, letting her do it!' She squeezed a little too hard and Bernadette moved sharply, just avoiding knocking the pail over.

'Sorry Bernadette! Only yesterday Eric said to her: "You're a remarkable woman, Mrs Carter. How do you pack so much in a day?" And do you know what she said, Bernadette? She said: "Well it has to get done, Eric." And then she took him inside the house, and showed him what she'd scrubbed, what she'd darned, what she'd fixed, and seven flipping blackberry pies she'd made ready for the freezer. The poor man came out exhausted, he did. What she really meant was look at me, I'm efficient, and look at that Janice, the useless slut. And do you know what, Bernadette?' Her monologue slowed as the spurts of milk lessened and became dribbles. 'I know she's right, I'm not the best at housework. And I know it's because I hate it. But she's making me feel inferior and Jim and the kids think it's funny. She's pushing me out in me own home. I know I should be grateful, because she's leaving me more time for looking after you and the other animals and working the nursery, but I'm not, Bernadette, I'm not!' She broke off and moved the bucket of milk out of harm's way. She scratched Bernadette's wiry white coat along the ridge her back. 'Come on, girl. Let's have you out in the fresh air.'

She began to lead the goat by the collar, and as she got to the door she saw Myra walking across the grass towards her, nylon housecoat flapping in the wind.

'Janice! JANICE!' she shouted, her voice partly carried away on a gust.

Myra had hung some white sheets on the long line, and they were thrashing about possessed, some already bunched and tangled up. The rest of the washing was still in the basket.

'Look! Me washing's all covered in smuts! Just like we live in a coalfield!'

'Wait until I've put Bernadette in the pen,' called Janice. 'She's partial to a bit of clean washing.' She noticed the breeze was carrying tiny black particles. No prizes for guessing where they've come from, she thought.

'What'll I do?' Myra yelled.

'Leave 'em out, it'll brush off when they're dry,' shouted Janice, tethering Bernadette to a post with a long rope. She knew they'd blow off the line and shamefully thought this was something she'd like to see, her mother-in-law chasing the sheets round the holding. The goat turned her back to the wind, bent her head and eagerly tucked into the grass. She was comparatively sheltered in her pen. Janice went to the gateway and plucked a few sow thistles. They made a hollow popping noise as the stems broke and the thistle-down burst and flew off into the air, lifted high on the breeze above the glass village.

Myra was shaking her head and tutting as she stuffed the smutty washing back into the slatted plastic basket. Then she balanced it on her bony hip. As she passed Janice the other side of the wire fence, she said:

'You can't leave it out! Our Jim'll not want to sleep in mucky sheets, he was always fussy about his bed. No, I'll 'ave to wash it all over again!'

Damn her. 'He wasn't so fussy about who was in it before I met him,' said Janice, partly under her breath. She hand-fed Bernadette who sucked in each sow thistle whole.

'What? What did you say, duck?' Her dangling Woodbine battled to stay alight.

'Nothing,' sighed Janice, and Myra heaved the basket back into the house, still chuntering. Janice walked back to the piggery to retrieve the warm milk. There'd been no talk of when her mother-in-law was returning to Nottingham, and now she had latched on to old Fred goodness knows when it would be. She had mentioned it to Jim but he reared up whenever she complained. She was an old lady, he said, and she meant well. Janice couldn't argue with that, but all she could see was the hidden agenda.

୭ ଓ

Later that day the first few spots of rain splashed onto Eric's windscreen. He had pulled his Volvo into a lay-by out on the back road, to eat his spam and tomato sandwiches and listen to *The Archers*. As the signature tune wound up the episode, he switched off at the button. He pushed his head-rest slightly so he was leaning back, and closed his eyes. He was weary and ready for a holiday, but he didn't have any annual leave due now until Christmas. He recalled his conversation earlier that morning with Jack Ball, the Estate manager...

Jack had summoned Eric by a telephone call to the ADAS area headquarters, and on his arrival at the LSA office Eric had been shown into Jack's lair by Muriel, the typist.

He'd found the boss of the Estate sitting with his legs crossed in an oval-backed wooden chair, and he'd motioned Eric to pull up a similar one. His body language appeared agitated; his right eyelid had a slight tick and as he drummed his fingers on the padded leather top of his carved walnut desk, two gold rings flashed, one on the middle finger, one on the little finger.

Jack launched in with: 'Now I know like me you're a busy man so I won't beat around the bush, I have heard from my sources and may I say reliable ones, that some of these foolish growers on this Estate are selling outside of the co-operative, in breach of the regulations. It's my job, nay duty, to bring these cheats to task. Now I know that you are welcome on all the holdings, whereas these malcontents are sly and devious with my staff.' He paused, to allow this abrupt shower of words to soak in.

Eric sat still and looked hard at him, guessing what was coming, but giving no hint of his feelings in the matter.

'Now I know that we work for different agencies but we both work for the future of horticulture as our government sees it. So in short Eric I want names, I say, I must have names. These people are making a laughing stock of us all!'

Eric appreciated his bluntness if nothing else. He hated people who skated around the point, life was too short for that. Apparently Jack felt the need for a little secrecy as he thrust his huge face towards Eric and his voice became a whisper, chin against chin, one sprinkled with stubble, the other dark and bristly. Jack's top lip curled away from his huge front teeth. 'And of course they must be the right names, Eric, if you take my meaning!'

Eric backed away slightly as the other man resumed his diatribe.

'I need to know, nay, have to know who these black-marketers are, they're letting the Association down, and we won't get a contract with the supermarkets if we can't guarantee the produce and that will affect everyone.' His large hands came to rest on his belly, but his neck and face were still thrust forward in earnest.

Eric cleared his throat and replied cautiously: 'In market gardening nothing is one hundred percent certain, no crop is one hundred percent definite..'

Jack Ball hated careful calculated replies. Text book talk, he called it. He nipped Eric's diplomacy in the bud.

'All the more reason to have the throughput of produce. The surplus can always be sold on the wholesale markets. It's in their interests, I say, it's in their interests!' He thumped flamboyantly on his desk in exasperation, because he had actually respected this man, and by evidence of what he wasn't saying, Eric seemed prepared to stick up for these no-hopers. He could see it in the Advisor's face.

'I've heard that many of them are in such hopeless debt that I wonder whether growing anything at all is in their interests,' Eric said patiently. It was quite a contrast of styles.

Jack Ball raised his eyebrows slightly in suprise, and the big tongue danced briefly around those teeth. 'That's true,' he agreed. 'You always get those who fall by the wayside in any industry, Eric, you should know that. Deadwood. That's the term. Leading a horse to water, come *on*, Eric.'

'Well yes, but I can't understand the Association letting the debts mount so high. Some people owe upwards of forty thousand pounds and with no equity apart from a glasshouse or two that's certain bankruptcy. And they'll be homeless too, don't forget that.'

Jack briefly considered this. Eric watched as his mouth made a selection of shapes as he chewed his tongue and licked his lips. The man is half animal, he thought. Then Jack selected a stance and opened his hands in a gesture of openness and honesty.

'I believe, between you and me, that the Association is about to pull the plug on them. And if they're homeless they'll get a council house. But nobody's going to escape from their financial difficulties by sitting on their butt. Get to work and sort it out, that's what I say to them!'

'Isn't it working that has got them into this position anyway?' asked Eric coldly. He wanted to disassociate from Jack Ball now, and he abandoned his calm manner, or perhaps it abandoned him. He continued with iron in his voice, face slightly flushed. 'Hasn't the debt accrued by buying more plants from the prop, and more packaging materials and fertilisers and things from The Stores – and on quarterly credit? And then finding the returns don't cover the outlay? It isn't as if they've been jetting off to the Bahamas for a fortnight every year, is it?'

'Come on Eric! Look at this motley crew. Yes, it's true that a lot is owed by way of materials. The rest is living expenses and equipment. I'm afraid that times are hard in the industry, as you yourself know better than anyone. We cannot afford to carry deadwood or freeloaders, I say we can't afford to carry deadwood.' He spat the words with contempt. 'And you would be doing some of them a favour by telling me who is breaking their tenancy agreement.'

Eric had stood up to leave. He shook his head firmly. 'Jack,' he said, 'I am an ADAS officer. I exist purely to advise the growers on technical matters, and since my services now cost I receive much less business from them than I used to. I do not know what happens to their produce after harvest, but I would suggest to you that if they are selling elsewhere then they're doing it because they feel that your marketing organisation is failing them, and that their debts force them to look for cash in hand. I hope you bear those facts in mind when you're carrying out your detective work, which, incidentally, I want no part in at all! Good day to you, Jack.' And Eric left the office, marched to his car, and drove to where he was now...

Reflecting now upon the events of the morning he was proud of his outburst, but he also knew he was unable to stay detached from the growers' plight. Try as he might, he couldn't help worrying about the future of families like Steve's, Eddie's and even Josh's, just like he couldn't help worrying about his daughter Gail, although it had been quiet for some time on that front, touch wood.

The sound of rain drumming on the car roof made him open his eyes and sit up with a start. Water streamed down the windscreen as if from a hosepipe, and he had to set the wipers to super-speed before he could see clearly. He tucked his empty Tupperware box into the glove compartment and waited for a lorry to pass, splattering the old Volvo with spray, before he could pull out on to the road to return to the office.

Thirty

The rain, which died away towards the end of the afternoon, refreshed the whole Estate. The moisture settled the dust on the surface of the Drift and deposited it as thin lines of mud caught in the ripples in the concrete. The earth smelt sweet again, a moist fresh smell which Karen always noticed when she switched the overhead irrigation lines on in a greenhouse.

Jim heard the telephone ring, courtesy of his outside bell. He came running down to answer it, cursing because he was measuring some concentrate, a tricky job. I'll kill our Marie, he thought, if it's another lovesick sod after her. But it was Adam the Packhouse Manager on the line. He only rang growers personally when he was desperate for produce, and desperation was the order of today. He wanted to know if Jim could send a hundred boxes of lettuce the following morning.

'What's the price like?' Jim asked automatically. If it was low he didn't want to be bothered with it. Now the weather had changed, the lettuce in his plastic tunnels would hold for up to ten days. He had examined them with Jonathan yesterday, and they'd both agreed it was a fine even crop; this new variety "soliloquy" gave solid, full hearts, leaves tucked in layers over tight centres, like a recently opened rose. Damn stupid name, mind. He could hardly say it, never mind spell it, and cut it he certainly didn't want to do today. He was busy feeding his cherries and courgettes, and wasn't keen to increase his workload at little gain to himself.

'Holding up,' Adam said, ambiguous as ever. Jim could

hear his shallow breathing. He had a list of these answers on his desk right next to his diary, Jim guessed. It included "well worth the effort" and "bearing up nicely." He'd learnt not to trust these catchphrases, and knew that if he pressed further he'd be told Adam didn't have a crystal ball either and could only go by what the salesman told him. Jim silently cursed himself for not just saying no. He could have said they weren't quite the weight or he hadn't the time. It was a pity Jonathan had seen them. If Jim hadn't read the warning in the Bulletin his answer would certainly have been negative.

'Okay,' he assented. 'I'll have to cut them tonight, though, and keep them in the shed. It's cool enough. I'll be up at crack o' sparrows fart anyway.'

'Fine by me mate,' was the reply. 'Cheers Jim'.

Jim replaced the receiver and looked around for his mother. He could do with a cup of tea. Then he remembered she was out gadding with Fred, and the teenagers were all away somewhere. Damn, he thought. A hundred boxes was tough going for the pair of them, whereas his mother could've made up the flatpacks and boxed the lettuce behind them. Janice wouldn't be too happy. He found her in the piggery, but he didn't go in, just rapped on the window. He didn't go into too much detail, and Janice could tell he was angry he'd been sucked in to cut them against his will. Not happy either, she accepted her fate and walked over to the house to fix a few sandwiches for an early tea, so they could be cutting by six pm.

Bloody woman, just when we need her she isn't there, Janice thought, slapping sliced cucumber and Shippam's shrimp spread between soft slices of recently thawed Mother's Pride.

By six o'clock the two of them were steering the jack-truck up to the tunnel, its flatbed laden with empty boxes, bags and the Avery scales. They fastened their plastic aprons, his a bra and suspenders, a present from the kids, hers Heinz Tomato Soup.

As Jim stooped over to cut the first lettuce, he cried out: 'What the bloody hell's this?' He bent down to look more closely, and then swivelled around to examine the lettuce behind him. He picked his way further into the crop, swearing to himself. 'Janice. Take a look. Can you see what's wrong with 'em?'

Janice bent to have a closer look. 'Looks like they're full of blackfly!' she said.

Every tight little heart was infested with black speckles. As Jim prised the surrounding leaves back, he saw the black particles had become lodged deep inside the head. He knew immediately what the trouble was although he hadn't experienced it before. With difficulty he picked one out and rolled it between his thumb and forefinger, and it disintegrated into powder just as he expected. In the middle of the tunnel the problem was less but still enough to make the crop unsaleable.

'It's smuts from that bastard farmer's field!' he said. 'The whole crop, all eight hundred boxes are ruined! They'll never sell like this!'

He aimed a kick at the tunnel doorway, and the tightly stretched plastic roof shook, showering droplets of condensation onto the crop. Some splashed wet and cold on Janice's neck, causing her to shiver.

'We had smuts on the washing today,' she remembered. 'I'm surprised they've settled inside the tunnel, though. Can't we swill them out with the irrigation?'

'Irrigation's part of it,' sighed Jim. 'I watered them today and didn't look inside. Just ran each irrigation line for five minutes. The water has washed the specks right deep into the hearts.'

It was obvious really. On hot days the growers removed tunnel doors to encourage through draughts. The burnt particles had blown inside. If the tunnel had run north-south instead of east-west the pollution couldn't have penetrated.

'What can we do?' asked Janice. 'Shall I ring Eric?'

'Not a lot of point,' Jim said gloomily. 'We'd do better to ring the NFU, see what they're goin' to do about it!'

He began to stack everything back on the truck. Janice noticed the resignation on his face, and she felt a rush of warmth for him. He forced a smile, and said: 'Come on, Jan, you put kettle on. At least we haven't got to cut them now.'

Janice thought about all the problems over the last few years, and she respected her husband for still being able to take a detached view, to realise a lost cause. He was angry, but he was philosophical and should there be no compensation, she knew he'd accept it and his good humour would soon be restored. She was grateful for this; she knew his disposition helped keep them both sane. She also knew their financial position was far from rosy. Just at a time when the family were growing up and leaving home, and they could expect to wind down a little they were having to work harder and grow more just to keep the status quo. Anything untoward, from the washing machine packing up to a lost crop could cause real problems for them although they were still a long way from bankruptcy. But she knew she had the solution, right there in the piggery, if only he'd take her seriously, at least listen to her ideas. Sadly she watched Jim trudge ahead of her into the house, she knew he'd ring Eric anyway, it was just what you did in the wake of disaster.

കെ ൬

Josh had the same problem, except his crop was totally outside and the pollution if anything was worse. He too had promised to cut some for Adam. It was the following morning when he discovered them. The lettuce were heavy and robust, and the heavy downpour had washed the smuts deep inside.

'Stick 'em in anyway,' he told Guy, but this time the boy stood firm.

'No way, Josh, you know you can't do that! We'll only get them back again and the boxes will be knackered,' he said. Familiarity with Josh had gained him the courage to disagree. Josh started to rear up, but thought better of it.

'Well then smartass, what the bleedin' hell d'you suggest?' He kicked the nearest lettuce and it erupted in a shower of leaves, leaving a pathetic looking battered green stump.

'How about we get a hosepipe up here, and I wash the black bits out with the force of the water?'

He was his Granddad's boy, thought Josh approvingly.

'Well it's worth a try, I suppose.' The circumstance was more serious for him than Jim. His financial situation was much more precarious, and he didn't have a crop of cherries with a higher price more or less guaranteed.

It took some time for them to drag hosepipes up to the top field, coupling them together, a long line of hose which would impress a firefighter. They then fitted the final length to the water supply back in the greenhouse. Josh turned the tap and Guy experimented with the spurt from the hose on one individual lettuce, and the excess water welled up and overflowed but the flecks became trapped and marooned on the leaves. He soon realised the only way to clean them would be to fully immerse them in water, preferably running water, hardly practical.

'How's it doing?' shouted Josh.

'No go,' Guy shouted back, shaking his head. Josh came to look, twisted a lettuce from its root with his bare hand and studied it carefully for a second or two, peeling back the tight central leaves. Then he flung the lettuce down.

'WHOA!'

Josh leaped into the fine even crop, booting and kicking at the lettuces with his Doc Martens as he ran, shouting every swear word he knew, and some more which he made up. Guy dropped the running hosepipe in amazement as showers of leaves and little green balls hit the air. His boss ran round like a demented animal, shouting and reaping destruction in large loops. He weaved around the half acre crop desecrating it with overlapping patterns, like a child running amok across a field of virgin snow.

Eric watched spellbound from the path. Having seen Jim, he was coming to check whether Josh had the same problem. He hadn't expected such a spectacular answer, and if he hadn't known the gravity of the situation he'd have been forced to laugh. He could see Guy was helpless with laughter, rolling around hysterically on the edge of the crop. Eric thought he'd better intervene before Josh noticed and killed him.

Josh eventually wore himself out, slumped down heavily and gasping for breath, took a ready-rolled cigarette from a tin in his pocket. He struck a match and lit it with precision, as if nothing had happened. Eric had sent Guy back to turn the water off.

Josh looked up and saw Eric.

'Hi ADAS advisor,' he said, grinning sheepishly. 'Gonna advise me about this crop, then? Mr. Sainsbury, Mr. Tesco, Mr. Asda, bring 'em on! Let 'em see how we grow on the Land Settlement Association.'

Eric sat down warily next to him. He really didn't know what to say – he wasn't used to characters like Josh – who was?

'Maybe you can claim under the farmer's insurance,' he suggested, weakly

'Oh yes, I bet,' said Josh. 'Anyway, what the fuck? At least I won't waste the boxes and bags.' He forced a smile.

'How about a beer?'

'It's only ten o'clock!' said Eric, shocked.

'Okay, a cup of coffee then,' Josh said pleasantly. 'Guy!'

'Go on then,' said Eric.

Thirty-One

Jonathan sat on his settee with Sara at his feet and he played with strands of her fine hair. The candles she'd painstakingly placed transformed the dark room into a cave of love. In the kitchen a bolognese sauce blipped away romantically on the stove, the aroma wafting through as in a gravy advert. Looking at her watch, she calculated it had another five minutes to simmer, before she should put the spaghetti on. The television was on silent but the on-screen action hardly needed sound; sometimes a gun is louder that way. The music centre played softly, Queen with *We are the Champions*.

'When's this feast ready?' he asked. Sara wasn't going to rush it, she was sticking to the recipe. It was her first bolognese and he her first lover. What a steep learning curve she'd had this summer.

'Almost time to put the spaghetti on,' she said.

'Good, 'cause I'm starving.'

'I'm surprised you're still hungry,' she said shyly, squeezing his calf gently, 'after this afternoon.'

He took her hand and placed it to show her. 'Turn the cooker off and let's go back upstairs.'

Sara was torn. 'What about the meal?'

'It'll keep. I won't,' he whispered.

Then there was a knock at the door. An ignorant, intrusive rap, the sort difficult to ignore.

Sara jumped up, pulling her dressing gown tightly around her. Jonathan just had his cords on.

'Ignore it,' he said.

The knock came again. Then the voice through the letterbox.

'Jonathan! Open the soddin' door, I've made a special trip and I'm warnin' you I ain't coming back!'

Sara recognised the voice. He often came to the office, complaining about something, or, she now remembered, looking for Jonathan. It was Sammy Dove.

'Get upstairs,' her lover hissed at her. 'Now. Go on.' He mouthed her a compensatory kiss.

'What about the bolognese..' her voice trailed off as she caught his expression, and she obediently climbed the stairs, doubt and uncertainty replacing the euphoria of a moment or two ago.

₨ ₧

Early evening was usually a quiet time for Midge, and this was a regular evening. He'd partially drawn a curtain to block out the glare for the lunchtime domino players, long since departed. As the late sun angled past the blackout it washed a section of the room with its glow. Midge walked over and rearranged the curtain, so the full width of the window was exposed. He liked the filtered golden light although it illuminated the dust and smoke in the air. The lattice windows didn't open; obviously this hadn't been a priority in the past, and the building now had a preservation order preventing a cheap remedy. The brewery had installed an Expelair which rattled noisily and was forever getting choked.

A bell rang, diverting his attention, and he sighed. He hated that bell on the bar in the Lounge. It reminded him of the contradictions of being both landlord and servant, in a way a shouted greeting never did. Somehow he hadn't got around to removing it.

'Same again, Midge,' said Martin Dickinson. Son of the

local landowner, Martin was a ladies' man, sturdily built with a ruddy face typical of a heavy drinker or one who worked out of doors, or both. He was in his thirties and had never been married, but he'd built the nest. A thatched cottage in the village, pastel pink and expensively gutted, waited soullessly for the chosen female to turn it into a home. In the past Martin had a succession of live-in girlfriends; usually he found them in the town and fetched them to the village on probation. Mostly they didn't last long, whether dissatisfied with Martin or rural reality no-one really knew. He'd told Midge he wanted a girl to act and dress like a professional model, clean and draw a pheasant for the table and maintain the sex drive of a female ferret. Midge had shook his head, realising he couldn't give Kim a tick in any of those columns.

Martin hadn't given up hope. Tonight he was drinking with his friend from the local Young Farmer's group, a small-time haulage contractor with ambition. Chas had a similar penchant for women, but didn't have the advantage of a period cottage to lure them with. He lived in a caravan next to his lorry yard, awaiting planning permission for a house. Chas concerned Midge because when he'd had a few he could become very contentious, voicing opinions most people only thought about. Like many potential trouble causers, Chas was a good customer, and Midge knew a lot of his provocation was tongue in cheek. And when harnessed it did relieve the boredom, and the Red Cow was a public house which valued its conversational opportunities.

'Have you finished the harvest, Martin?' asked Midge, coaxing a little conversation.

'Just about, bit more burning to do on the far side,' said Martin. 'Dad not been in yet? I wanted to catch him but we can't wait around. Me and superstud's off into Wansbridge.'

'We have a date with two young ladies,' said Chas. Chas

was lanky, gangly almost, with a shiny flickback of hair on his forehead. His style suggested another time, not too far back, rural glam rock perhaps. Midge had noticed that in the presence of women, Chas would use the term "fillies". He'd seen Chas get cocky with Hazel and her rair up in return. Chas obviously fancied her and taunted her just enough to get her eyes blazing and then moved in with oily compliments and superficial charm.

The men drained their pints and left. Midge heard their Land Rover crunch across the gravel and then roar into the distance.

Silence reimposed itself on the pub, it was unusual to be this quiet. Perching himself on a high stool the wrong side of the bar, Midge spread the *Daily Mirror*, two-way crossword page uppermost, across the shiny woodwork of the hatch. He could relax. But as soon as he picked up his pen, he heard the door swing and a grumble of growers marched in. Midge clocked the obvious discontent in their body language as the three approached the bar with uncharacteristic purpose.

'Usual, gentlemen?' he asked.

'Yep. Have you seen that bastard Dickinson, Midge?' said Jim abruptly. He looked over his shoulder. 'I'll get 'em in,' he said to the others.

That's good, thought Josh, because I haven't any money on me anyway. They were on a mission and money hadn't entered his head. Midge did run a selective slate, but Josh wasn't one of the chosen participants.

'His boy's just left,' Midge answered, curiosity restrained for the moment. He didn't add that old man Dickinson was due in soon. He wanted to measure the situation first.

'We'll wait then, hang fire 'til the old man comes in,' said Jim, still curt, no hint of his usual wit and good humour. He just stood at the bar and stared into the depths of his pint.

Well, thought Midge, he's mad at something. Didn't know he had it in him. Personally Midge liked both Dickinsons. When approached right, like most people, they were fine.

Sammy went over to play the fruit machine, and Josh trailed after him to watch. They all knew that David Dickinson J.P. was usually in the Lounge on a Wednesday night as he sat on the Bench that day.

Midge rarely asked delicate questions directly. Like all good landlords he didn't need to. Now he restarted the conversation casually.

'Yes, Martin was in with Chas. Left not five minutes since, gone chasing women in Wansbridge.'

'Effing rich farmers! If I see either of them first, they won't be much use to –' frustration wouldn't allow Jim to finish the sentence.

Midge quickly considered the implications, and then leaned across the bar towards Jim. He looked him straight in the eye.

'I know you won't let it get out of hand, but keep the animal under control,' he said in a low voice, nodding towards Josh. 'I don't know what it's about but I have my licence to consider!'

'Yeah, yeah, we will, but that pompous pillock Dickinson has it coming this time. We've lost hundreds of boxes of lettuce because of smuts from his damned stubble burning. All in their bloody hearts, it is. Have to plough the lot in, we will.' Jim was showing signs of real distress and anger. His face was red and his eyes bulged. A deep frown distorted his forehead, and he was clenching his hands fiercely as he spoke.

This is serious, thought Midge, and he leant thoughtfully on the bar, stroking the ash from his cigarette gently around the thick glass rim of the brewery issue ash-tray.

'Can't you get compensation?' he asked. 'Surely your crop was insured? I'd of thought they'd grow out of it, anyhow.'

Jim shook his head to all counts. 'Nope,' he said, and then explained: 'You see it wouldn't matter when the lettuce are young, wouldn't be a problem. It'd wash off the leaves. But once they develop hearts, well the smuts just get trapped in, deep among 'em. Would you want to eat lettuce full of black bits?'

'Well I suppose it'd swill out,' said Midge, for he dealt with lettuce on a purely culinary level. But then he sensed Jim's irritation. 'When you rinse it, I mean, in the colander. But no, I take your point. They wouldn't go a bomb on the open market, all full of muck.'

The heavy door banged again, and David Dickinson, magistrate and arable farmer, strode unsuspecting into the Lounge. In his loud fruity voice he called:

'Pint of the usual, Midge, when you're ready.' He climbed stiffly astride a barstool. 'And a little Highland tincture on the side.'

'That's the smug bastard!' growled Jim, knocking his pint clumsily as he stood up. Beer slopped onto his jeans. Josh and Sammy were still at the machine. Midge's eyes flicked over the bar into the Lounge.

'I'll be with you in a moment, David,' Jim heard the landlord say in his usual disinterested voice.

Jim called Sammy and Josh over, but like Francis Drake with his games of bowls they had time to wait until their last coin ran out. This gave Midge time to try last ditch diplomacy.

'Look, the best thing to do is to try reason first,' he said. 'Don't be doing anything you'll regret. He's sharp as vinegar. You never know, he just might compensate you hisself. They say he's a fair magistrate. And you know – jaw jaw's better than war war, Churchill I believe it was..!' And he went to attend to the man in the other bar.

Jim doubted that. Although he'd never had a conversation himself with the man, he felt the farmer regarded the growers with disdain. This attitude was even more pronounced in his son, who'd had several clashes with Sammy in the past, mainly to do with his inability to prove the pheasants Sammy ran a nice line in were in fact his father's.

Sammy scooped out his winnings with three fingers, and Josh collected what fell to the floor. Then they were ready for action.

Sammy, swelling his chest said loudly: 'Same again, Midge, and can you put them through to the Lounge? We fancy lording it a bit.'

Sammy hadn't lost any lettuce himself, he didn't bother growing it in summer any more, but he disliked the Dickinsons and was eager to be involved in any affray with them.

The three men swaggered into the Lounge. Old David Dickinson was mounted on his bar-stool, puffing on his cigar and set to enjoy his pint and whisky chaser. With his tweed jacket, corduroy trousers and his flicked up curly white moustache he could easily have been a military man. His bony face was flushed red with years of weathering, especially on the shiny bit of skin stretched tight across the bridge of his bony nose. His eyes were clear, intelligent and grey.

'Evenin',' the men said in unison. They weren't familiar enough with him to address him as David and they definitely weren't going to call him "mister."

Dickinson barely raised a bushy eyebrow.

'Evening,' he answered amiably in the educated accent which his son had apparently chosen to reject. Midge watched, anxiously towelling some glasses which had mysteriously appeared from somewhere.

'These two gentl'men ere's had to dump over a grand's worth of fine lettuce between 'em today, mate,' Sammy said in a conversationally pleasant voice. Sammy spoke quite precisely usually but he could change this if it suited proceedings and it did today. Now he leaned sideways on the shiny surface of the bar, his plump bearded face uncomfortably close to the bony aristocratic one.

'Is that so?' came the polite reply. If he objected to being called mate, it wasn't detectable. 'I hope it wasn't in the middle of the bypass like the last time otherwise I will see them in court, no doubt.'

Blue cigar smoke curled up to the ceiling above him. Both men made no attempt to move, and the other two clumped around in ambush. Dickinson remained outwardly cool and nonchalant, his hand rock steady as he raised his glass.

'This time,' said Sammy, still in a friendly tone, 'You're responsible, Mister Dickinson.' Midge thought he could just detect the sarcasm in Sammy's voice. David Dickinson still didn't flinch, despite the fact that the three men were standing menacingly beside him. You had to admire that, thought Midge, tea-towel twisting repeatedly around the same glass.

'And how,' Dickinson turned his long skinny neck around just enough to face Sammy eye to eye, 'do they arrive at that conclusion?'

'When your men burnt your stubble the wind carried the smuts into the hearts of these gentlemen's lettuce, and now they're buggered – can't be sold – not even to the faces down the auction. Unless of course your hounds fancy a vegetarian meal? I'm sure we could arrange a satisfactory price if you know what I mean!' Sammy's voice was soft, Midge could only just hear him. Four pairs of eyes were fixed upon the elderly man. He managed the slightest curl of a smile; his gander was definitely up now, Midge could tell.

'If you're referring to my 200 acres behind your salad factories, I seem to recall the weather was perfectly still when we burnt that field,' he said. 'You cannot hold me responsible if the wind got up overnight before there was any rain to settle it. I believe insurance companies term it an Act of God, do they not, Midge?'

'Sorry?' Midge pretended he wasn't listening, still polishing the same glass.

'I'm sorry for their misfortune,' continued Dickinson, addressing poor Midge, and allowing himself a sip of whisky. 'I know I own a lot of land around here but it is rather exaggerating to confuse my actions with those of God's!' And if there is such a thing as an aristocratic chuckle, he allowed himself one.

'You cocky piece of shite!' said Josh and went to spring at him, but Sammy was ready and grabbed the arms of the crazy one firmly from behind. Midge had set down the glass he was drying and his hand alighted nervously on the hatch. 'Gentlemen! Remember where you are please!'

All ignored him. Josh swore and struggled, and Jim helped Sammy to hold him, as he spat: 'How would you like it if I sprayed something which damaged your crop?'

'What could that possibly be?' Dickinson downed the whisky and quickly swallowed a mouthful of bitter. His adam's apple went into overdrive. 'Same again, please, Midge.' He said. Midge side-stepped, not wanting to turn his back.

'Come on, it's not worth it, he's a pathetic old man,' said Sammy. David Dickinson bristled at that remark and Midge now held a second empty glass. 'Let's go home and I'll give you a brace of pheasants for your tea, that'll cheer you up.' Sammy added with a wink.

This had the desired effect. Dickinson knew he was the only pheasant rearer for miles around, and he was aware that poachers were stealing upwards of twenty five percent of his birds. He turned angrily to Sammy, shaking a bony finger. Midge at last replenished his glass, the crisis had passed. Sammy let go of Josh.

'How dare you come in here and talk about my pheasants in front of me!' he said. 'I know exactly how many birds I've lost and I know where they've gone! And I'm very close to proving it!'

Sammy smiled at him, savouring the moment. 'Mister Dickinson, don't be like that. Have you considered it could be an Act of God?' he said. 'Poor dumb birds, all losing their way like that. Come on boys, lets go. Catch ya later Midge, tomorrow, in the Snug. We don't like the company in 'ere.' And they banged their glasses down on the polished wood, one, two, three. Clearly Sammy was Diana Ross and the other two the Supremes. They were gone.

Midge cleared his throat. 'Sorry about that. Do I take it you want another whisky in that glass, David?' he asked.

Thirty-Two

Hazel surveyed herself approvingly in the full-length mirror. It was Saturday afternoon and she was going shopping in Wansbridge. Eddie would watch the kids whilst she trailed round town and visited the supermarket. Stocks from the cash and carry were running low, and she needed a few essentials to "put her on." Often Eddie accompanied her but today there was motor racing on the television. He loved motor racing, it was the only sport he really bothered about. He apologised to her.

'Sorry Haze, you don't mind if I watch this instead?'

Minded? Of course not. She had other plans. They involved Jonathan...

'I've got something for you,' he'd whispered, as he passed her on the lawn on his way to speak with Eddie. 'If you call in Saturday after lunch.' She'd caught a wink.

'I bet you have, except I don't want it. I keep telling you. What bit of "no" don't you understand?'

Jonathan had smiled back at her. 'Not that, you cheeky girl! I've bought you something. I obviously can't give it you in front of your old man!'

'What if your little tart's there?'

'Avoid Sundays and evenings. That'll still give you plenty of scope.'...

So fate had intervened. She smiled as she twisted around to check her skirt was the best length to display her long tanned legs. Eddie never bought her presents, he wasn't that sort of man. They had both decided when the children were born that any surprise gifts should be for them, although he was always willing to pay for things for her, even when there weren't really enough funds. If she pointed to something in the catalogue he'd just say "send for it, gel." But apart from the occasional box of chocolates from the garage when he realised he'd missed some anniversary, exchanging gifts was history. A joint decision, she had to admit.

Now she felt the thrill of anticipation. And it wasn't as if she was going to "do" anything. She held back her head and smiled to the mirror knowingly. Well, she might kiss and cuddle and let him touch her as she'd done several times recently, but she knew she wouldn't go all the way. She just wanted a bit of fun, something to look forward to. In truth she didn't even fancy him that much, he was just the best of a bad bunch. Growers as a breed weren't smooth talkers, and Jonathan did have the gift of the gab. And she knew about Sara, whom he was surely sleeping with, so he'd be happy with that. On impulse she released her hair from its elastic band and allowed it to fall softly about her face. How fortunate her hair lightened as her skin darkened in the sunshine. Yes, she was satisfied for once with what she saw.

She kissed her children and her husband, who mumbled: 'Bye love,' his attention full on his programme, craning his neck to see the screen as she bent towards him to land a peck.

80   C3

She got into the car and drove to town with abandon, taking the corners wildly, excitement bubbling through her.

In order to make up some time she rushed around the shopping centre, and then decided to visit the supermarket on the way home. It would be less crowded, she convinced herself, but in truth she just couldn't wait any longer. She could call on Jonathan first.

She found his house and parked the car out of sight

around the corner. As she knocked on his door she could hear Adam Ant "standing and delivering" through the nets of a partially opened sash window. The door opened instantly, and Jonathan stood there, big smile, no sign of suprise. A blast of Brut hit her in the face; he had a towel over his shoulders so she guessed he'd just applied it.

'You came, then!' he said with direct eye contact. Hazel shivered inwardly with excitement but took care to appear cool and detached. He stood aside to let her pass. The room was dark and cool, and suprisingly small. It was also very tidy, nothing out of place. This wasn't a surprise, she knew he liked things ordered. 'D'you want a drink?'

'No, not just yet,' said Hazel. 'So this is it, then. Show me round your bachelor pad.' Her eyes moved cautiously around the room, her brain very alert.

She knew his girlfriend didn't live with him and she could see no obvious evidence of a female's presence. The biggest item of furniture was an oak table with solid legs, strangely out of place. It was obviously old, and really too bulky for the house. She guessed it was a family heirloom and he'd agreed to take it, perhaps sell it later. Apart from that there was just a drab two-seater settee in the way of furnishings.

He showed her the kitchen; sink, worktop, fitted cupboards all present and correct, nothing the least bit inspiring. Then he opened an insignificant door in the living room and pointed to a narrow staircase.

'I'll show you upstairs. You first.'

'No, you first.'

'Visitors and ladies first.'

'Your house, you go first.'

'No lady then,' he said, leading the way. 'I thought as much!'

She followed him, listening as he pointed out the bathroom and the spare room. He'll probably be an estate agent next, she thought, and proposition the seller if not the buyer too.

'This is my room,' he said. The double bed was made up with a clean bright quilt. Sunshine lit a pattern on the wall. Hazel decided it was the most pleasant room in an otherwise dull house. Of course this would be where his priorities lay.

'Do you want to test the bed?' He smiled at her, almost shyly, she thought.

'No,' she said firmly and backing away from him. 'I am not screwing you up there, where you probably had your little office slut last night,' she giggled.

He made no attempt to deny this or defend his girlfriend, but laughed. When he didn't answer, Hazel continued.

'I don't mind a bit of flirting but that's it. I'm not committing adultery. I've Eddie to think of.'

'Yeh, yeh, yeh.'

She knew that the bed would not be a good idea. She doubted her ability to hold back once they were laying on a bed. She walked back down the stairs, and he followed.

What the bloody hell's she playing at, he thought.

She sat down on the settee and he sat next to her, but he made no attempt to touch her. It was strange. The repartee which characterised their meetings on her nursery was strangely lacking now.

'So do you like my house?' he asked her.

'Yes, it's a nice house,' she lied. 'I often think I'd like to live in a town instead of being stuck away in the sticks like I am. Aren't you going to get me that drink?'

She stood up and moved to the sideboard, and began flicking through his collection of records. Jonathan disappeared to the kitchen. She selected and set up the *Best of Marvin Gaye* on the player.

He went to the fridge and took out a bottle of Mateus Rosé. He poured two glasses, and carried them over to the settee where she was sitting once more, one leg draped sexily but protectively over the other.

'I suppose you think if I drink this you'll get your wicked way with me?' She must have gone too far with the banter because Jonathan went to take it away again and she snatched it back quick. 'I'll take a chance!' she said. They chatted for a while, saying nothing consequential, keeping the banter light.

'Hazel, come upstairs,' he said suddenly, quite seriously. He put his arm around her and pulled her to him. 'You're doing my head in.'

'You don't listen to me!' she said, pulling away. 'I've told you I'm not screwing you, it's not my fault if you don't believe me!'

With a flash of her long legs she stood up to emphasise the point.

Fucking hell, he thought. I don't believe this. We've virtually done it anyway. He felt a huge surge of irritation, but somehow managed to keep it submerged. Why should she use him to get all horned up and then go back to finish the job with her old man? Jonathan still felt resentment over the stolen pump, which he was certain Eddie had somewhere.

He stood up as well and she let him kiss her, her tongue responding to his, and she pressed against him when he put his hands under her jumper and undid her bra.

'Let me see your breasts,' he whispered, and she didn't protest when he pulled the tight cotton top over her head, throwing it with her bra on to the settee. He undid his flies and put his cock in her hand, and she toyed with it for a while. All of this was old ground. When he reached to put his hand inside her knickers, however, she pushed it away. Looking at her watch, she said softly:

'I'll have to go. I haven't been to the supermarket yet.'

'Fuck the supermarket,' he said, but to his surprise he

could feel resistance in her body. As he kissed her breasts, she backed towards the oak table until she was pressed up against it.

Suddenly his hand moved from her thigh and began to tug at her knickers. He had taken her by surprise and they slipped to the floor before she realised. He trapped them smartly with his foot. Her wraparound skirt had been a bad choice, for it slipped off easily leaving her completely naked.

'NO!' she said. 'Jonathan, no, I don't want to!' He didn't seem to hear her. He pushed her backwards onto the shiny wood of the table. It felt cold to her bare back.

Suddenly she realised her predicament, and any desire drained totally from her body. She tried to sit up, but he forced her down again, banging her head. Although slighter than Eddie, she felt his iron grip on her wrists.

'Jonathan NO!' she shouted now. 'Please. I don't want to do it today! Not today! NO. Not this! Not now!'

It was as if he didn't hear her. She was talking to the west wind.

'It's okay darling,' he breathed, 'I know you want it really.'

The more she struggled the tighter he held her. She felt sure he was bruising her, but something inside prevented her shouting out any more. He forced her legs apart, and was now standing between them.

She could feel his hard penis stabbing at her, trying to find the entrance. Then he did, and he began to pump at her with long hard shafts. Each thrust reverberated through her body which was now just lying there limply, for she knew there was no use in fighting further. He didn't seem to notice, his eyes were glazed. She felt no sexual pleasure, she was aware of his body blocking the light from the window with each time he pulled back.

Suddenly he withdrew, and turned her over like a cut of meat. Again she didn't have the energy to resist. He continued banging her from behind now, and she felt the corner of the table digging into her flesh. She shut her eyes now; the jarring was making her feel sick. Then she heard him build to a crescendo and withdraw as he came all up her back. He leaned heavily on top of her and for a moment she could feel his hot rasping breath in her ear. She thought she had never ever felt so repulsed.

Then she was aware that he had moved off of her and was doing up his trousers. She heard him switch the television on, Marvin Gaye having played out some time ago. Ironically she could hear the drone of motor engines and the excited voice of the commentator as the Grand Prix was reaching the crescendo. She thought of Eddie, and felt sick. Her flesh was stuck to the table. She eased herself up from it and slid, naked and sticky into a heap on the carpet. He threw her clothes to her, and said as if everything was normal:

'How about a coffee and a sandwich?'

'No,' her voice sounded strange to herself, as if it belonged elsewhere. He didn't appear to notice.

'Well I do,' he said, and took himself into the kitchen to prepare it.

The programme broke to the football results, the first fixtures of the season. Hazel stood up with shaky legs, and with difficulty stepped into her knickers. Her hair was knotted and she needed hot water and clean clothes. Her priority though was to get out of this house and run away as far as possible. She pushed her bare feet into her high heels. Gathering all her courage she went to the kitchen door. He was slicing tomatoes on the work top. Everything was organised, there was a small mound of diced onions and some ham in a plastic carton. The bread was neatly buttered, ready.

'You lousy fucking rapist,' said Hazel from the doorway, her voice low.

He looked up from the task and glanced around the room, as if wondering whom she was addressing.

'What?' he said. Then he added, by way of admission: 'Well I could tell you didn't enjoy it. But I didn't expect such a fight. You came here, you knew the score. Exactly what did you expect?' And he had the audacity to smile at her.

'I'll make sure everyone knows what a rat you are,' she said with venom.

'I don't think so,' said Jonathan, nonchalantly patting the lid down on his sandwich. 'Who are you going to tell? Eddie? "I went round to Jonathan's house and I let him grope me and I played with his dick. When he fucked me on the table, I didn't like it." No, I don't think you'll tell anyone that!'

He heard the door slam. Unease must've come in as she went out for it hovered over him now. He hadn't wanted it like this. He preferred sex with full co-operation and this was honestly the only time it had ever happened like this, but she had been ready for it, all juiced up, certainly it wasn't rape. She came to his house looking for sex and got more than she bargained for, perhaps. He had thought the struggle was part of the game at first. Maybe he should have stopped when she shouted no. But how did he know she meant it? Her messages weren't exactly clear. He shook the speculation from his mind and settled down to enjoy his sandwich and check his Pools coupon.

Thirty-Three

Hazel drove the car out of town and on to the back road, her shaking hands gripping the steering wheel tightly. When she was clear of houses she pulled into the verge and broke into sobs for the first time. Her body shook with them. What should she do? She felt so desolate, as if somebody had taken her body and wiped the street with it. Her world had spun out of control. But he was right, the bastard, she knew she could never ever tell Eddie.

She realised she couldn't go home as she was. Focussing on survival she recalled an isolated telephone call-box half a mile up the road. She drove up to it, got out of the car and pulled open the stiff glass door of the booth. The enclosed space smelt strongly of urine and vulgar graffiti mocked her. She dialled Karen's number, thank God it was her and not Steve who answered.

'Karen! Is Steve listening? Good. Oh Karen, I'm in a mess. I've got see you, I need your help! No, of course I'm not all right. I've just had an awful experience and I need a bath.... I'll tell you when I see you. And Eddie mustn't know a thing!'

Karen listened without judgement, replaced the receiver and went straight to switch on the immersion. Obviously this was serious, and she needed to get her children out of the way so her friend could tell her about it in private. The girls were in the front room, watching the *A Team*, riveted. She felt bad that they'd have to be disturbed, but it couldn't be helped.

'Has it nearly finished?' she asked them.

The girls ignored her, craning their necks to see past her to the screen.

'Mam, you're in the way!'

'Daddy's going to take you out for a bit,' she said, squatting on the floor beside them.

She ruffled their hair, but they were oblivious. She went into the kitchen where saucepans simmered on the cooker, steam rising steadily. Dinner would have to wait, she decided, switching off the rings. She'd have to explain something to Steve, and of course it was especially tricky after the conversation of a few weeks ago, and Karen didn't know many men who liked their dinnertime messed about. Was it luck that he wasn't as narrow minded as many she could think of? No, of course it wasn't, she'd chosen carefully and her man would understand if it was "women's stuff". She found him in the packing shed, sorting out the red tomatoes from a tray of mostly green ones.

'Hiya luv, dinner time?' he said, above the radio.

'Sorry Steve, I've had to put it back.' He noticed the urgency in her voice as she went to unplug the radio. 'Hazel rang me from a call box. She's in a right state about something, and she's coming straight round here. Will you take the kids somewhere, while she tells me about it?'

'What's it about then? You know I like me dinner on time..'

'Steve, even I don't know yet. I think it's a bit of an emergency!'

'Well shall I take them up to Eddie's?' he asked. 'I'm bloody starving, mind, so it hadn't better be long.' They were walking back across the grass. It's getting long again, thought Steve. Maybe I'll mow it tomorrow if I get the chance.

'She don't want Eddie to know where she is,' Karen said, cautiously.

'Huh, it gets worse! Karen, I'm telling you I don't want to get involved in their affairs, Eddie's me mate,' he said defensively. 'I suppose she's been screwing around?'

'I don't know what it's about, Steve, but she needs my help, and she's my friend. And he's not your mate, I think you called him a Tory twat the other day? Could you take the girls to the Little Chef and we'll have bubble and squeak tomorrow morning?' They reached the back door. She passed him a crumpled note from the pocket of her jeans.

God, thought Steve, it must be serious if she's going to finance a Little Chef dinner for me and the kids. This was a first.

'She's trouble, that one,' he said. 'I knew it.'

In five minutes Karen had dislodged the children from the television using guilty promises, and Steve was heading towards the main road, the kids disgruntled in the back seat. He passed Hazel turning into the Drift, but her car flashed past like a stranger's.

Karen had the door open ready. She watched Hazel scramble from the car, dishevelled and wary, checking right and left. The road was empty.

'Steve's taken the kids to the Little Chef,' she answered Hazel's unspoken question. 'The water'll not be properly hot yet.' Karen decided against commenting on Hazel's appearance just yet.

'It's okay, I'll use it cold,' Hazel said, her voice abrupt and strange. 'Can I use the phone?'

'You know where it is. Shall I put kettle on?' Hazel ignored her, and went to dial her own number. Karen heard her speaking to Eddie, her voice just about controlled.

'Eddie, I'm at Karen's. She's upset about something. I'll be back as soon as I can... Use those gammon steaks and frozen chips... haven't we... Oh no, I didn't get them from the supermarket...' her voice began to trail of miserably... 'Yes of course I went... I just didn't get frozen chips that's all...see you later.' She slammed the receiver down.

'Shit!' she shouted. 'I forgot the supermarket!' and she disappeared into her friend's bathroom slamming the door and locking it behind her.

Inside Hazel stripped off her clothes. She turned the hot tap, the water was lukewarm. It gushed over a brown stain on the white enamel, the sort caused by a continually dripping tap and impossible to scour away. Looking around, she spotted a bottle of Dettol and she poured it into the bath. The brown liquid turned cloudy and yellow as it hit the water. She then soaked herself in the pungent antiseptic suds, twisting her arm over her shoulder to scrub her back which had been so abused, until it was almost raw. Eventually she stood up, drained the water and refilled the bath. The replacement was harsh and cold, but she needed to get rid of the stink of the Dettol. She washed her hair too because she could still smell his aftershave, now rancid with sweat, on that. She shivered with cold, teeth chattering and skin all goosey. Finally she reached for a big towel.

Karen banged on the door. 'Get a move on, Hazel. Steve and the kids'll be back soon, and I want you to tell me what's happened, I want to know what this is all about.'

'Can you lend me a bra and knickers and a blouse and skirt or something?' Hazel hissed through the door. 'And a plastic bag.'

When Karen returned with them, Hazel was wrapped in the towel. Karen passed her the clothes, turning away as her friend dressed. Nothing really fitted, but the clothes felt clean and pure against her skin. Using just her thumb and forefinger, she picked the soiled ones from the floor and dropped them into the black binliner. Karen noticed her top from Sacs, barely worn. Bloody hell, thought Karen. I helped her choose it too.

'Can you chuck these clothes away for me?' was all she said.

'Come into the bedroom. What the heck's this about?'

In the bedroom, Hazel curled up on the floor, tight against the wall and Karen sat on the bed, leaning slightly forward to hear the story.

'Come on Hazel. Why are you chucking perfectly good clothes out?'

'Because I've been raped,' said Hazel.

'You've what?'

'Raped.' She repeated, bitterly. And she recounted the tale, from when he had forced her onto the table. She had to clench her fists to repeat it and even then she left bits out. She didn't say how humiliated she'd felt, and how he climbed off leaving her sticky-backed to watch television without so much as a word. Karen hadn't spoken but her expression was suitably shocked.

'So where were you?' she quizzed gently, now.

'In his house,' replied Hazel. 'It was awful –'

'You went to his house!'

'Yes, he said he had a present for me,' she said. For the first time she remembered the present, another body blow.

'What was it?'

'Well, I don't know do I, I didn't stop to find out!' Hazel knew she wasn't really facing the stark facts here and it showed in aggression in her voice.

'So you called on him, then what did he do?' Karen persisted.

'He showed me his house, his bedroom, and I said I didn't want to fuck him. You know I didn't even fancy him really! He knows all I wanted was a bit of fun,' she wailed. She'd noticed a row of pink marks where the table had pressed into her thighs and she was familiar enough with her body to know what form they'd take. 'My legs will have bruises!' she sobbed. 'Eddie will see them. What'll I do?'

Karen ignored this. 'Did you kiss him? I mean a tongue one?' Hazel had told her that she'd kissed him in the field already, so there would be no denying this.

'Of course I did!'

'Anything else?'

'Yes, I think I let him touch my breasts,' said Hazel, miserably. 'And if you really want to know he took my top right off.'

'Was he undressed too?' asked Karen. She felt she needed to get the whole picture.

'No!' said Hazel bitterly. 'He was dressed all the time. He only had his trousers undone. That was one of the most awful things,' she cried. 'I felt like a whore!'

'Was his dick out? I mean when you kissed and things. Did you touch it?'

'YES YES YES! But then I told him I had to go to the supermarket. And I still haven't done the bloody shopping! What am I to do?' She held her head in despair.

'Well don't worry about that. I have some stuff I can give you, and some carrier bags. So you were going to piss off and leave him like that, with a bloody great stiff on?'

'I have always told him I wouldn't commit adultery,' she said, her voice deteriorating to a sob. 'And now I have. I can never face Eddie again,' she wailed. 'He forced me, Karen. He gripped me like – like iron. I tried to stop him, but he was too strong. If you're forced, Karen, do you think that counts as adultery?'

Karen thought for a moment. 'I think that the moment you let another man's tongue down your throat you've done that,' she said. 'Letting him fondle your breasts, touching his penis, yes, I think you've done that already. So I wouldn't let that worry you. Eddie won't find out, and I'm sure as hell Jonathan will never tell him.'

Hazel felt her anger rising, but she wasn't sure where to direct it. 'Don't mention that bastard's name in front of me,' she shrieked. 'I'll shoot him if he comes near our land!'

Karen ignored the hysterical outburst. She put her arm around her friend, but Hazel shook her off.

'Did you say he came in you?' Karen asked.

'No, he pulled out,' Hazel said, her voice quieter now.

'Well I suppose he did that because he was afraid of getting you pregnant. At least he thought about that.'

Hazel turned her head, her eyes full of tears. 'No, he came all over my back,' she said with a shudder. 'And he didn't even give me anything to wipe it off with. So that's how fucking considerate he is! Then he threw me my clothes. Do you think I should go to the police?'

'Only if you don't mind being all over the front page of the Gazette,' Karen said. She took a deep breath. 'Look, it's happened, and it's done with. You've got a husband and children to consider. You have got to face him, and act like nowt's happened. You've learnt a hard lesson.'

Hazel shook her tangled hair and her eyes blazed. 'You don't know how it feels to be raped!' she hissed. 'To have somebody forcing into you like – like you're a hole in a piece of wood! I think you think I deserved it! I can tell you do! Fine friend you are.'

But there was no point in her getting up to leave. She was hardly in the position to reject her only chance of help. Karen climbed off the bed and sat next to her, and this time Hazel didn't remove her friend's arm.

'Of course I don't! I just think you gave out the wrong messages. I don't think you deserved the brutal way he did it, but he obviously thought you went to his house for one reason. How many men have you been to bed with, Hazel?'

'Three, counting Eddie,' Hazel answered. Karen was surprised, she thought the number quite low for one as overtly sexual.

'Right, well now it's four,' said Karen. 'Put it down to experience. One day you may find a way to get your own back. And I heard a car pull up!' She got up and found a hair brush in a drawer. She tossed it to Hazel, who took it gloomily and began to scrape at the tangles with it. 'You haven't got the space to take this too much to heart. Or you'll end up losing your family.'

Thirty-Four

The summer was drawing to a close, and the August Bank Holiday beckoned with the likelihood of high produce prices as housewives splashed out on salads. On the bank holiday Monday an event was held in the nearby village and it was a big affair, drawing crowds from far and wide. A Charter Fair in the old English tradition, this one was still popular thanks to its ideal location.

The old village was picturesque in a way the glass village most certainly wasn't, and only a few open fields saved it from the indignity of having the Estate as part of it, attached like a great carbuncle. The Red Cow lay just on the fringe, the left-hand sweep of its tiled roof was the last village building before the open road led past the top of the Drift and wound onwards towards Wansbridge. The village was called Market Boulton, and as the name suggests it had once been an important agricultural trading centre. The core consisted of a line of old thatched cottages, ringed by tall brick houses. The flat roof of a purpose-built shop squatted awkwardly between two of them courtesy of the sixties and this was both post office and general store. Ribbons of council housing followed the main road, with new development springing up outwards and in between like a crop of weeds. Several back lanes twisted around just north of the road to give the village a centre next to the Norman Church. One of these lanes swelled out at this point into an open expanse of tarmac and some of the oldest cottages bordered this area, their irregular bay windows jutting into the street suggesting they'd been shops or inns, but sadly, they were all private houses now. To the north was a pantiled pumphouse and a regular war memorial. The churchyard dozed behind a row of tall limes, this summer's leaves still struggling to soften a brutal pollard the previous year. This ample open space, which a town would be proud of, would house the stalls.

Midge was a local boy and he discussed the fair with the growers, who weren't.

'There's been one here since the year dot. It's tradition, the Charter states it's to be August Bank Holiday, and it's been here ever since. We used to have a weekly market here and all, but that got shifted to Wansbridge, more's the pity. Good little market it was.'

'What's all this about teddy bears abseiling or parachuting off the church tower?'

'Yeh, some fancy idea of the new vicar's. To pay for restoring the tower, the bill still hasn't been settled. You sponsor your teddy or something daft. Kids'll like it. Stallholders are supposed to give ten percent of takings to the church, but it don't happen like that, it's a flat rate. But this vicar, he's said to be a bit of a joker, he's running the bowling for a pig. Not that I know him, mind. He don't visit this establishment.'

'Do you visit his, though, Midge?'

'Point taken. I met Kim at the Charter Fair, you know. She came up from the Smoke to stop with her aunt and I've been rueing the day ever since.'

'Go on with you. I wouldn't like to abseil my teddy past them gargoyles, mind. Where's the fair held, then?'

'Other side of the village, by the playing fields. There's so many stalls now, the fair got forced out.'

There was rich variety in these stalls. Maisie, Ruby and a few village women ran the WI stall. Eric watched as Maisie secured the top of a jar with gingham cloth and an elastic band.

'You go to a lot of trouble,' he said. 'It's good to see. That chutney's very nearly organic, you know, with you using predators instead of spray. Organic produce is selling for a premium in London, my daughter tells me.'

'More money than sense them lot. Oh, I ain't talkin' bout your Gail, Eric. I don't think of her as a townie. I remember her as a nipper. 'Ere, feast yer eyes on what we've got.'

There was lemon cheese and gooseberry jam, green chutney and vinegarised courgettes. If it was edible and preservable, the WI ladies would know how to blanch, steam, pulp, strain or stew it, and then present it in a clean recycled jar so its natural colour shone temptingly through. They also made iced sponge cakes and dropped scones, rock buns and Cornish pasties.

Flowing muslin drapes hung from Nicole's stall, she had used them cleverly to create ambiguity as well as to conceal certain wares from the casual punter.

'You need to be careful,' Simon warned her. 'You can't sell these things, you'll be had under the Trade Descriptions Act. You're saying these potions will cure things and they might not.'

'Oh, don't be so stuffy, Si. I'll stick them under the bench and get them out when I trust who I'm talking to. And I'm doing palmistry. Any boring old law about that?'

'No, that's traditional, but the women at the fairground mightn't like it. How much are you charging?'

'Only fifty pence. And can I have some of those flat peas you're growing? I can take the scales with me.'

'Nicole, you can't take the dopehead scales! I despair of you.'

So here she was with her re-packaged herbal teas and recently split Aloe Vera plants, and a dozen dreamcatchers swayed in the breeze. Re-worked antique jewellery was pinned to velvet cushion and in front of her stall was a plastic bucket full of flat podded peas. A discrete card advertised her palm reading service. It was a mish mash, but an interesting one.

Josh was taking his stall seriously. He needed the cash. He was prepared to sell his train sets and the associated paraphernalia. Angie had been surprised and she took it to mean he'd accepted she wasn't going to get pregnant, and he wouldn't have a son to pass them on to. The subject had been taboo since she'd told him her tubes and ovaries were in fine fettle, and the doctor suggested he went for a sperm count. He'd punched a hole in the wall and then, nothing, Angie spoke often of her disappointment to Maisie.

'Do you know any old wives' tales, Maisie? You know, to help me catch on?'

'Ooh, let me see. We used to reckon eatin' lettuce helped, you know.'

'Ugh. I hate lettuce. Anything else?'

'We-e-ll, there is one..a bit rude mind, but since you're desperate, they used to say as you should lay for half an hour wi' your legs up in the air, you know, after the deed, like.'

'Cheers, Maisie, you're a star.'

Now Josh had cleared his Hornby collection from the spare bedroom; wagon loads of track, boxes of lead trains, stations, bridges all the bits. Angie hugged and kissed him when she saw them stacked in boxes, asking him if he was sure.

George of course sold pot plants, and he would probably take the most money. His geraniums ranged from brash oranges through searing scarlets to plum reds and pastel pinks. They were ivy-leafed, trailing, climbing, bushing, squatting, and all were flowering or at least in bud. Nicole glanced sideways at the battle of colour, and it offended her eyes. Her Aunt Dorothy used to marvel at how colours could clash something shocking on a woman, yet harmonise perfectly in a municipal flower bed. She'd have liked Aunt Dorothy to take a look at George's stall.

Vera Clay was a needlewoman, and despite working full time on the nursery still managed to sew Crimplene skirts and cotton tops of the sort she wore herself. They were all pressed tidily into polythene bags, neatly labelled with the price. There would be no bargaining at Vera's stall. Everything was up front and open, no hidden extras. If Vera said you could wash a skirt at sixty degrees, then that would be the case. If she sold jigsaws and said there were no pieces missing, you could rely on that. Just like she lives her life, thought Karen who was taking a walk around to see who had what before the rush. No compromise, no backing down, that was Vera, and she expected everybody else to behave the same and have the same standards, because she *knew*. Consequently she spent her whole life in confrontation.

Janice too had been preparing for this day. She was still getting a surplus of milk from Bernadette, and now the pigs had been slaughtered she was unwilling to pour milk down the drain, partly through loyalty to Bernadette and partly because she thought it wicked, a legacy of poverty experienced as a child. From the Goatkeepers' Federation she'd learnt you could successfully freeze goat's milk. She bought a case of stiff greaseproof cartons and had been freezing the excess. When she told Nigel, he decided to do the same, and now between them they regularly froze several cartons a day each claiming "English Goat's Milk, the secret to a healthy skin" in blue and white lettering. She was convinced there was a business idea here but Jim steadfastly refused to allow her to buy any more goats. It was 1981 but Janice was financially disenfranchised. Everything was in her husband's name, and indeed this was true for many growers. So Nigel ran the business and Janice assisted him. They'd set up a freezer at the fete.

Nigel shunned activity. 'I couldn't be there, Janice, it'd do me head. Too many folk.'

'No problem, I'll sell yours too and we'll split the money.'

'You can't do that, lass.'

'Course I can. If it hadn't been for you, Bernadette would've had a burst bag back in the spring.'

Janice had been mightily relieved when Myra told her she'd promised to help Fred serve on the British Legion tombola.

Some growers sold a mixture of wares; a few second-hand items, some fruit and vegetables, especially things they grew for their own use, like kohl rabi and summer cabbages, Victoria plums and Bramley apples. Eddie and Steve had filled LSA trays with 'bits and bobs', excess gekas, useless lengths of hose, second-hand jubilee clips.

'You watch,' Eddie told Steve. 'They'll be fightin' over these.'

'You reckon?'

'Of course. Don't you think they envy us, stuck all day in their poncey offices? They'll never use them, mind. But it'll make them feel better just buying them. Poor sods.'

Sammy and Maureen were cagey about their stall, and they drew up the van but refused to unload it.

'Aren't you going to set your stall out?' asked Midge. As the Red Cow was too far away, he'd hired a marquee. The license was a formality, it had been granted for hundreds of years. His wife Kim was helping him today and Bank Holiday Monday was one time she didn't mind, because there was a bit of life about the place, she said.

'Nope, not yet,' said Sammy. Maureen leant lazily against the bonnet, her big thighs squashed tightly by the hem of her pink shorts, her bare feet stuffed into white plastic shoes.

'You'll have it all to do at the last minute,' said Kim to

Maureen. Kim was as slight as Maureen was large but the two women were firm friends.

'No mate, don't you fret,' she smiled. 'We ain't even gonna unload.' She leant her chins towards Kim. 'We're 'bout to run a spot o' a gamblin',' she whispered. 'That way we win both ways. We don't 'ave all that effort unloading, and we can bring out somethin' a bit dodgy when the coast's clear.'

Kim smiled. 'I don't know. You and your scams. And all the coppers care about is getting on the back of the poor publican, tryin' to catch him selling after hours.'

'Coppers could come for your ol' man, take 'im away, he'd be gone and I doubt you'd even notice, stuck in front o' the telly!'

'I can but hope Mo, I can but hope,' laughed Kim.

The playgroup had roped off an area for the children to play safely when their parents needed a break. Sara from the office was on her knees, arms waving as she spoke to a circle of cross-legged toddlers. Karen and Hazel caught glimpses as the crowd shifted.

'Oh my God. Is that who I think it is?' said Hazel.

'I think so. She's only young, can't be more than sixteen!'

'Look how frail she looks. Quite pretty though. Do you think that bastard's as brutal with her? Probably not or she'd snap in two. I feel awful now, looking at her..'

'How you getting on with Eddie now?'

'Steady. I'm steady with Eddie. Do you *really* think she's pretty?'

'Aye, in a little girl sort of way.'

'Sexless though.'

'Maybe that's what keeps her out of trouble.'

'Eddie's noticed that the J word doesn't come on the holding now. He said: "I used to think he fancied you but he must have gone off you."

'That's okay then. Sorted.'

'Karen, how can you say that? You don't get over that sort of thing just like it's a bad dream. I'm scarred you know, and then there's the guilt! Just looking at that poor cow brings it all back!'

'Hey, I'm sorry, I didn't mean it like that. And you're doing so well. Come on, let's try and enjoy the day.'

සිං ඟ

At eleven o' clock the fete was formally opened by Mr David Dickinson JP and the rush started. The weather held fine, a slight breeze swayed Nicole's ethnic drapes but wasn't strong enough to stir George's solid flower heads. The sky was blue, but a layer of high cloud clung around the sun filtering it and subduing the glare. People swarmed the stalls, and transactions came thick and fast. George had to abandon wrapping the plants in newspaper and was forced to shove them into outstretched hands as they were. He caught sight of his grandson and called him over to help out. It took Guy ten minutes to push a way through.

'It's quieter on Josh's stall,' he said, as they rooted simultaneously in the ice-cream box for change.

A determined woman helped herself to a geranium from the reserve stock under the bench, as the stock on display had all but gone. The plants in this tray were smaller and in early bud only.

'Scuse me. What colour's this one?' she asked.

Guy had learnt from Josh. 'Oh – yellow,' he said.

'Yellow? Really? I'll take four.'

Three quarters of an hour later the crowds had thinned, and they got the chance of a breathing space. George was taking stock. The boards which had been packed tight were nearly bare now. There were only a few of the common *Paul Crampell* red and *King of Denmark* salmon-pink remaining.

'Have you any more of those yellow geraniums left?' It was the pushy woman, back again.

'No, sorry, we've sold out,' said Guy quickly. George looked at him.

'Did I just 'ear that correct?' he asked, as the woman moved off.

Guy double-checked under the bench. Sure enough the tray was empty.

'Them ones without flowers on,' he explained. 'Someone asked me what colour they were, so I made a guess. They sold like hot cakes after that.'

'I'll bet they did an' all,' laughed George. 'Thing is, mate, God don't make geraniums in yellow!'

After the rush died down Guy met up with Janice's son Paul and together, heads down and hands in pockets, they slunk through the aisles like two lean tom cats, muscles understated, looking for girls. Approaching Josh's stall Guy could see his boss's agitation from afar. His hair was matted, his eyes wild and he paced up and down. He looked every bit an axe murderer. Guy clocked a couple of empty bottles on the grass. It appeared he hadn't sold a thing, and now the punters were giving him an even wider berth.

'Where the bloody hell's Angie? You seen her?'

'Nope, sorry mate,' said Guy.

'Well you've just come in time,' he said, hands gesturing wildly. 'All this fucking lot's for free now, cos I'm not taking it home!' He raised his voice along with his arms and addressed his fellow stallholders and the knots of customers still strolling past. 'Roll up! Roll up! Life collection! All free! Come and get it! Track, trains, all the gear! No price!'

Guy tried to shield the front of the stall, but he needn't have bothered, the crowd were much too wary of the crazy man. 'Don't be fucking stupid, man! You'll regret it tomorrow!'

293

'I need a drink. No one wants this crap, anyway. Can't give it away!'

'I'll fetch you some beer,' said Guy hastily. He didn't want to get landed behind this stall. He knew Josh wouldn't come back.

A man approached tentatively, neck protruding bravely. 'Free, you say? Er – do you have any carrier bags?'

Josh stared at him and the man shrank back. 'Carrier bags? Carrier Bags?' He addressed the crowd, ripping open his shirt to reveal his tee-shirt. Sticking out his chest, he prodded it with his forefinger. 'Not content with my life's collection, he wants to rip my heart out as well!' And he opened the door to his car and began stuffing all the empty boxes and carrier bags he could find on to the back seat. Middle England looked on uncomfortably, from the genteel stallholders surrounding him to the bewildered punters passing by. Maybe there are some things you just can't give away, and even more that a madman can't give away. Either way there were no takers. Guy and Paul managed to drag him away.

'Come on, let's get that drink.'

Gradually a crowd closed in on the abandoned pitch, but without the courage to touch.

Josh only reached the end of the row and said: 'Fuck me, what have I done?' And he turned and hurried back, his quick temper spent. The lads shook their heads, happy to escape.

Back at his stall Josh spotted an apparition. His wife the lovely Angie was stood on something and chatting to the crowd.

'Free? Don't be daft, this here's worth a fortune! It's his life's collection, this is. Got all the stuff, trains, stations, what have you! About three hundred quids worth, here, there is!'

Josh squeezed back behind the stall, and the crowd stirred uneasily. A middle-aged man with a bald head and chunky neck spoke up in an American accent. A wiry kid with an eager nose hovered by his elbow.

'This is for real? Is this how you folks do things over here? Is it street theatre?'

'You could say that,' said Josh, mild now the red mist had gone.

'Amazing! Never seen anything like it! Done the trick, though, got the crowds here. How much for the whole caboodle, buddy?'

This took Josh by surprise, he hadn't worked them out as a job lot, but £150 sounded a nice round figure.

The man turned to the boy and into the hush of the crowd said: 'I figure that I owe you for the last three Christmases son, so if that's what you really want!' He peeled ten pound notes from a money clip as the crowd looked on as if he was pulling a rabbit from a hat.

Josh's stomach gave a back flip and he didn't know what to say for once.

'Nice to do business with you, sir.' The man stretched his hand out across the table. Josh shook it, rapidly revising his often voiced opinion of Americans.

'Ange love, can you get the boxes out the car?'

She pretended outrage. 'No way I can't! I'm your wife, not your slave!' and she planted a kiss on his cheek and flounced off. The crowd clapped, relieved.

'Thank you Dad!' said the boy, obviously pleased, and they stacked the boxes as Josh double checked the cash. Strangely the boy sounded English, and posh at that. Whatever, thought Josh. He was on cloud nine. His stall was empty and now he was free to wander around himself, and his first priority was to find Midge as he needed that pint even more.

Walking between the stalls he spotted Nicole. She was weighing up some of the flat podded peas for an elderly woman.

'Are you sure I don't shell 'em, dear?'

Nicole handed her a leaflet. 'No, you fry them,' she said gently. 'Read this, it tells you what to do.' The woman thanked her, and disappeared into the crowd.

Nicole saw Josh and smiled, looking straight into his eyes. 'I'm not doing massage today,' she said. She could see Josh looked embarrassed. 'I'm reading palms, though,' she said. 'It's okay, I'll do yours for free since I know you rather well.'

'I don't believe in all that shite,' he said, but lingered anyway. She really did seem to cast a spell. Perhaps she was a witch. She'd learnt well at witch school, he thought.

'Well,' said Nicole, bewitching him again with her brown eyes. 'If you don't believe in it, it can't hurt you can it? Come on.'

'Suppose not.' So he followed her behind the drapery.

₭ ₠

There was a crowd around Sammy's van. When Josh managed to elbow his way closer he found Sammy and Maureen doing something with maggots. Half a dozen people were leaning intently over a wooden box illuminated at one end, shouting excitedly. Sammy was racing maggots of all things, and running a book on it. The crowd were loving it. Sammy caught sight of Josh, whispered in Maureen's ear, and came over to join him saying: 'Don't ask!

'Only you could pull a stunt like that,' said Josh, his mind still sifting the New Knowledge.

'Don't you dare leave me for long!' shouted Maureen. She had her daughter Michelle by her side.

'See ya later!'

Further along Midge joined the two men leaving Kim to run the tent. After all a man deserves a day off once a year, he told himself.

'How about bowling for a pig?' Sammy suggested. This seemed reasonable and they strolled across to where the Rector was running the bowling. In the shade of the churchyard wall, snout down and snuffling, was the pig, a barrel of a beast with a corkscrew tail and covered all over with ginger hairs. A jolly country parson with a red face and ripples of grey hair was touting for custom.

'Roll up, roll up, come on gentlemen! Who will take Priscilla back with them tonight? I think it may be one of you!' He had a deep booming voice, a real asset in a large church with a shrunken congregation.

'Your Maureen won't be too happy if you come back with another pig,' said Midge. 'She was just telling Kim her freezers are full.'

'Oh, I'd sell it,' said Sammy quickly. 'I'll have five goes to start, Your Eminence,' he said.

The Rector gave Sammy five hard wooden balls and said: 'Roll them through the hoops sir, they're all numbered. Highest score wins the lovely lady there, but don't ask me to perform the wedding!'

All the men had a go, but Midge produced a near perfect set. His score was far above anyone else's, although they'd have to wait until half-past four to see if anyone could match it.

'Well done, old boy,' boomed the vicar in admiration. 'I don't think anyone will beat this.' Midge wrote his name and phone number carefully in the vicar's notebook.

Midge leaned over the temporary fence and scratched the pig's golden rump. It squirmed in delight. The reluctant chef of the Red Cow could see pork and apple hotpot scrawled in chalk on his menu board alongside meat pie. His new dish would be nearly a hundred percent profit.

'Why d'ya 'ave to bowl a bloody great score like that, Midge?' Sammy asked crossly. 'I'm never gonna beat that, if I try 'til Labour gets in.'

Midge looked at him in surprise. 'You don't begrudge me winning that pig, do you Sammy Dove? And you with a freezer stacked like royalty?'

'No, course not mate! I don't want the pig, I jus' want that dickhead Dickinson to think I won it, 'cos he donated it,' Sammy explained, but Midge was not interested. David Dickinson was as valued a customer as Sammy, more probably, he certainly put more cash across the bar.

'You're a pratt, Sammy Dove,' he said. 'Get back to your maggots.'

Sammy stayed put as the others walked on, deliberately losing them in the crowd, scratching his beard as he considered his next move. Then he noticed the vicar, obviously bored, had strayed over to the children's enclosure and was chatting with Julie and Sara. He'd left his notebook open on his wooden chair and the breeze was flipping the pages. Sammy approached cautiously. Midge had written his score in pencil, the very one which was holding the place in the notebook, with rubber tip. Sammy quickly erased Mr Midgley replaced it with Mr Dove. And he walked casually back to his maggots.

℘ ℃

Late in the afternoon those interested grouped around the Vicar to hear the results of the bowling. Sammy stood close to Midge, and whispered in his ear:

'Midge – listen – he'll read out my name, but then, straight up mate, I promise I'll give it back to you. Look, I'll even throw in six sacks o' spuds and some nets of onions, so your hotpot can really be buckshee! Can't say fairer than that, mate.'

Midge turned and stared at him. 'Why, what you been up to?'

The Vicar was clearing his great throat, and the bulk of

the crowd quietened.

'Shh,' hissed Sammy.

The pig scoured obliviously in the dusty grass, late sunshine sparking his ginger hairs.

'Ladies and Gentlemen!' boomed the Vicar. 'The winner of the pig is – and may I say that as a believer in equality of gender I am very pleased...'

What? thought Sammy.

'Eh?' said Midge, nervous now.

'The winner is – MISS NICOLE HARVEY! Nicole won with an amazing perfect score of sixty –' he paused, beaming, 'And may I say it was like poetry to watch her!'

Josh's mouth dropped open, and he wondered. No! She couldn't have, surely not the vicar.

The crowd clapped and Sammy gawped. Midge turned around to him, his brown eyes uncharacteristically angry. The day's exposure to sunshine had already darkened his skin and he looked more Latin than ever.

'What did you do Sammy Dove? Did you bribe the Vicar?'

'Midge, I swear on my Maureen's life that's nothin' to do with me, mate.'

'You must've done something. I should've won that!'

'Well, what I done didn't work obviously,' Sammy admitted churlishly.

Nicole stepped gracefully forward, her chiffon skirt flowing, her legs bare and silhouetted through the material, Lady Diana all over again. She reached the Vicar and shook hands with him, and then unexpectedly raised her face up and kissed him on both cheeks. The Vicar grinned and blushed like a choirboy.

Nicole started to speak, and the crowd went quiet. 'I am a vegetarian,' she announced in a clear voice, 'So I plan to take this pig to West Wansbridge animal sanctuary where it will hopefully live to a great age!' The crowd roared, half amusement, half disapproval.

Midge had his head in his hands. He felt cheated.

Sammy craned his neck to see David Dickinson. He knew that in the JP's Venn diagram of contempt Nicole would fall in the overlap, being vegetarian and grower. So he'd got a result after all.

'Nice one, Nicole!' Sammy shouted loudly, making sure the farmer could hear. 'I know where there's some pheasants you could take along too!'

೫   ೦౩

Later that evening when the stalls were dismantled and the crowds died away the focus shifted back to the Red Cow. Angie had agreed to open the pub whilst Midge and Kim cleared away the outside bar. She stood in a cloud of perfume, and with a big smile on her red lips she dealt capably with the rush. When he returned to his pub Midge had to admit Angie looked the part; he might even have considered her as a barmaid had the Red Cow been "that sort of pub" all year instead of for just one day. Josh watched with pride as his wife ran the bar like she'd been born in a boozer, but this was tinged with annoyance that he wouldn't be able to spend quite as much or get quite as drunk as he'd planned.

The bars were both packed, regulars lost amongst strangers and as Midge ducked under the hatch to help Angie, Kim and Mo leant against the door to the garden, keeping a very vague eye on the children darting around outside.

In the car park groups of youngsters from surrounding villages sat on the wall, legs dangling, drinking too much and shouting. Behind an outbuilding on the edge of the field of stubble sixteen year old Michelle Dove stood pressed against Martin Dickinson, her pale skirt reflecting the moon

300

and her high heeled shoes sinking in as she stretched up to him. Sammy's earlier victory would have seemed hollow indeed had he seen them both slide into Martin's Land Rover and head for the back lanes.

Thirty-Five

Tim, Vice Chairman of the Growers' Association had a holding like no other. Originally an employee of the Estate propagation department, he had persuaded Jack Ball's predecessor to let him take on a bare six acres which were no longer used for production. The manager had been wary as no glass meant no collateral, but at least the land was surrounded by conifers which provided a good wind break. Single then as now, Tim had scoured the country for second-hand plastic tunnels, any size, any shape, bent frames, whatever, and he now had forty-six single span structures spilling onto an extra two acres which he now rented as well. His tunnels were all numbered, each numeral scrawled in indelible ink onto a piece of wood and nailed above the door. He grew only two crops – Cos lettuce and peppers. He'd never attempted aubergines, cultivated cucumbers or troubled himself with tomatoes. He'd chosen his couple of crops and that was that.

All this made for a soulless nursery and the other growers shook their heads, referring to it as the Factory. They couldn't understand his lack of aspiration towards good glass or multispans, and he kept no livestock and grew no pot plants. Twice a year the dark green rows of Cos lettuce crept up to his back door. What about crop rotation? What about variety? What about boredom? Tim was certainly an enigma although he did seem to be doing rather well financially, rumour had it.

Plastic sheeting on tunnels is supposed to be renewed every couple of years, but Tim hadn't bothered; maybe he didn't relish the thought of the amount of labour required. Consequently the covers, some as old as five years, were becoming very scruffy, criss-crossed with the gaffer tape he used to patch them.

Jim had asked him once: 'I'm not being funny mate, but how long d'you think you can go without changing the plastic? They'll all give up the ghost at once and you'll spend the whole year replacing 'em!'

'No need, my friend,' Tim had replied. 'I can't afford to go wasting money like that! They could last another six or seven years. The proof's in the crop, and I don't think you can argue with that?'

Jim couldn't. He'd bent to examine the pepper crop and it was indeed beautifully even, the rows straight and controlled as a topiary hedge. Tim used lengths of six-inch squared plastic mesh which he laid out on the soil before he planted up and as the plants grew, he gradually raised this mesh so the thin branches were supported fully. Most people just tied string along the sides in an attempt to stop the plants collapsing on the path, but this wasn't ideal and if a plant flopped you got uneven and misshapen fruit.

'I'm impressed with this,' said Jim, fingering the mesh. 'I haven't seen this in The Stores.'

Tim rubbed himself on his thin cheek with a blocky pepper he'd picked earlier, beautiful satin finish, perfectly hooked stalk. 'No, they won't stock this mesh. I'll give you the address if you like.' And next day Tim pushed a note through Jim's door with the contact number, good as his word.

So Tim was King of Peppers and King of Cos, and his vast throughput had helped Adam secure a contract with one of the supermarkets. He even devoted half a dozen tunnels to letting the fruit turn red, something nobody else could afford to do as the premium price for these didn't really compensate for time wasted waiting for them to ripen.

This year most other growers had a tunnel or two of peppers and a supermarket chain had been taking all the Estate could produce, until August when a glut meant they'd cut back their order. Adam continued to sell Tim's to the supermarket, but was forced to dump the rest on the wholesale market at a third of the price. The other growers were angry and stopped sending their peppers through the official channel, the "warning" having gone cold. Then suddenly the glut was over and the supermarket was screaming for peppers once more.

'Jonathan! We're going to lose that supermarket contract if you can't get some from somewhere,' Adam's voice crackled over the two-way radio. 'They can't have all pulled them out and planted lettuce!'

Jonathan's Astra was parked outside Jim's. 'Well I've tried, Adam, for heaven's sake. Jim says he's only got six boxes, and with a few from here and there I can muster about fifty but no more than that.'

Now peppers start producing slowly and build up nicely to a crescendo. It's just the shorter autumn daylight that slows them down. It was still only September so all concerned knew the plants would be producing in full swing.

Jack Ball must have snatched the mike at the other end. 'Jonathan!' he growled. 'Jonathan! We all know they're selling outside. How long, I say, how long ago did I give you that camera and tell you I wanted evidence? Now we're going to lose that contract. Who the hell are you working for – me or them?"

Up yours, thought Jonathan. Why do you put it all on me?

'Okay Jack,' he said meekly, for there was a reference request winging its way to his boss. He would have to act fast if he was to gain credibility in time. 'Leave it with me.'

'Huh. I want to see some action, and soon,' the big man snarled.

'You will, boss, it's in hand.'

'He'd better,' said Jack to Adam as he crashed the mike back on the desk.

୨୦ ଓ୪

Jim's son Paul backed the Bedford CF van up to the shed, leaning out from the sliding door so he could see behind. The shed lights shone warm and inviting on this dark windy night. It was late September but it could have been November as a cold wind from the north gusted and bent the trees which still held most of their leaves. His father and Eddie began to stack the van with boxes of peppers, most of which were their own but they'd topped up with some from other growers. Soon the back of the van was stuffed full. The load couldn't shift as they'd forced the top layer in tight to the roof and boxes were even wedged under the bench seat in the front.

'Same place as last week?' asked Paul. He regularly took produce such as this to various locations and enjoyed the excitement. He thought it a bit like the bootleggers in the *Dukes of Hazard*.

'Yep,' said Jim.

'I'm coming with you, I fancy a ride,' said Eddie.

Shit, thought Paul, who enjoyed listening to music radio and didn't relish the company of a sixties fanatic.

'Don't you trust me or something?' he asked sulkily.

'I'd sooner trust a cat with me pigeons,' said Jim. 'No, it's not that son, it's just that that lock-up's in the middle of nowhere and Eddie can keep an eye out.'

୨୦ ଓ୪

The wind howled. It was whipping the trees and ripping their leaves to the ground before the poor things had had

305

time to change colour. It was so strong it even rocked Jonathan's car, concealed as it was in a dark hedgerow. Jonathan pushed his seat back and stretched his long legs as far as the cramped conditions would allow. He was dreaming vaguely of other nights spent in dark hedgerows, much more rewarding ones. Now he was on a mission to catch a culprit red-handed. This was how he'd spent the last two evenings and both had been fruitless. The first night only cars had left the Drift, and yesterday he'd followed Nigel's van for miles along the winding country lanes...

His van had finally pulled into the drive of a large farmhouse. Confident this would be a dodgy deal, Jonathan left his Astra concealed under a large tree and crept like a stalker up the drive, hiding in a bunch of pampas as Nigel knocked the front door. A middle-aged woman opened it.

'They're in the back,' he heard Nigel say briefly.

I'm in business now, thought Jonathan, wondering how he was going to photograph the transfer without them spotting the flash. He was, after all, on private property.

The woman shuffled out of her slippers and pushed her feet into a pair of wellingtons, leaning on the doorpost as she wriggled. She followed Nigel to the back of his van and Jonathan skirted around the herbaceous border to get his view.

'Which billy do you want? Yours are British Alpines, I think, aren't they? It's eleven pounds a shot whichever one you choose, successful or not.' The woman had spoken in a very businesslike way. 'They usually catch on, as I'm sure you know and the kids'll have all the benefits of our excellent breeding.'

Jonathan couldn't see but he could hear well enough. Anger flooded over him. Nigel wasn't selling illegally, he was taking his goats for a shag! Now he could see the first animal, as it was dragged from the van, silhouetted in front of the lights of the farmhouse.

'Come on lass- coo coo shooo shooo...' Nigel cooed softly, but the poor goat obviously wasn't convinced. This is rape, he thought as they pulled and dragged the goat to her stud. Hazel had been positively willing compared to this. Then why did the episode still leave a nasty taste in his mouth? Irritated, he skulked back to his car, another wasted evening. Tonight really was his last chance...

Suddenly he heard a diesel engine and he recognised the number plate as the van slowed to turn into the lane from the Drift. There'd be no reason for this vehicle to go anywhere else. He quickly slid his seat back to position, turned the key and was in pursuit, tailing the van at a reasonable distance.

೫   ಄

'Bloody 'ell, you drive like a flamin' maniac,' grumbled Eddie as he grabbed a handle to save being lurched across the seat. Paul increased his speed slightly for effect. The road snaked so much it was only possible to see a short distance ahead. The headlights turned the trees ghostly against the dark sky, it was like driving beyond a photograph and into the negative.

'Didn't think you'd be chicken,' he said, crunching the gears slightly as he changed down into a sharp corner.

Eddie looked in the left hand mirror. 'You don't want the old bill to stop us do you?' He caught sight of a vehicle travelling as fast as them which took some doing on this dark windy night.

'Naw! They'll be back at the station drinking tea, or on the motorway,' said Paul, dismissively.

Eddie hunched his neck into his shoulders to get a better view in the mirror, as Paul turned left up an even smaller lane with a screech of tyres. 'Do you want us to end up in the bleeding DITCH!! It's still following,' he added in a more normal voice.

'Middle aged passengers!' sighed Paul, but he dropped his speed anyway to a more manageable fifty miles per hour. They didn't see the headlights any more, and soon forgot about it. Paul switched on and tuned to Radio One just as his favourite song of the moment came on. He sung loudly, moving his shoulders to the music as the van bounced along the narrow lanes, occasionally scraping the hedgerow.

"Sometimes I feel I've got to runaway
I've got to get away
From the pain you drive
Into the heart of me..."

'Hey, what's this?' said Eddie after a minute. 'This is better than the usual crap. Somethin' about this one.'

'Been number one – Soft Cell... *hey tainted love..*' and encouraged by Eddie's comment Paul upped the volume to full blast.

"Take my tears and that's not living
Oh, tainted love woh-oh-oh-oh
Tainted love..."

And the song bridged the generation gap for a couple of miles at least.

The lockup was on the edge of an isolated village; it was part of a commercial development by one of the larger farmers, perhaps searching for that magic state – diversification. It consisted of about twenty breeze-block buildings which were used for a variety of activities from motor mechanics to storage. It was easily visible as the hedgerows had been destroyed.

Paul slowed to a halt and Eddie jumped out and unlocked the padlock on the five-bar gate as the wind ripped at his body warmer and roared through a clump of tall ash trees behind him. Paul drove through, and Eddie didn't bother to lock it behind him, nobody was about. The headlights gave directional light, but it wouldn't have been pleasant to be alone, Paul thought. He jumped back in and they drove up to number six, its only distinguishing feature a maroon up-and-over door. Paul had a key; he found the lock without difficulty, swung the door up, and groped the ledge inside for the envelope with the cash.

Eddie, looking around cautiously, thought he heard a car engine stop, the sound just audible between gusts of wind. The moon which had previously been hidden, emerged just long enough for him to pick out and recognise a vehicle before scuds of cloud suffocated the light once more.

'It's Jonathan Foster! The sneaking bastard must have followed us, he's come to catch us out!'

Remembering his position here as minder, Eddie immediately took charge. 'Listen,' he hissed. 'Don't unload a thing. Keep stum. And mind you put that money back! Hurry up. Shut the door – we've done nothin' he can have us for. For crissake don't let him see in the van and drive straight back home.' The youth nodded and stuffed the envelope back on the ledge and dropped the door down. Then he realised Eddie wasn't getting back in.

'Why – where are you going?' asked Paul, grappling with the padlock.

'I'll see you back at your Dad's or I'll flag you down in the road. Don't worry about me – you just get the van back safe!' And Eddie was gone, disappearing between two of the buildings into the darkness and the roar of the wind.

Paul jumped back in the van, swung her round in the yard and drove with strong resolve back through the gateway. Jonathan, camera useless in his hand, flattened himself against the gatepost to save from being squashed. The youth kept his face a mask.

As Paul turned out on to the lane, he saw Jonathan's Astra completing a panicky three-point turn in the road in front of him. Then he remembered Jonathan always left the keys in his vehicle. It was the sort of careless habit which comes from getting in and out of your car all day. That crafty bugger Eddie, thought Paul with a grin as he accelerated to catch the Astra. They chased each other back home, blasting their horns all the way along the twists and the turns and the overhanging branches.

When they got back to the LSA office complex, Eddie parked the Astra in the space marked J. BALL MANAGER. As he climbed into the van he said to Paul:

'You know what, Paul old lad?'

'What?'

'I love it when a plan comes together!!!'

₳ ₳

The next morning no fewer than six different growers rang the Packhouse to tell Adam they'd miscalculated and would have more boxes ready for collection by lunchtime than they'd thought. Adam didn't ask questions, just assured them their peppers were wanted once again at the higher rate.

Jonathan was late showing his face at the office, and when he did arrive he was tired and irritable. It had been a long windswept walk to find a phone box and an expensive taxi ride back to the Estate, where, thank God, they'd left his company car. Now he walked in without his usual cockiness and silently sorted the mail on his desk.

'Good work old man,' Adam said to him. 'You look knackered, good night last night?'

Jonathan glared through narrowed eyes. Good work? Was he in league with the growers too, did he know something?

'I don't know what you mean,' he said coldly, tossing junk mail into a metal basket by his feet.

'I don't know what you did but the growers are all ringing up with peppers this morning. Was it your powers

310

of persuasion or did you put the frighteners on them?' Adam rubbed his large belly, ripe for a bacon buttie.

Jonathan took his time digesting this bit of information, pretending to study a letter so Adam couldn't see his face. Finally he answered, when he was convinced Adam was being genuine and not sarcastic:

'Let's say a bit of both. But will you do me a favour Adam?'

'Sure, I'm a happy bunny now I haven't got to cancel that big order. I'll do anything, well within reason..'

Jonathan stood up to go, colour back in his cheeks and his spirit restored. 'Just remind the Boss it's much better to take a positive stance rather than a negative one. He wanted me to catch someone red-handed at selling outside, but I don't much like making scapegoats of people. I think it's much better to draw them all into line, *get them on board, get them on board*, I say, by other methods!'

Adam laughed. 'Spot on, Jonathan. I'll do that old man!'

Thirty-Six

Eric often pondered which part of his job he enjoyed the most. Was it the detective work necessary to identify a plant pathogen to solve a problem with a crop or was it the social work element? He certainly liked the personal contact, aware that lives might be affected if he failed to diagnose and advise on a horticultural problem quickly and correctly. He was an agronomist by interest as well as training and even on holiday he carried his pocket plant identification books and was forever diving into hedgerows, much to the annoyance of his wife, but latterly he seemed to have become hooked on the social side. He was very aware of the sins of self-satisfaction, especially as some of tenants regarded him almost like a priest. He was bothered too because all the "Mr Nice Guys" of his experience were awfully tedious. Fortunately his wife reminded him daily of his unsavoury habits, and he thought maybe he should spend a Saturday morning parading them up the Drift with a banner stating: "hey, I'm human too".

The summer was nearly over, and so far this year no growers had actually been caught selling outside, none had gone bankrupt although he knew it was only a matter of time before the Association pulled the plug on some, and none had given in their notice so far as he knew. It was strange, thought Eric, how the winds of change move slowly time like a grumbling appendix. Then something happens abruptly which catches everyone by suprise. So it was with George and Maisie.

Visiting their holding he noticed they hadn't planted up

with autumn lettuce, something they'd done every year since Eric had known them. He realised they'd missed the date now. Something was amiss.

'What about your late lettuce George?' he asked. 'Aren't you leaving it a bit tight or have you got so many of those famous yellow geraniums you're in the export trade now?'

They were sitting outside the tomato house on upturned bulk bins in the warm September sunshine. Maisie looked tired and Eric wondered when she'd last had a holiday. He thought probably not since her children left home and like most growers, not many before that.

'Shall you tell him, Maisie?' George said with a wink to her.

Maisie's face brightened, and the weariness faded. 'We're packin' this lark in, Eric, and goin' to buy a little place with about an acre, so as he can mess with his geraniums and I can get a little part-time job, dinner lady or somethin'. Can you see me as a dinner lady, Eric?'

Eric privately thought she'd be wasted as a dinner lady, a pub cook might be better, after all don't they just eat beefburgers at school, these days? But he said: 'Well yes, Maisie, but I have to say I can't imagine you without a greenhouse.'

'Well, I'd still 'elp George, of course, with his pot plants,' Maisie explained. 'If he paid me right! I've had enough of these years of working for nothin', 'im bossing me about!' she laughed, jowls rippling and chest wheezing.

Eric laughed too, but then his smile faded as he remembered the rumours he'd heard, that the Association wouldn't be re-letting any holdings. This could present a problem for George and Maisie who might be relying on a new tenant buying at least half of their glass as it stood. Luckily the aluminium house which they were sitting in front of, could easily be dismantled and caused no such worries. He was reluctant to dampen their enthusiasm when his fears had no definite basis and he decided to keep quiet for now. He said instead: 'Have you anywhere special in mind?'

'No,' said George.

'Yes,' said Maisie.

'I've told you woman, that we got to give three month's notice and we'll be bound to lose that one. Eric, she's seen a bungalow and it's got one of them bloody fancy corner baths. Fancy buying a house just because you like the bath. Anyways, I told her, I like to stretch out in me bath.'

'And I 'ave to give him a hand to get out of it!' retorted Maisie.

'That's an excuse, Eric, for 'er to get 'er hands on my naked body!' They both roared with laughter at this, and Eric speculated how much they'd be missed on the Estate, not just as genuine characters, but as good practitioners of their trade too.

'It's got a Jacuzzi thingy,' continued Maisie.

'And it's got an acre of land,' said George, seriously now. 'I could grow me geraniums and sell 'em by post. I've built up enough stock 'ere. An' I can sell at the gate, cos it's on a main road. But it ain't no good you gettin' all worked up, my little Petunia,' he continued, as if it were only she who was. 'I only jus' handed me notice into the office, yesterday. We oughta be out by the New Year.'

As Eric strode back to his Volvo, he noticed the asters in Maisie's front border were flowering with an abundance they always achieve too late, for autumn would surely put paid to them before most of the buds reached maturity. Yes, asters definitely misjudge the English summer, he thought.

℘   ℘

Two days later, George was knocking on Simon's door. Nicole answered it, blinking at the bright light. Although it was two in the afternoon, she looked as if she'd only just got up. Pretty as she was, George mentally gave thanks that he had married a good strong workhorse like Maisie and not a wispy creature like Nicole, but then it struck him that Simon was as different from himself as the Tropics from the Arctic, so they were probably very well suited.

'Hello George. This is a surprise. Have you trouble with your back?'

'No- no...' spluttered George, filled with panic. 'I've a good strong back, like an 'oss! No, it's Simon I've come to see.'

Nicole laughed, leaned around the doorpost and pointed towards the chaotic holding. 'He'll be up there somewhere.'

He followed the trace of her delicate finger up the overgrown pathway and past dilapidated Dutch Light houses, to a more solid glasshouse. It wasn't aluminium because Simon didn't have any expensive glass. George was secretly shocked by its ramshackle condition.

'SIMON,' shouted George. His voice echoed loudly in the quiet of the afternoon disrupting the birdsong. Then he could hear the regional accents of a radio four play. Simon stuck his head out from a forest of triffid-like growth which wasn't quite contained by the walls. Shoots were escaping through doors, vents and broken panes.

'What on earth you got there?' asked George in amazement. 'Some sort o' peas?'

Incredible. Peas at this time of year, and under glass too. The fronds were trailing everywhere, like a grove of semi-cultivated tropical lianas. The crop wasn't under control and Simon appeared to be picking the pods before they were fully developed. He set the plastic bucket he was carrying at George's feet, then squatted down, all bony knees and khaki shorts, and dipped his hand in amongst the flat immature pods. They squeaked as they rubbed against each other.

Well, he must be as crazy as everyone reckons he is,

thought George. And I've always stuck up for him too.

'Mange-tout peas,' explained Simon with a smile. 'The French eat them, but they are catching on in posh restaurants across London.'

'Hmm, well,' said George unable to resist picking up a handful and squeaking them between his fingers too. 'I s'pose we could farm snails and all an' catch frogs and cut their legs off! But they ain't ready for harvest, mate.'

He held a flat pod in his hand, and split it open with difficulty. The undeveloped row of green peas was visible inside the pod and the unmistakably sweet smell of newly-popped pods took George immediately back to his childhood, when he used to trail behind his mother in the pea fields of Kent.

'Ah, well, I can see you didn't study French,' said Simon, smiling. He reached in the pocket of his baggy shorts and pulled out the duplicate of yesterday's ticket, which he'd sent with his produce to the Packhouse. 'Look, "mange tout". Manger is "to eat" in French. Tout is "all," or "everything." It translates to "eat everything peas." You eat the pod as well, in stir fries.'

'Well I'll be damned,' said George. He thought to himself, now I know I'm making the right decision. I'm much too old for this game, I can see that now. Laughingly he said to Simon: 'Are you sure you ain't supposed to eat the leaves an' all? You might be leaving 'arf your produce in the greenhouse!'

They walked companionably towards Simon's packing shed. Like George, it had seen better days. Simon put his bucket in a space which he cleared of clutter with a sweep of his forearm. Behind him was a large cardboard case containing transparent plastic punnets of the sort George had seen Jim use for his cherry tomatoes. Simon carefully arranged the flat green pods in a punnet, making sure they were all perfectly aligned. He placed the lid and pressed with his thumb to snap it shut. George had to admit the result was most attractive.

'Hmm, nice. What 'ave them lot made of 'em in the Packhouse?' he asked.

'I haven't had the returns yet,' Simon admitted, 'But apparently there shouldn't be any problem shifting this small amount. The beauty of it is that I harvest in just a few hits, and then the crop is finished.'

George knew that this was a feature of peas. They didn't keep coming like beans. He could imagine how this would suit Simon, who liked intensive bursts of work, rapidly becoming bored with anything approaching the steady.

'Let's go down to the house for a drink,' Simon suggested.

When they reached the overgrown lawn, Simon indicated two bleached wooden chairs set in a pool of warm sunshine, and he went inside the house to put the kettle on. Nicole was now lying in a hammock close by, one leg trailing over the side, lost in a book. George watched some dragonflies basking in the sun on a five-barred gate, and wondered if they'd known yesterday the weather would change, as they sheltered somewhere from the torrential rain. Simon stuck his head out of the kitchen window.

'Camomile, wild blackberry or peppermint?'

Oh no, thought George. I forgot about this. 'Peppermint,' he replied, after a second or two. His mother used to make peppermint drinks when he and his brother were small and suffering from stomach complaints. How strange he should think of his mother twice in so short a time. Maybe it was because Simon and Nicole, despite being young, seemed to exist in limbo between the reality of today and idyllic dreams of yesteryear.

The two men relaxed with their tea. Simon advised George to leave it to cool a little, not having added cold milk to reduce the temperature. George filled his pipe as his tea steamed.

'Simon, I'm packin' it in, I give me notice in last week,' he said simply. Simon merely raised his eyebrows. 'Then Jack Ball sent for me today, an' he told me that the Land Settlement ain't letting any more holdings as they become vacant fo' the foreseeable future, he said. 'Course I asked 'im why, an' I've a good idea meself like, but he weren't lettin' on. He jus' said it was orders from above.'

Simon listened intently and his sharp brain digested and arranged the facts as he blew gently to cool his wild blackberry tea. A couple of wasps which had hung benignly in the warm air now homed in on the fruit teas. George barred them with the wall of his hand but Simon batted at them and they rose to the fight.

'Well I'm not surprised,' he said slowly. 'They obviously can't keep going as they are, with growers' debts mounting all the time. *Pesky things!* But I see the problem for you, of course. You'll have nobody to sell your fixed assets to.'

'Aw, it ain't the end o' the world for me,' George said. 'I'll still be able to dismantle me Fen houses an' Dutch Lights and sell 'em as individual Lights, at fifty pence a go. I ain't in debt, thank God, and the aluminium should fetch a pretty penny. And I've got me a small insurance policy about due. What I really wanted to talk to you about, mate, is the future of this Estate. You being a scholar, like, 'ow do you see it?'

Simon stretched out fully tilting the wooden chair onto its back legs. With his wiry brown legs covered with golden hairs and his shorts he looked even less like a grower, more like an athlete. He knew what a dedicated chairman George had been, and it was typical of the man to be bothered for his fellow growers, even though he knew his own future was secure. The wasps appeared to have gone but it was just that their circle had widened.

'My opinion is this,' said Simon, 'and may I remind you

it is only an opinion. I think that the marketing association as it exists in its present form will cease. The market is so tight at the moment that it's unfair to restrict growers to only one outlet, or only one source of supplies, come to that. *Sod these wasps!* The LSA have recently failed, for whatever reason, to obtain competitive prices and they will recognise that if things continue they'll be liable to be sued for malpractice. They'll need to place responsibility for marketing and everything else squarely on the grower.' He sipped his tea reflectively. 'Remove the stabilisers from the bike, if you like. The idea of the co-operative is outdated now, I'm afraid, in Maggie Thatcher's Britain. *Get lost, will you!* The question is this, will the growers, many of whom have little knowledge of how the markets work and no business training, be able to do any better?'

'A chimpanzee could do better 'n them!' said George with contempt. 'When I stop an' think about the prices just five year ago.......' One of the wasps paused for a breather and George squashed it easily with the base of his cup. The other flew off to report it. George used his cup again to push the crushed corpse off the edge of the table.

Simon leaned forward, eyes earnest, voice just short of patronising. 'George, you said earlier that times have changed. We're in the Common Market with countries which have all kinds of advantages and I don't just mean climatic. Our five acres are desperately undersized now. Why, there's a lettuce producer just north of London who has fifteen acres under glass! That's yours, mine and Jim's holding completely covered with glass, just growing lettuce. I ask you, how can we hope to compete? I think you're probably doing the right thing wanting to get out.'

'Hmm, that bloody Common Market. I never ever agreed wi' it. Least me and Maisie, we voted against it in that refer.. refer whatsit, our consciences is clear. Course it's too late now. But what'll you do, Simon?' George asked, refilling his pipe. Simon couldn't possibly be surviving. The general disrepair of buildings, the empty houses full of weed bore witness to this. Simon smiled wanly.

'We'll stay, partly because we can't afford to move right now, but partly because I'm sure that once the marketing organisation pulls out, the government will sell off the holdings, as they're doing with council houses. We'll get a bridging loan, hopefully, to buy then sell the holding as it has potential as an executive house with paddock or suchlike, and after we've paid off our debt we should have enough left to buy elsewhere. You know, you should really consider that, George. If you've no real liability you could buy your holding and become potentially wealthy. If you just hold on.'

George considered this for a moment, his pipe working overtime, smoke rising in short sharp bursts. He shook his head. He couldn't imagine anyone wanting to buy the holdings, with the pokey little houses. His "tea" was now cool enough to be gulped down like evil tasting medicine, back again to his childhood.

'Maisie has 'er heart set on a fancy bungalow,' he explained. 'No, I've made me decision, we 'ave. You pays your money, you takes your chance.'

Simon laughed. 'Well, just remember there's the possibility the Drift will become Millionaire's Row.'

George giggled at this as he stood up to leave. Nicole's book lay discarded on the grass, and her leg was tucked back up in the hammock. She looked as if she was asleep.

'Wait a minute, present for Maisie,' said Simon, and he ran into the packing shed, his action reminding George of a giraffe. Perhaps not an athlete, he thought. Simon returned with a punnet of peas.

'Maisie will know what to do with these,' he said. George took them and thanked him, but he doubted she would. On the other hand, she never threw anything away so they'd probably appear boiled and steaming next to his mashed potato. Maybe he should chuck them in the hedge now? Then he laughed again. 'Mangy peas. Not a good name for marketing your own produce!' he said to himself.

Thirty-Seven

It was half-six on a late September morning, and it had rained lightly during the night, enough to dampen the concrete and darken the mud without leaving puddles. Now the sky was clear but for stripes of cloud in the east which almost blocked the yellow light of dawn. The autumn air was cool and moist, and spiders' webs sparkled in the tired hedgerows linking grasses at the side of the road. Birds congregated on the telephone wires presumably discussing travel arrangements, and the occupants of two police vans on the Drift were presumably discussing how they'd carry out instructions.

$\wp$ $\text{\calligra}$

Karen slid honey from a heated spoon and stirred it into her porridge and Steve shovelled sugar onto his. She was puzzling over a sheet of paper, he stared into space. The radio played softly as the children were still sleeping and Karen hoped they'd stay that way until she had to get them ready for nursery school in an hour and a half's time.

All at once they were startled by a loud clattering on the front door, the sort which strikes irrational fear into your very being.

Bewildered, Steve went to open the door.

'Who the hell's that at this hour?' he said. 'OK– I'M COMING!'

What happened next was a blur.

Steve thought he heard: "this is a drugs raid" as three

men rushed past him, and a uniformed police officer positioned himself at the conservatory door. Karen found herself stranded at the table unable to move. Her heart was beating wildly for the situation was utterly incomprehensible. Steve also stood and watched in a trance.

The three men, dressed for the town, would have looked totally out of place in this room even if they hadn't been pulling open drawers and rifling through cupboards. It was bizarre. They searched systematically, from the food cupboards to the deep dusty crevices down the side of the old settee.

At first Karen watched with the detachment of somebody observing a scene from a movie, one which you haven't watched from the beginning but catches your attention on the television as you're doing something else. Then harsh reality dawned on her. They really were in some kind of trouble.

'What the hell's happening? What on earth's this about?' she cried.

The uniformed officer, leaning casually against the doorway, looked hard at her. He was young, about her own age she guessed, and tall and slim. As the others continued their orderly ransacking of the room, he said conversationally:

'We have a search warrant as we have reason to believe that we will find drugs in this house. It's no use you running away, if that's your intention. We've a road block outside.'

She stared at him incredulously. This was the Drift, a respectable estate with reputable residents. Could this possibly be right?

'Steve! D'you hear this? For Christ's sake do something! Tell 'em, they've got the wrong house! How dare you touch that!' She was referring to her diary, which one of the plain clothes officers took from the top of the television, a large Letts type in which she kept personal comments along with crop data – planting dates, harvesting amounts, that sort of thing. He flicked through it briefly, as if to check for loose papers, his eyes cold and expressionless.

Karen moved to snatch her diary from the policeman, but he swung it high above her head.

'You bastard!' she screamed. 'My diary! How dare you! You can't do that!' They completely ignored her, apart from the uniform who said in a condescending voice: 'You'd be surprised what people tell their diaries. Usually a lot more than they tell us.'

She looked around desperately for Steve, who was stood by the window staring at the cotoneaster as if counting the berries. Why wasn't he doing something to stop all this? She shook him, and he shrugged her off, his body tense as iron.

'STOP HIM!' she cried. 'STEVE!'

'How can I? It's a drugs raid an' they can look at owt they want. You'd do best to co-operate, make a cup of tea or summat.'

Karen couldn't believe it. What was wrong with him? Why wasn't he fighting? A cold shiver spread across her. Surely he didn't have any? She knew Steve had smoked marijuana in the past, but he knew how she felt about it, and there certainly hadn't been any sign of him doing so since Yorkshire. Sammy! Oh no, she thought miserably, anything's possible with Sammy.

Incredibly, the men had already scoured the lounge and dining room. Contents from drawers lay strewn across the floor. The only thing they attempted to replace was the carpet, which they'd ripped up in places, and one of them now poked it back flat with the side of his foot. They made to go upstairs.

'NO! NO!' she shouted. 'Let me go into the children first!'

At first she thought they weren't going to, but then they agreed to let her go into the girls' bedroom ahead of them. She ran up the stairs and into the bedroom, where the children must have been awoken by the noise. The two little ones were both on one bed. They sat huddled together, for once speechless, eyes wide. Trying to act as normally as possible, Karen walked over and put an arm around each of them, and the men hesitated in the doorway.

'Don't worry chickens, these men are policemen, and they want to look for something, something that the people who lived here before left behind.' She'd harnessed her voice, and it didn't shake.

Two of the men, it wasn't possible for three, squeezed into the room, ignoring the children, pulling out drawers, first those stuffed with clothes and then the ones filled with toys. And again tearing back the carpet, which fortunately had never been fitted anyway.

'They don't look like policemen,' said Mandy in a clear voice, and Trudy began to cry and cling to Karen. Usually it was Mandy who cried, but she was dry-eyed now. They all had to move off the bed, so the men could grope beneath the mattress.

'Right, you can go back.'

The other man reappeared in the doorway. 'Anything?'

'Nope.'

'It'll be outside then.' And they were gone with the same purpose they'd shown with the search in the house.

Karen told the children to stay, promising all sorts of things, and ran downstairs after the men to look for Steve. She felt a little more confident, because she guessed they were now looking for plants, and she was completely certain they hadn't any.

A police dog had arrived from somewhere, a perky looking Cocker Spaniel, and it trotted straight towards the prop house. Three of the four men followed. Again the uniform hung close to Steve and Karen, bringing up the rear.

Steve had gone pale. It was truer to say that he turned a sort of yellow.

'See! Nothing! They found nothing!' Karen was shouting to the officer in uniform. 'You've terrorised my kids. You wicked bastards! I'm going to make a complaint!' She was interrupted by a shout from the prop house.

'BINGO!'

Another policemen swung in closer to Karen and Steve. They now had one each.

'*What?*' she asked. 'WHAT?'

'I swear to God she didn't know,' said Steve, miserably. Karen eyed him with disbelief.

'You IDIOT!' she screamed, aiming a kick at him. The policeman held her back, his hard hands gripping and probably bruising the flesh of her upper arms.

'Twenty plants,' said one of the officers, 'That's all. We'll probably find more up here.' They set off with the dog, its nose to the ground, curled tail swinging gently.

ഇ ൬

They didn't find any more. Steve went willingly to the Police station and Karen was allowed to stay with the girls. She walked back to the house, and shouted for them to come down.

'Did they find what they were looking for, Mam?' asked Trudy, from the stairs. 'Ahh!' She clapped her hand to her mouth as she saw the mess.

'Yes they did, and that's why Daddy's gone with them to explain.' Her legs were weak so she sank into an armchair.

'Why did he go in the police van and not ours?' asked Mandy, tear-stained face anxious, big eyes watery.

'I'll tell you later. Don't worry.' She forced a weak smile. 'Lets have breakfast and then I'll clear up this mess.'

'The policemen are very naughty to leave all this mess, are they coming back to clean up later?'

'I hope not,' said Karen wearily.

After settling the children to their Weetabix, she went to telephone Hazel, who could now repay her debt. She found the telephone was dead, it had been pulled out at the wall. With shaking hands she replaced the plastic connection, and the line purred once more. Whatever had they hoped to find? This operation must have been massive. Her head spun as she tried to take stock.

Hazel told her the police had raided them too, and also Josh. They'd found nothing. Hazel listened, shocked, as Karen told what had happened to Steve, but Eddie came on the line.

'Listen, Karen, don't worry girl, it'll be okay.'

'How the hell d'you know?'

'Because it's nothin' twenty plants! Classed as personal use. It'll just be a fine, and maybe probation. Pull yourself together!'

'You seem to know a lot about this sort of thing.'

'I don't, but I know he's not done that much wrong. Listen, Hazel says she'll be straight up. You have a nice cup of tea.'

Eric was there when Hazel arrived, sitting in the chaotic dining room and drinking tea he'd made himself and comforting Karen. The children had gained confidence with his arrival, because he represented normality. They were playing happily in the new topsy turvy landscape of the lounge, rooting through the emptied upturned drawers, uncovering items they hadn't seen for ages. Karen had her head in her hands fighting back tears.

'They did you over too?' asked Eric, as a breathless Hazel came in and flopped at the table, still gasping from her run. He told how he'd had to explain who he was and his purpose before the police allowed him onto the Drift.

'Yes, but they didn't find anything. Did you know Steve had those plants, Karen?' She got up to fill and switch on the kettle, a task too complex for her poor friend at present.

'No, of course I didn't. You know what I think about drugs. The prop's used as a dumping ground ever since we cleared out them early cues. I never ever went near there, always too busy grafting, making honest money! My God, what did the stupid bastard think he was doing. Look at the state of this house. It was bad enough before those pigs came in, now I'll never sort it out, I might as well set light to it! But I suppose that moron spent the insurance premium down the pub,' she added bitterly.

'Well, I think you're getting it out of proportion,' said Hazel, easily. 'Nobody cares about dope any more. Most people don't think it's any worse than beer and fags.' Eric nodded in agreement.

But Karen wouldn't be subdued. 'That's not the point! Look at the trauma the girls have suffered! And the house! All our belongings. I feel like..' she was going to add "I've been raped" but she caught Hazel's eye, so she didn't.

'Where did he get them from?' asked Eric trying to change the subject. He remembered in his student days finding the seeds in Trill bird food, soaking them in water and germinating them, but then again he had been a student of horticulture. Personally cannabis didn't bother him, he rather hoped the government might legalise it soon, not for his own interest but because he was following the situation in Holland and could see the reasoning.

'Sammy, I bet, bound to be,' said Karen. 'I wonder if he's been caught? No, not 'im. Not our slippery Cockney wide boy.' Her voice had a hard edge quite unlike her, Eric thought.

A shadow passed the window, and there was a knock at the back door.

'I think this might be your answer,' said Eric, hurrying to the door to head off Sammy.

'Just keep 'im away from me,' said Karen. 'He's not

welcome here, ever!'

The two men were talking in low voices and Karen and Hazel couldn't catch what was said. Eric had wisely detained him on the doorstep.

'Tell him to piss off,' shouted Karen, not trusting Eric to deliver a blunt enough message. 'He's done enough damage to this family!'

'Charming,' said Sammy as he retreated to his van. 'Ungrateful cow. And there's me thinking I've done 'em more than a few favours.'

Thirty-Eight

Sammy saw Steve getting out of a taxi and pulled up next to him. The clock on his dash made it eleven o'clock. So he could speak to Steve, he reached across and unfastened his passenger door by pulling a wire looped to the broken latch.

'They let you out, then mate?'

'Aye, couldn't keep us. You comin' in?' He didn't know who else had been raided. Still buzzing, he wanted to talk about it.

'No, I ain't flavour of the month with your missus. I'll see you in the Cow for the lunchtime session. I don't think you're much more popular, mind. Good luck mate, I reckon you're gonna need it. Remember, what you've got to do, mate, is show her who's boss! That's how I handle my Maureen.'

'Oh, she'll be right. It was just the shock,' said Steve, adrenaline still pumping. He was up for anything. 'Cheers, pal.'

However, all his new-found bravado drained at the sight of Karen's white face and tight lips, and the realisation hit him that his worst ordeal was yet to come. Eric and Hazel had gone by now. Her eyes pierced him, filled with venom. He walked casually past her and into the dining room. The state of it unnerved him further.

'You're back then.'

'Aye. No problem.'

'I can't believe you were so stupid. Thanks to you, we'll probably get kicked off the Estate, now.' She got up and began to rush about tidying frantically and frenetically, crashing things deliberately.

'Don't you be so stupid,' said Steve, conscious suddenly that his mouth was dry. 'It was nowt! Just a few plants. Do you know how little that is in the scheme of things? I'll get away wi' just a caution, the solicitor reckons it'll not even get to court, and nobody will know owt about it. I'd just like to get me hands on the bastard who tipped them off! I think I'll ring Eddie, find out what happened to them.'

Karen stopped and stood stock still. She fixed him with a withering stare and said quietly: 'Then you'd best hang on to that solicitor's number and hope he does divorces as well. Now piss off out of here, you're not touching my phone!' Steve retreated quickly. He knew he was no match for her in this mood. He treated himself to a door-slam, though.

Alone again Karen's anger gave way once more to worry and distress. She felt Steve had deceived her and that was the worst thing. She'd always known he was easily led, but this was such a foolish thing to be involved in. You could compare it, she thought, to robbing a bank for fifty pounds. Pathetic.

Later she and the children walked up the Drift towards Hazel's in the late September drizzle, the girls in their cagoules but Karen in just her tee-shirt and jeans, as if the rain couldn't touch her. The Estate lay law-abiding and peaceful, empty apart from a solitary tractor or the odd car. Even the glasshouses seemed lined up in submission, and the morning's events appeared even more ludicrous, looking at them. She hadn't decided yet if she could forgive Steve. All they had worked so hard for, put in jeopardy.

৪০　ত্ব

It was lunchtime and the Red Cow was packed. Midge was eager to glean more information, sort rumour from fact. Gradually the "villains" drifted into his bar, all eager to tell their tales. The mood was buoyant and Steve was still elated and for once he was at the hub. Midge called Kim to take a shift behind the bar, so he wouldn't have to miss anything.

Josh had been raided as Angie was cooking herself egg on toast. He'd been lazing in the dining room drinking his first coffee of the day. He'd spotted the van drive up and had time to hide a lump of foil-wrapped marijuana deep inside a trade packet of seeds and now he was proud he'd outwitted the drugs squad. They'd found nothing in his greenhouses because there was absolutely nothing to find. 'I have enough trouble growing lettuce,' he laughed.

Simon and Nicole had been turned over too, not surprisingly, thought Midge. God knows how they'd found nothing there. Nicole was perched on a bar stool, legs swivelled round facing away from Midge, drinking red wine. Head down, hair full of wispy plaits, she swirled the red liquid gently around the bowl of her stemmed glass and reflected patterns from the sun onto the far wall.

'They took some of your fruit teas to analyse didn't they Nic?' said Simon. 'And some irrigation pipe glue.'

'Mmm,' she said.

'Did they strip out your cupboards, then?' asked Kim.

'No. We don't have cupboards. Or drawers. They ripped apart Si's bureau, though, didn't they Si? Only found boring old paperwork though, nothing as exciting as drugs.'

'How d'you manage without drawers?' said Kim, deliberately or not, it was hard to tell. They all laughed. Nicole caught Josh's eye, but he glanced away, embarrassed. As general conversation drifted away from her she turned to Eddie and whispered:

'How's the back? Need any more treatment?'

Eddie stammered: 'It's good, yeh, great. Er, I'll be fine, erm thank you.'

Sammy strolled in, chest out, shirt tucked in one side, loose the other. He walked over to Steve and clapped him heavily on the shoulder. Eddie was watching with a sly eye. 'Sort out the missus then, mate?' asked Sammy.

'Aye, no problem mate!' lied Steve.

Sammy said: 'Shame about them plants, Stevie boy, you should 'ave turned 'em into hard cash by now. Expect you was waitin' for the market to pick up. Mistake, that.'

Eddie looked at Sammy incredulously. 'Are you telling us they didn't get you then?'

Sammy didn't even have the grace to look sheepish. 'No mate,' he said. 'I cut 'em down and sold the lot last Tuesday. You should 'ave seen the sniffer dog though, it went bleedin' berserk, tried to dig in the ground, chasin' round in circles. I thanked mi' lucky stars that dogs is dumb! But they couldn't prove nothin' 'cos I got Mo to clean up, roots and all. She's very thorough when it's summat a little bit bent, you know. The devil must be looking after me, mind, 'cos I lent the rewinder to Nige only last night. I'm too slippery for them,' he said. 'There's no flies on Sammy!' He stuck out his chest out further and one of the buttons gave up, revealing a patch of red hairy chest.

'Regular Jack Dawkins, ain't you, Sammy.' Midge's wife filled the pint glasses, carelessly slopping ale into the drip tray. How she hated this pub, she couldn't treat it seriously. She imagined herself in a wine bar, serving businessmen and women, not in a small time country boozer where the customers thought they were class one criminals just because they'd been caught with a few hash plants. Stepney had been the backdrop to her formative years and she'd seen real crime. Even she had to admit that the raid had been a big operation, albeit unsuccessful. She watched Sammy, his head tilted in boastful arrogance and she wondered just how long he'd last on the shady streets of her own East End.

'You got away with it!' Steve was suddenly amazed he hadn't thought to ask Sammy that question earlier. He must have been too relieved to be out of his cell to think clearly.

Karen was right, he thought, he truly was the fool. Elation sank to embarrassment as he measured the extent of this betrayal. He realised Sammy was still talking to him.

'Steve! Did they question you 'bout who you got them plants off?'.

'He told 'em you!' Eddie put in quickly.

'I know old Stevie boy better'n that,' Sammy said, and he didn't even wait for confirmation, so sure was he of Steve's loyalty. 'Who d'you think grassed? Whoever it was, they must know everyone pretty well. I mean the old bill didn't go to George, or old Vic. Or Jim's. Or Dennis'.'

Kim returned with empties fanned out in each hand. She crashed them down on the bar-top. 'Oh yeh,' she said. 'They'd be top o' my list, that lot! And don't forget Gerry and Vera Clay and what's 'is name, Bernard, 'im who's only forty but looks about ninety. You can tell he's at it!'

Midge looked at his wife in alarm. 'Put a sock in it, now!' he said. 'You an' your acid tongue. You'd 'ave us out o' business. Perhaps you'd better go back to your *Pebble Mill.*'

'No way! I'm enjoyin' this,' she said.

Eddie began to laugh. 'You know old Maurice who delivers the bacon?'

They all did. They were all customers.

'He was trapped in my shed for half an hour. When the van pulled up, he thought they'd come for him.' They all laughed for it was easy to imagine him cowering with his plastic carrier, waiting until the coast was clear before he made his escape.

'What's puzzling me,' said Midge, slowly. 'Is why spend all that taxpayer's money looking for a few plants? Or a bit of wacky baccy?'

Simon said: 'Whoever gave the tip-off must have thought there was a big-time operation, growing them under ultra violet, that sort of thing. Because the Drift's a private road and not terribly accessible to the public, and we have all sorts of growing equipment and three phase electricity right up the holdings, we'd have the ideal opportunity to conceal something big. It's another take on diversification.'

'Well it's bloody obvious that none of you lot's making a fortune!' laughed Midge, condescendingly. Josh picked up this comment from the small time publican and felt insulted. It was never difficult to make Josh feel insulted. His whole being was tuned to the recognition of it.

'What's that supposed to mean?' he asked, aggressively. 'This ain't exactly a high class boozer!' All eyes turned on the landlord. He had a point.

'Come on now. Look at your motors!' Midge justified, somewhat bravely. 'You'd drive brand new Volvos, at the very least.'

'It could be a cover,' said Simon. 'Anyway the dealers would be the ones with the wealth, it's the middle men, like in every other aspect of life.'

'So who tipped them off?' asked Midge again, and they sifted through each other's ideas. But not one of them guessed the truth. Top of the list was Jonathan.

Sammy said: 'Nope, it ain't 'im. Guaranteed.'

'How d'you know? I wouldn't trust that tosser as far as I could throw him,' said Eddie.

'Let's just say he'd have to pay more elsewhere. 'E might be a tosser but he's as tight as a duck's arse. No, not 'im.'

Eddie shook his head in disbelief and said: 'Ever heard of principles, Sammy Dove?'

'Nope. Can't spell them long words,' Sammy said. 'Who else we got in the frame then?'

The list included Mike Taylor, the retired tractor driver who lived opposite Sammy and David Dickinson, the farmer and magistrate who had signed the warrants. None of them seemed terribly likely. They decided it must be someone who knew them all well.

'It could be you, Midge,' his wife said from behind the bar, her face straight. For a second or two there was silence. 'Only joking!'

'Stupid cow!' said Midge, angrily. 'They called this pub after her. She was wearing a red dress the day we went for the interview.'

Thirty-Nine

Eric pulled into Dennis' roadway and drove up to his packing shed. He could see activity as he drove past span after span of the giant glasshouse, some bays a jungle of tomato plants, the labourers splashes of colour amongst them like cockatoos in an equatorial forest. Others were scraped bare, ready for cultivation, and in the final few row upon row of lettuce stretched into the distance at various stages of development. He guessed Dennis wouldn't be in any of these, much more likely he'd be busy in the office he'd constructed for himself in the corner of the shed. He guessed right. In the stud wall was a small window, and as Eric walked up to it he could just see the back of Dennis's bent head. He was deep in his paperwork.

Eric hesitated before he tapped on the glass. He was unsure what he was going to say. Dennis looked up and beckoned him inside.

'It's Mr. Adas advisor!' he greeted the visitor. 'Long time no see. What brings you here?'

Dennis spun his swivel chair to face Eric, who sat down in the only other seat in the narrow office. Eric noticed how organised he was. The secondary wall above the desk was slotted with pigeonholes, all neatly labelled and carrying paperwork. The other wall was divided likewise into boxes and Dennis had organised it into screws, bolts, nails etc., the sort of paraphernalia that most other growers shoved haphazardly in trays which were in turn often lost under heaps of boxes. Most growers hung a trade calendar somewhere in their shed, showing voluptuous trusses of

337

tomatoes or bunches of perfect runner beans. Dennis's was a glossy English Country Life one, and huntsmen and hounds splashed colour above September. He also had a wall clock, and a telephone, a separate line from the house. This office was impressive, demonstrating what could still be achieved on the Estate.

'No, no, I know. Just passing.'

'What's new, then, on the Estate?'

'You live here, Dennis, not me.'

'True, but I keep my head down. Busy working. A place like this takes some running.'

'I'm sure it does. You must have heard about the drugs raid, though, yesterday morning.'

'Well yes,' said Dennis. 'The women have never stopped gassing about it since they got here this morning.'

Eric took a brave deep breath. The two men had been quite close years ago.

'Everyone has their own ideas about this, but I think I know who may have informed the police.'

Dennis kept his gaze steady. 'I should think a lot of people could of done it. Drugs is a terrible business, and whoever done it will've done the rest of us decent people a favour, if you know what I mean.'

'Well, apparently several people had their houses turned over in a dawn raid. Not a pleasant experience. And they only found something on one nursery.'

'That so?' said Dennis nonchalantly. 'This Estate is riddled with rubbish now. Remember Eric, when only the cream got onto places like this? Now we have any Tom, Dick or Harry and they've ruined it. If we're harbouring drug addicts then let's paste 'em on the wall for all to see.'

Eric sighed. 'I wouldn't mind betting that the only drug addicts as you call them on this Estate are those who take prescription drugs for stress. Coffee and alcohol aside.'

Dennis winced. Sylvia flirted with Valium. Why, he'd

been almost tempted to see the doctor about getting some himself recently.

'Well, that remains to be seen. Nobody who's innocent will suffer, but let's face it, there's no smoke without fire. Anyway, why are you here going on about all this to me?'

Eric said nothing. After a few seconds Dennis answered himself.

'Oh I see, Mister Adas Man. You think I called the cops?'

Eric seized his chance. He didn't think; he was almost sure.

'Dennis, I've known you a long time. I respect you as a grower and a friend. I know you don't do things without good reason. So what was it?' He judged the direct approach would be best here. He didn't want Dennis to start spinning a web of lies, and anyway he'd got so far, best to grasp the nettle.

Dennis glanced at Eric, and the ADAS Advisor's face told him that he knew, but goodness knows how. And anyway, he hadn't told the police about anyone else, so he thought he couldn't have been the only informant if they'd raided so many. In fact, as the morning wore on, he'd felt sure the operation couldn't have had anything to do with him. It was much too big, stupidly and ridiculously over the top.

'If you must know, though what's it got to do with you I don't know, I only informed on that wastrel. Not on anybody else. I've never heard that any of the others was involved with drugs, but someone else must have known about the others.'

'You think Steve's a wastrel?'

Dennis looked up sharply. 'Steve?'

'Steve was taken to the Police station. They found some plants. It's possible that he and Karen will be thrown off the Estate when word gets back to Jack Ball.' Eric spoke quietly.

'Karen is distraught, because she knew nothing of it!'

Dennis played with the wooden knob of his rubber stamp. He drew small circles in the palm of his hand with it.

'Well I'm sorry for Steve's missus. She's a hardworking sort. Often it seems that some of these men don't deserve their wives....didn't no-one else get done, then?' he asked, just as quietly.

'No, they were all clear, didn't even find red diesel. Goodness knows how!'

'What about that Ogden character?' Eric recognised a vicious edge to Dennis' normally pleasant voice.

'Josh? No, nothing,' said Eric. 'Did you think there would be?' He pressed gently, sensing the truth.

Dennis scooted the chair round and thumped desk-top with his fist, and sending papers fluttering to the floor.

'So he got away with it! The evil nasty-tempered bastard! Yes, I told the police that – that – Josh, as you call him, was involved with drugs.' His voice was its calm self again. 'But I didn't, I swear, mention anybody else. That Steve's an ignorant fool. All the years I've been on this estate and we've never had anything like drugs. He hasn't been here two minutes.'

So this was it, thought Eric, it had something to do with Josh, the change in this normally mild mannered man. 'Why, Dennis? If he does smoke marijuana, and there's no evidence that he does, he's hardly a risk to anyone else.'

'You're going soft in your old age.'

'I'm being realistic.'

There was a silence and Dennis stared through the internal window.

'He went for me, would you believe!' said Dennis, 'the nutter! Just drove up on his tractor, got off and struck me! True as I'm sitting here. For no flamin' reason. Just because his wife's working for me! I couldn't believe it. Poor Angie, what she has to put up with. He don't know when his bread's buttered. Anyhow, she told me that he smokes drugs every night, to relax, she says. One night I couldn't sleep for thinking about it, and I just did it, I telephoned the station there and then. But that's all I did, Eric, and I'll stand up and be counted if that's what you're after. I don't like drugs, never have. So how did you find out?'

'Let's say I guessed,' said Eric. This wasn't strictly true. 'Don't worry, your secret's safe with me, Dennis. You are entitled to take whatever action necessary when you hear of an offence, I suppose. But as I said before Josh is hardly a risk to anyone, he hasn't even any children. And I suspect Guy will come across much worse when he goes to college.' Eric's voice was bleak and cold. Dennis sensed his disapproval.

'It was Angie I was considering,' said Dennis, his voice small, his head bowed. 'Look, I don't know why I'm being made to feel the guilty one. And you're treading on sticky ground, Eric, it's not about growing and it's flaming well not your business.'

Eric chewed his lip, considering hard, eyes linking patterns on the lino.

'No you're right.' Maybe he was being too hard on this man who was once his friend. 'Perhaps I shouldn't be poking my big size tens in. Just with us going back a long way, you know. Forget I said anything. My lips are sealed.' He got up to go. 'I'll be seeing you, Dennis.'

Dennis grunted something and stayed motionless as he heard Eric reverse down the drive. He sighed deeply, he felt sad and confused. He hadn't wanted to cause trouble for Steve and Karen, indeed he knew how desperately hard it was for any newcomers to make a living at the moment.

Meanwhile Eric had spotted Sylvia vigourously shaking a tablecloth or sheet or something just outside her back door. She hailed him, beckoning him to stop and talk. He switched off the engine as she walked over to his window, which he wound down completely.

'Long time no see. Is everything okay?'

'Yes – just having a word with your good husband. How's the bank?'

Sylvia neatly completed the final fold of the tablecloth and positioned it across her forearm. She smiled.

'Hectic as ever. Tell me Eric, are we any nearer to the government selling off these rabbit hutches?'

'I've really no idea,' Eric replied honestly. 'Are you looking forward to that?'

'Eric, I dream about it every night. Then we'll do it up, extend, sell it for a fortune and you won't see us for dust!'

In his mirror he saw Dennis scuttling towards them across the landscaped lawn.

'Eric!' he said as he got near. 'Could Steve and Karen do with a couple of girls helping out tomorrow? I'm a bit overstaffed at the moment. Charged to me, of course.'

'I'm sure they could,' said Eric. Clever move, he thought. 'You give them a ring. They've a crop of chinese cabbage in a tunnel which the slugs are starting to attack.'

Sylvia frowned. 'See, Eric, we must be making so much money he's paying for other people's labour. Shall I book a holiday in Florida tomorrow before he funds the whole Estate? What a good hearted man I married!'

What indeed, thought Eric.

Forty

October is a fickle month for growers. It can be mild and miserable, and therefore little use for plant growth or it can toy with them giving bright sunny days, only for temperatures to drop sharply at nightfall forcing a frost fierce enough to threaten crops under glass. For successful growers like Dennis, George and Jim who had thermostatically controlled heat sources this wasn't a problem. Huge blasts of warm air would roar across their autumn lettuce like the exhalation of some fire-breathing monster, keeping the frost at bay. But for those tenants who had entered the Estate in the last five difficult years and couldn't afford the heat, an eye was always watching for clear skies at night and they were forever telephoning the Weatherline. Often a teasing wind would lift just before temperatures fell too far and the month would drag past without a frost serious enough to cause any damage.

There was always the question of how long growers should keep their tomato crop running, because if the frost does hold off and there is enough sun to warm the air through the glass, tomatoes will still continue to ripen and green ones will continue to slowly make the size.

The alternative had been to tear out the tomato plants during September and quickly fertilise, rotovate and plant up with autumn lettuce. If a grower had no heat source, this was risky too as a frost at harvest time would rupture the veins and make them unsaleable, although the lettuce could stand any amount of frost as young plants. It was a gamble either way, and Karen and Steve chose to keep their tomatoes, but Eddie had ripped his out in favour of autumn lettuce. So far there hadn't been a really hard frost, but the long range forecast said a cold snap was approaching.

'Time to pull them out, I'd say,' said Eric to Steve. 'Spray them off with ethanol, then pick everything. They'll turn colour in trays in the shed. If you leave it too late and the weather turns it won't work.'

'Sounds a bit unhealthy to me,' Steve said. They were standing in the tomato house and the crop looked tired and scruffy. The dense fog had even penetrated the greenhouse and the far end of it had all but disappeared. The morning was strangely silent, the fog suffocating sounds or the birds stopping in bed, perhaps. Steve had floaters in front of his eyes as he looked at the white wall of mist. Eric reached up to touch a truss of large green fruit, and as the plant moved a shower of white-fly took off into the damp atmosphere like a snowstorm in reverse.

'I've not kept to me spray programme,' Steve admitted, slightly embarrassed. 'It was a case of having to buy a new bottle of pesticide and at the price it didn't seem worth it.'

'We-ll, perhaps it wasn't,' agreed Eric, 'as the cold will knock them back anyway. It's not good husbandry, though. The fly will over-winter in the woodwork if we don't have a severe enough winter to kill them. Then your problem will be magnified next summer, unless you plan to fumigate or sterilise the house.'

'Well, I don't want to pay out for methyl bromide just yet,' Steve said. 'Eddie reckons it's really dear and Karen thinks it should wait while next year. She's the boss of the money, tha' knows.'

'And a very shrewd boss she is, I'm sure,' said Eric. 'It's good to see you working so well as a team. Talking of pests and diseases, though, aluminium has a big advantage over wood. Much less hospitable to both.'

'Makes you wonder how they coped in the old days,

before aluminium and fancy sprays.'

'Oh – they'd have burnt sulphur in the houses,' said Eric. 'Some growers of the old school still do. It's still relatively easy to obtain, but you couldn't get it in The Stores, though. I should think your friend Sammy Dove would be your man.'

'Not if Karen has owt to do with it!' said Steve gloomily. 'She's barred him from the house, and the holding too. She's still not forgiven him over the raid. Says he's a bad influence on me.'

'And is he?'

'Well, I admit I'm easily led. And she's certainly straightened me out. Saved me from a life as a Hells Angel, she did!'

Eric laughed. He really couldn't see Steve with a long ratty beard, biting heads off chickens.

'If I was you, then, I'd stick with her and do as she says!'

'Mebbe I should. Listen to you, Eric. You sound like me Dad!'

Eric laughed. He did indeed feel like a father advising his son and it seemed a piece of cake compared to advising his daughter.

'So what about these tommies?' Steve reminded him.

'I should spray with ethanol tonight. And no, it's not nasty or anything. It's actually very clever. All you're doing is adding a natural hormone the plant produces anyway. It just triggers the ripening process. You must have noticed that if you put a ripe apple in with a bowl of green ones, they'll turn more quickly.'

'Will it ripen these 'uns?' Steve pointed to a truss of marble-sized fruit, up in the eaves.

'No, they'll probably drop off. They have to have reached an optimum sized to ripen,' he said. 'Then you'll have no income til the spring, I take it?'

'Just a bit of outdoor celery, nothing chunky though,

just thin sticks. Come and see what you think. Oh, and two tunnels of late lettuce. Bit o' a risk, like, but you never know, do you.'

Eric sighed inwardly. This had started out a social visit – was still a social visit, so far as ADAS was concerned. He knew he couldn't keep doing this indefinitely but he also knew Steve needed his support.

They walked up beyond the greenhouse to where the top field lay fallow. Steve had sprayed with Roundup and now the dying weeds coloured the field with deep reds and dark oranges. It was no good growing anything up there; without a pump and storage tank you couldn't retain water pressure. The large square of celery standing green and proud marked the limit. Around this crop Steve had laid a thick layer of straw to help maintain temperatures. Inside the square the celery were planted as densely as possible so this would help keep them snug as well. Obviously the longer they could be left, the weightier they'd become. Another balancing act.

'I'm glad you've banked the straw up,' said Eric. 'Don't forget too, the wetter you keep them the better they'll handle the frost.'

They walked back towards the house, Eric glancing at his watch.

'So how do you think you're doing financially?' He felt he knew the answer to this, but he wanted to test Steve's awareness.

'Not bad,' said Steve. 'Difficult to tell, mind. I haven't had time to study the figures. We're just keeping as tight on spending as possible, which i'nt hard to do here.'

'What you need to watch is your LSA account,' Eric persisted gently. 'That's the killer.'

The accounts department only published quarterly statements, and the growers were often horrified when they discovered just how much they'd spent on sprays, plants, boxes, bags, fertilisers, slug pellets, heating oil, the list was endless.

'I figure that if we just spend what we desperately need, then we'll not run into problems.' Steve said.

Eric had seen that school of accounting before. He knew the list of things you desperately needed had a nasty habit of expanding like the contents of his wife's suitcases.

They had reached the lawn, still looking good in the cool sunshine which had briefly beaten the mist. The Bramley apple tree which the children played on was still studded with fruit, the ground about it littered with windfalls. The mountain ash looked stunning, red berries glowing against a patch of blue sky. The ducks had matured, they were grouped around the pond and a light wind ruffled their feathers. As well as the plump white Aylesbury's Karen now had Rouens (which were really rather obese mallards, Eric thought, their colouring being the same) and several Indian Runners with their peculiar upright bodies, reminding him of penguins. They were less sedate than their plumper "table duck" cousins, running around the lawn and reminding Eric of a Benny Hill chase. Sitting snobbishly apart from the others were the Muscovies, curious fowl which seemed undecided as to whether they were duck or goose. He considered them ugly with their stark eyes and lumpy red beaks.

Eric could see the attractions of living here and for a moment was almost envious. There was something about simplicity which he found tempting. He lived in a large red-bricked semi, its elegant bay window facing the River Wan. Whatever the charms of its high-ceilinged rooms, decorative cornices and slate fireplaces, his lifestyle couldn't be described as simple. He was once-removed from the land, and occasionally he just wanted to be in there, back to basics and honesty. But in truth he loved the academic part of his job like he loved his study, a shell of books with a desk overlooking a small walled garden.

In reality he feared for these two; Steve with his capacity for dogged hard work, sometimes misplaced, and Karen with her instinctive acceptance and determination, sometimes blinkered. At least she hadn't been tempted with goats and pigs and lambs; she was content to concentrate on ducks, chickens and the cockerels which were eating themselves towards a Christmas slaughter in the piggery.

'Whatever happened about the dope plants?' Eric asked suddenly.

'I got let off with a caution and a year's good behaviour by the judge, but our lass still hasn't sentenced me yet,' said Steve. 'It'll likely be all over the *Gazette* this week. I just hope Jack Ball don't read it and kick us off.'

Eric shook his head. 'He'd need a bit more than that, I would think. You just need to make sure you don't do anything else stupid. No more winding back the meter, or using red diesel in your motor. And absolutely no selling outside.'

'D'you know about all that then?' asked Steve in surprise.

'I know about everything,' joked Eric. Too damn much, he thought to himself.

He needed to make a move, he wanted to catch Jim before it got dark.

ℰ ℂ

Jim had just finished clearing his cherry tomatoes and the huge glasshouse stretched vast and vacant once more. The only clue to the previous crop was the pathways, stamped down so hard by continuous harvesting, and the holes where he'd dragged out the root balls. He'd called Eric because he was concerned about residue left in the soil for his next crop.

'I need a soil sample,' he said. 'Look, Eric, you can see the chemical. Bound to be too strong for me Christmas lettuce, it'd be like dipping a baby's dummy in Marmite.'

Eric, who hated Marmite, winced. 'Yes, I can do that, and the lab can give you an idea how much water to put on to leach it out.'

'Then the soil'll have to dry out before I can cultivate it. Only us lot spend money heating bare soil. No wonder the farmers laugh at us.'

'If you time it right, though, you'll get the Christmas price.'

'There is that.'

Eric collected the soil samples in plastic bags and he used his thigh to lean on as he squatted down to write the labels. Soon both men were leaning on the fence watching Janice's livestock. Although the lambs were now in the freezer, like her pigs, she still had the dopey turkeys and a couple of sheep as well as Bernadette and lots of unusual hens. There were Silkie bantams with their wonderful metallic colours and flamboyant tails as well as many species Eric couldn't recognise, and lop-eared rabbits and guinea pigs hopped around the enclosure as well.

'Do they pay for themselves, overall, this lot?' asked Eric.

'Well they do,' said Jim. 'But she's fartin' around selling goat's milk now, her and Nigel. Gives her a bit o' pin money. They like that, women, don't they? She can't get enough milk to satisfy the weirdo's, can't understand it myself. I drank some once, and it upset me stomach, had an arse like the Japanese flag for days, I did. She keeps on about getting more goats, you know. But we're growers, not flaming farmers,' he said.

'Any money helps, doesn't it? You said yourself she's found a market.'

'Hmm..it's a paying hobby, that's all. I might give her a

bit of business tuition come January,' said Jim. 'You know, when it's thick snow and there's sod all else to do.'

Eric wondered how his own wife would react if he belittled her that way. In a few years time it may well be Janice's milk business that saves the day for them. But he merely said:

'I've been meaning to ask you, but I keep forgetting. What happened to the old billy?'

Jim laughed. 'He's living the life of Riley, he is. He's a stud, lucky bugger! Nigel took him to this woman what lives over the back, she's got all the breeds, you know, apparently she charges a tenner for three thrusts. Another example of a woman making money off a man's hard graft!'

Eric laughed. He was pleased the animal hadn't ended up in a curry despite eating his cherry tomato specifications. He recalled the ribbing he'd had to suffer in the office about that.

Myra came out of the kitchen and threw the tea leaves onto the lawn. She didn't see the men watching her.

'Janice hates her doing that,' Jim laughed. 'Says it treads in everywhere. I don't think it's been easy for her, having Ma around,' he admitted.

'She's stayed longer this year, hasn't she?'

'Well yes. Between you and me, I think the old girl's smitten. With old Fred, from the council houses. I don't much care for him, finicky, like a woman. But if it makes her happy, and she's been twenty six years on her own, you know. And she's been able to help with packing the cherries. What a bloody job that is.'

'Would you grow them again?' Eric asked.

'Ye-s, I reckon so, because the price has been guaranteed all summer long. The only trouble is that I'm still waiting on me cheque for August.'

Eric could see the potential for cash flow disaster, and he'd heard this criticism levelled at the supermarkets before.

Obviously this was how they paid all their suppliers, by contrast the wholesale markets paid out straight away and the LSA had the cheque with the grower in a fortnight. He would have to raise this potential problem at the trial evaluation.

'What would you do differently next year?' Eric asked. He needed to glean these nuggets of information, and he was quite skilful at avoiding making the grower feel he was being interrogated.

'Next Year eh? Well, on New Year's Day I'd wake up with a stinking hangover in the Bahamas, with only Debbie Harry's naked body blocking my view of the sea, and... oh you mean about growing cherry tomatoes? Nothing so far as the cultivation is concerned, I suppose,' Jim pondered. 'But the picking process is so slow and I can't really see how that could be speeded up. It would be a piece of cake if the whole truss ripened together, but it don't. They ripen all over the damn place and I'm up and down like a bride's nightie. Actually though, I sussed it in the end. I had Janice doing the top half of the plant and Ma the bottom, because she's so short. Bless her.'

'Not at the same time, I trust!' said Eric.

'Good God no,' said Jim. 'They'd rip each other's eyes out. I reckon I could sell tickets. You know it's a pity the housewife won't buy a truss at a time, and keep picking 'em off as they ripen. Would be fresher for her, and all.'

'Sell them on the vine, d'you mean? It would be easy to harvest. Just clip the whole truss with a pair of secateurs. Nice idea, will never happen though.'

'Why not? Look at them Cabbage Patch Dolls. Anything can be sold if it's marketed right.'

'No, it's all going the other way.' said Eric. 'Cling film, bubble wrap, plastic punnets. That's the future. What sort of return did you get on them, though?'

Jim was cagey as ever. 'Well I won't be going to the

Bahamas, and Blondie'll have to come to me. But yeah, it beats ordinary tommies, even if the goat ate the lot tomorrow.'

❧   ☙

As George and Maisie were not replanting they had let their tomato crop run its course. With the spare time created they were busy house hunting, and George needed to sort all of his equipment ready for auction. He would hold the sale on his own lawn, the lawn which would soon no longer be his, and which technically had never been his, and the lots would be advertised to the growers on other LSA estates as well as locally in the Gazette.

Maisie was reminiscing as she hung out her washing, large comfortable white knickers and sensible brassieres stitched in sections for maximum support. They billowed voluptuously in the strong breeze. She remembered when she'd first arrived, pegging out narrow cami-knickers and flimsy little blouses. She'd been slim then, and George had been wiry. The lawn didn't exist at that time, it had been a yard which poultry scuttled about in, and she had hung her washing out over a narrow patch of grass, hens clucking and nodding beneath the clothes. She'd been bothered her washing would smell of the farmyard, and George had teased her. "There ain't no better smell," he'd laughed.

Now her capacious underwear soared above reels of black hosepipe and spiky metal implements. George was adding daily to the assortment, and she knew it was a difficult task for him because each article told a story, each rusting piece a memory.

'What in glory's name is that?' she pointed to a vicious looking tool she didn't recognise at all.

'That, my little Gloxinia, is a de-beaker,' said George. Once used on capons, they had long since been outlawed.

'Out o' fashion now.'

'Who on this earth's gonna want it then?'

'Collectors, my sweet,' said George. 'They paint 'em and hang on 'em on the wall.'

Maisie was not convinced. 'If they 'ang that there horse plough thingy it'll fetch the house down!'

'They put 'em out on their front lawns on them new housing estates, woman, like where you want to live.'

Maisie considered this. She had seen old wooden cartwheels often enough, all brightly painted, she had to admit. 'We'd better keep that ol' plough then even though it looks like junk to me.'

George surveyed the paraphernalia with pride. 'The money earned from this ol' junk as you call it is what we're gonna pay for your new carpets and fancy curtains with.'

'I'll be gettin' 'em from the Oxfam shop, then!'

Forty-One

Angie hoped to finish work early today. She had spent all day setting lettuce, a heated crop timed for Christmas, in Dennis' multispan greenhouse. The electric planter purred along so different to the noisy, smoky petrol version Dennis used outdoors. This one was so quiet you could still hear the radio, and that was a big plus to Angie because she loved music. Her favourite station had a slogan, "music first talk second", and she approved of this, and she was irritated by dee-jays who talked over the introduction or faded out the best part of the track. She and workmate Joanne rode the planter, its lever set to full speed, and sang loudly to the music. Dennis was pleased when they finished the greenhouse in record time.

As they crawled around hand-planting the corners where the machine couldn't reach and filling gaps they had missed, the girls chatted and joked together.

'I'm surprised the dirty old bugger isn't in here watching you planting these,' said Joanne. 'He could see right down your front.'

Angie laughed. As she bent double, the cheap material of her tee-shirt couldn't cope tipping forward her deep cleavage.

'Go on with you,' said Angie. 'He's more of a bum man, haven't you seen his wife? Anyway I'm a married woman, in love with me old man.'

'Not what I've heard,' said Joanne, reaching as far as her arms would allow so as not to squash those she'd already planted. 'I heard you two would've killed each other if you hadn't of come here, that you used to throw pots at each other and smash windows.'

Angie stood up, put her hands on her hips and stretched the rest of her body. Her tight jeans had left weals around her stomach and were visible for a moment. How stiff you got doing this job. A smile played around her bright lips.

'Yes, that's true,' she admitted. 'Not windows exactly, greenhouse panes. We're not made for working together, me and Josh. You could say old Dennis saved my marriage. And we haven't got fancy equipment like this,' she indicated the planter. 'I'd have to plant the whole house by hand.'

'Never!' said Joanne, horrified at the thought. Planting by hand made her legs tremble and her shoulders ache.

'Seriously though, it's twice as hard to split up in this game, living on the Estate, I mean.'

'How's that then?' Joanne lived in the sanity of Market Boulton.

'Well, if you split and take half, then the other one's out of work and homeless as well. They'd have to leave the Estate, 'cos we all only own the greenhouses, not the house. They'd have to be sold off.'

'Wouldn't stop me if I lived with a bastard.'

'Makes you think, though, maybe try a bit harder. You see for most people, this Estate's their dream.'

'Bloody hell. Is it really?'

'Look at Sylvia and Dennis..' She broke off, as he opened the door catching the crop wires and vibrating them the length of the house.

''Talk of the devil.' said Joanne. She addressed the boss. 'You're too late. Missed it. She's stood up now!'

Angie ignored this. She respected Dennis, didn't want him to think they'd been dissing him. 'Yes, we're getting on well now.' She shifted the subject as Dennis approached.

'Who with?' said Dennis amiably, but his face clouded as he instantly realised who she meant.

'Josh – I'm just telling Joanne how working for you's saved me marriage..'

'Don't tell me about that obnoxious man, Angie,' he said, and his face flushed with something; embarrassment, anger, Angie wasn't sure.

'But I'm saying he's not so bad really,' Angie persisted, for she felt guilty now. A lot of what she'd told Dennis had been out of context and she wished she could suck back the words. Now she wanted everyone to be happy, like a child from a broken marriage. 'He's different now.' Her mind raced. She looked at Dennis's face, a mask of contempt. It wasn't a pretty sight. How could Dennis hate Josh so much. Had she really been that disloyal?

'You're kidding yourself. Leopards don't change their spots. You'd be better –' he stopped himself. 'Oh, it's not for me to say.'

Angie was bewildered. She'd never found out about her husband thumping Dennis in the face, or suspected her boss as the grass and she couldn't understand his attitude now. Well sod him, if that's what he thinks. She mentally closed a door, couldn't be bothered with this. Dennis plummeted in her estimation but she wouldn't dwell on it. Dwelling was not in her nature. She shook her dark hair in a sort of shrug and looked at her watch. Dennis took the hint.

'Anyway girls, you've done a good job here, you may as well get yourselves home,' said Dennis. As he said it he straightened a plant, moved it an aggravating quarter centimetre. Joanne elbowed Angie in her fleshy ribs. Angie winked back. The girls hurried to the packing shed to wash their hands, and Dennis watched them disappear with a sigh. Just what did Josh have going for him? Try as he would he could think of nothing.

Released into the fresh air, Angie cycled cheerfully along the Drift in the gloom of a mild autumn day, waving to a lorry driver who was unloading a mountain of LSA trays onto the grass outside Karen's holding. Karen had been hidden by the bulk of the wagon, but now she shouted out as Angie passed.

'It's WI tonight, Angie. See you there?'

Angie squeezed her brakes and stuck out a leg, bumping to an undignified halt. 'Oh, is it tonight? I'd forgotten. Yes, all right. Don't suppose I'll get a better offer!'

The lorry driver, a thin man in his late thirties, laughed loudly.

'WI?' he mocked. 'I thought that was for old grannies.' He and Karen were now taking turns heaving stacks of trays off the tailboard and onto the grass.

'Yes, and lifting heavy boxes is for men!' said Angie. 'You go in, Karen, and leave him to do it himself. Where's Steve?'

'Sor-ree,' said the lorry driver, sarcastically.

'Cash and carry,' Karen explained briefly. She was proud of her strength, liked to think she could do anything a man could do and more. This didn't impress Angie, she'll grow to be like Myra, she thought. As if she could read Angie's thoughts, Karen added: 'Don't forget the Sick and Sorry box this week!'

'Sick and Sorry Box!' laughed the driver.

'Shit,' said Angie under her breath. 'As if I would!' she added.

Remounting her bike, she felt slightly annoyed. She wasn't keen on Karen, thought her too pushy and organised, not only remembering everything in her own life but carrying responsibility over to other people's. Angie's life was a good example of relaxed chaos. Too serious, that Karen, she thought, poor hen-pecked Steve.

Unfortunately she knew where the Sick and Sorry box was, and it may as well be in Ethiopia for what chance she had of retrieving it. Tonight she was going to have to confess.

Then a more agreeable thought tossed the worry aside. If it was the monthly meeting of the WI tonight, then her period must be late. Excitement mounting, she remembered calculating she'd be due at the end of the month, and WI was always the first week of the month.

She quickened her pace, realising she didn't really have any of the signs either; no dull ache above the groin, nothing. By the time she reached her house, her heart was thumping in her chest as if she she'd ridden a mile uphill and the Drift was pancake flat. She threw her bike carelessly against the hedge.

Common sense took over though. She wouldn't entertain false hopes. All the time she'd wanted to become pregnant, at least nature had never paid that cruel trick of delaying her periods only leading to disappointment when they arrived. She'd never really had opportunity to properly raise her hopes. Anyway, she felt they'd both reached an unspoken acceptance; hadn't Josh sold his train set at the Charter Fair? So it didn't really matter then, did it?

Despite her logic, she went quickly to the bathroom to check anyway. She would visit the clinic if there was no sign in exactly a week's time.

It was quiet in the house, just the usual creaks and scrapes you hear when the radio is silent. The battery must be flat, she couldn't remember turning it off. There was no sign of Josh, or Guy, they must both be working outside. She plugged in the kettle and extricated a mug from the clutter on the draining board. The pile slipped a little, but nothing actually fell off. What a mess, she'd have to clear up tonight. Then she remembered that she couldn't because it was WI and the urgent problem of the Sick and Sorry box resurfaced in her mind.

80 03

Meanwhile Janice, head crammed full of business plans, was on her way to Nigel's packing shed to discuss a proposition. She'd been helping him milk his goats and cool and pour the milk ready for freezing in those blue and white waxed packets for weeks now. She's seen a chance to really profit from her animals, but Jim was the keeper of the purse and was resisting strongly her plans for more goats. He was dismissive to the point of scathing, so she was biding her time, helping Nigel and learning all she could, hoping Jim would cave in eventually. It would just take a cropping disaster and he'd be putty in her hands. But Jim was a canny enough grower that complete fiascos were usually avoided; hadn't he taken 'diversification' by the throat? But yesterday Nigel told her he had a proposition, although he hadn't been specific. Maybe he would put up some money in a partnership until she got on her feet. A proposition might bring her business dream closer.

When she caught sight of him, Nigel was closing the shed door, methodically, tediously, bolt after bolt. He looked all wrong but for a second she didn't know why.

Then it dawned. He was dressed differently. An almost feminine patterned sweater stretched too tightly across his chest, distorting the design. His trousers were the pale herringbone of a distant age, and he wore shoes. Black shiny lace-ups gleamed where his green wellingtons should surely be. His face radiated from scrubbing or sunburn or something. Janice was as startled as if he'd dropped from Mars.

'Are you going out?" He never went out, Julie his wife did all the shopping, unless it was to do with goats or waterfowl, and then he'd wear his oldest clothes.

'Nay, lass,' he said. 'Would you mind accompanying me to the house?'

The house? Nobody she knew had ever crossed into that house – it held as much secrecy as Nicole's and Julie's neighbourliness had never exceeded a nod. Nigel must be taking this business proposition seriously. Perhaps he'd invited the bank manager, but she hadn't noticed a car.

Past the immaculate glasshouses, not a weed out of place, Janice followed Nigel, gripping her books and file with her elbow. Nigel opened the back door, he had no conservatory, and they entered the gloom of the house. Silence swallowed them as Nigel ushered her into a spartan room.

She settled uneasily on the edge of an upright settee. Nigel went off to make the tea, and she looked around. The metal bars of the window dominated the room, the skimpy curtains unable to soften it. The wooden mantleshelf was lined with goat trophies, and a small cabinet was crammed with cups and rosettes. If Julie was here, she must be under the floorboards.

Nigel came in with two mugs, steaming in the chill of the room. Janice moved up and he sat on the other end of the settee.

'Where's Julie?'

'Julie?'

'Your wife, you know, Julie.' Janice put the hot cup on the lino to save her fingers.

'Oh, aye, Julie. She's gone, lass, a while since.'

'Gone? We never knew. You never said!' Her mind raced and her head was dizzy with bewilderment.

'Did I not mention it?'

'No, Nigel, you didn't. When did this happen?' Then she said, more kindly: 'Are you all right? I mean, all on your own. Who cooks for you?'

'Cooks? Well, me. I don't do nowt fancy, mind. She's away to Middlesborough, months ago. Thought I'd said.'

'No you didn't, and I just can't believe this can happen down the Drift and no one know. You suffering like this and nobody to help you..'

She looked up at Nigel's face, the shiny expanse of his

balding head, and his chubby pink cheeks swollen with a smile. In a flash she knew he didn't need her sympathy for his feelings lay elsewhere. The word proposition sprang to life. She spread her business file across her knees and shut off the eye contact.

'Shall we talk about business?' she said coldly.

'Aye, this is a difficult business.' He leaned forward and she tried not to recoil too much, desperately hoping she'd misunderstood. 'Janice, I'll come straight to th' point. I'm not one for beatin' about the bush. Nay, lass, stay there, don't be embarrassed. It's the power of love as I'm talking about. I'd be good for you, Janice, and I want you to move in an' set up home with me.'

The room spun. Fifty chubby faced men grinned at her, all of them loving her. She stood up and the file of goat papers emptied, knocking the teacup and spilling the tea. Flooding the lino. So crucial earlier, these documents were useless now.

'How – what – how can you say such a thing? What about Jim?'

'Well you've nowt in common wi' him, now, 'ave you? I should know, I spent a lifetime wi' a lass what cared nowt about goats. Me and you – well we're made for each other!'

'I thought we were going to talk about a business proposition!' She backed away towards the door. His face still wore the smile but his eyes were dulled and desperate.

'Well, it's about business too, lass! The business of life.. hey Janice don't go, lass, sit and have your tea. I'm not practised in these things.'

Janice reached the door. 'You can say that again.'

'Lass, sit down, let's talk -'

The door slammed in his face. He saw her shadow pass his window, out of grasp. Nigel sat back down on the settee, alone with the tea-stained papers and his trophies, and he cried.

Maisie was cooking. Angie could smell it as she approached the house and a blast of warm air hit her in the face as she entered the conservatory and knocked the back door. She must be frying onions with steak or something, thought Angie. She'd read somewhere that if you wanted to fool people into believing you were a brilliant cook, fry onions. After that they were hooked and however ropey the dish you eventually served they'd be sure to enjoy it.

The door opened and a flushed Maisie welcomed her into the steamy kitchen. Aluminium saucepans rattled away on the cooker and condensation trickled down the walls.

'Angie! Come on in, gel,' she said. They didn't see as much of each other now the evenings were dark and the short grey days not so conducive to fencetop chatting.

Angie liked to get things over with quickly. There was no space in her head for harbouring or hedging. 'It's the Sick and Sorry box,' she blurted out straight away, slumping down in a chair at Maisie's formica-topped table.

Maisie wiped her plump hands on her apron and folded herself into the only other chair. She looked at Angie expectantly.

'It's gone.'

'Ooh. Lost it, 'ave you?'

'No, I've not lost it! I know where it is.'

'Well then, we'll get it back, dear.'

'No, we can't – it's been scrapped, Tom, Ruby's son, he scrapped it when he scrapped our old Mini!'

'Bit thoughtless of 'im,' said Maisie. 'It's a heirloom, ain't it. Ruby ain't goin' to be pleased he done that.'

Angie was getting irritated, but she pushed some patience into her voice. 'He didn't *know* it was in there. I put the box in the Mini, to hide it from Josh, cos he kept borrowing money from it! It was our car, and Josh swapped it for a crate of beer.'

'Oh dear,' said Maisie. 'Let me just see to me saucepans.'

Angie followed her, burbling into her ear, competing with the bubbling liquid.

'I've got the money, I can pay that back. It's the flippin' fancy box. Their pride and joy. What'll I do, Maisie?'

Angie backed along the narrow kitchen and into the small dining room so they could sit down again.

'Let me get this right, gel. You ain't got the box cos it's all squashed up into bits at the scrappers, by one of them great big machines – did it 'ave any lolly in it?'

'Only a few quid an' Josh's paying me back. He's been brilliant lately. A changed man. Chased up to the scrappers with me, to try and save it.'

'What a story. You don't 'arf lead a life, gel.' Maisie threw back her head and laughed loudly. She rocked to and fro, a big fruity laugh. She gave herself a stitch.

'Oh, I know I oughtn't!' she gasped. 'It ain't funny really! Ha ha! Oh what'll Ruby say? She'll 'ave your guts for garters, she will. An' er son what done it, too.' Angie laughed too, until the tears rolled down her cheeks.

'Best get all the giggling out of the way before I confront Ruby,' she said, as they sobered themselves up.

Maisie as usual had a practical suggestion, and switching the cooker off, she went upstairs. The saucepans now silenced, Angie listened to the tick of a carriage clock. She could also hear the floorboards creak above her head as Maisie rooted for what she wanted.

After sitting a moment or two, Angie got up and had a quick peep in the oven to identify the wonderful smell. It was a casserole, sweating gently in a very low heat. Her eyes scanned the kitchen, same as her own if both were gutted. But this kitchen was from a different time; rack upon rack of labelled glass jars with glass stoppers, the ink smudged and the paper yellowed with time and forty years of regular meals. Probably just a handful of menus, too. Angie turned her attention to the dining room. A couple of framed photographs on the radiogram, one of their wedding day, George standing stiff in a suit, strangled by an unaccustomed tie and his large hands exposed by the ill-fitting jacket. Maisie, feet placed carefully, looked young, fresh, and even slim in a pale costume and feathered pastel hat. The other photograph showed a bunch of cows pressing against a five-barred gate, with George standing proud and confident in the foreground. This very house was visible behind the cattle. And it hadn't changed at all.

Maisie clumped down the stairs clutching a wooden box and she set it on the formica table, wheezing heavily from the activity and the dust. The box was light brown wood patterned by a distinctive green grain. It had an exceptionally glossy finish and was deeply carved everywhere but the base, which was covered in a red baize. The metal clip was very fancy. The box was quite different and Angie guessed it to be foreign.

'Now ain't this lovely?' said Maisie, stroking the grooves gently with her finger. 'Ow about this?'

'It's a cracking little box. Don't you want it?' asked Angie. She preferred it to the metal one.

'No, I ain't used if for twenty years. Me sister Violet fetched it back from foreign parts, donkey's years ago. Reckon I'll live without it now!'

Angie leaned across the small table and gave her a big squashy hug. 'Oh Maisie, I shall miss you!' she said.

Forty-Two

The first week in November saw a full moon and a few days of severe frost. It penetrated the glass and snuffed out any lingering tomato plants, creating a real problem for Karen and Steve who had some lettuce in full heart. Although the skies were clear in the daytime, the ground where the sun didn't reach stayed crunchy and white and for the first time that winter Karen's duck pond iced over. She watched with the girls as the ducks tried to jump in as usual, and saw their confusion when they found it solid ice. Then they experimented walking across but their legs slid out from under them and Karen felt embarrassed for them as they toppled, webbed feet in the air. Funny it's not instinct, she thought. A homing pigeon can find its way back to Yorkshire but nothing's prepared a duck for something as dramatic as this. Eventually they learnt how to waddle across.

When Steve heard that a long cold spell was approaching, he'd discussed the implications with Jonathan. They'd stood at the foot of the crop which stretched evenly the length of the tunnel, punctuated with just a few gaps where plants had rotted off. Disease was always more prevalent this time of year but a conscientious spray programme had prevented any disasters. There was just one more tunnel but they'd been a week later in planting it which meant it was further behind for harvest, so it posed no immediate problem because they hadn't hearted up.

'These'll be ruined tonight if you don't get some heat on,' Jonathan said bluntly. Steve didn't have electricity that far up the nursery, so a supplementary heater wasn't a feasible option even if he could obtain one large enough. 'If I was you I'd cut like hell now. In fact if I was you, I wouldn't have risked a cold crop at this time at all.' He stamped his smart black shoes in an effort to warm his feet.

Steve looked at his watch and ignored Jonathan's taunt. It was ten o'clock already. According to the forecast they had about six and a half hours until darkness and the temperature inside the tunnel dropped like a stone,.

'I could ring Eddie, if he isn't too busy,' he said thoughtfully. 'And maybe Jim.'

Even so, there was a limit to what they could cut in the time, and Karen and Hazel found it difficult to spend time on the holding now it was too cold for the children.

Jonathan relented. 'You could cover up what you can't cut today,' he suggested, more pleasantly.

'Cover them up? With blankets?' said Steve sarcastically. 'Do they want hot water bottles an' all?'

Jonathan forced a smile, but in reality he was irritated. When Eric suggested a course of action, it was accepted and he was praised for it. When he made a similarly valid proposal it was generally ridiculed. He kept his voice even, though.

'Newspapers, polythene, whatever you've got. Rizlas, I hear you've got some of them going spare! I take it you do want to save this crop?'

Steve ignored the jibe, he still wasn't convinced this bastard wasn't behind the raid.

'Aye, course I do, but we don't bother wi' newspapers and Karen chucks everything out. If in doubt chuck it out's her motto,' said Steve. Then he remembered something. 'Eddie's got a load of old polythene sheeting, I s'pose we might cut that up and use it. Can you ask him if you're off up there next?'

Jonathan stared at him. Just what did they expect?

'No, I'm not going up there,' he said. In fact he rarely went near their nursery now. He felt contempt towards Hazel after she led him on, making him treat her like a whore. He'd confirmed his original conclusion that she deserved it, and he contrasted the episode to his lovemaking with Sara. He was also embarrassed and angry with Eddie for taking his car and leaving him stranded. 'That's what telephones are for!'

∞ ⅆ

Half an hour later, the crop of lettuce was being slaughtered by the task force. Jim and Janice came to help and Jim fetched his mother to watch Karen and Hazel's children so the women could work as well. The lettuce were good, most of them making six ounces which meant they could be sent as first class. By half past three a pale white moon was already up, as yet benign, but the day was fading rapidly and the sky flushed red from the west. Their breath turned to smoke and they stamped their feet and wriggled their toes inside their wellingtons. Temperatures were dropping fast, and Karen, Hazel and Janice walked over to the house while the men tucked the remaining lettuce under their polythene quilt. Two hundred and fifty boxes were stacked ready on pallets in the packing shed, protected by some lengths of old carpet, and Steve was proud. By rights he shouldn't have planted these, it had been an unsafe bet and he'd had to really argue with Karen, who'd been wary of spending money at the time. But it had paid off, they should break even with what they'd harvested and would be cutting into profit tomorrow.

When they reached the house, Myra was busily polishing the white tiles around the cooker.

'Look what I've done for you,' she said, reeling off a list which even included cleaning out the light fittings.

Oh here we go, thought Janice. Why can't she just relax like other people? The children have probably killed each other in the front room, but so long as the kitchen's a new pin. What will Karen think?

Karen seemed pleased though. Myra told everyone to sit down while she made them all a cup of tea. The children were absorbed in cartoons so the women sat down in the dining room.

'It's Bonfire night on Friday,' said Hazel, warming her hands around a big mug of tea. 'Midge is doing the fireworks, and Sammy makes his own. It's always a good laugh, isn't it Janice?'

Janice nodded. She was busy reading a magazine she'd found on the side. She wouldn't be going, she'd be comforting the animals, who were as fearful of fireworks as they were of thunder. The embarrassing episode with Nigel still burnt in her mind, undiluted because she hadn't even been able to voice it to Bernadette. She now avoided Nigel like the plague.

'Bound to be dangerous,' said Karen. She still hadn't forgiven Sammy.

'And -' added Hazel, realising Janice was in a world of her own, and Myra duster-happy in the kitchen, 'Martin Dickinson and that Chas Barnes will be there. They're good for a bit of a laugh with, Martin is quite good looking, and,' she added, 'did you know he's filthy rich?'

Karen shook her head incredulously. 'You don't learn do you?' she whispered.

൪   ൙

Midge enjoyed Bonfire Night. Christmas and New Year he could do without, all those decorations to put up, the tree to dress, and the once-a-year drunks to humour. Guy Fawke's Night carried none of this tedium although he'd heard on the licensed victualler's grapevine that some foolish landlords were now making something of Halloween, decorating their pubs with spiders and witches and leaving the paraphernalia in place until after November the fifth. Heaven forbid he should ever have to mess around like that. This is Britain, for God's sake, not America.

The annual Red Cow Bonfire party had indeed gained a reputation due to Sammy's powerful fireworks, and the pub was in an ideal situation, standing on the edge of the village. Already this year the growers had been adding to the bonfire, delivering broken pallets and waste wood in their pick-ups.

'We always have a competition for best guy,' said Kim to Karen, on a chance meeting at the supermarket in town. 'I run it. Reminds me of me lost youth, big thing was made o' guysing around where I come from. Your kids could enter, it's all for charity. And tell that flouncey mate of your's.'

'You know,' said Karen to Steve later, 'everywhere has different traditions. She hadn't heard of Mischief Night, or chubbing. You know Steve, I'm glad you made me take a chance with those lettuce. That's six hundred quid we wouldn't have had.'

'Should listen to me bit more, then!'

'Don't get too cocky,' she warned, but she smiled and gave him a big hug.

෯ ෬

On the night itself only Midge and Sammy set off the fireworks. They ran a double act, pretending to withdraw in fear, then tricking each other. It was tired but the punters loved it, another little piece of tradition. The night was clear and cold with several degrees of frost, you could raise your head and breathe out steam towards a sky speckled with stars. The moon was on the wane but still buxom and bright.

Cars and vans were parked along the roadside so the crowd could gather in the old coaching yard. It was packed. The bonfire gusted and sparked like a volcano behind a rope on the edge of some wasteland. Its plume of smoke rose straight up into the still of the night.

Kim was serving hamburgers and hot dogs with Maureen assisting her, squirting each open bun with a dollop of tomato sauce. You had to be smart to avoid it. Maureen failed to see how anyone could possibly enjoy food without it.

Karen handed out sparklers as her twins and Hazel's two youngest watched their guy meet his fate. Hazel had dragged Karen around every charity shop in Wansbridge to find black clothes and sunglasses like Jonathan's, then she'd spent hours unravelling a gold curtain tassel and stitching it on for his hair. It didn't win, though; Kim wouldn't allow that, but she'd propped him up at the base of the fire and sparks were pock-marking his face. Despite this timely reminder, Hazel was already exchanging repartee with Chas and Martin, Karen thought maybe one of them would win the competition next year. The children drew squiggles of light, chain lighting sparklers like Myra did her tabs, and losing concentration as a huge bang split the air showering bright lights high above them. Nathan came running up, with a couple of lads from the village. How fast he was growing up.

Myra and Fred were arm in arm, Myra raucously joining in with the oohs and aahs, her face lit up by the glow from the bonfire and showing the pleasure of a young girl.

'I've always loved fireworks, Fred,' she said as she cuddled up closer to him. 'Ever since I was a lass.'

'They don't remind you of wartime then? All them bangs?' Secretly Fred didn't like them; this time last year he'd shouted at youngsters for letting them off early and had been a lynchpin in the campaign to stop a bonfire party in the field behind his house. And here he was now, enjoying himself like he'd forgotten how to. Funny what love can do.

'Wartime? Naw,' said Myra. 'That time's best forgotten. The future's what it's all about. Roman candles! Them's me favourites.'

Maisie, George, Ruby and Vic were huddled together, collars up, hands in pockets, Vic wanting to make his escape to the bar but Ruby preventing him. Both couples had plenty of family somewhere in the crowd, or squashed in the crush of the smoky pub.

'The next do'll be Christmas, and then after that we'll be gone from the Drift.' said Maisie, sadly.

In truth she was excited, but events like this made her want to remain part of this community.

'You'll not be barred, you know, just cos you've moved a mile down the road! We might even let you come back next year.' said Ruby. Maisie laughed, but she secretly thought it wouldn't be the same.

Dennis and Sylvia stood together, her with an upright fur collar and her arms folded, he with his hands behind his back, obviously enjoying the fun. They were each making efforts to partake in the other's world, and it seemed to be working. Conversation was slowly starting to germinate again in their lives.

Angie was feeling smug. Today she'd been to the doctor for the result of her pregnancy test. She parked the car and clattered along the road towards the crowds, her high heeled boots zipped under her jeans and her jacket unsuited to the winter night as usual. The curls at the back of her head were still damp from her shower, and now felt cold against her neck. None of this bothered Angie. She hadn't told Josh the news yet, and she wanted to pick her moment. Guessing where he was, she opened the heavy oak door and noise, light and hot air all hit her in the face with equal force. She soon spotted him, thanks to her heels. He was playing dominoes in the bar with Eddie, Steve and Jim. She edged carefully through the throng into the Bar, instinctively shielding her stomach.

'Josh, come outside for a sec!' she called to him.

Josh looked at her like she was crazy. 'What for?' he asked.

'To see the fireworks!' she said.

He looked up fleetingly and shrugged.

'Too bloody cold,' he said. 'Come and sit down – you like a game of dommies. Anyway I see fireworks every week in me own house.' He rapped a domino twice on the table to signal that he couldn't go. Then he added: 'Only joking, Ange.'

'I'm up!' said Eddie, as he placed his final domino with a flourish.

'I'm with you Angie,' said Josh, trying to slip from the table.

'Hey! that's a quid you owe me!' said Eddie, jumping up. Angie struggled with her tight jeans for some money and passed a pound note to him. Josh's eyes widened.

'Have you won some money or something?' he asked, as they pushed through the crowd.

'Oh, better than that, Josh. we've won the pools!' said Angie, as she led him behind the old stables which edged the pub yard. Away from the bonfire it was even colder but there was enough natural light to see by, just.

'We don't do the pools, do we? I thought you said you didn't trust the collector after watching Kes...'

'No, stupid, much better than money.' Angie put her arms around him, and he noticed her eyes shining as she looked up at him. 'Guess what it is!'

'I think I must've left me fags in the pub,' said Josh, giving her a squeeze back. 'Angie, what is it? It's too cold for a knee-trembler behind here, woman!'

Angie wouldn't let him go. 'What is it, what we've wanted for so long?'

Josh was shivering, he'd left his jacket along with his cigarettes. He looked down at her smile, and it left him in no doubt.

'You're not? Really? Angie!' He grabbed her and swung her around like a toddler. She screamed, and as he put her down he said: 'So.....so......my swimmers.....I'm not a jaffa then?'

'You most certainly are not, Josh Thomas!'

'And you – well if it didn't sound soft I'd say I love you,' he said, grabbing her hand. 'And not just because you're pregnant. Come on, let's go tell the pub!'

Forty-Three

By mid-December winter had sunk its teeth into the Estate. Most of the glasshouses lay fallow, although a few large growers such as Dennis could afford to heat theirs. There had been too many fierce frosts for any cold crops to survive, and the panes of glass were opaque with ice. This was an advantage, the frost accentuating cracked or missing sheets, for winter was the season of repair. This job had to be attended to swiftly for a January gale funnelling inside a greenhouse could lift it up and destroy a whole bay. Steve left the doors open on his old Dutch Light houses as someone might leave a key and a box of matches in their old banger. Sadly, the howling winter wind had only managed to shatter a few more panes and the bare ground was covered with broken glass.

George was scraping up the remnants of his tomato crop with a hand-rake. The spent plants were already piled up and rotting on his compost heap and the glasshouse was technically sold, just waiting for the buyer to come and dismantle it. Most people would have left the small tomatoes which littered the ground, and the leaves and other scattered debris; there wasn't really any point to his efforts other than finishing a job properly and enjoying the company of the little pied wagtails which bobbed companionably alongside him, and had done so for thirty years, scrounging the tiny red chats.

His auction had been a great success, and there was little left to place in the Wansbridge Sale or throw in a skip. Buyers and spectators had huddled on his lawn, collars up against the keen wind, Maisie and Angie ladling cream of tomato soup into double plastic cups. He'd seen many friends from the past, a few who were now farming successfully elsewhere but the majority having long since turned their backs on horticulture and now working as groundsmen, in factories, or for security firms. George was grateful he had managed to continue so long in the business he loved. For years now he felt he'd been clinging to an industry which was spinning into a different world; luckily he'd been able to jump off in time. At the last Growers' meeting he'd been presented with a clock which was ironic as he hardly ever bothered to look at one. He always knew roughly the time from the sky, and he had never felt the need to consult one out of boredom. He hoped that wouldn't change now. They had found another bungalow, having lost the one with the corner bath. George had been secretly relieved at that, he couldn't imagine sitting scrunched up in it, gold taps or not. The chosen one had an acre of garden and a big through-lounge where Maisie could entertain the family.

The Grower's Association had voted Tim to the chair, with Simon as his assistant. George had strongly supported Simon, who although he couldn't really be respected as a grower he would be invaluable in the coming months as tension between the LSA and its tenants looked set to accelerate. Simon's expertise in law and his incisive brain would be crucial in any future negotiations.

He paused in his work, and re-lit his pipe. His gloveless fingers were almost numb with cold and patting tobacco firmly into the warm bowl he glanced to the sky. The grey blanket of cloud had a yellow-green tinge to it, and with the wind blowing steadily from the east George knew there was a strong chance of snow. As he pondered this, the thinnest and driest of flakes stung his face. Time to go into the warm house for Maisie's mid-morning milky coffee.

Josh, Eddie, Steve and Jim were playing dominoes in the Snug of the Red Cow. The only clue to Christmas was a bunch of holly taped to the wall, leaves now tinder dry and curling. And someone had twisted a strand of tinsel around the "dirty old men need love too" postcard rack. Midge leaned on the bar and tried his hardest to engage two strangers in conversation. They escaped to the fruit machine and then Midge watched the domino players with envy, he'd love to join them but he couldn't at this time of the day. The only other person in this bar was Simon, who'd pulled his chair up to the fire and kicked off his wellingtons. A paperback was suspended in his left hand and he stretched his wooly socks towards Midge's log fire. The great mound hissed and rained sparks, and Simon dealt with them by rubbing his feet together. Midge could smell singed wool.

'Simon,' he called loudly enough to get his attention. 'I haven't seen Nicole lately. I've got a crate of red wine in, new stuff from Chile or somewhere, with her in mind. Classy wine, I'm told.'

'Oh,' said Simon, looking up. 'I should have told you, we've split.'

This titbit reached the domino players, and they paused their game. Midge opened the hatch and came over. He squatted in front of the fire, out of range of the sparks.

'I'm sorry to hear that. Gone to her mother's, has she?'

Simon lost his page in his paperback. He stared at Midge. Her mother's? he thought. How strange.

Midge caught his look and explained: 'Kim ran off back to her mother's once. Soon came back though, tail between her legs.'

Eddie stirred his dominoes. The players contributed to the hush.

'Well I suppose I'd better tell you all she's not gone to

her mother's, father's or even the vicar's. Fact is, she's living with someone, with a woman, as it happens.' He stared defiantly around him, but he moved his feet to safety.

Eddie's hand froze on his dominoes like a crab stranded by the tide.

'Piss off!' Josh said. 'You're having a laugh.'

'Holy Moses,' said Jim. 'Straight up?'

'I'm afraid it's true,' replied Simon, without malice. 'I always knew she had been bisexual in the past, and we both thought it was a phase. I felt it was coming, and we'll always remain good friends.'

'You don't mean – can't be – she's a lezzie?' Josh's dominoes were in total disarray. It was then Eddie realised he hadn't been the only one.

Simon had looked irritated. 'It's no big deal is it? I mean lots of people are, it's just this place which is so damn conservative, so locked into itself! It's the sodding dark ages. Why can't you all judge Nicole for herself?'

Midge, more accustomed to the role of voyeur, returned to his lair. There was a second or two before anyone spoke.

'Oh, no mate, Nicole's great!' said Eddie.

'Nothing against her,' stammered Josh. 'Why not?'

Jim raised his eyebrows at Josh, then addressed Simon. 'I hope you gave 'er what for, though mate. Can't let 'em walk all over you. Don't know what I'd 've done, if it was our Janice. Reckon I wouldn't 'ave been responsible for me actions.'

Midge leaned eagerly forward, his neck protruding further than usual. This was the first real excitement since the dope raid. 'Only yesterday I was reading that statistically –'

Simon cut him short. 'It's in the past now. I'm sure you'll sell your crate of vino.'

Steve watched, thinking if it had been him, he'd could never have shown his face. He felt admiration for Simon, who sat so cool, confident, matter of fact. He raised his glass.

'Well here's to the future, Simon,' he said. The others joined him.

'Well she cured my celery rash and my bad back. You know, with her lotions and suchlike.' Eddie still couldn't leave it alone.

'An' she predicted about me being a Dad. Not in so many words, like, but that's what she meant, when I went and had my fortune told,' Josh said.

The game was lost, nobody seemed to know the state of play so Steve scooped up the dominoes with his two hands ready for the next game. 'You had your fortune told? Never!'

Josh, embarrassed, was glad to be able to show a bit of aggression to hide behind. 'So what?' he said. 'What's wrong with that? Law against it, or somethin?'

'No law, you muppet. Can just see you, though. You'll be doing yoga next.'

        ∾   ∾

Eddie answered the telephone in his house. It was Adam, from the Packing Shed, asking if he had any lettuce.

'Nope, last lot got frosted a fortnight ago.'

'That's a pity,' Adam was saying, 'because they're treble the price now.'

I bet they bloody are, thought Eddie as he replaced the receiver. He and Hazel were painting the lounge. As he walked back to his tin of paint he mentally returned to the gossip which had blown his mind in the Red Cow the night before.

'How long are you going to stir that emulsion?' Hazel asked, irritably. 'It's snowing and I need to get to town before it comes in dark.'

Eddie jumped. 'I was just thinking – just can't believe it about Nicole running off with a woman!' he said. Hazel was painting the ceiling, poised on a pair of wooden steps. Luckily the ceiling was low. Her right arm was stretched up, and the other had to keep balance and hold the paint kettle. It was very hit and miss and slicks of emulsion splattered everywhere. The stretching movement emphasised her slim waist in her tight jumper. She brushed a swath of blond hair which had escaped from her ponytail away with her forearm.

'Oh I can!' said Hazel. 'You could tell she wasn't interested in men. I bet she wouldn't know what to do with a dick,' she added vulgarly. Eddie was lost in thought, and a dee-jay blabbered into their silence, followed by:

'*You were working as a waitress in a cocktail bar...*'

Hazel joined in: '*when I met you..*'

❧ ☙

Janice was in the piggery, milking Bernadette. Her milk yield was greatly reduced now, and it would be necessary to get her sired in the spring, in order to up the volume again.

'And this time, Bernadette,' Janice pressed close to the warmth of the goat's flank. 'This time, you'll be able to keep your kid, I promise you that.'

Bernadette munched happily at the meal. The piggery was comparatively warm and cosy, her pen stacked snugly with clean straw. Janice was supplementing her food with molasses for extra vitamins. She waited as the last trickle dwindled. The pail of milk steamed in the cold atmosphere. Janice loved the warm animal smell, and she stroked and scratched Bernadette as she talked to her.

'Myra is getting married, would you believe. To finicky old Fred, and they're going to live together in the village. That will be great, because she'll be near but I won't have to have her living in my house for months, taking over everything! Out of my hair at last. On Christmas Eve, Bernadette, we're off to a party, a surprise leaving party for George and Maisie. No, I don't mean you, old girl, you can't come. It's in the village hall, and goats aren't invited, of course, in case they drop their currants on the floor.' Bernadette obliged with a steaming shower there and then, and rubbed her hairy chin affectionately against Janice's hand. In response Janice fondled her beard.

As she stood up to leave, she caught sight of the white flakes, still tiny but very dense and so dry they were already sticking to the glass.

'It's snowing,' she told Bernadette, as she patted her warm back. 'Good job you're all safe and cosy in here. I'd better get back to the house – they'll all be looking for their tea.'

ഇ ଔ

Karen and Steve leaned on the bottom half of the split cubicle door and watched their cockerels, too weighty now for comfort. Some had already begun to "lose their legs" due to excess weight, and had to be killed before they were attacked and pecked to death by the others. They hadn't lost many; there were about twenty left now, which according to Eddie was a good survival rate. They planned to give the birds as gifts to immediate family and closest friends, and still have a few for the freezer.

'I'm having nowt to do with the killing,' said Karen. How quickly their time had come. She was still unable to accept the 'barbarous attitude' of most of her neighbours.

'Don't worry, no one's asking you to,' Steve said. 'Eddie and I will do that. I'm not exactly over the moon about it meself.' He gave Karen a bit of a squeeze which she hardly felt on account of her layers of clothes. The smoke from their breath danced in the electric light which struggled against the gloom of the shed. 'But I know I can do it, mind. D'you think you can manage to help Hazel pluck 'em, though?'

Karen shivered but Steve failed to notice. 'I'll try,' she promised. Then she gave him a big hug, snuggling up against the vicious cold. 'Our first Christmas in the country. Er, Steve...'

'What?'

'Are you happy?'

'Well it's too bloody late if I'm not, woman!'

She broke away to look up at him. She didn't really need to ask. But she never presumed anything.

'Don't mess around. Are you?'

'Yes, you daft thing. You know I am. Broke but happy. Happier than them, anyway!'

The birds, warmed by a small heater scratched and scuffled aggressively as far as they could in their cramped surroundings. If you give them too much space for exercise, Eddie warned, they won't make the weight.

'I've seen more space on Brid beach on a Bank Holiday,' said Karen.

'Poor bastards. I don't reckon I'd do them again. Not much of a life, hardly any daylight, no fresh air.'

'And never feeling the grass beneath their feet. Hey, shall I release them, let 'em take their chance?'

'For Christ's sake woman, no! It might be a bit cruel but they've saved us this Christmas.'

They both guessed they'd made a financial loss, and this Christmas was set to be a spartan affair but with plenty of good food and ale. They'd bought toys for the girls from the Cash and Carry, and these birds would save the day so far as presents for the family were concerned. They planned to spend New Year in Yorkshire.

Karen bit her lip: 'Yes, I will help pluck them. I don't

want to, but I will pluck the birds, because we are so broke. And that's the *only* reason. And definitely, it'll be the first and last time.'

She went to open the door, and a blast of cold air hit her face. She tasted ice on her tongue. 'It's snowing!' she cried, and raced to tell the twins.

℘ ℘

Dennis and his workers were busy in the glasshouse, a merry band of lettuce slashers, full of Christmas cheer. The price was so high even Dennis himself was hard at work. He had a whole acre ready to cut, all timed perfectly. He tried not to mentally count the profit, but he couldn't keep the figures from his head. He stood up and looked around him. The snow was melting as soon as it hit the glass but despite the comparative warmth inside, it was still quite chilly. The cold reflected light from the snow outside would have made for a gloomy atmosphere but for the bright clothing of the women and the radio blasting out Christmas crap, as Dennis called it. He looked over at the pregnant Angie, her cheeks glowing and her dark curls shining. He couldn't pretend to approve of her reconciliation with Josh, but he'd managed to come to terms with it. He and Sylvia were attending the Bank's annual dinner tonight. He had begun to feel more affinity to the people he would see there than his neighbours on the Estate. The gulf between the successful grower and the struggler was now wider than the Packhouse door.

℘ ℘

Sammy and Maureen shared a flask of sweet tea in a lay-by on the main road, side by side in the front seat of their van. They had four Christmas trees left. The snow was quite deep now and still falling, whirling in the car headlights as

382

people left work early, fearful of drifts blocking the road which was already reduced to two narrow tracks in places.

'Well, we'd best call it a day, Mo old thing,' said Sammy, tightening his flask top. 'The snow's settled so much no-one'll spot our notice.' He opened the door and jumped into a drift. He padded through the powdery snow, bent against the wind, to retrieve his sign. As he tucked it under the sleeve of his donkey jacket, a car ground to a halt next to him. It was Jonathan.

'Well, well,' he said, smiling as he wound down the window. Snowflakes blew inside, dampening the dashboard and the passenger seat. 'Dealing in Christmas trees now!'

'I deal in everythin' mate, would sell you if you stood stock still and anybody wanted you,' said Sammy, pulling his woollen hat down further. Snow was caught in his beard. 'You know me. Tell you what, if you pull up to the back, you can have one, no charge, seeing as you've been a good customer!'

'Cheers, mate.'

'You're not givin' that useless lump one for nothin', surely?' said Maureen through her teeth, cigarette glowing in the corner of her mouth as she passed the tree out to Sammy.

'Why not? Regular customer, ain't he? Anyway the dog pissed up this one. When 'e gets it in 'is little warm 'ouse it won't 'arf pen and ink!' joked Sammy and his wife cackled obligingly.

Jonathan accepted the tree graciously, he knew Sara would be pleased. She moved in with him last week, the same day he heard he'd got a new job in Surrey. A new life surely beckoned and he couldn't be bothered to tell the growers about it. He wished Sammy and Mo a merry Christmas.

Now Sammy just had to drop a tree off to Midge (he'd protested but Sammy decided the miserable old bugger would get one if he wanted it or not), save one for Eric, then the final one they'd keep. He had already traded trees with most of the growers for meat, greenhouse glass, even duty-free tobacco from someone who'd been on a day trip to France. He pulled out into the blizzard, and they headed for home with a full bag of money.

℘ ℘

A week later shrunken patches of snow lingered where the weak winter sunshine couldn't reach. Eric steered the Volvo down the Drift, slush splashing out from its wheels, back seat covered with gifts from the growers. There were four Christmas cockerels, trussed in plastic, de-gibleted and oven-ready, and frozen joints of home-reared lamb. Bottles of home brew, jars of pickles, leeks and lettuce and a couple of Christmas trees. He was meeting his daughter, Gail, in a pub in Wansbridge. Still estranged from her mother, Eric was pinning his hopes on a Christmas reconciliation, he had the letter in his pocket.

Tonight he and his wife would attend a surprise party for Maisie and George, and this time next week they'd be aboard a plane taking them to the Canary Islands to spend New Year in Tenerife. Eric was sure this would be the last year of the Land Settlement Association as it had existed for so many years. But then who knew what a new year might bring?